He tilted her chin and studied the pale features in the lantern glow. His fingers lightly brushed her cheek, and he stared at the tears that clung, like diamonds, to his fingertips. Without thinking, he bent his lips to hers, covering the trembling mouth, kissing it with more tenderness and longing than he had felt a need to express in a very long time.

The softness, the vulnerability he discovered startled him. Earlier he had kissed a willful, defiant creature who had asked for a lesson in gamesmanship and had won one. Then it had been her spirit and energy that had challenged him; now he found himself kissing a warm, accessible woman who was tempting his body with exactly the kind of release it craved. . . .

He felt her lips quiver and begin to move beneath his. Hands that had grasped him for comfort moments before now clung to him with a new urgency and sent a chill rippling through his body.

What was he doing? What insanity had gripped him?

Adrian started to pull away but the softness followed him and this time his flesh met a greater temptation: the bold firmness of a breast found its way into his hand, the crown thrusting eagerly to fill his palm. He lifted his mouth from hers, his lips bathed by the sweet tang of her tears. His hand cupped her flesh and even though there was a layer of cotton obstructing his way, the velvet softness branded its imprint onto his skin. The ache grew, robbing him of the ability to think clearly or to move. His breathing labored; blood pounded into his senses, drowning them, drenching them with need. He knew he had to fight the weakness in his arms and the hunger flowing into his loins. God, the hunger!

"No," he muttered hoarsely. "No, dammit. . . ."

**THE WIND AND THE SEA**

# THE WIND AND THE SEA

### Marsha Canham

*PaperJacks* LTD.

TORONTO   NEW YORK

AN ORIGINAL

# PaperJacks

## THE WIND AND THE SEA

**PaperJacks** LTD.

330 STEELCASE RD. E., MARKHAM, ONT. L3R 2M1
210 FIFTH AVE., NEW YORK, N.Y. 10010

PaperJacks edition published April 1986

Cover design: Brant Cowie/Artplus
Cover illustration: Rick Ormond

ISBN 0-7701-0415-0
Printed in Canada

To the black sheep, whose characters I draw upon liberally, with affection. And special thanks to the real Davey Dunn — how could I have invented him?

# Prologue

Between the line of thick green foliage and the sparkling sweep of azure water lay a stretch of blindingly white sand. The sun was directly overhead, a fiery orb that caused the surface of the water to shimmer with vapors and the trees to droop. Now and then a gull circled, screaming mock commands at the row of sweating men and cannon strung along the beach below. Now and then a bleary eye was raised skyward and a curse was muttered; the absence of the normally huge flocks of scavengers was taken as an ill omen.

Everart Constantine Farrow crooked an eye above a dust-laden stone wall and peered out to sea. His voice was as ominous as approaching thunder as he spat a low warning over his shoulder.

"Any time now, lads. She's got 'er arse to the wind and she's comin' in fast. Keep yer 'eads low and yer guns warm. She can't be takin' too much more punishment the likes we been givin' 'er, mark me."

Several red, powder-burned faces glanced in Verart's direction but no voice contradicted him. It was the truth as far as Farrow was concerned; he was not a man to admit defeat easily. The siege cannon had replied enthusiastically all morning to the broadsides unleashed from the warship *Eagle* and had left many marks on the oak decks of the American frigate. Still, a glance past the battlements would see the Barbary defenses badly mauled. Of the fifty-eight massive cannon originally commanded by Farrow's men, fewer than twenty remained seated and functional. Of a force of three hundred eager, strong men attempting to stave off the naval assault, fewer than one hundred and thirty were still alive. The stand of palm trees behind the line of defence was littered with the dead and dying. Pieces of bone and flesh hung from the branches, and the sand underfoot was stained crimson from the spill of blood.

" 'Ere she comes," Verart murmured, watching the ship tack expertly to take advantage of the full lift of the wind. There were gaps blown through her sails and rigging, holes gouged in her sides, and at least one of the three main masts was cracked, rendering the top steering sails all but useless. Still the *Eagle* came on. Whoever was at her helm was a master of the sea.

Through his spyglass, Verart could see gaffers scrambling in the rigging, beginning to bend the fighting sails on orders from the helm. He could see the gunnery crews at their stations and the two decks of gleaming black cannon presenting their iron maws. In the stern, on the quarter-deck bridge, stood a group of uniformed officers, their white breeches and dark blue jackets unmistakable even at such a distance. A sudden flash of light skipping off brass made Verart's skin prickle with the knowledge that he was being just as closely observed by the enemy.

The enemy, he mused, and spat in disdain. How in blazes had the Yankee warship found Snake Island? Surely none of the Pasha's men would have betrayed them: the Farrow stronghold represented staggering profits for the Dey of Algiers, as well as irreplaceable firepower to guard the approach to Tripoli. He could only assume that the war for control of the Mediterranean had taken a turn for the worse. If the Yankees could spare their ships to search out pockets of corsairs along the coastline, then it did not bode well for the fate of his brother, Duncan Farrow, and Duncan's two ships, the *Falconer* and the *Wild Goose*.

Verart lowered the spyglass and growled loudly, "Court!"

A slender figure — features buried beneath layers of grime and oily sweat — jumped up at once. "Yes, Uncle?"

"How do we stand for shot?"

"We've more than enough to hold them off," was the confident reply. "We've double and grape aplenty. Seagram's brought down more incendiaries, and we've enough to pepper a hundred fires if the bastards will just hold course."

Verart chuckled and thumped the narrow shoulders affectionately. Huge emerald eyes shone up at his and startling white teeth broke through in a smile that stirred the man's heart.

"Ah, Court, your father'll be proud of ye this day. I always 'eld you'd do a proper turn when 'e needed it. I always told 'im 'avin' a sprout like you was nothin' less than the grandest feat of 'is miserable life."

Courtney Farrow beamed under the praise, knowing her uncle rarely bestowed compliments and never unless they were heartily deserved. It made the aches and bruises in her body seem insignificant; it made the bleeding wound in her upper arm more of a trophy than a nuisance; and it made her wish more fervently than ever that she could single-handedly destroy the Yankee ship that was even now backing its sails into raking position.

The daughter of the most notorious pirate along the coast of North Africa was as slender and fine-boned as a young doe. She had the brilliant, bold green eyes of her father, the same dark auburn hair and quick Irish temper. She had lived among the corsairs for nearly ten years and was as apt to be found drilling on one of the smoking cannon as she was to be running her hands covetously over the rich silks and satins confiscated in prize cargoes.

"We will get her, won't we, Uncle?" she asked tersely, her eyes blazing with sudden hatred. "We will be able to hold her off until Father returns?"

"Bah! Hold 'er off! We'll sink the bitch into 'er own beakheads, we will. Moffins! Willard! Polks! Look lively on the guns, boys. A gold sovereign goes for each sharpshooter ye send to look sharper in the never after!"

The words had scarcely cleared his throat before a cheer went up along the beach and the guns roared to life. Clouds of grapeshot the size of musketballs, screaming tangles of chain, rockets, red-hot iron balls, and howling storms of nails and assorted razor-edged missiles were hurled across six hundred yards of churning blue water. The reply from the *Eagle* was swift and spirited. Her starboard battery erupted with fire from both decks and in moments cloaked the sleek lines of the frigate in clouds of white, drifting smoke.

Captain Willard Leach Jennings paced the width of the *Eagle*'s bridge, hands clasped behind his back emphasizing the bulk of his girth. He was a short, stubby strut of a man with a florid complexion that did not take kindly to the Mediterranean sun. His ferret-like eyes were set between pudgy, red-veined cheeks, beneath a brow that arched high on a dome-shaped pate. Beside him, similarly attired in immaculate white breeches and dark blue naval tunic, was the *Eagle*'s second lieutenant, Otis Falworth.

"Well, Mister Falworth," the captain mused, "I see Mister Ballantine is in his full glory."

"Indeed, sir." The junior officer sniffed. "He does seem bent on winning the day unassisted."

The officer to whom they referred, First Lieutenant Adrian Ballantine, stood with his long legs braced against the roll and sway of the ship. His tunic was discarded, his shirt torn open from throat to waist, baring a wide vee of coppery brown hair. His face was sunbronzed and angular; his thick wavy hair, once brown, was now bleached to a pale gold by constant exposure to sea and sun. There were fine creases at the corners of his eyes, gained from squinting at tall, sunlit masts and distant horizons; deeper lines were etched into the square jaw and around the firm, resolute mouth — lines drawn by experience and cool efficiency. He stood six feet tall, although the breadth of his powerful shoulders and the length of his tautly muscled legs made him seem far taller.

One of his arms was raised. His steely-gray eyes were fastened on the shoreline as he issued commands to his gun captains, directing the ship's long guns for the most effective range of fire.

Each time his arm descended, the starboard battery erupted with clouds of orange-flecked smoke as the twelve eighteen-pounder guns exploded almost simultaneously. The *Eagle* lurched violently with the recoils, the motion helping the crews who immediately hauled on the thick breeching tackle to pull the guns inboard for reloading. The snouts were reamed out, and fresh powder cartridges were fed into place. The iron shot was rammed into the muzzles, they were packed and primed, and one by one the gun captains turned their sweating, smoke-streaked faces toward Lieutenant Ballantine and shouted, "Clear!"

Ballantine was justifiably proud of his crew. They could fire three rounds per minute, if pressed, and their aim was so precise that even as formidable an emplacement as the defense of Snake Island was being systematically destroyed.

He shouted encouragement to the crew of bare-chested, blood-smeared gunners who fired steadily even though the rails and planking were being shot out from under them. The lower tier of guns was blasting as quickly and as efficiently as the upper. Ballantine mentally praised the chief gunner, Danby, and the helmsman, Loftus, who was holding fast to the course he had ordered. The men were eager and superbly trained. The *Eagle* was handling like the predator she was named after — there was no earthly possibility they would not emerge as the victors this day . . . or any other.

In one of the cramped, mud-daubed huts that clustered in a deep valley sheltered by sand dunes, Miranda Gold raised apprehensive, amber-colored eyes from the thatched cot of the wounded man she was tending. Miranda was a blend of striking features: slim of waist and hip, but possessing the full-blown, voluptuous bosom that bespoke her Castillian bloodlines. Her hair was the color of ravens' wings, her skin a warm olive shade. The lashes framing the almond-shaped, seductive eyes were long and lustrous and guarded the windows of a soul wise far beyond her nineteen years.

"What do you make of it, Drudge?" she asked in a husky whisper. "Do you think we will hold the day?"

Drudge's right leg was shattered from the knee down. He could only close his eyes weakly and run a dry tongue over his parched and cracked lips and hope that his lies sounded convincing. "We got a good chance, Mistress Gold. But the fox at the helm knows no backin' down. He's a fair shot, a worse sportsman. He t'inks if he keeps rammin' iron down our t'roats we're bound to choke. But he don't know Verart, now do he? He don't know that Verart'll take a chokin' in stride then spit out the bile twice as fierce as afore."

"If Duncan was here," she murmured bitterly, "or Garrett, the Yankee ship would never had come within a thousand yards. Damn the pair of them. Damn their souls for insisting on running to aid the Pasha. They should have left Karamanli to stew in his own treachery and stayed here to protect us."

Drudge's eyes opened a slit. He would rather cut out his tongue than harbor any ill thoughts toward "Golden Miranda," but only a week ago it had been Miranda, the high-spirited, outspoken mistress of Duncan Farrow, who had sided with Garrett Shaw, the captain of the *Falconer*, when he demanded that the Farrow ships keep the rendez-

vous with the Pasha's messengers. Ten thousand gold ingots were at stake, and all they had to do was escort a fleet
of five grainships past the Yankee blockade and run them
into a beleaguered and starving Tripoli. Easy work, for the
*Wild Goose* and the *Falconer* were as slippery as eels; they
had run the blockade so often in the past it was child's
play.

Drudge's wandering thoughts were brought sharply
back to the present by a thunderous volley that shook the
dust loose from the walls of the hut.

Miranda screamed and dropped to her knees as stones
and debris fell around her. The roof began to cave in, and
clouds of dirt and dried grass swirled in through the
paneless window. Searing heat roiled through the gaping
doorway, and Miranda screamed again as she realized that
a shell had struck close to the hut and that the outer walls
were in flame. There was no water, no men to fill the
buckets they kept handy for just such a dreaded occurence.
Miranda started to crawl toward the door, her eyes blinded
by the acrid smoke, her lungs fighting for every scalding
breath.

"Please . . . !"

She stopped, halted by Drudge's weak cry. He could not
move because of his leg, but fear was driving him upright
as he struggled to support his weight on his elbows.

"An arm, lass, there's a good girl. An arm, and I can
make it."

Miranda looked at the door, four short paces away, then
at the straw cot, fully ten paces from where she knelt.

"I . . . I'll send help," she said, and started to crawl for
the door.

"There ain't time, lass! See, the walls are aflame!"

The wooden supports behind Drudge's cot were
smoldering, and licks of flame were darting through gaps
between the wall and roof.

"Just an arm to lean on, lass," he pleaded. "Or a stick,
for pity's sake. The sweep handle! The musket!
Anyt'ing!"

"I said, I'll send help!" she screamed, and ran for the door. She did not straighten fully until she was well away from the danger, and when she looked back it was with a brief, whispered thanks for her own quick thinking. Three of the four walls were alight and the roof was blazing. Two seconds elapsed — the time it would have cost her to go back for Drudge — and the structure collapsed. The roof crashed in in a shower of spitting flames, the walls quivered for the spate of a deep breath and then they too folded inward. The sound of tearing wood and stone almost drowned out the shriek of Drudge MacGrew as a flaming ceiling beam severed him in two.

Miranda swallowed hard and staggered the few paces necessary to fall into the outstretched arms of the three women who had come running out of nearby huts.

"Miranda! Miranda! What happened?"

"A shell," she cried, and began to sob uncontrollably. "It struck the side of the hut. I called for help but no one came and so I had to try to move Drudge by myself. We almost made it. We almost . . . but when he saw it was too late . . . he pushed me out the door! He saved me! He pushed me away so that I wouldn't go back for him and because of that he . . . he. . . ."

The women did not need to hear the end of the grizzly story.

"There, there," said the eldest with admiration in her eyes. "Hush now, girl. You did what you could to help. No one could ask more of you."

Miranda raised her tear-stained face. "But I just know I could have saved him. If he'd just tried harder, if I was just a little stronger. . . ."

"I said hush," the woman commanded. "And dry your eyes. We've no time to be weeping over what could have been and what should have been. We cannot mourn the dead when there's still the living to tend to."

A few more moments of offered comfort, and the three crones hurried back to the horrible wounds and mutilations they had become hardened to over the years. Miranda dashed away the tears that shone on her face and brushed away the thick layer of ash and soot that coated her damask skirt. By habit, she adjusted the neckline of her sheer cotton blouse, scooping it lower so that her shoulders were bared along with a breathtaking expanse of bosom. With a toss of her ebony hair she left the circle of huts and climbed the dune that overlooked the scene of the battle. Her eyes narrowed and the amber shimmered, alive with bright green flecks of anger.

The cratered, pockmarked beach stretched out below her. A haze of smoke and drifting sand hovered over the line of palm trees like a cloud of ash over a volcano. Men were running everywhere: carrying powder and shot to the cannon emplacements, buckets of water to the many fires, litters to remove the bodies that peppered the beach and dunes in unbelievable numbers. Most of the wounded hadn't made it up the shallow hill; a trail of broken, bleeding bodies lay face down in the hot sand.

Her sharp, quick eyes located the center of activity on the beach. She easily identified Verart Farrow and the hovering bulk of the giant Seagram. Between them was the nimble, darting figure of Courtney Farrow.

The tiger eyes glittered with sudden, malicious pleasure as she envisioned the slim, auburn-haired daughter of Duncan Farrow being thrown on a heap of lifeless bodies. She relished the thought of ants and maggots feeding on the hated face, of crows and scavengers picking the bones clean and leaving them to bleach white under the sun.

"Perhaps some good will come of this day after all," she murmured. "Fight on, sweet Courtney. And be sure to lead the charge when the Yankees put their boats ashore."

# Chapter One

Captain Willard Jennings stepped from the bow of the longboat that had transported him ashore from the *Eagle*, and surveyed — with great satisfaction — the damage inflicted on the pirate stronghold of Snake Island. Flanking him on either side were his lieutenants — Otis Falworth and Adrian Ballantine.

"A splendid job, I must say, Mister Ballantine," Jennings nodded, his eyes darting along the smoking ruins of the beach. "Convey my congratulations to your gunners for a job well done. Extra rum all around, I should think, and . . . er, whatever else we keep in stores for special occasions."

"Salted mutton, sir," Lieutenant Falworth supplied dryly. "Unless we can find fresher fare here."

"By all means. By all means. Rout it out, Mister Falworth. I'll put you in charge of the acquisition of whatever goods you deem acceptable to our needs."

"Aye, sir."

The captain kept walking, his head swiveling on his stocky neck as he absorbed the full extent of his triumph. Lieutenant Ballantine was a pace or two behind, his expression blank, his body taut, as if it was taking all of his willpower to endure the formalities. Unlike the captain and Otis Falworth, Ballantine disliked gloating over the devastation his guns had wreaked. He was impatient to return to the ship and to determine the condition of his own crew and armaments. But he knew too well that Jennings needed this moment of glory and that the men had earned this frenzied release from such a close brush with death.

The looting was already well underway. The village was being systematically ransacked, the women driven screaming out of their hiding places and herded together for future selection. Bedlam would reign until the small hours of the morning, and even then the rum would be flowing from the scores of puncheons the men would squirrel on board away from the quartermaster's prying eyes.

"Down this way, I see," Jennings said, pointing toward a huddled group of prisoners surrounded by a marine guard. "God's teeth, is this what we've been fighting for two days?"

The lieutenant's gaze swept over the ragged group of sullen-faced men. Most were bloodied from wounds sustained in the hand-to-handspike fighting that had been necessary to finally win the beach. Ballantine was surprised by the numbers. Barely three score raised hate-filled, glowering faces to the trio of approaching officers.

Courtney Farrow crouched near the center of the group with her uncle and Seagram. The short, squat captain and the lean, arrogant-looking officer earned hardly more than a disdainful glance; it was the third man, the tall lieutenant, who drove the film of sullenness from Courtney's eyes. She had seen only half a dozen fair-haired men in the past ten years or so. The inhabitants of the Barbary Coast were all dark skinned, with dark hair that never sunbleached gold. And his eyes. They were the color of polished steel, cold and distant. They never stopped moving, assessing, contemplating (no doubt) the size of the reward that would be forthcoming on surrendering the prisoners to a Yankee court. His was the face of a man she could easily hate, and Courtney felt better for having acquired a focus for her hostility.

Captain Jennings halted beside a deep crater in the sand and puffed out his chest in an attempt to disguise the expanse of his belly.

"Which one of you is in command here?"

Not a single pair of eyes flickered, not a single head turned to betray their leader. For eight months the American forces had been actively engaged in fighting a war that had been dragging on for three years; for eight years the Mediterranean had been a hotbed of piracy; for eight centuries the northern coast of Africa had been the thriving center for white slavery. The corsairs of the Barbary Coast were among the most vicious, cunning, and ruthless breed of criminals imaginable. It was unlikely that any one of them would falter now.

"I want to know the identity of the man in charge," Captain Jennings bristled. "I know his name is Farrow. Everart Farrow, brother to Duncan Farrow, who at this very moment swings from a yardarm on board our flagship, the *Constitution*, anchored off the coast of Gibraltar."

Lieutenant Ballantine's eyes were drawn away from the *Eagle* as he noticed a brief scuffle near the center of the prisoners. A wounded man and a young boy sat together, the man's grizzled head cradled in the lap of a large man who resembled a well-fed gorilla. The wounded man's hand clawed at the boy's wrist, apparently to caution him to silence. Ballantine guessed the age of the man to be about fifty, but the thin, wiry appearance was deceptive. He had wispy brown hair shot through with gray and gathered untidily at the nape of his neck. Torn clothing revealed skin turned leathery by the sun and rock-hard flesh covered with a laticework of sinews and blueish veins. Despite an ugly bleeding wound that covered the whole of the corsair's chest, the dark green eyes were clear and alert.

The lieutenant felt a tingle skitter along his spine and realized that he, too, was being carefully studied. The lad's huge green eyes were devouring every detail of his face and uniform — not out of casual curiosity, but out of the age-old need to know an enemy well. The centers of the emerald eyes glowed with an inner fire unlike anything the lieutenant had seen before. The boy was otherwise un-distinctive. He was thin and scrawny and wore a dirty blue bandanna tied on an angle over greasy brown hair. The boy, like most of the survivors, was wounded, but he ig-nored the blood seeping down his arm and seemed to be more concerned with the comfort of the other man.

The third member of the group was plainly awesome. Even seated, there seemed to be more than seven feet of him, Ballantine judged, all of it gnarled muscle and seething hatred. The giant's hair was jet black and hung shaggily to his shoulders; his mouth was scarred cruelly from a knife wound that had left him with a permanent scowl. His hands were like slabs of ham but, astonishingly, held the wounded man as if he were a piece of delicate china.

The lieutenant's concentration was broken by the sound of the captain's voice demanding once again the identity of the leader.

" 'E lies wi' 'is skull stove in down yon beach," a man near the perimeter of the group sneered. "We leads ourselves now, we do."

"Identifying marks?" Captain Jennings shrilled.

"Eh?"

The captain's face turned a dark, ugly red. He tapped his ivory walking stick against his thigh in a gesture of im-patience. "Everart Farrow is known to have a tattoo of a boar's head across his chest. Should I walk down the beach in this sweltering heat and find that this . . . this man with his skull stove in . . . is not so adorned, I might be tempted to disembowel the cur who gave false information."

The corsair looked away in feigned boredom while his mates hurled insults at the American officers.

"On the other hand —" The captain crooked a fore-finger at one of the nearby marines. The soldier immediately seized the man who had spoken and dragged him clear of the others.

"On the other hand," the captain continued, "I could order this dog gutted now. And each man-jack of you in turn thereafter until either I have my answer or you are all dead. Now then. Where is Everart Farrow? If he is dead, I wish to know the location of the body. If he is alive and listening to me, let it be known that he was given fair warning of the deaths of his compatriots and that the blame therefore lies solely on his shoulders."

He waited a full minute in glowering silence before he struck his thigh impatiently with the ivory cane. He glanced at the marines, who held a now tense and cursing corsair between them, and nodded curtly. A third marine stepped back a pace, and his saber sang in the bright sunlight. The tip of the blade slashed down faster than the eye could follow it, leaving two torn halves of a shirt and vest in its wake, and a bright red stripe of blood welling from the man's breastbone to his navel. The prisoner gaped down in horror at the parted edges of his flesh. The curses ceased but he did not flinch as the sword began a second descent.

*"No! Enough!"*

Lieutenant Ballantine focused swiftly on the man and the boy. Their positions had reversed. Now the boy attempted to restrain the man from rising.

"Nay, Court, leave me be. I'll not be the cause of more good men being put to the sword for the sake of a Yankee bastard's pleasure." Verart raised his voice and shouted scornfully, *"I'm* Everart Farrow, ye murtherin' sons of whores. I'm the one ye seek and have the mark to prove it."

Captain Jennings held up the ivory cane to halt the gutting.

"Show me."

Verart struggled one-handed to bare an enormous reproduction of a charging fanged boar on his chest, barely discernible through the slick, fresh blood. The effort cost him dearly, and he slumped back into the giant's arms, the angry color draining rapidly from his cheeks.

The captain gloated as he turned to the lieutenant. "Mister Ballantine, I'll want this man transported to the *Eagle* at once. It should be dusk in two hours; I'll want the trial and the hanging over with by then. The rest of this scum is to be chained and locked in the *Eagle*'s brig. Mister Rowntree" — He lifted his cane to signal the sergeant-at-arms — "I'll not want to see a single tree or piece of thatch left standing on this island. Have it thoroughly searched and anything not of value burned to the ground."

"Aye, sir." The sergeant of the marines stepped aside as the captain passed, with Lieutenant Falworth close behind. They walked a dozen paces to the well-guarded pen of women prisoners, and would have passed them by with no more than a cursory glance if the raven-haired beauty had not moved — just enough to be noticed — as they neared.

Jennings came to a dead halt and stared.

The woman looked almost untouched by the battle, unlike the others who were caked with grime and filth, their hair matted and greasy, their clothes torn and sweat-stained. Her blouse was pure white and pulled low enough on her shoulders that the fabric was threatening to pop off the magnificent fullness of her breasts. A hint of the dark aureoles was visible through the flimsy cotton, and the sharply defined peaks strained against the cloth like ripe berries. Her waist was incredibly narrow, her calves slender, and her ankles trim where they peeped out from beneath the hem of her skirt.

Jenning's eyes devoured the woman's face and a tremor slithered through his loins at the thought of having such a wench beneath him. She was a rare find indeed. The un-blemished oval face and the shimmering cascade of black hair surrounding it were enough to render his mouth dry and his palms clammy.

"You," he rasped. "Come here."

Miranda walked with the grace of a cat, her hips playing with the sway of her skirt as if she had practised the effect in a hall of mirrors. She was conscious of the eyes of Verart's men following her, as well as the lustful gazes of the Yankee guards, the sailors, the stubby little captain, and his officers.

"You have a name?" the captain demanded.

The delicately shaped nostrils flared slightly as she nodded. She allowed the captain and Falworth an unimpaired view down the front of her blouse as she leaned forward to gingerly rub her thigh.

"You have been injured?" Jennings asked, over the catch in his throat.

"A scratch. Nothing more."

"Your name?"

The black lashes lowered and lay in a crescent on each cheek. "Miranda," she murmured.

"Miranda." Jennings tasted the name and found it to his liking. He smiled and turned to Lieutenant Falworth. "She seems to be the least likely of the lot to be harboring the pox. Have her brought to my cabin after the prisoners are all on board."

"Aye, sir," Falworth replied, his eyes still fastened to the dark-haired beauty — as were those of nearly every other man on the beach.

Jennings noted the absence of activity and scowled at Sergeant Rowntree. "Well, sir? What are you waiting for? I believe I gave you your orders. I want this business with Farrow over and done with before nightfall."

Rowntree snapped to attention. "Aye, sir! Sorry, sir." He watched Jennings and Falworth stride away and added beneath his breath, "And bugger you, sir."

"Careful, Sergeant, he just may take you up on the offer."

Rowntree whirled, startled to find Lieutenant Ballantine standing directly behind him. He flushed hotly and stiffened, waiting for the inevitable reprimand and probable arrest for insubordination.

But the lieutenant only arched an eyebrow and turned his attention back to the prisoners. Recognizing a reprieve, Sergeant Rowntree shouted to a pair of guards to separate

Verart Farrow from the others and bring him forward. At the sound of the order, Courtney leaped to her feet. A dirk appeared out of the folds of her clothing and was held unwaveringly in an outstretched fist.

"Stay away from him." The warning hissed through almost bloodless lips. "I'll geld the first bastard who dares to lay a hand on Verart Farrow."

"No! Court, no!" The man grunted and craned forward to snatch at a slim ankle. "D'ye hear me, I say no! God love ye, but can ye not see I'm a dead man anyway. Leave it be, Court! Leave it, I say."

"I'll not let them hang you like a thief," she said. "I'll see us all dead here where we stand before I'll allow that."

The vow was scarcely past her lips when Courtney heard the smooth slip of steel leaving leather. She dropped into a crouch and spun, but the tip of Ballantine's saber was there to meet her. She stared along the gleaming steel, past the carved hilt, the rock-steady arm, and up into the deadly calm, gray eyes.

"Drop the knife, boy," he murmured.

Courtney's heart pounded within her breast. Her fury was so great she was willing to die at that moment if she could take the golden-haired bastard with her. In a movement so deft it barely caught Ballantine's eye, she flipped the dirk so that the blade was held in the throwing position.

*"No, Court!"* Verart leaned forward. A cough halted him before he could reach her, and a terrible gurgle of blood surged from the cavity in his chest.

Courtney tore her eyes away from the Yankee. The rage died as swiftly as it had risen, and she fell to her knees by her uncle's side, the dirk thudding forgotten to the dirt. Some of the tension left Ballantine's arm, but he kept the saber pointed warily at the trio — especially at the giant who looked to be on the verge of erupting into violence. Ballantine bent over and retrieved the dirk from the sand, fingering it thoughtfully for a moment, noting the sharpness of the blade.

Courtney was bowed over her uncle, clutching his

shoulders as if she could infuse him with some of her strength. The coughing spasm continued until it seemed there could be no more breath in the ravaged chest. Verart's head sagged against Seagram, his eyes glazed over with an unnatural brightness, and the blood-flecked lips moved feebly.

"Court. Court, can ye hear me?"

"I hear you, Uncle," she cried softly. "Oh please . . . please don't die. You're all I have now. *Please* . . .' "

"I'm sorry, Court," he whispered. "Truly I am. But there's nought to be done for it. I'm all broken inside. 'Tis up to you now to see that the Farrows survive."

His eyes softened, and a hand quivered as it reached up to rest against her cheek. "Lord, how I wanted to see ye grown, child. How I wanted to see ye off this heathen land and into the likes of as fine a home as ye deserve. 'Twas what your father and I both wanted and worked for. He never liked this life, ye must believe that. He only kept it up for you." A coughing spasm gripped Verart again, and it was several moments before he could continue. "There's land for ye, Court, land in America. And a fine big house with servants to care for ye. Promise me" — his voice faded to a dry rasp — "promise me ye'll live to claim it. Promise me your father and I've no' died in vain. . . ."

Courtney had to place her ear against his mouth to hear the final few rattled words: a name, a place — things she cared nothing about at that moment. Tears blurred her vision, and her throat was scalded with helpless rage. When she raised her head she saw a faint, proud smile on her uncle's face, and a hard shine in his eyes as they flicked to a point over her shoulder.

She looked up and saw that the blond-haired officer had replaced his sword in its sheath and was silently observing them.

"Court —"

She looked back down at her uncle, her chest constricting in the rush of confused emotions. Verart used the last of his strength to twist his fingers into the coarse homespun cloth of her shirt and drag her close again.

"Court, there's more . . . something ye should know . . . ye must be warned . . . Seagram . . . Seagram knows." — he rolled his eyes up to the black-haired giant — "and . . . and . . .*oh, God*" — his mouth stretched into a rigid O and his tormented body arched upward. The hand twined in Courtney's shirt tightened enough to tear a section of the shoulder seam, then went suddenly slack.

"Uncle?" she gasped. "Uncle Verart?"

The glow faded from his eyes, and a final, weary groan emptied his lungs. Courtney stared at the wizened face for a long moment, her eyes huge and swimming with horror. She drew the lifeless head to her breast, and the tears slid hotly over the fringe of her lashes, leaving two shiny, wet streaks in the filth on her cheeks. From her chin, the tears dripped squarely onto her uncle's brow and trickled into his creased eyelids so that it appeared as if he too was weeping.

Lieutenant Ballantine knelt on one knee and pressed his fingers against the man's throat. There was no sign of life, no pulse, no flicker of a heartbeat. He glanced around him at the sea of hostile faces, then beyond the corsairs to the circle of waiting guards.

"I wouldn't let it become common knowledge that you are related to this man in any way," he murmured. "Do you hear me, boy?"

Courtney did nothing to acknowledge the Yankee's warning.

"The captain will feel cheated when he hears about this. You'd be wise not to offer him a substitute."

Ballantine pushed to his feet and strode briskly out of the ring of prisoners. He snapped out a series of orders to the guards and without a backward glance, headed along the beach to the waiting longboats.

The sergeant of the marines approached the burly, shaggy-maned giant with trepidation. Bloodied from a dozen scratches and in possession of two of the blackest, fiercest eyes Rowntree had ever seen, the pirate stood protectively by the young boy's side, his massive hands flexing and unflexing in a mute challenge. His arms were as solid as tree trunks, his torso powerful enough to rival Ulysses'. The sergeant halted and a dry tongue scraped nervously around his lips.

Seagram, Courtney, and six others were the last of the prisoners waiting on the beach for transportation to the ship. Behind them, belching clouds of black smoke curled over the knoll that concealed the main village from sight. Every hut, shed, and fencepost had been smashed and set afire, and no one on the beach had needed to see the nestled village to know how widespread the destruction was. Stores of food, caches of gold and silver plateware, silks, priceless gemstones, as well as a small mountain of rum puncheons and rich madeira wine casks had been carried down to the shoreline and were surrounded by grinning, clawing men whose task it was to sort and itemize the booty before transferring it to the *Eagle.* The grinning and clawing extended to the huddled, bedraggled group of women and children who had been herded together on the sand dunes. They too would be taken on board the *Eagle*, their fates etched plainly on the leering faces of their captors.

Musketfire sounded sporadically from beyond the dunes. Once, an immense explosion ripped the evening air wide apart, signifying that the powder magazine had been found and the surplus destroyed. The smell of smoke and charred flesh stung the nostrils; dozens of glowing fires robbed the summer sunset of its cool beauty.

"I'm ordered to put you all in chains," Rowntree said, fortified by the presence of muskets on either side of him. "Anyone resisting is to be shot."

Seagram's eyes narrowed. "You'll not be putting chains on me, Yankee. I cut my teeth on bones larger than you."

The seageant paled. He was young and earnest-faced, and the chains trembled in his hands. "Y-you have my final warning: the manacles . . . or a lead ball."

Courtney raised her head and laid a hand on Seagram's

forearm, halting the rumble of anger that was rising in the corsair's throat. "It would serve no purpose to die for such a trifling matter," she said softly.

She stepped out from behind the shield of Seagram's bulk and walked rigidly toward the marine, meeting his gaze unflinchingly as she held out both wrists.

Rowntree faintly smiled both his thanks and his apologies as he snapped the heavy iron bands around her slender wrists. The weight of the manacles and their linking chain dragged Courtney's arms downward, but she countered the strain and determinedly raised them to chest level again, holding them steady while the bolt was threaded and locked.

A four-foot length of iron chain separated her from the next pair of manacles, and she felt the startled tug as the guard looked up to find that Seagram had moved forward. The bracelets proved too small for the hairy wrists, and it took several minutes for the marine to jury-rig an adequate way to lock Seagram in line. In the end there were two twisted bolts and a good deal of damage to the hard flesh, but Seagram only grinned and glared down at Rowntree with a silent promise.

The rest of the men shuffled forward, accepting the manacles with balled fists and tautly compressed lips.

The sun had dipped below the horizon and the sky was tinted pink and gold as the prisoners were led through the shallow lapping surf to the waiting longboat. The water was surprisingly clear and dark where it rushed across the shale and, farther out, was like a velvet seat on which the graceful silhouette of the *Eagle* gently rocked. Damaged spars and rigging had already been removed and men were busy making repairs by lantern light. Marines had shed their battle dress and toiled alongside the ordinary seamen to haul away debris and wash down the bloodstained decks. Cannon blown from their carriages were being winched upright and reseated. Torn canvas sails were spread out on the spar deck and were being set to by the sailmaker and his league of frantically stitching apprentices.

The *Eagle* was a commerce raider, one hundred and fifty

feet long from bow to stern, carrying an armory of forty guns and crew of two hundred and seventy-five. Her three masts rose high above the cocoons of lamplight; her rigging sparkled against the sunset, jeweled in fine, clinging evening mist.

The longboat scraped against the hull of the frigate, and a bowline was tossed to a waiting sailor. A huge pair of emerald eyes gazed slowly up the curved side of planking, halting only when they came to the yawning lower level of gunports.

"On yer feet," a guard ordered gruffly, prodding the prisoner closest to him with the butt of his musket. "Step lively now. One slip and youse all go down. Ain't a one of us about to jump in the drink to save youse, neither."

Seagram tilted his head, and a small, scruffy buccaneer stood and grasped hold of the first ladder rung. He moved nimbly despite the cumbersome chains and led the seven others up and over the curve of the ship. Courtney was last in line, grateful to have Seagram ahead of her to take up the slack of the chain; she doubted whether there was enough strength left in her legs to make the climb without his help.

She stepped through the open stern gangway and down onto the main deck. All around them sailors stopped working to stare, curse, or jeer at the last of the Barbary captives. Many had stained bandages to show for their efforts in battle; many more fingered the dirks they wore strapped to their waists as if desirous of continuing the fight. That the crew did not appear to have been excessively depleted by the day-long battle was yet another blow to the men of Snake Island. Would that they had had the support of the *Falconer* or the *Wild Goose*! The Yankees would not be standing quite so smuggly on their deck now; they would not be looking quite so contemptuous of the men filing slowly past them.

Courtney felt a resurgence of the hatred that had been numbed temporarily by the death of her uncle. She stared at the neat row of bodies stretched out under canvas and knew there would be great pomp and ceremony accompanying their burial at sea. The brave men of Snake Island lay where they had fallen, exposed to the broiling sun and flies, defenseless against the two- and four-legged predators that would strip them to bare bone before many days had passed. She thought of Everart Farrow, sprawled with the other corpses on the pure white sand of the dunes.

They will be made to pay, she vowed bitterly, casting her eyes around the cluttered deck. All of them. Somehow, in some way, they will be made to pay for Verart's death and for the death of each and every man left behind to rot on the beaches of Snake Island.

The creak of tackle overhead caused Courtney to lift her gaze to the upper mainsail yard. The Yankee captain had said that Duncan Farrow swung from just such a yard, but she refused to believe it. Handsome, daring, and reckless, Duncan Farrow had commanded the men of Snake Island with a skill and boldness that had kept the rival bands of corsairs at a respectful distance. He had no use for the Dey of Algiers, no interest in the petty squabbles between the ruler of Tripoli and the nations whose merchant ships were regularly plundered and held to ransom. Farrow's was a private odyssey and if, as it happened, his goals coincided with those of the Tripolitans, he took advantage of the Pasha's protection, just as the Pasha took full advantage of the reputations of the *Falconer* and the *Wild Goose*. Courtney could not believe, she *refused* to believe, he was dead. The idea that Duncan Farrow could have been caught by these primped and overstuffed Yankees was laughable. It had been a ploy by the captain to shock Verart Farrow into revealing himself, and it had worked. But she, Courtney Farrow, would make them pay dearly for their treachery.

A pair of pale, blue-gray eyes stole into her consciousness.

*He* was standing on the quarter-deck, his hands braced on the carved oak fife rail, his tall, broad frame highlighted by the blood-red sunset. He wore a slight frown, as if he had been observing her for some time and suspected that something about her was wrong, out of place.

The bindings Verart had insisted she wrap around her breasts cut into her flesh, preventing Courtney from taking the deep swallows of air that would have helped control the anger rising within her. She knew her only chance to survive — and possibly to escape — lay in her remaining an anonymous face among the prisoners. To reveal her sex or identity would place her in the hands of the *Eagle*'s captain and expose her to his thirst for retribution. At the very least it would leave her to share a fate no better than that of the other women of Snake Island. Both Verart and Seagram had insisted on the ruse; it was necessary for her survival. That the Yankee lieutenant knew at least half of her secret should have prompted her to lower her eyes and keep them lowered, yet she was drawn to the gray threat like a magnet: the Irish curse was with her — the need to see and know an enemy, to show a lack of fear so there could be no doubt about the outcome of a confrontation.

Lieutenant Ballantine felt the hatred ripple across the open deck, glowing from the depths of the eyes that had turned almost black with intensity. The blood pounded in his temples, and his knuckles turned white on the railing. He felt as if he was staring at death itself — his death. The challenge was unmistakable. Moreover, he had the distinct feeling he would come to regret not having used his sword earlier that afternoon.

The spell was broken by the rough hand of a guard shoving against Courtney's shoulders. The line of prisoners was ushered along the main deck to the afterhatch and led down two levels of steep, dark stairs to the musty airlessness of the orlop deck. They were below the waterline, and the sounds of the chains clinking and dragging were muted in the dankness. A command was barked from somewhere ahead in the narrow confines, and the line moved again in darkness.

This deck housed, among other things, the infirmary and the surgeon's cockpit. Courtney tried to block out the groans and the cries of the wounded, but she could not avoid glimpses of the two lighted rooms they passed where men in white aprons leaned over bloody worktables. Nor could she completely ignore the stench of cauterized flesh, of boiled tar and sickly sweet camphor. She saw a man, dressed in a chaplain's collar and black apron, holding a cup of rum to a sailor's lips with one hand, and making repeated signs of the cross over the patient's legless stumps with the other.

A strained, weary voice halted the prisoners.

"Any wounded in this lot?"

The guard shrugged and waved a hand casually. "Dunno, doc. This is the last of 'em, though."

The doctor moved slowly along the manacled line, studying limbs and faces and torsos for signs of damage. When he came to Seagram, he stopped and tilted his head up in appreciative awe.

"I don't suppose you want medical attention for any of those scratches, do you?"

Seagram bared his teeth and grunted, "Bugger off."

"I didn't think so." The doctor's mouth twisted wryly, and he was about to return to his small anteroom when he caught sight of Courtney's blue bandanna. He craned his neck to see around Seagram and saw the ugly, weeping wound high on her arm.

"What about you, son? Care to let me take a look at that?"

"Bugger off," she said, duplicating Seagram's low hiss. "I'll live."

"Perhaps." He limped slightly, favoring a game leg, as he moved past Seagram. "And perhaps not, if you keep losing blood at that rate."

Courtney's eyes narrowed, but she said nothing as the doctor's hands deftly probed beneath the soiled bandanna.

"Right," he pronounced crisply. "I'll see this one. Cut him loose."

The guard warily unlocked the bar connecting Courtney's chains to the others. "You want me to wait, doc?"

"Are you suggesting the boy could overpower me? Or perhaps you think he'll try to make a run for the side and swim ashore? No, corporal" — the doctor sighed when his sarcasm was lost on the soldier — "leave the boy and leave the key and get on with what you were doing. I'll send him down when I've finished."

"Aye," grumbled the guard, clearly not pleased by the tone of the dismissal.

The doctor started back for the surgery. "Come along, lad. Quicker in, quicker out."

Courtney exchanged a terse glance with Seagram as he was led away, down the dark corridor. She remained standing in the spill of light from the surgery, listening to the fading clink of chains. When there was nothing more to see or hear she moved tentatively toward the lantern light, blinking uncertainly as she stopped in the entranceway.

The doctor was busy as the far side of the room pouring clean water into a chipped enamel basin. He was of medium height and build, and his hawkish profile was softened by curly, cropped chestnut-brown hair. He could have been any age: a young man cursed with a mature face, or an older man favored with smooth features. Only the deep-set hazel eyes betrayed the fact that he would probably not see his thirtieth year again. They were haunted by the many hours spent witnessing the suffering of others.

"Come along, boy," he muttered, noting the inspection. "I haven't all day."

Courtney ventured into the surgery, warily examining the dreadful assortment of files and pincers, saws and knives that lay spread out on a long wooden bench. Her gaze was drawn to a particularly thin, razor-like blade that seemed to beckon to her from across the table.

"I can move surprisingly fast," the doctor murmured, not looking up from the basin he was filling with water, "crippled leg or not."

Courtney released her pent-up breath, acknowledging the warning. She also saw that they were not the only ones in the surgery. A thin, wide-eyed boy of ten or eleven years stood by a steaming vat of hot water into which he stirred soiled rags and bandages to be washed and reused.

"That's Dickie," Dr. Rutger said, by way of an introduction. "Dickie Little. He helps out with odd jobs."

The doctor smiled at the boy and moved his hands in a series of gestures. The boy studied the doctor's hands, nodded, and crossed over to stand by the table of instruments.

"He's deaf," the doctor added. "The ship he was on exploded, taking his family, his identity, and his hearing with it. We've developed a rather crude method of communicating. Crude, but effective. Have a seat. I'll need to clear away a few layers of grime on your arm before I can see what has to be done. How did it happen?"

Courtney sat on the edge of the chair and kept her lips pressed firmly shut. To her chagrin, the doctor smiled again.

"So I've got myself a tough, seasoned pirate, eh? Well, let me see then — " He rolled her sleeve up to her shoulder and swabbed at the crusted blood and dirt. The scrap of cotton that had been tied around the wound to staunch the flow of blood came away with difficulty, leaving Courtney's cheeks drained of color. It took three squares of linen to completely clean the wounded flesh, then a separate dry cloth to dab at the fresh trickles of blood while the doctor decided what to do.

"I'd guess it to be from a fragment of an exploding shell. Would that be close?"

The emerald eyes lifted to his.

"Among my other attributes, I've been in the navy for seven years." His smile slipped under the intensity of her gaze, and he straightened. "How old are you, son?"

"I'm not your son."

"True enough. You do have a name though, don't you?"

"Court," she said after a pause.

"Curt? Very well then, Curt, how old are you?"

"Old enough to slit your throat ear to ear and take pleasure in doing it."

The doctor glanced up, mildly startled. He almost laughed at the attempted bravado, but thought better of it. Instead he gestured to Dickie Little which instruments to fetch from the table. "Then I suppose you are old enough to sit still while I attempt to sew this together?"

Courtney glanced involuntarily at the wound. She had not seen it without benefit of dirt and ragged cloth but she knew by the pain and the amount of blood clotted on her arm that it was no small cut. The sight of the jagged, furrowed flesh caused a bubble of nausea to rise in her throat, and she swiftly turned her head away.

"The lacerations go rather deep, I'm afraid. Lucky for you the main artery was missed and the bone seems to be in one piece." He saw her eyes close and her throat move in a heavy swallow. "You can take your shirt off before we begin. I'll find something cleaner for you to put on later."

"No," she said sharply, the queasiness vanishing instantly. "No, I — " She clamped her mouth shut and turned away.

"Suit yourself," he shrugged. "Although I fail to see how an absence of odor could be construed as cowardice by your associates. Here, take this."

Courtney frowned at the wedge of wood he held out to her.

"What's this for?"

"You hold it in your fist and squeeze," he said gently. "Or if you prefer you can bite down on it when I begin. Even the bravest of men have limits to the amount of pain they can endure in silence."

Courtney looked from the doctor's face to the chunk of wood.

"By the way, my name is Matthew. Matthew Rutger. You may, from time to time, hear the men address me fondly as 'Rotgut,' but pay no heed. They know full well their wretched lives depend on my mercy. Consequently they know when to lose at dice, the type of brandy I enjoy in the evening, and the general temperament of the women I prefer. It helps if you breathe."

Courtney gasped and squeezed her eyes tightly shut. He was talking to distract her, to divert her attention from the needle and thread punching through her flesh, but he was unsuccessful. She felt the sweat beading across her brow, and she gripped the edge of the bench so hard her arms trembled and her fingers burned with the agony.

"Almost done," he murmured. "Two more . . . one . . . finished."

Courtney exhaled loudly, shuddering as the shock jolted through her body. Her arm throbbed so badly it took several minutes for her vision to clear and the pounding to leave her temples. The deaf boy touched her shoulder and held out a cup of rum. "Go ahead," Rutger said. "Drink it. The worst is over."

Courtney accepted the cup and swallowed the strong rum in two desperate gulps. It landed in her empty stomach like a fireball. While she collected her breath and her wits, the doctor finished bandaging her arm.

"Better?" he asked, with a smile.

"Yes, I — " she stopped, sensing they were no longer alone in the room. She glanced toward the door and saw the tall blond Yankee officer leaning casually against the jamb.

"Ah," — the doctor followed her gaze — "Lieutenant Ballantine. Is this a social visit or are you in need of my services?"

"Neither." The lieutenant straightened from the doorway, a movement duplicated by a suddenly nervous Dickie Little, who backed away from the table as the lieutenant approached. "I was just on my way to the brig to see if our guests were comfortable." He nodded at Courtney. "Is the boy ready to join them?"

"His arm is patched, if that's what you mean. I'm not so sure I'm ready to condemn him to the prison hold."

Ballantine shrugged. "He fought as hard as any of them. Seems to me he's earned the right to share in their reward."

"Adrian, for God's sake, he's only a boy."

"Weren't we all at one time or another?"

Rutger sighed. "And look at how you turned out. Perhaps given half a chance — "

"Softening in your old age, Matthew?" Ballantine's

mouth curved down at the corner. "Or is this just a desire to adopt another stray?"

"I don't call it soft to try to give the boy a chance. You know damn well what will happen to him if he spends the next two months locked away in the hold like a rat."

"What would you have me do?" Ballantine asked, with gentle sarcasm. "Convince the captain to take him on as a bootboy?"

The doctor shook his head and grimaced. "No, but maybe you could arrange a parole to the galley, or let the boy work with the sailmaster, or the carpenter, at least during the day. It's been done before with good results."

The lieutenant glanced pointedly at Dickie Little, who was trying unsuccessfully to blend into the shadows. His eyes narrowed and raked casually over Courtney's tattered clothing. "Your . . . friend on the beach — was he your only family?"

The emerald of her eyes flared darkly with an unspoken retort. *As if he cares. As if any of them care!*

"Speak up, boy. Do you have anyone else on this ship? Any other family?"

"No," she spat. "You bastards have done your job well."

His jaw squared into a ridge. "I see. Matthew seems to think you deserve an opportunity for redemption. What do you think?"

Courtney smiled tightly. "I think you're a pair of filthy Yankee sods and I'd shoot you both dead if I had the chance."

Rutger sighed audibly. Ballantine simply stared.

"Have you ever had a taste of the lash, boy?" he asked finally.

Courtney's response was to tilt her chin defiantly higher.

"I'll warn you not to test my patience too far, or you will," he promised. "Now thank the good doctor for his services."

"Go to hell, Yankee."

The lieutenant reached forward suddenly, grasping the

chain that linked her manacled wrists together. He twisted it to take up the slack, causing the iron bracelets to bite deeply into her flesh. She was yanked off balance at the same time and only saved herself from a bad fall by bracing her hands against his chest.

"I said, thank the doctor," he hissed. His eyes had become darker, angrier, hinting at a violent temper beneath the cool exterior.

"Thank you, doctor," she spat contemptuously.

He shoved her toward the door and scoffed, "Any more humanitarian suggestions, Matthew?"

The doctor avoided meeting the lieutenant's gaze as Courtney was shoved roughly again, this time hard enough to strike her wounded shoulder against the bulkhead in the companionway. She choked back a cry of pain and stumbled ahead of the Yankee's impatient bootsteps, half running along the dimly lit corridor. When they arrived at the farthest, murkiest point in the hold, he barked at her to halt.

Three lounging guards, alerted to the lieutenant's black mood, jumped to attention at once.

"Put this boy in the cage. He wants a few days alone to learn some manners."

"Aye, sar." One of the men saluted and stepped forward. "And 'is bracelets?"

Ballantine glanced down at the chafing manacles. "Leave them. It'll give him something to sharpen his teeth on."

With that, the Yankee officer turned on his heel and strode back along the passageway. Courtney felt a tug on her shirt and heard the guard grunt an order to follow him. Tears, pressing and unwanted, burned behind her eyes as she inwardly voiced every curse and invocation she could remember. She passed the barred entrance to the brig and felt some relief when she recognized Seagram's scowling face peering out from the dark interior. He roared a stream of oaths when he realized she was not to be put in the same holding pen, and his voice was joined instantly by a rousing chorus of oaths from deep in the darkness.

The guard muttered a Scottish oath and banged on the iron bars with his truncheon. The din only increased in volume, and several arms snaked out from between the bars in an attempt to grab the wooden club.

"Gi' on wi' ye," he snarled, pushing Courtney away from the bedlam. There was a squat iron cage at the far corner of the hold, three of its sides made of rusted bars and the fourth of moldy, slime-covered planking. Something dark and furry darted out from behind the crates stacked nearby, and she could smell and feel the vileness accumulated an inch thick beneath the soles of her feet. There was no source of light other than the yellowish glow that came from the lantern at the guard station. There were creaks and drips and constant groans from the outer hull, and for the first time since the attack on Snake Island began, Courtney experienced a shiver of fear.

"Couldn't I be put in with the others?" she whispered, facing the burly guard.

"Ye heard the lieutenant's orthers. And I'm nae the man to go agin 'im." The Scot hesitated, seeing the bright shine in the lad's eyes. "Ach . . . I'll fetch ye a crate to sit on. Keep yer feet up off the muck and gi' a rattle on the chains noo an' then to keep the rats away."

Courtney shuddered. She watched him slot a thick iron key into the lock, twist it, and swing the cage door wide. She looked up into his face once, steeled herself against the pity she saw there, and ducked slowly inside.

# Chapter Two

Miranda Gold yawned and stretched, arching her golden body into the stream of sunlight that filtered through the open gallery door. From habit, she slid her hand along her thigh and inspected the single bruise she had earned during the fight for Snake Island. It was low on her hip, and she hadn't the faintest recollection of how she had come by it — probably in the hut with Drudge. At any rate, it had faded nicely over the past six days, changing from an angry, mottled purple to a sickly yellow.

She was alone in the huge tester bed; the curtains were still in place, the sheer netting draped from canopy to floor in an effort to deter the intrusion of night bugs and mosquitoes. Filmy enough to let her feel the gentle morning breezes against her body, the net was thick enough to give her the impression she could see without being seen. Jennings was seated behind his desk. She could clearly make out the shiny top of his head, the brow pleated in concentration, the fat, spatulate fingers scratching a quill across the pages of his journal. The man was obsessed with recording the hours and minutes of his life, as if they were of importance in the grand scheme of things. As if in years to come the volumes would be exhumed from some dusty vault and held aloft for all to see and praise.

Miranda sighed and rolled onto her side, and her gaze followed the slash of light from the gallery window. The greatcabin was not as large as either the *Wild Goose*'s or the *Falconer*'s, but what was lost in size was made up for in comfort. No spartan, military basics for Captain Willard Leach Jennings. His desk was carved oak with brass inlays; his chairs were upholstered in thick rich velvet; the carpet underfoot was Persian, the pile deep enough for one to lose sight of toes and heels. A china washbasin and pitcher sat atop a priceless gilded nightstand; the lower tier housed a solid gold thunderpot. There were two enormous ebony sea chests, oriental in design, with a pair of rearing dragons inlaid in ivory on the sides and lid. A wire-fronted cabinet was stocked with silver goblets and china dinnerware. The candles on his desk were seated in gold bases, and even the lantern on the ceiling beam was brass, not pewter or tin.

Yes indeed, she mused, Jennings was a man consumed by self-interest and creature comforts, a pompous man who used and abused his power. It had taken less than two minutes for Miranda to assess his character and to determine he was the type of man who could be cruel and vicious when the mood was upon him, or as malleable as a hungry puppy when the events of the day agreed with him. A conceited fool, a blow-hard: the kind of man she normally associated with French uniforms and tastes that ran to young boys.

The amber eyes clouded a moment as they stared through the film of netting. She had assumed, with the entry of Duncan Farrow into her life, that the need for such games would be over. Sold to a Spanish marquis at the age of nine, traded to a Dutchman by the time she was twelve, won on a dueling field at fourteen, then kidnapped by a

Frenchman and forced to work in a bordello, she had developed early on the instincts of a survivor. A multilingual survivor, she reflected wryly. And that talent, more than anything else, had earned her the notice of Duncan Farrow.

She had been sixteen and serving aboard a French merchantman in the capacity of captain's plaything, when the ship, *Triomphe*, had been attacked and destroyed by the *Wild Goose*. The corsair, Duncan Farrow, had shown little interest in Miranda's more obvious charms, and even though she had targeted him to be her protector, it was not until she had off-handedly cursed him in four languages that she had earned a second glance. His own talents, although impressive, were confined to a brilliance in naval tactics and a wild fearlessness and cunning in the face of adversity. He had sheafs of captured documents he could not translate: a treasurehouse of shipping schedules and manifests he had no means of interpreting — until Miranda had come along. "Golden Miranda," he had laughingly dubbed her, after the first documents she deciphered led to a prize cargo of ten chests of gold coin.

She spent hours poring over ledgers and manifests, and hours studying the tall, enigmatic Irishman whose smile was as quick as his temper. He was the first man — the only man — Miranda had encountered who appeared to be completely immune to her powers of seduction. Rum did not affect him, regardless of the quantity, nor did provocative clothing — or the lack of it. Subtle invitations were refused; not so subtle attempts to arouse him won black moods and even blacker threats of violence. Yet she had heard of his prowess between the sheets from a dozen sources. There were no apparent grounds to question his manhood, yet he seemed loathe to touch her even by accident.

After a week of mounting frustration, the reason for his bizarre behaviour was introduced to Miranda on the shores of Snake Island: Courtney Farrow.

Duncan's daughter, his protégée, his conscience.

She and Miranda had been the same age: sixteen. They

had been the same height and had a similar fine-boned structure, but they shared little else beyond an ability to convey entire worlds of emotion in their sparkling eyes. At sixteen years, Miranda possessed a face and body that turned heads in awe, whereas Courtney was all legs and eyes. The dress she consented to wear on special occasions hung from her slender shoulders like a sack. Her hair was a lustrous auburn but it had been cropped boyishly short by the hand of a butcher. There was nothing soft or pretty about her, nothing promising in the gawky, suspicious way she shunned everything feminine. Miranda had been told the blood of the French aristocracy flowed in Courtney's veins, but it was obviously in short supply, a supply that rapidly became shorter. It flowed daily from cuts and scrapes, from scuffles with the young boys on the island, from rope burns and splinters when she worked on the rigging of her father's ship. It flowed most stubbornly during the lessons she sought with sword and dirk and pistol.

The woman and the girl hated one another on sight. Miranda was sensual and voluptuous, with flowing black hair and proud, jutting breasts. She could seduce a man with a single glance, promise him pleasures beyond his wildest imaginings by a pout on her gloriously red mouth, and speak volumes with the silent language of her body. Only Duncan Farrow eluded her. And only because he associated her with his daughter.

Accepting the challenge, Miranda had become like a panther stalking its prey. She concentrated on Duncan Farrow with a singlemindedness that doomed him from the outset, despite the strength of his own resolve. She attacked him through Courtney, his weakest link, by assuming the role of motherly advisor. She suggested to Duncan that he persuade his daughter to learn at least the rudiments of femininity, and then she proceeded to show the chit how to dress, how to arrange what little hair she boasted into an attractive style, how to wear a corset, and how to add to the meager allotment nature had provided in order to fill out the bodice of a dress.

Courtney had rebelled, as Miranda had known she

would. Humiliated, she had hurled accusations at both her father and his supposed mistress, compounding Duncan's frustration by declaring an abhorrence for everything soft and feminine. Duncan had been startled into realizing what everyone else had seen from the outset, that Miranda and Courtney were as different as the wind and the sea. He had retreated in glowering silence to the solitude of the *Wild Goose* — where Miranda had been waiting with open arms.

Miranda inhaled deeply and smiled at the memory of her lean Irishman standing rock-like and immobile as she slowly pulled away the layers of their clothing. Her body had glowed in the shadow-haunted cabin: the curves had been accentuated, the ripeness of her flesh had been presented like an offering of pure gold. And such discoveries she'd made! Her reluctant lover was sculpted from mahogany, honed to athletic perfection with not an inch of excess flesh anywhere on his impressive frame. His arms were like iron and rivaled Seagram's in strength; his legs were sinew and bulging muscles. His flesh bore a hundred scars, some from his youth in Ireland, many from his days as a mercenary in Europe, most from the years he spent plundering the shipping routes of the Mediterranean. Savagely demanding in his lovemaking, he was able to render her breathless and trembling and utterly satisfied. So satisfied, she probably would have been content to keep him as her only lover, despite his infuriating obsession with his daughter. Yet, while he had admitted Miranda to his bed, he was as cool and indifferent to her as if she were only a vent for his physical needs. Ten minutes prior to leading her to bed and ten minutes after leaving it, he was a stranger — a dangerous stranger with black moods and an impenetrable wall around his innermost emotions that only Courtney had access to.

It had been maddening and demeaning, and more than once Miranda had sought to punish him by going elsewhere for the attention she craved. Never within his notice, however. He was not a forgiving man, or one likely to look on cuckolding with much favor, but it gave her an inner satisfaction to know she had cheated him, that she could leave him any time she chose.

Well, there were no alternatives now. Duncan was dead, and she, Miranda — Golden Miranda — had changed hands again. If she tried very hard she might be able to coax forth a tear or two for her lover's fate — he had been a man who deserved better than a dog's hanging — but tears were not a part of her character. She shed them often, certainly, and always to good effect, but she could not recall the last honest tear she had parted with. She was a survivor and, moreover, she knew how to survive with a minimum of discomfort. It was another glaring difference between the Mirandas and the Courtney Farrows of the world: some were born to languish on silks and satins, others were driven to prove their merit in fetid prison cells.

The image amused her and Miranda snuggled deeper into the cool, slippery sheets. A smile pulled at the corners of her mouth as she thought of Courtney Farrow battered and bleeding, dazed to insensibility and broken in spirit as she was dragged out of the dank hold and passed among the leering, lustful crew members for the dozenth time. It would be the end of her; Miranda only wished she could have been present to witness it. Surely after a week of captivity the little bitch was dead.

Lieutenant Adrian Ballantine studied the toe of his polished leather boot and frowned over a salt stain one of the cabin boys had missed. He was freshly bathed and shaved. His damp hair trapped the soft rays from the lantern and gleamed the color of burnished brass.

He was dressed in a loose-fitting shirt and breeches, having decided it was too early in the afternoon and too hot in his cabin to bother with the heavy woolen tunic and formal collar. His snowy white shirt was open at the throat and contrasted vividly with the deep tan and the wealth of coppery-brown hair on his chest. His feet were crossed at the ankles and propped carelessly on the corner of his desk; his long tapered fingers were steepled beneath his lower lip. His brow, furrowed in concentration, cleared suddenly as he noted a subtle change in the ship's motion.

A summer storm had kept them anchored in the shelter of a friendly bay for the past forty-eight hours, giving them extra time to lick their wounds and effect minor repairs to sails and rigging. They had sailed around Cape Blanc with the early-morning breezes, and if the weather held they would be anchored at Gibraltar within three days.

Lieutenant Ballantine blinked and raised his head at the sound of a knock on his cabin door.

"Yes, what is it?"

"Rowntree, sir."

Ballantine was about to object to the interruption, then recalled that the sergeant-at-arms was present by his request. He sighed and lowered his feet from the desk.

"Come in, Mister Rowntree."

The cabin, located amidships, was windowless and ten paces square. Comfortable enough for a man of Spartan tastes, it contained a sleeping berth, a desk and chair, a bookcase, and a narrow wardrobe. It seemed overcrowded, however, with the introduction of two more bodies.

As soon as the sergeant ushered the sorry-looking bundle of rags through the doorway, the lieutenant's gray-blue eyes widened and his nose wrinkled in protest at the indescribably foul odor that accompanied the prisoner into his cabin.

"Good God. Couldn't you have thrown a bucket of water over him before bringing him here?"

"I did, sir," Rowntree assured him, his own nose twisted in distaste. "But it comes with the accommodations. Sort of grows on them, if you know what I mean."

Ballantine stared at the boy and debated the wisdom of his impulse.

"See if you can locate Dr. Rutger for me. The boy has some stitches that may require attention."

"Aye, sir. Anything else?"

The lieutenant hesitated, wondering if it was his memory playing tricks on him, or if the boy had actually shrunk inside the folds of filthy clothing. His face was gray from lack of fresh air; the downcast eyes seemed sunken in hollows the color of old bruises.

"When was the last time the prisoner ate?"

"Damned if I know, sir. According to MacDonald, he throws most of what he's given right back in their faces."

"He does, does he?" Adrian lowered his hands to the desktop and drummed his fingers lightly on the wood. "Thank you, Sergeant. That will be all for now."

"Aye, sir."

When the door was shut again, Ballantine sorted through a sheaf of papers on his desk and stacked them neatly in the corner. He could feel the wary eyes of the prisoner on him, following his every move, and Ballantine had to resist the urge to smile.

Courtney only noted the grimness of his expression and the power that rippled through the muscles of his chest as he moved. She was bewildered by the unexpected summons, uncertain of what this arrogant, self-righteous officer might want of her. Forced to the back of her mind was the terror of her confinement in the small iron cage, and the very real dread she had of being sent back down to it again. She had always loathed tight, confined spaces, and the cage had been one of the toughest tests of her will and endurance. She had repeatedly fought the urge to scream, to weep hysterically, to tear at the planks and bars and beg her captors to give her a single dry blanket, a single small light, a single deep breath of fresh salt air. But she had done none of those things. She had spent the time crouched in silence and darkness, and while her cheeks had often been damp at times, she had no recollection of feeling any emotion other than hatred.

She felt it now, stifling her ability to hear and think clearly. Her eyes burned from the brightness in the cabin; her muscles were cramped from the sudden ability to stand straight; her skin was clogged with dirt and sweat and drying salt water, and bore welts and raw patches from the manacles and the rigid bars. She had lost the blue bandanna, and her hair hung about her shoulders in a greasy snarl; her clothes were mildewed and stank of dampness.

Yet, when she raised her downcast eyes for the first time and met those of her hated enemy's, they were bright and clear and burning darkly with green fire.

"Well, boy, what have you learned over the course of the past seven days and nights besides how to waste good food and stink up my cabin?"

Courtney stared at him hard. Seven days! She had lost track of the time in the airless semi-darkness.

"How to reply smartly to a direct question, I see," the lieutenant mused. "Perhaps you need another week in solitude to loosen your tongue."

To Courtney's chagrin, a gasp escaped her lips. "No. No, I —"

She bit down on the inside of her lip, but the smug smile was already curving his mouth.

"You what?"

"I don't give a damn what you do, Yankee," she spat defiantly. "But to answer your question: The food was crawling with maggots and you have your own hospitality to thank for the stink."

Ballantine leaned back in the chair. "You're accustomed to better living conditions, are you?"

"I'm accustomed to living like a human being, not an animal."

"You sound educated, boy," the lieutenant observed, after a lengthy pause. "Does that mean you were not always in the company of pirates?"

"I fail to see why my upbringing should interest you."

"It doesn't," he said crisply. "I merely find the notion that Duncan Farrow might have intended his son for better things entertaining."

The emerald eyes narrowed. "A pity *your* father did not have a similar ambition."

Ballantine regarded her in mild astonishment. A week in the cage would have demoralized a man twice the age of this urchin, not fired his spirit.

He smiled briefly. "You seem bent on testing my patience, boy. Have you that much contempt for the value of your life?"

Courtney did not answer. Her hands curled into fists around the heavy link of the iron chain, and she glared at him with as much loathing as she could muster. It did not have the effect she intended, for he merely looked into the snapping fury of her eyes and his smile developed into quiet laughter.

"All right, boy, you've proven how fierce you can be. I'm impressed, truly I am. And against my better judgment, I'm even prepared to offer you a way to help yourself."

"Help myself?" she asked suspiciously, still bristling from his laughter.

He laid his hands flat on the desk. "A hot meal, a long hot *bath*, and perhaps even a chance to earn a parole in the galley."

"In exchange for what?"

"A little information."

Courtney stiffened. "Go to hell."

"Your father was running the blockade out of Tripoli, was he not?"

Courtney tightened her grip on the chain and said nothing.

"How did he know where and when to cut through the blockade?"

She looked away disdainfully.

"What was he carrying through the blockade? Was he planning to return directly to Snake Island?" Again the long fingers drummed noiselessly on the desktop. "I have the duty watch in two hours, boy. I'd like the answers before then."

"You'll get nothing from me, Yankee," she snarled.

Ballantine drew a deep, patient breath. "You and your uncle were not taken along on this raid. Why was that?"

"You're smart, Yankee. You tell me."

"I'd rather *you* tell me," he said silkily, and Courtney found herself staring into the wintery gray eyes.

"Verart had a wound in his leg," she said shortly. "It hadn't healed properly."

"Ships sail with wounded men."

She barely missed a beat. "They also sail with peacocks at the helm."

"And you?" Ballantine asked easily. "Why were you left behind? A man like Farrow" — he shrugged — "one would think he would be proud to have his son fighting by his side."

Courtney felt the blood rush warmly to her cheeks. The deliberate insinuation that Duncan Farrow did not think his son worthy to fight at his side begged for a retort, but Courtney refused to rise to the bait. Son or daughter, she could fight as well as any man, could wield a cutlass or a musket with as much confidence and skill. Years of living among the hardened corsairs had taught her much — including unquestioning acceptance of orders as they were given her by her father. He had ordered her and Verart to remain on Snake Island, for reasons the Yankee would never learn from her.

Ballantine stood up suddenly and walked over to the nightstand. Courtney tensed as she heard the soft trickle of water being poured from a pitcher into a tin mug.

"Are you thirsty?" he asked, half turning. "Or hungry?"

She watched the icy clear water tip out of the jug and she ran her tongue across her parched lips. "No."

He smiled and extended the cup. "Here, boy. Drink it. You aren't breaking any unwritten codes by doing so."

The cabin swayed giddily beneath her feet for a moment and to Courtney's mortification she began to tremble. She squeezed her eyes shut against the temptation, but when she opened them again, it was still there. The Yankee had moved closer. He had detected a weakness and would use it to soften her, to befriend her and then ply her with questions.

"I want nothing from you, Yankee," she rasped, her mouth so dry her tongue seemed to scratch against its roof as she spoke. "I only want to be treated like the other prisoners."

"But you aren't like the other prisoners," he said pointedly. "You're the son of Duncan Farrow and you'd be quite a feather in the captain's cap were he to discover you are on board.''

"Then why haven't you told him?" she whispered, trying not to imagine the taste or feel of the water he still held out to her.

"I haven't told him because he'd be just as apt to hang you from the nearest yardarm as deliver you to the authorities for trial."

"That idea troubles you?" she snorted, mockingly.

He smiled and sat on the edge of the desk. "Not at all. Certainly not as much as it would trouble you."

"I would look on it simply as another demonstration of Yankee justice."

The bitterness in her voice scraped a nerve along Ballantine's spine. "Your people have earned whatever form of justice they get. Piracy, extortion, white slavery, murder — those are hardly acts deserving leniency."

"My father is not a murderer," was the taut response. "He does not deal in slavery and has never once extorted a ransom for any captured Yankee crews."

"What about the French and the Spanish?"

"He treats them as they treat us. A lesson I can only hope you learn in the near future."

Ballantine's temper was prodded, and he set the tin mug on the desk. "But you don't deny the charge of piracy — of attacking shipping lines and taking vessels by force. Or perhaps you have a means of justifying that as well?"

"You Yankees have already found a means," she said, dryly. "I believe you call it privateering."

"You have your definitions a little twisted, boy."

"Do I? Your merchantmen are armed. They open fire on French and Spanish ships, do they not? They waylay cargoes of spices and sugar from the West Indies, and they transport shiploads of Africans to sell as slaves to work your fat cotton plantations. Tell me, Yankee, how do you define those *honorable* practices if not as piracy and slavery?"

She had the satisfaction of seeing a warm flush spread upward into the lieutenant's face.

"You have your father's nerve, boy," he murmured, after a tense moment. "I'll say that much for you. And frankly, I've about reached the end of my good humor. I want answers and I want them now, or so help me Christ, you'll come to think of the cage as a holiday."

"You don't frighten me, Yankee," she said, squaring her shoulders. "And you're wasting your breath if you think a few threats will make me quail before you."

Ballantine's eyes were cold and hard as he crossed his muscular arms over his chest. "We know quite a lot already about your father's . . . business. We know Duncan Farrow was in the employ of Yusef Karamanli, the Pasha of Tripoli. We also know he had dealings with Rais Mahomet Rout, the Dey of Algiers — an odd combination of associates, since the two despots are sworn enemies."

"Are they?" Courtney asked mildly. "I wouldn't know."

"And you wouldn't know what your father was bringing through the blockade that was important enough to deserve the cooperation of both Arabs?"

"My father's business is his own."

"I'm making it mine."

"Then I wish you luck," she countered evenly. "You'll have a great need for it."

Adrian contemplated the hard set to the boy's jaw, the deadly earnest green eyes, as well as the unspoken challenge. Always challenge, never defeat.

"Duncan Farrow's ships are destroyed, boy; his stronghold is in ruins, his life forfeit — the games are over. There is nothing left but your own fate to bargain for, and nothing standing between you and survival but your own foolish notions of sacrifice. As I recall, your uncle's last instructions to you were to live, at any cost. I imagine Duncan Farrow's last wish would have been the same. If you won't do it to help yourself, you should at least consider doing it for them."

It was a cruel blow, given with cold dispassion, and Ballantine disliked himself for having to resort to such methods. But the boy had to accept the fact that he was alone now, that he would find no sympathy anywhere else on this ship. In somewhat less than three days, he would be set ashore in Gibraltar bound either for a hanging, or for a long prison sentence — unless he did something to help himself.

"Well?"

"My father is not dead," Courtney whispered hoarsely. "I refuse to believe it."

Ballantine was transfixed by the glowing eyes. The centres had expanded until only a thin rim of green remained.

"Your father and Garrett Shaw are both dead," he repeated, his voice like ice.

"No."

"The *Wild Goose* has been destroyed, so has the *Falconer*. Karamanli sold them both out. Someone did, because the word was leaked through to the American patrol ships telling them where and when to intercept."

Courtney felt the clutch of raw fear in her chest. "No! You're lying!"

"Am I? Then how did we know about Snake Island? How did we know the strength of your uncle's defenses, the number of men he would have by his side to protect it? Your father was sold to us, boy, and if not by Karamanli, then by one of his own men."

Courtney reacted with the instincts of a trapped animal. A blurred movement of her hand beneath the waist of her shirt produced the gleaming knife she had taken from the surgery the first day. She thrust it out in front of her, gripped tightly in bruised and swollen fingers.

Ballantine's astonishment was genuine, and it slowed his reactions. He saw the glitter of steel slashing toward him and twisted to one side a fraction of a second before the blade hissed by his throat. With one hand he grabbed for the outstretched arm and with the other shoved against Courtney's chest and spun her off balance and back against the wall. She recovered swiftly, pivoted around, and lashed out with her nails. Adrian felt flesh and hair torn in thin runnels from his scalp. He slammed a brutal punch into her midsection, one that drove the air from her lungs and left Courtney doubled over in agony.

Ballantine kicked savagely at the knife and sent it spinning safely out of reach before he grabbed a fistful of her hair and used it to brace her as he cracked the flat of his hand in a series of stinging slaps across her cheeks.

She continued to fight him, to flail at his chest and face with her fists, scarcely able to see past the wall of pain. He lost his grip on her hair and sought a firmer one on her shirtfront, but the cloth tore and the buttons popped as she struggled to break free. The sudden release sent her sprawling backward, and as she raised her hands to protect her face from an impact with the wall, the heavy chain whipped up and grazed her temple.

Ballantine was by her side in two strides. He reached for the remnants of her shirt and held her braced against the wall. The blow from the chain had dazed her, and she could no longer summon the strength to resist as he drew his fist back for the final blow. Something at the last possible moment made him look down — down to where the binding cloth had been wrestled awry.

His fist froze by his shoulder. He stared first at the torn garment in his hand, then at the firm, upthrust breasts that pointed accusingly at him. Courtney's head lolled weakly to one side, and he felt the splash of a hot tear on the back of his hand.

He lowered his fist slowly, then, as if he had discovered he was holding burning coal, he jerked his hands free from all contact.

He opened and closed his mouth. Then he simply gaped at her speechlessly.

Courtney turned her face away and fumbled to cover herself. Her motions were clumsy, slowed by pain and humiliation. Ballantine reached out a hand, but drew it back again when he heard a muffled sob and saw her fold her knees up so that they were tucked protectively against her chest. A thin trickle of blood seeped from the cut on her chin, and he saw, to his growing horror, red welts rising on her cheeks from the imprints of his hand and fist.

The initial shock that had drained Ballantine's complexion now darkened it painfully. He was stunned by the knowledge that he had struck a woman — a girl — one who looked to be hardly more than a child.

A grimy fist was knuckled into the green eyes to force away the tears.

"Good God," he muttered. "What kind of game are you playing? Why the devil didn't you say something when you were brought on board?"

"Why?" she demanded bitterly. "So you could have sent me with the other women to be put to better use? I knew what was planned for them on the beach. I know what has been done to them every day and night since." A sob caught in her throat. "At least I've cheated you of seven days and nights, Yankee."

The lieutenant took a deep breath to reply, but the denial had to be swallowed unheard. Since the ship's captain had a healthy interest in female captives, the crew saw no reason not to follow his example.

The sight of the girl cringing against the wall was fraying Ballantine's nerves. He took a step toward her, but stopped when he saw her flinch even farther back. The torn edges of her shirt were brushed open, and he marked the gleam of a gold locket where it hung from her neck on a leather thong. That and the sharp contrast between the soft unmarked flesh of her breasts and the harsh black iron chains caused him to curse aloud. He strode over to his desk and yanked the center drawer open, snatching up a ring of keys before he went back to where Courtney was crouched.

"Hold out your hands," he commanded.

When she did not budge, he cursed again and dragged one resisting arm forward.

"I'm not going to hurt you," he said impatiently. "Now hold still or by God —"

Courtney winced under the pressure of his fingers as he

twisted the manacles up to receive the key, but her eyes did not leave his face, not even when the two inch-thick bands of iron were unbolted.

"Who in blazes dreamed up the idea for you to pose as a boy? And don't try any of your cat-and-mouse ploys with me — believe me, I'm in no mood for it."

"Verart," she muttered sullenly. "He thought I would be safer this way."

"Safer? In a prison hold?"

"Seagram's there. He would have looked after me."

"Seagram? Don't tell me — the giant?"

She nodded and gingerly massaged the chafed flesh on her wrists.

Adrian Ballantine looked down at her, still unwilling to believe what his eyes were plainly telling him. She spoke like a young ruffian, she dressed like one, and she certainly acted like one. If it wasn't for the obvious physical contradiction . . .

Courtney dashed a hand across the persistent film of tears, smearing the dirt on her cheeks in the process. She peered up at the imposing form of the Yankee; he hadn't moved for a full minute. She felt a growing discomfort when she saw where his eyes continued to wander, and she struggled to clutch the tattered folds of her shirt more closely around her body.

The gesture at modesty brought a vein throbbing to life in Adrian's temple.

"How old are you?"

"Old enough," she murmured.

*"How . . . old!"*

"Nineteen!"

Ballantine scowled and the pale eyes narrowed. "I'll ask once more —"

"I was born January third, 1785!" she hissed, through clenched teeth. "If you can count, Yankee, it comes to nineteen years, six months, and . . . and some days."

His mouth curved down skeptically. "Well you look ten years younger. Do you have a name?"

"Farrow," she spat.

"A *first* name," he said coolly, prickled by her murderous stare.

"Court." And after another stubborn pause, "For Courtney."

She saw the doubt in his face, and she balled her fists.

"My mother was French, if you must know. From the court of Louis XVI."

Ballantine was unmoved. "She must have found life with an Irish exile-turned-pirate a humbling experience."

Courtney's slender shoulders stiffened. "She was not given the opportunity, Yankee. She found herself humbled by Madame Guillotine first. And now, if your curiosity has been satisfied —"

"How long have you been with your father on Snake Island?"

"A thousand years," she said tonelessly. "What difference does it make?"

The Reign of Terror had swept through France eleven years earlier, the blades of hundreds of guillotines slashing off the heads of the ruling aristocracy with bloody vengeance. If the girl had somehow been smuggled out of the country and had kept company with corsairs since then, it would go a long way in explaining her anger, her mistrust.

It did nothing to ease Ballantine's discomfort or his guilt, and as he paced slowly to the far side of the cabin, his brows crushed together in a frown. What the devil was he supposed to do with her now? He certainly couldn't hand her over to the captain, nor could he, in all conscience, send her to join the rest of the women. Not that he gave a hang one way or the other if she was raped by half the crew: hell, it might be exactly what she needed to bring reality crushing down around her once and for all.

But he didn't believe that either.

He cursed softly and raked his fingers through his dark blond hair. "What the devil am I supposed to do with you now?" he asked aloud.

"Send me back to the hold. Let me be with my father's men."

"Your father — he approved of this way of life for you?"

"He approves of me. And as far as I'm concerned, that's all that matters."

"But the bloodshed, the violence. . . ."

"I was weaned on bloodshed and violence, Yankee. The guillotine granted no favors to anyone waving a lace handkerchief or swooning from fright." She paused and used the wall for support as she struggled to regain her feet. "I don't frighten easily. And you can beat me until your knuckles bleed, Yankee, you'll not see me cry again."

Ballantine almost believed it.

"You won't last ten days if I send you back to that pestilent hold," he murmured.

She kept her glowing eyes locked to his. "Gibraltar is less than a week away; I heard one of the guards talking about it."

"Norfolk is six times that. And a rough ocean crossing in between."

"Norfolk?"

"The jails have stronger bars, I'm told."

"A noose is a noose wherever it's strung," she shot back.

"You won't live to see either a jail or a scaffold if you're beaten to death over a few scraps of food."

"I told you, Seagram's there, and —"

"He can't watch out for you twenty-four hours a day. And he can't guard you against an informer."

"An informer?" She scoffed at the notion. "There are no informers among my father's men. They would follow him to hell if he asked it of them. And so would I."

"Hell is quite possibly where you'll end up if you persist in this stubbornness. The naval courts in Norfolk are not known for their tolerance of pirates — or daughters of pirates."

"Tolerance? You've kept me chained and locked in an iron cage for seven days with only rats and maggots for company. You've threatened me and beat me, and you warn me the naval courts will not be tolerant? Your compassion is overwhelming, Yankee. Dare I ask if you have more of the same in mind?''

Ballantine was momentarily distracted by the edges of her shirt falling open. Her breasts, firm and ripely formed, made her bruised and chafed flesh all the more ugly. This time she did not scramble to cover herself. She endured his stare with calm resignation and contempt.

"Will you take what you want now, Yankee?" she hissed. "Or do your fists need to prove themselves further?"

Ballantine met her gaze unwaveringly. She expected rape. Damn her, she was defying him to do it, and no doubt would fight him tooth and claw for his trouble.

He almost laughed aloud. "My dear girl, I can think of several infinitely more pleasurable ways to take the pox, if I was so inclined. Happily, I am not. What I will demand of you, however, is to make liberal use of the soap and water you'll find on the table."

He strode to the door and paused with his hand on the latch. "I'll be back shortly. I won't guarantee the condition of your hide if I return to find anything amiss. And that's not a threat, it's a promise."

Courtney continued to stare at the oak door long after the key had twisted in the lock and the sound of his footsteps had faded from the companionway. She shuddered violently and hugged her arms close to her sides, doing nothing to staunch the flow of scalding tears that welled over her lashes and streaked down her cheeks. Her stomach muscles were bound in a tight knot; her legs were shaky from the painful effects of the confrontation. Where was he going? Had she pushed him too far? Angered him enough that he would consider going to the captain?

Of course he would go to the captain, she thought derisively. He was a Yankee, he was an officer, and he was a bastard. Obedience came with the fancy uniform and the stiff upper lip.

Courtney shuddered again as a wave of nausea swept over her. She stumbled to the desk, and her hands were trembling so badly she needed both of them to steady the tin mug as she raised it to her lips. Even so, half of the water spilled down her chin and splashed icily onto her breasts. But it tasted good, so good she eagerly refilled the cup and drained it without taking a breath.

She cried out softly when the open sores on her wrists came in contact with the cold water in the basin, but she ignored the pain and used a scrap of toweling to bathe her arms, her throat, her face, to scrub some of the slimy memories of the cage from her skin while she had the opportunity. The Yankee was not the type to waste his time or his sympathy. And if he had gone to fetch the captain, she would be ready for whatever came next.

She gasped and leaned over the basin as the nausea persisted. She had not eaten more than a stale biscuit over the past few days and the hasty mouthfuls of water were stirring false hopes in her stomach. Not knowing how much time she had alone, she forced herself to scrub her face with the strong soap, and then to remove the useless strip of cotton from her breasts and carefully wash her bruises and scrapes. There was not much remaining of the front of her shirt, but she was able to overlap the ragged halves and tie them in place at her waist.

By the time she had finished, the wound in her upper arm was throbbing with a dizzying vengeance. The wound made her think of the doctor; thinking of the doctor made her drop to her knees and search below the desk for the knife she had lost in the tussle with Ballantine.

She had just located it in the shadows and had stretched out a hand to grasp it when she felt the hair on the back of her neck rise. She whirled and gaped at the open door where the lieutenant stood, his face as ominous as a thundercloud. The flinty eyes snapped once to the knife, then returned to her face.

"You can always try," he said quietly. "And frankly, you'll save me a great deal of trouble if you do decide to take this way out. But I will not make another stupid mistake. Touch that knife and I'll break you in half."

Courtney was held by his icy gaze for several long moments, then her fingers slowly curled away from the temptation.

Ballantine banged the door shut behind him. The vein in his temple was pulsing furiously, and the muscles in his jaw were flexed into a hard ridge. As she stood and faced him, his attention was drawn to the cinched waist, to the very definite feminine curves of hip and thigh, and to the noticeable strain of her breasts against the tight fabric.

He remembered the bundle he carried under one arm.

"Here," he grunted, tossing it to her. "Strip out of those rags and put these on."

"Why?"

"Because I told you to," he said evenly. He went to his desk and retrieved the knife from the floor. Courtney glanced around the tiny cabin but there was no place that offered protection from the probing gray eyes.

"Before my duty watch," he reminded her with a scowl.

She muttered a ripe curse under her breath, which earned a narrow glance from the lieutenant. She squared her shoulders and set the bundle of clothing on the berth, then, keeping her back to the Yankee officer, she pulled her shirttails free and shrugged the garment from her shoulders. She unfastened her trousers and let them fall around her ankles, and Ballantine had a fleeting glimpse of slender legs and rounded buttocks before the clean breeches were hurriedly drawn on. He also had time to frown over the multitude of purpling bruises that dotted her skin before the new shirt was shaken out and pulled over her head.

The breeches were knee length and baggy, the shirt a stout homespun and shapeless enough to camouflage her figure. Most of it. There was no mistaking the shape or fullness of her breasts, or the way the coarse fabric worried the nipples into prominence. Another moment of study sent Adrian to his own wardrobe to find a long, wide, linen neckcloth.

"You'll have to flatten yourself again," he said matter-of-factly, and handed her the cravat.

This time when she faced him, the inspection resulted in a nod and a faint smile of satisfaction:

"Come along," he said gruffly, and scooped up the discarded chains and manacles.

Courtney shied back against the wall and held her breath until she realized he was walking past her and had no intentions of replacing the iron bracelets around her wrists.

"Where are you taking me?" she asked, haltingly.

"To see if you can pass a test, Irish. After that, it's up to you."

# Chapter Three

Matthew Rutger washed his hands fastidiously, his thoughts divided between the festering wound he had just lanced and drained for the third time, and the problems of listing the provisions he would need when the *Eagle* stopped at Gibraltar. Many of the powders and unguents he used were in short supply and would need replenishing.

He splashed water on his face and dried it vigorously hoping to erase some of the fatigue that had been plaguing him for the past week. Most of the ship's normal routines had been restored, but the sick bay was still crammed to capacity with lingering casualties. He had lost five patients in the past three days — not a poor showing considering the ferocity of the fighting that had taken place on the beaches. Still, it troubled him.

With seven years of naval service behind him, Matthew found himself yearning more and more for the common-place ills of gout and dry throat. He'd had enough of shattered, bloody limbs beyond salvage. He'd seen enough healthy young men brought below on litters, their eyes blinded by powder flashes, their bodies burned and horribly mutilated by enemy cannonades.

The sedentary, gentlemanly practice he had shunned half a lifetime ago was looking better and better to him. His father had been a doctor, as had his grandfather and great-grandfather. If he, Matthew Rutger, wished to carry on the tradition, he would need a wife and son soon.

He reached down and absently massaged the welt of scar tissue distorting his left knee. There were more reminders of his way of life — scars on his back and his ribs, shiny patches of skin where he had suffered burns while attending the men on the battle decks. He was getting too old for all the violence, too sickened by it all — too human, as Adrian put it.

The doctor sighed and began to rinse the instruments he had used. He made a mental note to ask the chief sailmaker for more thread, and the carpenter to fashion a new handle for the bone saw. The last time he had used it, he had driven a splinter deep into the palm of his hand. It was still there and it was beginning to burn like the fires of Hades.

A physician's worst patient, Matthew mused, will always be himself.

Selecting a needle from the table, the doctor perched on the corner of the bench and angled his hand toward the lantern light. The splinter was embedded in his right palm, the shaft completely enclosed in swollen flesh. He was berating himself for his clumsiness with a less dextrous left hand when he heard a laugh from the doorway.

"You look like you could use a little help."

Matthew glanced over. "Adrian. Sorry about the delay but I had to see to a couple of our men. Nasty business, powder burns. Sometimes they heal right away, sometimes there's more damage than you realize at first and —" He stopped when he saw the slender form standing behind the lieutenant. He noted the clean clothes and the absence of manacles, and offered a friendly smile.

"Hello, Curt. How's the arm?"

Courtney said nothing, and shifted so that she was deeper in the shadows.

"Had a change of heart, have you, Adrian?" Rutger asked.

Ballantine leaned casually against the wall. "Let's just say I'm considering the options."

"Well, it's a start anyway," the doctor grinned. "All right, Curt. Come over here into the light and let me have a look at your arm. Any burning sensation? Any fever or bleeding?"

Courtney shook her head, heeding Ballantine's crisp warning to keep her answers brief and her eyes lowered. She moved reluctantly out of the shadows and rolled the sleeve high over the soiled bandage on her arm. The doctor indicated the corner of the bench he had just vacated and proceeded to unwind the cotton strips.

"Taking the threads out isn't nearly as bad as putting them in," he said. "And" — he leaned over and startled her by sniffing the cleanly healed wound — "since there doesn't appear to be any sign of corruption, there may not even be much of a scar."

His smile was not returned. The thick sweep of lashes hid the boy's eyes, but Matthew sensed the tension keeping the full lower lip curled between the even line of teeth. He glanced up at Adrian, but there was no hint of what was going on behind the cool gray eyes.

Rutger frowned and began working at the crusted stitches with a small knife and a pair of pincers. The blackened threads came out easily enough, their exits marked by tiny beads of bright red blood. The scar itself was a jagged pink welt on the pale flesh, and in examining it he noticed what he had missed before — the youthful pliancy of the arm, the lack of developed muscle that should have been there, even in a boy of nine or ten.

"Ow!" Courtney jerked her arm out of range of the distracted doctor's knife.

"Sorry," Matthew murmured. "My hand slipped. Still hating the world, are you?"

"Only certain parts of it," she replied evenly.

He smiled and resumed snipping and plucking. "You could do worse, you know. A lot worse than having Lieutenant Ballantine watching out for you. He usually only kicks where it doesn't show."

The emphasis was placed gently on the word "usually" as the doctor's gaze move pointedly to the puffy fresh cut on Courtney's chin. There were other indications that Adrian's authority had been challenged — fresh red marks on the lad's forearms and the decidedly cautious way he had taken a seat on the bench.

Matthew had served with Adrian Ballantine for six years. He knew the deceptively cool manner masked a will of iron and a razor-edged temper. Those who were not attuned to the subtle warning signals could find themselves talking to an amiable, relaxed man one moment, and the recipients of a verbal lashing that could flay to the bone the next. The men respected and admired Adrian as a leader, and followed his command without hesitation.

"There," Matthew said, the pincers pulling the last stitch free. "You'll have to be careful with the arm for a few days. Keep the wound clean and out of the air — *damn*!" The knife handle had slipped and pushed the sliver deeper into his palm. "Adrian, can I trouble you for a steady hand? There's half a yardarm wedged under my skin and I can't seem to get the blasted thing out."

Ballantine's gaze flicked lazily to Courtney. "Let Curt try. His hand is steady enough."

Matt's expression altered noticeably at the suggestion, and Adrian laughed, a deep throaty sound that was seldom heard within the walls of the sickbay.

"It was your idea to try to rehabilitate the urchin — or do you only participate in good deeds from a distance?"

Matt scowled at Courtney as he held out a needle to her. "Here. And by God if your hand slips —"

Courtney looked at the outstretched palm, at the embedded sliver, then at the needle.

"I don't think I want to do it."

"Do it," Ballantine ordered quietly.

She took the needle and glared at Ballantine.

"I don't believe I want to watch this," Matthew muttered, and turned his head. His whole arm tensed when he felt Courtney's cool fingers close around his wrist. He held his breath and waited for the plunge and slash of the avenging needle, and Courtney smiled faintly for the first time, knowing she had perfect opportunity to cause the Yankee doctor a few minutes of discomfort. She was still staring at him, her eyes huge and luminous, when he swore and turned to her.

"Well? What's wrong? I — " Matt glanced down and saw the needle with the offending splinter of wood impaled on its tip. He looked down at his hand, at the droplet of blood beading over the hole in his palm. "I'll be damned. I didn't feel a thing."

"I told you he had a steady hand," Adrian drawled. "Care for a shave?"

"No! I mean . . . er, no thanks, but I —" Matt stopped, his attention drawn swiftly to Courtney's face. She had dropped her guard for a split second and smiled openly at the doctor's hasty reply. The effect was astounding. The smile revealed soft generous lips and drew Matt's attention to a slight self-conscious blush on cheeks that never had and never would show a trace of masculine hair. The long slender throat was far too delicate to lead to brawny shoulders — an observation confirmed by a gap at the collar of her shirt.

Rutger's jaw slackened as the bits of the puzzle came together like metal scrapings to a magnet.

"Good Lord!" His eyes sought Adrian's for confirmation. "He's a girl!"

The lieutenant sighed expansively and pushed away from the wall. "I didn't think she'd make it past you a second time."

"Make it past . . . *what are you saying*? You mean you've known all along that he . . . that she —"

"My introduction to *Miss* Farrow came as unexpectedly as yours," Adrian assured him dryly. "About an hour ago and twice as abruptly."

The doctor stared at Courtney, who had backed away

again, her face taut, her eyes moving warily from one man to the other.

It took several seconds of strained silence for the name to register on Matthew's brain.

"Farrow?" he gasped. "Did you say *Farrow*?"

"I did."

"As in Duncan *Farrow* and Everart *Farrow*?"

"Father and uncle, respectively."

That was too much for Matthew, and he sat down heavily on a nearby chair. He took in Courtney's appearance — the loose-fitting shirt and dark breeches, the stringy mop of hair. His gaze moved down her arm to the wound that stood out pink and swollen beneath the rolled sleeve, and he thought of the treatment she had endured from his overtired hands that first day.

"Dear God," he murmured, as he turned to Adrian in disbelief. "Why didn't you say something? And what do you intend to do about her now? Adrian . . . you can't mean to hand her over to Jennings. Why he'd . . . he'd. . . ."

"I know damned well what he'd do with her," Ballantine interrupted grimly. "That's why I've brought her to you."

"Me?"

"I am loathe to keep repeating myself, but this was your idea."

"My idea?" Matthew frowned, then looked at Courtney's clothing and was jarred by another thought. "You can't seriously be thinking of keeping her disguised as a boy?"

Ballantine spread his hands wide. "Have you a better idea?"

"Not off hand, but —"

"We don't have a wealth of time for debate," Adrian countered evenly. "But since it isn't uncommon to take the younger prisoners and put them to work, there is a chance — a slim one, I agree — but a chance the charade could work. She'd have to stay out of the way of the rest of the crew, naturally."

"Naturally," said Matthew, as if it was the easiest thing in the world to manage on a ship one hundred and fifty feet long and twenty-five feet wide. "And I suppose you're about to tell me now that you've also decided this" — he indicated the infirmary — "is the safest place to keep her?"

"I considered it, believe me," the lieutenant admitted with a grin. "But unfortunately there is far too much coming and going at all hours. Someone'd be bound to notice something . . . different about her. No —" He paused, and the next thought was obviously a distasteful one. "I'm afraid she's going to have to remain with me — work for me as my personal steward. That way she'll need only report to me, and there should be few, if any, questions asked."

"Well, I have about a hundred!" Courtney cried angrily, her cheeks flushed with indignation as she listened to the two men discussing her like they would a piece of furniture. "You could ask me what *I* want to do!"

Both men turned to her, but it was Ballantine's voice that cut through the air like an icy blade.

"What you *want* to do has absolutely no bearing on what you *will* do. I thought I made myself clear on that point."

She planted her hands on her hips. "And if I refuse? If I scream from the top of my lungs who I am and who it was trying to keep me apart from the rest of the prisoners? The cage you so generously made my home for the past week may have been dark and airless, but it wasn't without sound. I heard the guards talking. I heard how the captain would dearly love to have a reason to break you, *Lieutenant Yankee*. Protecting the daughter of Duncan Farrow — or worse, saving her in order to add to your own fame and glory — might provide him with the excuse he needs!"

Ballantine's eyes darkened ominously. "Are you attempting to blackmail me? To blackmail a man who'd sooner toss you over the side than waste energy flogging you?"

"I doubt very much whether you'd do either, Yankee."

"Really?" Adrian arched a brow in amazement. "And why wouldn't I?"

Courtney caught a movement out of the corner of her eye and saw Rutger shake his head in warning. And a closer look at the lieutenant revealed a man taut with fury. Violence was in his clenched jaw, his poised stance, in the tiny vein pulsing at his temple. A chill swept through her but she did not turn away. *Let the enemy see your fear and you are lost*. Duncan Farrow's words. Sound advice — but what if you were facing a man like Adrian Ballantine, and if you knew, suddenly, his were no idle threats?

Matthew cleared his throat cautiously. "Shouting your identity, Miss Farrow, might cause the lieutenant — and myself — some discomfort, it's true, but I rather doubt we would regret it as much as you would. We try to discourage it, but the crew has taken out their frustrations on some of the women we brought on board from Snake Island. Learning that they had the daughter of the man who was more or less responsible for the recent loss of their crewmates . . . well, they would all insist on their turn, if you understand my meaning. I don't think you'd last more than a couple of hours."

Courtney's cheeks stained a dull red. "Will I fare any better with the likes of you?"

Matthew smiled hesitantly. "If that's what is worrying you —"

"Speaking for myself," Ballantine broke in savagely, "I can only repeat what I said in my cabin, in plainer language. I am not desperate enough to want to fight my way past the foul language and ever fouler disposition in search of what could only be a moment's relief. I prefer my *whores* to offer tenderness, not the smell of a slops jar. The only thing you will have to fear from me is the touch of the lash against your backside — something, to my mind, that should have been done a good many years ago.

"As for threatening me, *miss*, I wouldn't attempt it again or not only will you be thrown to the crew with my blessings and encouragement, but I'll make damned sure you never get within smelling distance of your father's men again. Do we understand each other?''

Courtney looked past Ballantine while she swallowed her anger in silence. With visible effort, Ballantine regained control and addressed Rutger again.

''I've been without a boy for three months now and, as my personal steward, she'll be left on her own with few questions asked. She can take her meals alone and sleep in the small anteroom next to mine. She'll have to work for her keep — and work hard, by God — but if she's careful and if she wants to live to see Gibraltar'' — he shot her a glance — ''she just might pull it off.''

''She did raise an interesting question: What about Jennings? He'll be bound to notice her.''

''Jennings?'' Ballantine snorted. ''He's hardly been out of his cabin all week. But even if he does see her, he'll be looking at a scrubbed mouse of a lad who's striving to earn his parole outside of the prison hold. With luck they'll not get closer to one another than the width of the ship.''

''But if they do?'' Matt persisted, his concerns suddenly grave. ''If they do, Adrian, and if Jennings finds out —''

''Then neither one of us will make the history books — not that that should come as any surprise.''

''And Falworth? He sniffs around you like a bloodhound. What he wouldn't give to hand your head to Jennings on a platter!''

''Let me worry about Falworth,'' said Adrian firmly. ''He has his nose in so many dung heaps it won't be difficult to send him off on a false scent.''

''But —'' Rutger saw the cold, hard light enter Adrian's eyes and he ended his resistance on a sigh. ''What do you want me to do?''

''For a start, you can keep her here during my duty hours. I don't want her roaming around the ship unattended. She's far too imaginative for that. Let her scrub floors or tables. Put her to work and keep her occupied and out of sight.''

Matt nodded, "That should be easy enough. I'm always short-handed down here. She can work with Dickie. Anything else?"

Ballantine headed toward the door. "Since I'm due on deck soon, you could see that she has something to eat. And you might introduce her to a bath. As it is it will take a week to air the stench out of my cabin."

He paused in the doorway and grinned wryly as he removed the knife from his waistband. With an expert flip of his wrist, he sent it to a quivering halt, embedded an inch deep in the tabletop.

"I'd also take a careful tally of my instruments if I were you. She appears to have a fondness for squirreling away shiny objects."

When the door closed, Courtney and Rutger simultaneously released a pent-up breath. Neither of them moved for several minutes. Their eyes met and held; hers were filled with distrust, his with lingering reservations.

Adrian Ballantine was taking a hell of a risk, whether he admitted it or not, Matt thought. And keeping the girl on as his own cabin boy was lunacy. Jennings had spies all over the ship. If just one of them found out, if just one breath of suspicion was passed to the captain. . . .

"There are worse ways of spending the next few days," he said finally. "I only hope you realize that, and how much trouble we could all find ourselves in if you're caught."

Courtney regarded him without comment, and his complexion deepened a shade.

"You were incredibly lucky it was Adrian who found you out first. Any one of a dozen others would have presented you to Jennings like a ceremonial haggis — and handed him the dagger to carve with."

Courtney massaged a bruised wrist. "He isn't exactly a gentleman-prince. And I don't understand why I cannot simply be put in the hold with the others. I'm one of them. I belong with them. I'm not asking for any better treatment, or for any special privileges. And I'm certainly not asking either of you to risk a precious hair on your head for me. I just want to be put with my father's men and left alone.''

Matthew sighed. ''Surely you can see why it just isn't possible. You've been in the cage; you've seen the conditions in the hold. . . .''

''I've seen them. I've also seen my father's men and I can't stay here in warmth and comfort while they suffer. If the rest of your crew was being beaten and starved to death in a stinking prison hold, could you think only of saving yourself?''

There was no way to answer her. She was right, of course. How many times had he put himself into danger without thinking of the consequences, without considering anything but the welfare of his crewmates. He had the scars to prove it and so did Adrian.

The emerald eyes were burning into him, and he had to look away.

''Come along. As luck would have it, I had ordered a hot bath be put in my cabin, and I must agree with Lieutenant Ballantine: you need it far more than I.''

The doctor's cabin was located on the same deck, farther astern. They passed two sailors lounging at the foot of a ladderway but neither seemed to notice anything worthy of comment. They touched their forelocks respectfully and nodded a greeting to Dr. Rutger and stepped aside to clear a way through to the narrow companionway, then picked up their conversation without marking the interruption. There was noise and boisterous laughter filtering down from the gun deck overhead. Men recently relieved from their watches were greeting those who were already relaxing over a pipe and a mug of ale. The air was musty with the scent of sea water and tobacco smoke and with the earthy smell of unwashed bodies crowded together in cramped quarters.

The doctor's cabin was smaller than the lieutenant's. It housed a plain wooden cot and a single bookcase, the lower shelf of which opened down into a desk. All the free space was taken up by a brass half-tub filled with luke-warm water.

The books on the shelves were medical journals with long, unpronounceable titles and dog-eared pages. There was a tin cup containing goosefeather quills on the desk, and a pot of ink sitting lidless on a badly stained blotter. Papers covered with a tight slanted script were stacked an inch deep on the chair and the desk, and lying expectantly by the tallow candle was a long-stemmed clay pipe and a pair of square, wire-rimmed spectacles.

"It isn't exactly palatial," Matt said, noting her inspection of the cabin. "But it suits me. You'll find soap and a towel on the sea chest, as well as a stout brush for scrubbing. I'll come back in, say, an hour and bind up that arm for you again."

Courtney clenched her hands tightly in front of her, torn between the lure of the bathwater and her need to hide any and all weaknesses from these Yankees, regardless of their soft eyes and even softer words. Her throat felt scalded by unshed tears, the knot in her stomach took an extra twist . . . a twist that was sensed halfway across the room.

"Listen, you asked me a few minutes ago if I could think about saving myself while the rest of my crew was suffering . . ." Matthew paused uncomfortably. "Well, no, I probably couldn't. But I might be able to look on it another way. Outside the bars, I might be able to find ways to help them. Extra food, extra water . . . I'm not saying it could be done easily — or even that it could be done at all. In fact, I'm probably committing a mild form of treason in even suggesting it but" — he saw the tears vanish from her eyes as a sudden spark of attentiveness brightened them. It was not an altogether false hope he was giving her — "I have access to the holds several times a week. Normally I find myself short of volunteers willing to help out with the prisoners, but —"

"You would do that?" Courtney whispered, not entirely believing her ears. "You would allow me to help them?"

"I'm a doctor, Miss Farrow," he said quietly. "Not a

soldier. I might be able to arrange to have my back turned on occasion, providing it was only food and water you were smuggling in to them. I would need your word on that."

Courtney was startled a second time. "You would accept the word of Duncan Farrow's daughter? A pirate? A thief? A murderer?"

Matthew grimaced. "I don't believe you are any of those. And yes, I would accept the word of Duncan Farrow's daughter — if I thought she would honor it."

The dreadful, smothering panic in Courtney's chest eased slightly, and she could almost breathe normally for the first time since being summoned to Ballantine's cabin.

"You have my word, doctor," she said slowly. "I'll not attempt to arm a full-scale insurrection."

Matthew nodded and turned to leave. As an afterthought, he added uncomfortably, "And providing there is never any mention of this conversation to anyone — not even Lieutenant Ballantine."

*"Him,"* she bridled, "I wouldn't mention the time of day to that insufferable bastard."

Rutger winced at how easily the profanity slipped from her tongue. "Adrian is a good man to have on your side. You should be thankful he didn't call your bluff back there and toss you to the wolves."

"I'm so grateful I can hardly wait to scrub his floor and empty his slop jar," she said acidly. "What happened to his last cabin boy? Did he die of gratitude?"

Matthew reacted as if he had been slapped. "Alan was killed in a freak accident on deck. A winch cable came loose, and he was struck in the back of the head."

Courtney fidgeted a moment with the frayed end of twine that served as her belt. "Well . . . if it happened three months ago, why hasn't anyone else rushed forward to take his place?"

Matthew's shoulders sagged, and his expression altered again. "Alan was the lieutenant's brother. Adrian hasn't allowed anyone to take his place."

# Chapter Four

Miranda dragged her fingers along the oak rail, tracing over the myriad of dents and scratches that marred the polished surface. She inhaled deeply of the clean salt air and looked out longingly at the shiny swells of green water. Jennings permitted her two brief strolls on deck each day in the company of one of his junior officers. Most of them were young and plainly in awe of her raw beauty, and she took some amusement in guessing how long it would take for their appreciation of her to show in their breeches. Sometimes it only required a softly spoken compliment, a knowing glance, or a smile. Other times it called for a subtle play of gestures — a finger trailed suggestively along the arch of her throat, a smoothing of nonexistent wrinkles on her blouse or skirt. They all succumbed eventually.

Her most constant watchdog was Second Lieutenant Otis Falworth. He was of medium height, average build, with nondescript features that brought to mind a belligerent clerk. His only notable characteristic was two wide silver streaks of hair that grew like wings at each temple, slashing through his wiry, jet black crop and pinned, finally, in a neat tail beneath the cockaded bicorne. His uniform was always starched to military precision. His fingernails were as buffed and glossy as the black kneeboots that clumped behind her the required two paces.

Falworth needed only a smile from her for beads of sweat to appear across his stiff upper lip. A crooked eyebrow had him dry in the mouth and breathing oddly; a casual brush of arms had him all but dragging her into a shadowy corner. She had not allowed him more than an occasional breathless glance down the front of her blouse, and perhaps a peek or two at a shapely thigh when she climbed the ladderways. She wanted to be absolutely certain of her chosen champion, and she wanted to be certain she had given each candidate a fair chance. It was obvious from the desultory greetings Falworth received from the men on deck that he was not well liked: a point in his favor. He was in the captain's good graces, which also benefited Miranda, and she knew his loyalties were founded on ambition and greed, which made him a devious man: two points in his favor. His sole drawback thus far was the fact that he was too *eager*. A man whose brains were between his thighs thought of little else, and Miranda wanted to be sure her champion would be level-headed enough to carry off her escape. Cool enough to be clever when the situation required it; hot-blooded enough to deserve the rewards she was capable of bestowing.

The golden eyes slanted upward and studied the officer standing casually by her side. Adrian Ballantine. Even the name caused a tingle to race along Miranda's spine. Golden-haired, broad in the shoulder, lean in the waist and hips, he had enough muscle to make a woman feel dominated, enough leanness to suggest he knew exactly what to do with his brains, wherever they were.

So far there had been no visible evidence of Miranda's charms at work, but she had hardly warmed to the challenge. He had certainly noticed the way the wind molded the thin cotton blouse to her breasts, and the cool gray eyes had shown definite interest each time her shawl slipped from her bared shoulders and nudged her neckline down another inch. Discounting his brief appearances in the captain's cabin to deliver his daily reports, this was the first opportunity Miranda had had to closely inspect the ship's first officer.

When they arrived at a secluded area of the deck, she stopped and leaned her hands on the rail.

"What land are we passing now, Lieutenant? Still Algeria?"

Adrian gazed out over the marching whitecaps to the low slash of purple hugging the horizon. "We have been in Moroccan waters since noon."

"Morocco," she murmured and took a deep breath, as if she could smell the steamy incense from the bazaars. "I was in Casablanca once . . . under happier circumstances, of course. Much happier. My father was a very wealthy merchant from Madrid, and he occasionally took me with him on his travels."

Adrian said nothing; he merely glanced at her as he drew on a thin black cigar.

The sparkle dimmed from her amber eyes, and she bowed her head slowly. "I don't blame you for not believing me. It was many years ago and I . . . I have almost come to doubt it myself."

Ballantine exhaled slowly. "I have no reason to disbelieve you."

"But it is easier to think of me as a whore." Her eyes flashed up and captured his before he could avert them. "Indeed, it would be difficult to justify your captain's behavior if you had to think of me as the daughter of a Spanish Grandee!"

"A grandee?"

"I was kidnapped while on a journey from Madrid to Cadiz, to be with my betrothed. We were to be wed in Cadiz and then sail on to Mexico, where my father had provided land for my dowry." Her face assumed the guise of sadness again. "Instead, our ship was attacked. I was taken to Snake Island where I was beaten and threatened with slavery, and finally forced to serve the barbarians in the only capacity they alot to women."

"What about your father and your betrothed? Didn't they search for you or try to buy back your freedom?"

"My father searched. My Manuel searched. But they are saints, Lieutenant. How could I possibly return to them . . . soiled? I pleaded and begged with my captors, and finally did this" — she held out a tapered wrist, displaying a scar she had earned years earlier in a tavern brawl — "until Duncan Farrow agreed to send a message to my father saying I had perished in the attack. In exchange I agreed to be . . . docile. Afterward, nothing mattered to me anymore."

Ballantine looked deeply into the amber eyes, drawn skillfully, painlessly into their depths. He was teased by flecks of green and brown, taunted expertly by sparks of fiery gold. Good God, he thought. First the daughter and now the mistress — Duncan Farrow had needed to keep his wits sharp surrounded by these women.

Miranda frowned slightly, the meaning of the sudden gleam in his eyes eluding her. "Do you think it fair all of this should happen to me just because I'm cursed with the body of a temptress? I have tried to make myself ugly. I have scratched my face and torn out my hair; I have starved myself until I was nothing but loose flesh and bone . . . but to no avail. I am doomed, it seems, to give pleasure and receive nothing in return. When your captain tires of me — as surely he must — he will pass me on to another, just as insensitive, as brutal."

Miranda edged closer and her hand came to within an inch of Ballantine's on the rail — close enough for the fine coppery hairs on his wrist to prickle with the warmth. He was fascinated, despite himself. What had he said to the Farrow girl? That he liked his women to smell of tenderness? Miranda Gold fairly reeked of passion, a trait shared by all prime courtesans. Yet passion did not light the eyes, not the deepest part of the eyes where the soul was. These same eyes glowed in a hundred cheap taverns, a thousand furtive beds. The gold in them might well have come from the taint of coin. But just what was it she wanted from him?

"I only want kindness, Lieutenant," she murmured, the answer to his unspoken question bringing a smile to his lips. "Gentleness, compassion . . . All these things I see in you." Her fingertips touched his hand, traced a feather-light path to the cuff of his tunic, then back down to the strong, tanned fingers. "You are not like the others. In you I can see . . . appreciation."

Ballantine watched the luscious red lips form the words and was genuinely engrossed by the way she used her body to underscore her meaning. She was standing so close that the fabric of her blouse was pressed to his tunic. While it was impossible to feel anything through the heavy layer of wool, he could swear he felt the impression of her firm breasts burning their offer into his chest. In any other frame of mind, he might have succumbed to the temptation, if for no other reason than to coldly and clinically relieve himself of some of the tensions of the past months. Cuckolding Jennings would not have caused him any loss of sleep, but he wasn't prepared to stoop quite that low just yet.

"This, er . . . appreciation, I gather it would be for some form of reward, which in turn would be for an understanding we would come to? One that perhaps involves my smuggling you ashore when we dock in Gibraltar?"

Miranda felt a flush of satisfaction tint her cheeks. So much for thinking that Ballantine was different from any other hot-blooded male. Men were such fools! Such children! So easily governed and manipulated by the press of warm flesh.

"Unfortunately," Adrian said with a wry sigh, "I'm not very adept at smuggling. And I'm certainly not interested in being court-martialed for the sake of a little slap and tickle beneath a dark stairwell. I'm afraid you've wasted your time, and your tale of woe on me, Miss Gold, but I'd be only too happy to point out a more receptive . . . er, ear.''

Miranda's Castillian blood boiled instantly, and her arm drew back in preparation to lash out at his arrogant jaw. He caught her wrist with ridiculous ease and forced it down by her side.

"Ah, ah. We wouldn't want to see me lose all this gentleness and compassion, now would we?" A half-smile played on his lips, an arch lifted his brow, and a maddeningly amused glint shaded the gray of his eyes. Miranda drew her fists into claws and her wickedly long fingernails seemed to long to be set free to rake the laughter from his face.

Adrian laughed softly and turned toward the sound of boots approaching from behind. "Ahh, Mister Falworth. We were just discussing you.''

"Me?" The second lieutenant halted, his limpid brown eyes sliding from Miranda's face to Ballantine's. He stood with his hands clasped behind his back, his right foot poised at a studied angle to display to advantage the fine tailoring of his uniform. "Me?" he said again, "I can't imagine why.''

Adrian released Miranda's wrist and took a last draw from his cigar before flicking the two-inch stub over the rail. "Indeed we were. In the abstract, of course, but I'm sure Miss Gold would be only too happy to satisfy your curiosity, if you'd like to accompany her on the remainder of her promenade. Unless you have more pressing duties elsewhere?''

Falworth took a breath. "Why no. Not at all.''

"Good, because I was about to cut my stroll short.'' Ballantine bowed curtly to Miranda, his eyes still dancing with humor. "It is my watch. I trust you have no objections.''

"By all means," she said, seething, "go about your duties.''

With a mildly derisive salute in Falworth's direction Ballantine departed the quarter-deck, leaving Miranda to gaze blazingly after him and Falworth to look on, blatantly inquisitive. He was not the only curious observer, as a hasty glance told him. Crewmen were hanging by a crooked arm or leg in the nearby shrouds. Overhead, men were grinning at each other in the yardarms, their work interrupted by the enticing play of the wind on Miranda's clothes.

Falworth's pinched features went rigid as stone and a trace of color leaked into his cheeks.

"The wind seems to have picked up a chilling edge," he mused. "Perhaps we should go below where we won't be quite so exposed."

Miranda was still glaring daggers into Ballantine's retreating form. Falworth took her by the arm and ushered her firmly toward the hatchway. As soon as they were under cover of the shadowed entrance, a burst of ribald laughter broke out on the deck above them. It startled Miranda out of her blind rage and heightened the flare of displeasure in Falworth's face.

"Just ignore them," he advised her brusquely. "They have the manners and breeding of apes. They'll laugh at anything."

"What?" Miranda halted abruptly, almost causing Falworth to collide into her.

"Oh, I didn't mean anything by that . . . I mean, I didn't . . . I wasn't implying . . ." As he faltered his eyes were drawn down, unable to resist the swelling globes of her breasts as they brushed against his tunic. His legs seemed to fail him. He could not take the step necessary to break the contact.

Miranda's pride stung from Ballantine's mocking abuse; the anger trembled through her limbs, her belly, and demanded retribution.

"I'm glad he had other things to do," she murmured. "I'm glad he went away and left us . . . alone."

Falworth licked his lips and cursed the sweat forming on the palms of his hands. A quick glance told him they *were* alone. The companionway was deserted, the door to an empty storage locker only a few paces away. He gasped as he felt her hands on his wrists, guiding his hands up along warmed cotton until they were cupping her breasts. He dared not move or breathe. He could feel her nipples budding against his palms, growing hard as tiny buttons in the overflow of surrounding flesh. Conscious of the laughter still drifting down the ladderway, he took a bold step and urged Miranda into the deeper gloom of the storage locker. She was quick to drop the shawl and pull the thong that was holding her bodice together; he was even quicker to shove the cotton aside and fumble her glorious breasts free.

His groan was muffled against the soft pillows of flesh as he licked and suckled. The sweet, exotic musk of her skin sent blood racing through his body; his heart pounded desperately to keep pace with the flow and felt as if it would burst through the wall of his chest. He felt her fingers working nimbly on the bottom buttons of his tunic, then on the waist of his breeches.

"Wh-what are you doing?"

"You wish me to stop?"

His body tensed and his brow beaded instantly with sweat. "Someone could walk by."

"Then you must be quiet, my lieutenant," she purred huskily and slowly dropped to her knees before him.

Falworth's eyes squeezed shut and his teeth ground together in a shudder. He swayed drunkenly for a moment, but then there was nothing to do but curl his fingers into the silky raven tresses and hope the explosions he heard and felt were only in his mind.

Lieutenant Ballantine was relieved at his watch at precisely four minutes before eight o'clock. He remained on the bridge to savor the last inch of a cigar and to appreciate the effortless beauty of the *Eagle*'s motion as she was bathed in the fading russet glow of sunset. Her sails, tinted pink and bronze against the sky, were trimmed to a steady four knots and strained overhead. The tackle creaked and the rigging hummed. The sound of the bow carving into each successive wave was comforting like a low pulsing heartbeat.

He had spent the last twelve years of his life at sea, the last six months on board the *Eagle*. He had served under five captains in all, in various capacities, working his way up from ordinary seaman to first lieutenant in less than ten years. He had not taken the easy route of buying a commission with his family name and money; rather, he had learned the way of ship and sea through hard work and skill.

In all that time he had been content to call the sea his home, the ship his mistress. The latter had as many moods as a woman. She had her tantrums, her rages, her moments of hostile beauty. There were nights of holding down a solitary ghost watch when he could imagine nothing more peaceful, nothing more sensually perfect than riding his ship under moonlit sail, her canvas wings teased and lulled by the gentle hands of the wind.

The attraction had begun to sour lately. The ugliness of war, the deceit and intrigue were beginning to take their toll. His temper was shorter, his moods blacker. He even found himself being deliberately rude to men he had long considered to be friends. He knew the *Eagle* was not to blame for his changing attitudes, but the appeal of his highspirited mistress had altered drastically in recent months — the past six, from the moment he had stepped aboard the *Eagle* and saluted Captain Willard Leach Jennings.

His previous captain, James Sutcliffe, had been retired from service in disgrace. He had been blind drunk on a day when their ship had crossed paths with an Algerian merchantman; drunk and prepared to hull the unarmed vessel for the sake of adding an easy kill to his record. Ballantine had interceded to prevent the slaughter and, by doing so, had won himself charges of misconduct, of striking a senior officer, of intent to commit mutiny. For a lesser man, the charges alone might have been enough to destroy both his resolve and his ambition, but Adrian had stood his ground. He had refused to bow to demands for his resignation, and he had defended his actions to the Admiralty by substantiating countercharges of drunkenness and incompetence.

As a result, Sutcliffe had been quietly retired to a hog farm in Pennsylvania. In a private hearing before a naval tribunal, Ballantine had been declared innocent of the grave charges of mutiny and assault, but he had been branded a hothead and placed on a year's probation for his breach of discipline. He had been transferred to the *Eagle* for the duration, and for the past six months, subjected to the supreme test of his willpower in serving under Jennings.

Whereas he had occasionally been able to tolerate Sutcliffe's excesses, and had even shared them at times, he could barely conceal his loathing and contempt for Jennings. There were moments when the injustices and cruelties enjoyed by his new commanding officer stoked Adrian to such a rage that he was tempted to sacrifice what was left of his career for the pleasure of feeling his hands close around Jenning's throat. Only Matthew Rutger, his friend and shipmate for half of his life at sea, kept him sane. The sight of Matt's face beaming from the deck of the *Eagle* upon his arrival had been the only glimmer of light on a dark day. The darkness had deepened when Jennings had made it clear that he disagreed with the findings of the tribunal and considered it his personal duty to correct the gross error in judgment.

Perhaps that was why Adrian's thoughts drifted with alarming regularity to the sprawling plantations owned by the Ballantines of Virginia — to the rich tobacco fields, snow white acres of cotton, and all the comforts and luxuries afforded by the accumulated wealth of generations. His father, Samuel Ballantine, and Adrian's brother Rory controlled the empire, but there was room for Adrian in the fold. He could mend the rift with his family that he had caused through his demand for independence; he could settle down and marry a suitably well-bred, well-versed woman and raise a passel of well-bred, well-versed children who would no more consider running away to sea than they would lying in the path of stampeding wild horses.

Samuel had been ailing on Adrian's last visit home. He had looked like an old man for the first time in his sixty-three years of hard living. He had exacted a promise from Adrian to consider — *consider* — leaving the navy, a promise that did not seem so onerous now. The recent victory over Snake Island would assure a hero's welcome for the *Eagle*'s crew and her officers. It might even remove the cloud of disgrace that still hung over his head from the court-martial. And with the capture and execution of Duncan Farrow, the war would almost certainly draw to a swift conclusion.

Commodore Edward Preble had been in the Mediterranean less than a year and had accomplished more to hasten the defeat of the Pasha, Yusef Karamanli, in eleven months than his two predecessors had in the three previous years. Where the other commodores had been content with a token blockade and an occasional scowl at the Tripolitans, Preble had openly attacked the Pasha's weak spots. He had intercepted grain shipments and merchant vessels carrying much-needed supplies and weaponry to Tripoli. He had also gone after the Pasha's mercenary support forces. Snake Island had been the last major offensive, and its destruction would clear the way for an assault on Tripoli itself. Without mercenaries and Barbary corsairs to assist him, Karamanli's power was reduced to curses and fist-waving.

Duncan Farrow's feats had become legendary throughout the Mediterranean in the past five years. His ships, the *Wild Goose* and the *Falconer*, had never met defeat in a battle at sea. His victims claimed they had never met a more formidable, more cunning enemy. Farrow's men were seasoned veterans, utterly without fear; their commander was a brilliant tactician and a master at deceit. Both Farrow and his senior captain, Garrett Shaw, were singularly ruthless when it came to attacking and capturing merchant ships — and here Courtney's vehement defense of her father's actions categorically refuted official reports. On several occasions the crews of such vessels had been handed over to Yusef Karamanli to dispose of as he saw fit — the officers, for the most part, were ransomed; the ordinary seamen were sold into slavery. True, no American crews had met such a fate, but then no American merchantman had had the misfortune to be actively sought as a prize by the Farrows. Duncan Farrow seemed content to concentrate on the richly laden French traders and, to that end, he stalked them with an unholy fervor.

But Farrow was only one of a handful of vicious corsairs employed by the Pasha to help win the war against the only country whose president dared to refuse a demand for tribute, whose ships dared to use the Mediterranean shipping routes without paying for the privilege, and whose navy dared to send warships to defend their right of passage.

Commodore Edward Preble was the newest affront and was proving to be fervent in his intentions to bring about complete victory for the American forces. Not only had he whipped his band of young, ill-trained officers into a team of skilled and effective fighters, but he had established an intelligence network that spanned all of the major ports along the Barbary Coast: Tangier, Oran, Algiers, Tunis, even Tripoli itself. With the help of this network, Preble was kept abreast of Karamanli's movements, his shipments, his strategies, and thereby was able to do damage where it would be felt most.

With the help of one spy in particular, he had been able to methodically strip the Pasha of his mercenary support forces, most notable among them: Duncan Farrow.

What would the haughty Courtney Farrow's reaction be if she knew her father's camp boasted the highest-paid informant along the Barbary Coast? The man had not only sold out the rivaling bands of corsairs who raided the commerce of the Mediterranean, but he had arranged the trap that had ensnared Farrow and Shaw and the attack that had destroyed the stronghold of Snake Island. The man's identity remained a closely guarded secret. He was known only by a code name: "Seawolf." It was not known if Seawolf had escaped the trap for the *Falconer* and the *Wild Goose*, or if he had been among the defenders of Snake Island — no one knew if he had been captured, killed, or set free.

One thing was known for certain: As much as the idea of spies and traitors lodged in a man's throat, without Seawolf's greed, Commodore Preble would not have been able to affect the capture of the Farrows without paying a horrendous price in human lives.

Ballantine squinted at the falling red sun until it melted into the sparkling line of water. He flipped the cigar butt over the rail, watching it sink into the wash of foam creaming off the *Eagle*'s hull. He nodded to the helmsman, issued a few final orders, then left the bridge.

The girl's presence on board was definitely an unwelcomed turn of events. There wasn't a hope in hell of keeping her disguise effective for any length of time, especially if she persisted in arguing herself into confrontations. At nineteen years of age, she was not a child. She was aware of the consequences of the life she had chosen and despite his grudging admiration for her pluck and spirit, Adrian Ballantine was not about to place her safety above his own career. She would have to be put in her place and she would damn well have to keep to it or she would find herself back in the hold whether it spelled her death or not.

Neither Matthew nor the girl were in the infirmary when Adrian checked, nor had they been there for an hour or so. Matt was not in his cabin, or in the officers' wardroom, or gathered with the rest of the crew on the lower gundeck to participate in the evening weevil races. Ballantine arrived at his own cabin in a mood that sent the door slamming back on its hinges. The sleeping form on the bed sat upright with a stifled scream.

Ballantine glared at the occupant of his bed for a full minute before he connected the clean, wide-eyed young woman who was hastily scrambling to her knees, with the evil-smelling, rag-bound corsair's daughter he had left in Matthew Rutger's care. Her skin, cleaned of the layers of sweat and grime, was shaded honey-gold from the sun and glowed like warm marble. Her hair had washed into a soft mist of auburn curls that the lantern light teased with glints of fiery red. Her throat was a slender arch, luring the eye downward to where her breasts strained against the fabric of the shirt.

Ballantine narrowed his eyes and glanced briefly around the cabin. Nothing appeared to be out of place; there were no overt signs that things had been tampered with or disturbed. There was a tray of food sitting on his desk, and a small tin pot of coffee warming over a spirit lamp.

"How long have you been here on your own?" he demanded gruffly.

Courtney looked around the cabin, startled to see she *was* alone.

"I . . . I don't know. An hour, maybe more."

"Doing what?"

She flushed. "Trying to dig my way out! What does it look like I was doing?"

Ballantine scowled as he locked the door. "Where is Dr. Rutger?"

"I don't know. He was sitting behind your desk the last time I saw him."

Adrian crossed the width of the cabin, and his frown deepened when he saw the crumbs and drippings that were all that remained of his dinner.

"I presume you found your appetite again?"

Courtney stiffened. "I was hungry and it was getting cold. If you'll recall, I haven't had much to eat over the past week — not that I've missed much. Your Yankee food is as palatable as shoe leather."

"I'll see what I can do about getting you croissants and caviar," he snorted testily. "As for your sleeping arrangements, you'll find a hammock rolled under the cot. It fits between those two hooks" — he crooked a thumb at the wall opposite his berth. "It will do until you clean out a space in the storeroom next door, and until I think you can be trusted to be left on your own."

Courtney bit back a retort. He had been in the cabin less than two minutes and already she was longing to gouge his eyes out. So he intended to watch her like a hawk, did he? To keep her tethered like a slave with threats and warnings? He would not be as easy to fool with promises and imploring glances as the doctor had been, but she was not discouraged. His arrogance was his weakness.

Courtney lowered her eyes and forced a meekness into her voice. "I'm sorry if I have done something wrong again. You've been very kind to me and —"

"*What*?" The words had been strained through her teeth and Ballantine was not sure he'd heard what he thought he'd heard. "What did you just say?"

Courtney kept her face averted. "I said I was sorry. I did not mean to eat your food and I did not intend to fall asleep on your bed."

Ballantine folded his arms across his broad chest. "Four hours ago you were spitting at me like a cat, now you're apologizing? What are you up to, Irish?"

"I'm not *up* to anything," she said irritably. "I had a hot bath and a hot meal, and I've had a chance to think, and —"

"Look at me."

She hesitated, but before she could obey, Ballantine was beside her, his hand tucked beneath her chin, tilting her face roughly upward to meet his probing gray eyes. What he saw infused his voice with scorn.

"Don't make the mistake of thinking me a stupid man, *Miss* Farrow." His hand moved away. "You'll only wind up learning your lesson the hard way."

Courtney's eyes blazed a brilliant hot green as he turned away. "I just want to find out exactly what my position is, Yankee. In spite of your *honorable* claims to the contrary, you must have a price in mind for all this *generosity*."

A faint, amused smile tugged at Adrian's mouth. "And if I do?"

"If you do" — her smile was equally sardonic — "I'm not about to fight you for it. I've earned enough bruises from you for one day."

Something in Adrian's brain snapped and lifted the black mood that had plagued him all afternoon. First she had expected him to rape her; now she was offering her services like a penny whore.

His smile broadened to a grin. "I've already seen what you have to offer, Irish, and to be honest, there is nothing about an undernourished, ill-bred pirate urchin that rouses me. However, if you are determined to play the martyr, I suppose I could oblige. Begging was never much of an inspiration for me, but perhaps after a hearty meal, and with the help of a few mugs of rum . . ."

Courtney launched herself off the bed, her hands and nails clawing upward toward his face. Laughing, he ducked to one side to avoid the slicing talons and in an easy motion, caught at the flailing arms and twisted her wrists down behind her back. She was crushed against his chest and had to tilt her head back in order to see his face. Their eyes met and it was like the clashing of steel swords.

"Bastard!" she hissed. "Filthy, sodding, bas —"

Adrian silenced the tirade by the only means at his disposal. His mouth plunged down over hers, smothering the gutteral oaths, muffling the shocked cry of outrage. Like a virago, she writhed and twisted within his grasp. She kicked out with her feet and brought her knees gouging up along the inside of his thighs. Adrian shifted his hold, taking both of her wrists into one hand and using the other to capture and hold her arching throat. His fingers dug into the tender flesh and found a nerve, the pressure causing her to gasp and cease her struggles.

Spurred on by the challenge, Adrian forced her resisting lips apart, his tongue plundering what she had contemptuously offered.

It was impossible for Courtney to breathe, to think, to reason past the aggressive intrusion. The lash of his tongue sent panic spreading throughout her body, and she became shockingly aware of the solid shield of muscle that comprised his chest and shoulders. His arms were like iron, his thighs taut and unyielding. She felt her limbs grow weak under the assault, her skin flushing ferverishly. Her heartbeat raced and pounded in her ears, drowning out everything but the sound of his harsh breath against her cheek.

Courtney's lashes fluttered like dying butterflies and her body went limp in his arms. A swirling blackness threatened to descend over her, a blackness that sparkled with thousands of dancing pinpoints of light. His mouth was her only link to consciousness. She was amazed by its softness and warmth, driven to shivers of unwanted pleasure by the rasp of new beard on his chin. She moaned breathlessly and began to probe and question the curiously pleasurable sensations. She molded her body tentatively to his, then burrowed deeper into his embrace with a newfound strength, unlike anything she had experienced before. Her hands fought his grip at the small of her back, but this time the struggle was fueled by a desire to reach up and cling to him, to bring the ravaging mouth closer, to bury her fingers in the glossy thick mane of golden hair.

Without warning Ballantine released her. Her wrists stung from the pressure of his strong fingers but she lacked the presence of mind to massage them. Her mouth throbbed and ached from his assault, her body swayed as if her spine was inadequate to the task of holding her upright. Her eyes were locked to his. He was a breath away from finishing what he had begun — she could see it in his face; she could feel it pulsating from his body in waves. She was torn by an instinct to fight him, and a need to feel the heat of his body join commandingly to hers again.

"You're full of surprises, Irish," he muttered softly. "That was almost as fine a performance as the one I was subjected to this afternoon from one of your compatriots."

Courtney wiped the back of her hand across her mouth as if that would dull the burning brand he had left upon it. "I don't know what you're talking about."

"No?" The flinty eyes roved casually over the heaving breasts, the cheeks that were flushed a faint pink, the lips that were moist and parted slightly with breathlessness. "She has a few more weapons in her arsenal to call upon, but you have the technique fairly well honed. With a little more practice —"

"What are you talking about? *Who* are you talking about?"

Ballantine looked down at his hands, startled by his inability to stop their tremors. He forced a chill into his answer.

"I'm talking about the captain's newest plaything. Miranda, I believe her name is."

Courtney recoiled from the name as if she had been slapped. "*Miranda*!"

"A charming wench, as you must already know. She has half of my officers drooling around her skirts like imbeciles, and the captain . . . well, as I said before, he hasn't come out of his cabin much this past week."

Courtney had backed up against the edge of the bed. Miranda! Her father's slut! Alive and well and whoring in comfort while the rest of Duncan's people endured the filth and starvation and humiliation of a moldy prison hold. *How dare this insolent Yankee bastard compare me to her!*

Ballantine was studying the subtle changes on the girl's face. The dark eyes had seemed to go out of focus for a moment, staring inward, but now they were smoldering, directing at him the same incendiary hatred he had noted when she was first brought on board. It had caused the hairs to rise at the nape of his neck then, and it caused them to prickle now. Dangerous eyes, he thought. He could almost feel himself bend under their power.

He broke the visual bond abruptly and turned toward the wardrobe.

"I think we should set something straight here and now," he said brusquely. "Not that I owe you any kind of explanation or excuse . . . but I happen to be engaged to an extremely beautiful, extremely desirable woman whom I plan to marry as soon as this ship returns to Norfolk." He turned and the emerald eyes were still on him. "As much as I enjoy a warm bed at night, it would take a visit from the devil himself to entice me into dishonoring the commitment I have made to my fiancée. Can you understand that, Irish? Finally and absolutely, can you understand that?"

"I understand, Yankee," she murmured.

He held her gaze a moment. "Good. Then perhaps we can both rest easier at night."

It was Courtney's turn to smile faintly, hauntingly. "I don't intend to rest at all, Yankee. Not until every last one of you has paid for what you've done."

Ballantine stared. His rejoinder was forming on his lips when the tense silence was shattered by the loud, incessant clanging of the ship's bell. Ballantine jerked his head toward the door as an urgent knocking rattled the oak panel.

He brushed past Courtney with a hissed order to hide herself. From the shadowy corner between the wall and the opening door, she could not see the visitor, but she recognized the agitated voice as belonging to the sergeant-at-arms who had escorted her from the cage to the lieutenant's cabin that morning. She forgot everything in the rush of excitement his news brought.

"What do you mean," Ballantine demanded, "the prisoners have broken out of the hold?"

"Half a dozen of them, sir," Rowntree gasped. "They tore through the bulkhead somehow, got their hands on some muskets, and . . . We stopped four of them before they could clear the guard station, but two got past our men."

"Where are they now?"

"The aft powder magazine, sir. Them and three hundred kegs of black powder. They say they want to talk to someone in charge or they'll touch a flame to the lot and blow us all sky high."

# Chapter Five

Ballantine dispatched Rowntree with a hail of orders and closed the door. The deep-set lines around his mouth became etched in granite as he unlocked a drawer in his desk and removed two deadly looking Queen Anne cannon-barreled flintlock pistols. He poured a measured charge of powder down each barrel and rammed a ball flush against it. The pans were primed with more powder and the flints scraped to ensure a good spark on contact with the steel hammers. The procedure, almost second nature to Ballantine, was completed in less than thirty seconds. He was tucking extra shot and powder into the belt at his waist when he glanced up at Courtney and saw the triumphant smile on her face.

"You knew about this?" he demanded harshly. "You knew it was going to happen?"

"I knew there wasn't a prison or cell that could hold Seagram for very long." Her laugh was brittle. "And if it is Seagram, you'll never get close enough to use those fancy pistols, much less bargain for your miserable lives."

"Your miserable life is at stake as well," he reminded her coldly. "Yours and sixty other prisoners'."

"I'm sure Seagram has taken that into account. You can't stop him, Yankee."

Ballantine was by her side in one long stride, his fingers clamped around her wounded upper arm.

"Maybe I can't, Irish," he agreed blackly. "But I think we both know someone who can."

Courtney gasped against the waves of pain in her arm as he hauled her toward the door. The heat of his breath was on her skin; an echo of her own furiously pounding heartbeat was drumming within his broad chest.

"He won't listen to me," she cried. "He won't listen to anything but his own conscience. He's a very simple man, Yankee. Simple and loyal and completely without fear."

"The most dangerous kind. And the kind who take the vows they make very seriously — especially vows to dead men."

On the beach of Snake Island, he had seen Verart Farrow issue his final command to Seagram — to protect Courtney at all costs, even at the cost of his life.

"It won't work," she snarled. "Seagram will never pass up the opportunity to destroy this ship. Not even for me."

Ballantine's grip tightened, his fingers laced into her flesh until she feared the bone would snap.

"We'll see about that, Irish."

He shoved her ahead of him out the door. The companionway was deserted. Shouts and sounds of confusion rumbled down from the main deck as lifeboats were lowered, crates and barrels thrown overboard to act as floats. The corridors were dark, the lower gun deck littered with debris from the hasty evacuation. Ballantine ran into the stern, bypassing the first hatchway they came to in favor of the ladder that decended directly to the storage holds. It was steep and the rungs seemed to sag under the slightest weight, but Courtney followed the lieutenant resolutely into the blackness, trusting his hand to guide each ankle to the rung below. They saw few of the crewmen along the way. The stragglers were in too much of a hurry to detain the lieutenant with needless questions or to notice the slender figure dragged along at his heels.

There were fewer lights on the lower deck, and Courtney had difficulty distinguishing the huge coils of cable and spare rigging from the crouched marines who were guarding the approach to the powder magazine. Smoke was thick in the air, as was the smell or cordite and black powder.

"Anything?" Ballantine demanded in a whisper.

"Nae a blessed sound, sar," came a hoarse rasp.

"What in blazes happened down here?"

"They took the lads by surprise. Eight o' them went trompin' through the boards afore there were e'en a musket to hand. Ne'er had a chance to leave go a warnin' shot. We was fair damned lucky the sergeant were takin' our lads a cup o' brew to see 'em through the watch. We managed to cut six o' the bastards doon — dead as cobbler's nobs they are — but two o' the biggest and meanest sons o' bitches went chargin' fair through the line o' fire like it were nae more'n bee stingers. We ken one o' them is hurt fair bad, but the other'n" — Angus MacDonald shuddered — "he's nae human, tha' one. Nae human, I tell ye."

Courtney's eyesight began to adjust to the gloom, and she saw evidence of the swathe Seagram had cut from one end of the ship to the other — overturned barrels, smashed planks, spilled coils of rope. Two half-starved, supposedly beaten men had managed to bring a mighty Yankee warship to a complete standstill and gave every indication of keeping it that way.

Ballantine sensed her excitement, and the iron grip tightened around her arm.

"Try anything," he hissed, "anything at all, and my first shot goes directly between those big green eyes."

He steered her against the bulkhead and signaled to MacDonald.

"Keep a sharp eye on the boy. When I tell you to, bring

up a lantern and shine it on his face. And if anything goes wrong, kill him.''

MacDonald acknowledged the order with a curt nod. He accepted one of the Queen Annes from Ballantine as the lieutenant stepped in front of the smashed door to the magazine.

There was absolute darkness inside. The faint light from the companionway made the back of Ballantine's white shirt glow eerily and set him off as a perfect silhouetted target for the men inside.

"I'm coming in," he said clearly.

"Hold up, Yankee," a voice growled. "Or the next step you take is into eternity."

"You asked to speak to someone in charge. If you've changed your mind ——"

"Ye ain't the captain."

"No. I'm not. I'm the best you'll get, however."

There was a pause. "Ye wouldn't be the yellow-haired bastard, now would ye?"

"I believe we met briefly on the beach."

"Aye," Seagram chuckled dryly. "That we did. And before that, methinks. Gun to gun. It was you at the helm during the fighting, was it not?"

"It was."

"Then come away, Yankee," Seagram growled. "I'd never refuse a brave man the chance to die in my company. Just remember, I've a bit o' powder here and a pistol primed and ready. The banter ends when ye step through that door."

"Fair enough."

Ballantine's shoulders disappeared into the cavernous gloom. Courtney's heart had begun to pound even harder at the sound of Seagram's voice. Her brow was moist, her palms clammy from the tension. She glanced sidelong at the Scottish jailer, but he was watching her as warily as he would a coiled serpent. She had to find a way to reach Seagram! She had to get inside the powder magazine and *make* him blow up the ship!

Ten feet away, Ballantine was searching the blackness with every sense tuned for a sign of movement. A shuffle, a scrape of wood or cloth, a heavy breath would give him some idea of where the danger lay. Until he could pinpoint both men, he was at their mercy. Felt-encased cartridges for the cannon were stacked floor to ceiling all around him, the powder inside so volatile that a single spark would bring a swift, explosive end to all discussions.

"You sent for me with a specific reason in mind, I presume?"

"Aye, Yankee. To send you and yer ship to hell."

"You'd be sending yourself and your men along with us," Adrian pointed out calmly. The remark was met with a snort of contempt.

"We're halfway there now, Yankee. We'd just be making quicker work of it."

"Then why the delay? Half my crew have already abandoned ship."

Seagram's chuckle drifted as he moved a step to the side. Directly ahead, Ballantine decided. Probably shielded by casks — powder casks. He also detected a hint of sulphurous smoke in the vicinity, smoke from the type of slow wick kept alight during battle.

"Ye're a cool one, Yankee. But I've a trade in mind."

"A trade for what?"

"Yer ship. In exchange for a day's sail to land. I want the chains struck and my lads sent ashore — then ye can have yer lives and yer ship and sail to perdition for all I care."

"And if I don't consider the trade a reasonable one?"

There was another heavy pause. "Then we've nothing to discuss. My men are dying from weakness and fever. If they live, they live to see a hangman's noose for their trouble. We've nothing to lose. I have their heartiest wishes with me — and you have the length of a wick to decide."

Ballantine flinched involuntarily as a spark and hiss crackled out of the shadows directly beside him. He had not sensed that the other man was so close by, nor would he have believed anyone to be insane enough to hold a burning wick in the midst of a mountain of black powder.

"I cannot make the decision myself," Adrian said quickly. "I would have to consult with the captain."

"Ye barely have time to consult with the Devil," Seagram growled. "Nilsson's waving a two-minute wick there and his eyesight is so poor, it will take him that long just to find the bucket to douse it in."

"In that case, I have a counteroffer ——"

"Nilsson!"

Ballantine raised his voice. "I have a friend of yours standing in the companionway now. A friend whom I'm sure you would be eager to see."

"A friend? What trickery is this, Yankee?"

"No trickery. There were three of you together on the beach. Farrow died, you're here, and so is the . . . *boy*."

A minute passed before Ballantine heard the corsair rasp an order to his companion. The wick spluttered into silence as it was plunged into a bucket of water. Adrian felt a sudden cool shiver of relief wash over him; instantly, it was lost to fiery rage when he heard a brief commotion in the outer corridor. A blurred shadow hurled through the doorway leaving a stream of hot Scottish oaths in its wake.

An instant's hesitation on Courtney's part as she plunged in the darkness allowed Adrian to snake an arm around her waist and spin her off course before she could join Seagram.

"Damn you, let me go!" She writhed against his arm and kicked out sharply with her heels. "Seagram! . . . *Seagram*!"

Adrian ignored the flaying arms and feet and backed up toward the door so that the pistol he held against Courtney's temple was revealed by the light. Her struggles ceased immediately, as did the stealthy movement he had detected in the darkness.

"Seagram," she gasped weakly.

"Court? Court, is that you?"

"Oh God . . . *Seagram*!"

The cold snout of the pistol nudged more forcefully into the underside of her jaw and choked her into silence. Seagram had risen from behind a low wall of powder kegs, and Ballantine could barely distinguish the giant's frame against the surrounding casks and shells. A stray beam of light centered on the glittering black eyes and made them glow out of the darkness like two hellish embers.

"Now that I have your attention," Ballantine murmured. "I believe we can settle this situation quickly."

"Don't listen to him, Seagram!" Courtney cried hoarsely. "Don't do anything he says! Don't *believe* anything he says! Do what you were going to do. Blow them up!"

Seagram stared at the silhouette of the gun held to Courtney's throat. One of his massive paws came up, and Adrian saw a gleam of metal hover over an unstoppered bunghole in a powder cask.

"Do it," Ballantine said evenly, "and have the pleasure of seeing me blow the top of her head off before your finger finishes pulling the trigger."

"No, Seagram! No, don't listen to him! We'll never have another chance like this. Think of Verart! Think of Duncan and Garrett!"

"Think of the *promise* you made Verart on the beach," Adrian said silkily. "The vow you made to protect her."

"You *will* be protecting me, Seagram," she cried desperately. "We'll never leave this ship alive — not with the chains and cages and puppet trials they have waiting for us. I don't want to die that way, Seagram. *I don't want to die that way!*"

The air rumbled in Seagram's chest, and the pistol moved fractionally closer to the open spout.

"And I'll swear to you here and now that nothing will happen to the girl," Ballantine countered smoothly. "She'll travel to Norfolk in safety, and she'll have a fair trial at the end."

"That's no kind of a guarantee, Yankee. Especially from the bastard who ordered her locked in an iron box for a week."

Adrian's jaw tensed. "I had no idea who she was. Neither does anyone else, and I'll see to it things stay that way. No one will find out who she is, not even when we've made the crossing. She'll be put back with the other women then and ——"

"*No!*" Seagram roared loud enough for the crouching marines to scramble back from the entrance of the magazine. "No, by God, I'll not see her condemned to a whorehouse."

Ballantine was losing grip on his patience. The sweat was forming runnels from his hairline to his neck, and his hand was slippery on the brass stock of the pistol. He could feel Courtney poised to take advantage of the slightest mistake he might make, and he already knew the second corsair had maneuvered to within arm's reach, waiting.

"I'll see that she's set free when we land," he said through clenched teeth. "It's the best offer I can make — the only offer I can make. If she behaves and causes no trouble, and if she can manage to stay disguised until we reach Norfolk, then I'll see her taken safely ashore and set free."

The black eyes wavered from the lieutenant's face to Courtney's.

"I gave my word to Verart Farrow," he said slowly, "As long as I was alive, no harm would come to her. I want the same from you, Yankee. Ye're word on it. Ye're word as an officer in ye're bloody navy . . . as long as ye're alive, no harm will come to her."

"No, Seagram," Courtney gasped in disbelief. "Oh no, Seagram, *no*. . . ."

"Give me that, Yankee, and a promise of decent treatment for the rest of my men, and ye have yer ship."

Ballantine stood rigid, the urge toward violence pulsing through his veins like liquid fire. If he refused, it was certain death; he had no doubt the corsair would carry through on his threat to blow up the *Eagle*. If he agreed, it was on his word, his bond, his honor, and that could mean being saddled with the girl's welfare indefinitely.

"You have my word," Adrian said and removed the muzzle of the gun from Courtney's throat.

Seagram's great shoulders appeared to slump as he placed his gun carefully on the lid of the cask. Courtney wrenched out of Ballantine's arms and stumbled forward, fighting tears of anger and frustration. They had the Yankees by the throat! They had their revenge for Verart, for Duncan, and for Snake Island within their grasp! She couldn't allow it to slip away on the wings of a foolish promise!

Courtney ran with her arm outstretched, her hand clawing for the gun Seagram had set aside. But this time it was the solid sinew of the corsair's arm that stopped her. She felt it come between her and the gun, and the next thing she knew, she was sobbing her anguish against Seagram's chest. It was only when she heard the stifled groan and felt the tremendous body shudder that the full horror of the situation became clear.

Seagram was hurt. She felt a slippery warmth on her hands, and the shock of it froze her tears on her lashes as she gaped up at him.

"S'nothin', lass," he said quietly. "A pinprick from a toy soldier. He paid dearly for the insult." The black eyes found Ballantine's over the top of Courtney's head. "Almost as dearly as the fancy lieutenant here."

Adrian's jaw flexed as he acknowledged the man's cunning. The wound had to be fatal and Seagram knew it. And so he had bought safe passage for Courtney Farrow, fulfilling the vow he had made to Verart.

Ballantine barked a crisp order to the marines out in the companionway. He placed a hand on Courtney's shoulder to pull her from the corsair, but she savagely pushed it away.

"No! I won't go with you! I won't play your stupid games any longer. I release you from your promise, do you hear me? The oath you gave Seagram means nothing — *nothing*!"

Several burly, heavily armed marines crowded the entrance to the powder magazine. Ballantine looked coldly at

Seagram, who nodded and pried Courtney's arms away from his waist.

"Court, ye've got to go with him," he urged in a low voice. "It's ye're only chance to walk away from this."

"But you, Seagram . . . what about you?" When there was no response, she turned to Ballantine, her eyes stinging with unshed tears. "What will happen to Seagram? He'll be punished for this, won't he? He'll be punished and he'll die and it will all have been for nothing!"

"Not for nothing," Seagram said. "I couldn't've lived with Verart dead, ye know that."

Courtney's eyes shimmered in the lantern light that spilled through the doorway. Nilsson was outlined in the yellow light; the short, brawny man stood braced against the large water barrel in the corner. The front of his shirt was soaked through with blood, but the soldiers paid little heed to his wounds as he was hauled upright and prodded toward the door.

Seagram grunted in pain as two marines locked his arms behind his back and jabbed a musket against his ribs. Courtney started toward him again, but Adrian held her firm as did Seagram's dark, commanding eyes. They flicked up to lock on the lieutenant's for a long moment.

"Ye're word had best be good, Yankee," he murmured ominously. "If not, I'll be back for ye. One way or another, I'll be back for ye."

Ballantine returned the penetrating stare before he nodded to the guards. Courtney's final, futile cry was stifled by a hand that was longing more to wrap itself around her throat than her mouth. When the congestion of soldiers had dispersed in the outer room, he dragged Courtney along beside him. He did not trust himself to speak, did not trust his anger to be satisfied with words.

Matthew Rutger looked up, startled, as the slender figure was propelled violently through the doorway to the surgery. Two of his assistants and Dickie Little were present so there was not much he could say beyond a lame, "What on earth has been going on? I've got seven dead men on my hands, and three more who look like they will be dead shortly. I've got more wounded than I've got beds for."

"How many?" asked Adrian.

"Wounded? Enough to make you think we were attacked by a small army."

"Have them on their feet and outside the captain's cabin in five minutes. He'll be calling for blood any time now, and for my dollar, I'd willingly hand the lot over to him."

Adrian strode back to the door but paused long enough to shoot a withering glance at Courtney. "Keep our friend here with you until the excitement dies down. And if he dares to open his mouth or to disobey a direct order, you have my heartiest encouragement to thrash his hide raw."

Matt was silenced by the degree of venom in the lieutenant's voice and he tensed when he saw Courtney take her life in her hands by reaching out to clutch at Adrian's arm.

"Please," she cried softly. "What will happen now? What will happen to Seagram?"

Ballantine's mouth pressed into a thin line, and he glared at her hand until she removed it from his arm.

"If he's smart, he'll find a way to end it himself before morning. If not, the captain will be only too happy to oblige."

Ballantine checked the conditions in the brig and ensured there were sufficient guards posted to discourage any further troubles. Ten wounded marines were assembled at ramrod attention in the wardroom and dared not meet his eyes as he and Sergeant Rowntree entered. Also present were the second lieutenant, Otis Falworth, and the ship's chaplain, John Knobbs. The latter looked plainly ill at ease as he acknowledged Adrian's arrival.

"He's in a less than amiable mood, Mister Ballantine. He was already aboard the gig and had it halfway to land when the word came that the ship was out of danger. The alarm apparently roused him out of a warm bed and interrupted some rather . . . er, athletic endeavors."

"Thanks for the warning, Chaplain," Adrian said dryly. He rapped lightly on the captain's door.

"*Come!*"

The lieutenant drew a deep breath and turned the latch. Captain Jennings was standing in front of his desk, his back to the door, his hands behind him clasping and unclasping in irritation. His bulbous figure had been clad in haste. The buttons down his shirtfront were mismatched to their loops, his breeches sagged without benefit of braces, his ankles showed bare over the tops of his buckled shoes.

The cabin was a shambles. Desk drawers had been opened and their contents dumped onto the floor. Clothes had been torn from the shelves of the wardrobe; the sheets were tossed back from the bed and draped to the floor. The sole incongruity in the storm of confusion was the olive skinned, raven-haired beauty who sat perched in a wing chair looking as unruffled as if she had just attended a Sunday picnic.

Miranda was clad in a scanty silk and lace camisole, the garment far too skimpy to adequately contain her voluptuous breasts. Her short, crimson skirt accentuated her dusky, shapely calves. Her hair was scattered in careful dishevelment around her shoulders and lured the eye to the breathtaking expanse of flesh swelling out of the camisole. As Adrian watched, she raised one bare leg and hooked it lazily over the arm of the chair, an action which caused the skirt to ride farther up on her thigh. Her sultry amber eyes made a contemptuously slow inspection of the lieutenant from boot to hairline. She sighed and looked pointedly away, her hand tracing suggestive patterns on her lap.

Adrian looked at the captain.

"You took your time reporting to me, Lieutenant," Jennings scowled.

"I wanted to be sure all stations were back to normal."

"And? Are they?"

"I've placed extra guards in the hold and ordered a work party to repair the damages immediately."

"Which you will personally surpervise?"

"I had planned to."

Jennings's hands unclasped, then clasped together with an angry slap. "Can you tell me what in hell went wrong? I have a ship in chaos, bodies to dispose of, wounded men by the droves, and it should take at least six hours to retrieve lifeboats and other equipment from the sea. I want explanations, Mister Ballantine."

"As far as I have been able to determine, a section of planking gave way in a bulkhead dividing the brig from a storeroom. By the time the guards were alerted, several of the prisoners were free."

"And?"

"And they have all been accounted for."

"By *accounted for*, I assume you mean they are dead?"

"Six of them, sir, aye."

"And is that the lot of them?"

"Two additional prisoners were badly wounded, but recaptured. They're being held apart from the others."

"They surrendered?" Jennings's porcine eyes squinted over the glow of the desk lamp as he half turned to question Adrian. "Without making any demands? I was told they had us by the crotch."

"They were more concerned with bargaining for better conditions than they were with blowing themselves to hell," Adrian answered carefully. "And, as I said, they were both gravely wounded."

"Better conditions?" Jennings scoffed. "Where do they think they are? *Who* do they think they are?"

"Eight of their number have died in the past week from fevers and corruption in their wounds. They only ask for clean air and a chance to wash down the hold once in a while. The ration of a cup of water and two moldy biscuits daily is not enough to keep a healthy man alive, much less a wounded man."

"What would you have me do?" Jennings arched a brow. "Feed them rack of lamb and pease pudding?"

"No." Ballantine tensed under the sarcasm. "But

perhaps we could give them enough nourishment to keep them alive through the ordeal. Even slavers know the benefit of a live cargo. And if we have to transport them to Norfolk ——"

"Slavers, Mister Ballantine, transport for profit. If I am forced to carry these misfits to justice, it will be for the sake of expediency and because the other prison ships are full. I had hoped to make the journey to Norfolk with empty holds, but you did not see fit to oblige me during the cannonading."

Ballantine's jaw clenched. He had ordered the *Eagle*'s guns to cease firing on Snake Island when the last of the siege cannon on shore had been silenced. Jennings would have preferred to shell whatever humanity remained alive on the beaches.

"I did not want the battle to turn into a slaughter," he said, and saw Jenning's eyes glitter. "Our men fought too well for that."

"Your remarks border on impertinence, Mister Ballantine, as did your actions that day. Those men and women are pirates. Thieves, whoremongers, murderers, outcasts . . . they deserve precisely what we gave them. Perhaps your sympathies are beginning to cloud your sense of duty. I've even heard a disturbing rumor that you now want to parole one of their whelps as your own personal steward. Is this true?"

Ballantine was not ready to defend his actions so soon. How had Jennings found out?

"He's only a lad. Hardly past the breeching age."

"Youth does not seem to affect their sensibilities, or their penchant for slitting throats." Jennings threw himself into a nearby chair and laced his fingers together over his mountainous belly. "These people only understand authority, Mister Ballantine, not weakness. They respect disciplinarians, not milksops. I am surprised you feel inclined to offer a position of some trust to one of them, rather than to one of our own lads. How long has it been now since the death of your former steward?"

"Three months," said Adrian guardedly.

"Your brother was a fine sailor. He showed promise. It is truly unfortunate that he was cut down so young. You must have grieved deeply for him."

"Alan's death was an accident. I have accepted it."

"An accident," Jennings mused. "Stoically said, Mister Ballantine, and indeed I envy your ability to stand back at times and regard the world as if you were not a part of it. As if you were here to *judge* and not *be* judged. In some men, such righteousness eats away at the gut until they simply explode one day from the incredible burden of constant perfection. Is that what happened to you, Lieutenant? Is that what will happen again?"

"With regards to what, sir?"

Jennings leaned forward and his face blossomed a mottled red. " 'With regards to what, sir?' To your past, present, and future attitude on board this ship, sir. For your ingratiating contempt for anyone's authority other than your own. *My* authority, for example. I have long felt that you hold my position on this ship in contempt. Is that not so?"

The question was a leading one and Adrian remained unflinchingly silent.

"There are times when I plainly detect a burning need within you to speed me on my way to Glorious Judgment." Jennings continued and smiled malevolently. "I have often wondered if Captain Sutcliffe, my unfortunate predecessor, was so forewarned?"

Adrian barely managed to keep his voice even. "The incident with Captain Sutcliffe was an extreme case."

"Nevertheless, you did strike a superior officer. One would imagine with the ice broken, so to speak, the second plunge would not require half as much provocation."

"On the contrary. There would have to be a great deal more."

"A wise attitude to assume, Mister Ballantine, since you know full well you face a tribunal eager to see you cast out of the navy in disgrace should you give anyone in authority the least cause to lay further charges. You have earned the wrath of several high-ranking officers by daring to expose Sutcliffe as a drunkard and an incompetent — myself among them. But then'' — Jennings leaned back again and clasped his hands tightly together, savoring the flush of anger on his first officer's cheeks — ''you are already well aware of that. You are also aware that your fate rests squarely in my hands. Your good name, and that of your family, hinges or whether or not *I* decide you have redeemed yourself.

''Redemption is not won by displays of arrogance or incompetence. With that in mind, understand that I hold you personally to blame for the lax security which allowed the fiasco this evening to take place. Further, I shall hold you responsible for any such occurrences in the future, petty or otherwise.

''As to the business at hand, you may inform sergeant Rowntree that it will be my pleasure to witness the punishment of the prisoner responsible for holding my ship to ransom, tomorrow at eleven sharp. Three hundred strokes apiece to the pair who dared to instigate the riot, three dozen strokes to each guard who failed to contain it. The rest of the prisoners are to be put on half rations.''

Ballantine stood in rigid silence for a long moment. ''Sir, might I *respectfully* remind you the two prisoners were gravely wounded. Neither will survive three hundred strokes.''

''Precisely, Lieutenant. Let that be a warning to the others on board who may harbor similar fantasies of escape. And any further whining entreaties for clemency'' — he raised his voice to a hollow shriek for the benefit of those gathered in the wardroom — ''will earn the petitioner a place of honor on the shrouds beside the condemned men. Do we understand one another, Lieutenant?''

Ballantine's lips were drawn into a bloodless line. He looked from the captain to the girl and was enraged further by the smug gleam in her eyes.

"I asked you, Lieutenant," Jennings repeated slowly, "if your orders were understood?"

"Three hundred strokes," said Ballantine tersely. "Will there be anything else?"

"Yes," Jennings said, watching the lieutenant's face closely. "This lad you feel so charitable toward — does he have a name?"

"Curt," Adrian said slowly. "Curt . . . Brown."

"Well?" Jennings turned to Miranda. "Do you know the lad? Is he apt to be repentant for his crimes, or is he likely to stab my officers in the back while they sleep?"

"Curt?" The tiger eyes narrowed and Miranda's swinging leg faltered to a halt. A frown creased her brow as she searched the lieutenant's bland countenance. "Curt *Brown*?"

"It was the name he gave," said Adrian evenly.

For a moment longer Miranda continued to puzzle over the name. Curt Brown? She knew no lad by that name. Curt? Court? *Courtney?* No! It wasn't possible!

Miranda stiffened as the shadows cleared from her eyes. In the next instant she was struggling to regain her composure, but not before Adrian had seen the same glint of naked hatred he had witnessed earlier in Courtney's eyes. He tensed, waiting for the hammer-blow to fall, knowing Miranda would delight in repaying him for his earlier slight to her vanity.

"Why yes," she murmured, conscious of the watchful gray eyes. "Yes, I know *Curt*. He's an extremely stubborn lad when it comes to following orders, and I wouldn't trust my back to him at all."

Jennings stared at Miranda, then his gaze flicked to Ballantine. He laughed suddenly, the uncosseted rolls of fat around his girth jiggling obscenely. He reached out a hand, still laughing, and signaled her to move over beside his chair. When she complied, a pudgy hand slid up beneath the crimson skirt and began to roam enthusiastically between her thighs.

"By all means then, Mister Ballantine, keep the boy with you. Share him with that other paragon of virtue, Rutger. Perhaps I'll be spared the trouble of having to appear at your court-martials."

And Miranda smiled, the message in her eyes as clear as a spoken promise: *Enjoy your little masquerade, Lieutenant. Until it pleases me to end it.*

# Chapter Six

Lieutenant Ballantine lingered in the wardroom only long enough to convey the captain's orders and dismiss the men. The ten marines were shaken upon hearing the sentence of three dozen strokes; the chaplain had to sit down abruptly and seek some inner consolation before he could properly digest the horror of it all. Adrian strode into the companionway and was nearing the aft hatchway when the burly Scottish corporal cleared his throat and stepped apologetically into the lieutenant's path.

"Excuse me, sar. A word wi' ye, if I may?"

"What is it, Corporal?" Adrian demanded gruffly. "If it's about the sentences ——"

"Nae, sar. Nae. I ken ye can dae nothin' aboot that. It's another matter. I didna ken how to say it before, and I wisny all that sure, but ——"

"Yes?"

The corporal glanced over his shoulder and lowered his

gravelly voice. "It's aboot the prisoners, sar. They had guns. It were guns they used to break oot."

"*Guns!*" Adrian's temper flared. "Dammit man, weren't they searched?"

"Aye, sar! They was all sarched! Right doon tae their willies, they was sarched. And I'd be willin' to swear it on ma faither's soul — God rest 'im — that nothin' bigger'n a belt buckle went in the hold wi' them."

Adrian stared at the flushed, indignant features. "Then what are you telling me, Corporal? That the guns came into their possession *after* they were locked in the hold?"

"I'm nae sayin' nothin', sar. Only tellin' ye what I know."

Adrian swore under his breath and dragged a hand across his brow. How . . . *why* would anyone smuggle guns in to the corsairs?

"Have you told this to anyone else?"

"Nae, sar. The two guards what could've spoken aboot it are both dead. Mine are the only other eyes what seen it happen."

"Good. Good." The anger in Ballantine's voice receded and he laid a hand reassuringly on the corporal's shoulder. As powerfully built as Ballantine was, the Scot had him by at least six inches and several stone, and made him look a featherweight. "You did the right thing, Angus. Goddamn, I wish there was something I could do about the floggings."

"I've nae doot ye've done ye're best already, sar. The men and I ken that." He straightened and glanced warningly past the lieutenant's shoulder. "Will ye be wantin' me tae strike up a work party, sar?"

Ballantine half turned and saw Otis Falworth and the chaplain approaching. "Give me ten minutes, Corporal, and I'll join you below."

The Scot nodded and excused himself just as the chaplain reached Adrian's side.

"I'm so glad we caught up to you, Lieutenant," Chaplain Knobbs said, his brow pleated with concern. He was a gaunt, earnest man whose hands fluttered as he spoke.

"What is it, Mister Knobbs?"

"The prisoners, sir. Is there nothing we can do?"

"You heard the captain. You also heard his warning. It was quite clear. I don't think it would be in the best interests of your health or mine to plead their cases any further."

"But . . . three hundred strokes, Mister Ballantine. It's . . . it's inhumane."

It was not unheard of throughout fleets of all nations to pass sentences of three hundred lashes when the gravity of the crime demanded it. And they had certainly seen more than a fair share of bloody floggings on board the *Eagle* since Jennings had assumed command. But such punishments were usually dealt out in lots of three dozen, four dozen at the most, and given over a period of days or weeks to insure that the recipient survived to repent. Three hundred strokes of the lash, by lot, was a sentence of death. Neither a quick one, nor a clean one.

The chaplain was still grasping for words to convey his revulsion. "Three hundred strokes is . . . is . . ."

"Is what the captain has ordered," Ballantine said harshly. "The bastards likely won't survive beyond the first fifty anyway, so save your prayers for a time when they might do some good for someone."

Reverend Knobbs flinched at the insensitivity of Ballantine's statement. Adrian was aware of it too and was disgusted by it. He murmured an apology, but it was to the back of the chaplain's head as he hurried away down the companionway.

"Damnation," Adrian muttered, half to himself, half to Falworth.

"Self-righteous fools have no place on a warship," the second lieutenant sniffed. "It's obvious he hasn't the stomach for this life. Whatever made him choose it?"

"Why did any of us choose it?" Ballantine said, shaking his head in reply to the snuff Falworth offered him.

"I know why some of us did. Family tradition, what?

All of the men in my family have served in the military in some capacity or other. Few below the rank of Admiral — British Navy, of course. My father was the only disappointment. He emigrated to the colonies and fought for independence and, for his troubles, never survived past junior captain. A mini-ball, straight through the brain. From an American gun, no less.''

"My sympathies. Now, if you will excuse me ——"

"I don't imagine the Old Man thought to commend you on the way you averted a total disaster?"

Adrian sighed. He didn't need this. Not now. "I really wasn't expecting him to."

"Nevertheless" — Falworth tested Adrian's patience further by selecting a fine pinch of tobacco, sniffing it, and holding a breath through the resultant sting in his nostrils and throat — "you deserve a pat on the back. Not many men would have walked blindly into an explosive situation of that kind — no jest intended. Certainly not our fearless leader. And then to turn around and adopt one of them as a cabin boy — well, I can tell you, Jennings almost split his truss when he heard about it."

"I'm flattered he bothers to take notice of what I do," Adrian said bluntly. "Now, if you don't mind, I'm due below."

"Oh, he takes notice, Mister Ballantine. In fact he watches you like a starving vulture. He'd like nothing better than to dock in Gibraltar and be able to hand the Admiralty your head, broiled and carved."

"You're not telling me anything I don't already know."

The thin mouth slicked into a pretentious smile that did not quite touch the liquid brown eyes. "Do you know he has you followed? Day and night. I imagine if you were to rattle a few of these shadows you'd find a midshipman or two striving to earn extra stripes on their cuffs."

Adrian stared at the sub-lieutenant, a man he neither liked nor trusted, and wondered what was behind the sudden gesture of confidence. In no mood to deliberate subtleties, he asked outright.

Falworth's smile tilted. "Why, because I'm on your side, believe it or not. And because, in a way, I admire the task you've set out to do and I should hate to see you or your merry band of patriots fail this close to achieving success."

"You're speaking in riddles, Falworth. Make your point."

"The point, *sir*, has to do with your little witch hunt. Your game of spy-catch-spy. It would be a shame to have it compromised this late in the play, wouldn't it, *Captain*?"

Ballantine's manner betrayed nothing, but his eyes darkened at the pointed emphasis on the upgraded rank.

The snuffbox closed with a snap. Falworth's smile broadened until the gleam was reflected in Adrian's eyes.

"Walk with me to my cabin, Lieutenant," Adrian said evenly. "We can talk while I change clothes."

"Delighted to."

When they were safely in Ballantine's cabin, away from prying eyes and ears, Ballantine rounded on the junior officer.

"You may explain your remarks now, Mister Falworth. And the explanation had better be good."

"Shall I start with your court-martial?"

"What about it?" Adrian snapped.

Falworth strolled to the desk and fingered the ormolu facing on the humidor for a moment before he opened the lid and helped himself to a thin black cigar. He ran it under his nose, his nostrils flaring slightly with the rich fragrance, and glanced speculatively at Ballantine.

"I followed the trial with some interest — we all did, as you can well imagine. Engaging in fisticuffs with your commanding officer is decreed an act of mutiny, whether justifiable or not, and in the navy, mutiny is punishable by hanging."

"There were innocent lives at stake, and Sutcliffe was too drunk to give a damn."

"Testimony amply supported by half a dozen officers and crewmen present on deck at the time. Yes, I know."

"Then I don't understand the problem, or the connection."

"The problem is that James Sutcliffe had never been known to take a drink on board ship before. Not even a tot of grog. On shore, yes, in spades. But then you should know that, since you were often his drinking partner during some of his more astounding bouts."

"Is there a point to all of this?"

Falworth pursed his thin lips. "Several points, actually. First, as I said: the court-martial. Regardless of how valiant or eloquent or *justifiable* your defense was, at the very *least*, naval precedent should have seen you relegated to a dusty room somewhere counting gull eggs well into senility. And frankly, it looked as though that was how the ruling would go — until Commodore Edward Preble appeared. Which brings us to the second point: a long, closed-door conference later and you emerge with a slapped wrist and a year's probation in which to 'redeem yourself.' Sutcliffe conveniently retires and" — he held a candle to the end of the cigar and watched Ballantine's face through the cloud of blue-white smoke — "our fire-breathing lieutenant is suddenly as meek and repentant as a beaten dog. A lesson learned? Possibly, but I think not. And that brings us to point three."

Adrian waited, the fury and tension building within him.

"That being the glaring leak in naval security that has been plaguing Commodore Preble's efforts to end the war for the past year."

Adrian stared. Hard.

"Coded dispatches," Falworth continued blithely, "secret orders, vital strategies have all somehow been winding up in the wrong hands. It's difficult to believe we harbor a traitor in our midst. I mean, one expects that sort of behavior from these sand-hill bandits — it's inbred, after all — but from a fine, upstanding American naval officer? Hardly."

"How did you hear about this?" Adrian asked coldly.

"Ahh, the look of the betrayed. Really, Captain, you've

been in service long enough to know by now that nothing remains a secret for very long." Falworth paused and grinned cryptically. "Especially when one's cousin happens to be adjutant to one of Preble's senior captains."

Adrian made a mental note of the source. "How far has this information gone?"

"Are you asking if it's reached the Old Man's ears? If it has, he hasn't said anything to me — which would be strange indeed, since he considers my assistance invaluable in gathering nails for your coffin."

Ballantine forced himself to take a deep breath before he made any further attempts to untangle the net he could feel tightening around him. What the hell had gone wrong? How could such carefully made plans have been compromised by a starch-necked incompetent like Otis Falworth?

"From your silence, *Captain*, may I assume I have scored a bull's-eye on all counts?"

Ballantine glared at him, rankling at the deliberate usage of the rank known only to a handful of people. "From your persistence, *Lieutenant*, may I assume you have a definite purpose in mind for all of these revelations?"

"Let's just say I'm hoping we can arrive at some mutually satisfying arrangements in exchange for my continued silence."

"Such as?"

Falworth spread his hands expansively. "With Jennings out of the way and you surely in line to join Preble's inner circle, who would there be to assume command of the *Eagle*?"

"Jennings? What makes you think Jennings is the man I'm after?"

"If he isn't, why the elaborate hoax? Why were you transferred to this ship? Why was Sutcliffe so agreeable to the ruse, and why, in heaven's name, would you have permitted your reputation to be savaged, even temporarily? The grand Virginia Ballantines must have collectively turned blue at the news."

"Leave my family out of this," Adrian quietly insisted.

"But not Jennings. Brother-in-law to Commodore Morris; first cousin of one of Britain's most illustrious heroes, William Bligh. Good Lord, you don't take on a man like that as prime suspect without taking very special precautions yourself."

"No one has said Jennings is the prime suspect," Adrian reiterated, but he did not sound convincing, even to his own ears. Falworth merely smiled and tapped the ash from his cigar.

"Everything points to Jennings and everything points to you belonging to one of these new breed of clever, fearless men who work out of a department at the Admiralty known to a few as *naval intelligence. I* am one of the few. And I could prove invaluable in your efforts to expose Jennings as a coward and a traitor."

Adrian fought to contain his fury. Heads were going to roll in the War Department, beginning with that of the officious adjutant to one of Preble's senior captains!

"Conversely," Falworth added, "I could rethink my alternatives. I could impart all I know to Jennings, then simply stand back and watch him unleash the dogs on you." He grinned faintly and his voice was little more than a murmur. "Or perhaps he'll arrange another little . . . *accident*? With breaching tackle?"

Adrian's head jerked up. "*What do you know about that*?"

"About your brother's death? Nothing beyond speculation. It seemed odd at the time that he could be agile enough to survive the heat of battle, yet too clumsy to avoid tripping over a length of cable. One could speculate that he overheard something. Or saw something he shouldn't have, perhaps. I don't know, Captain. Do you?"

Adrian's fists trembled by his sides, and his cheeks were bloodless beneath the tan. "If I ever find out you *do* know something, Falworth ——"

Falworth held up a hand. "There is no need to go into

details. I'm well aware of what you can do with your hands, and your skill with both sword and pistol is legendary. As I said before, I am on your side."

"For a price," Adrian snarled.

"We all have one," the sub-lieutenant said. "Mine just happens to be slightly more tangible than yours. Think about it, Lieutenant Ballantine, and do let me know your decision."

He walked past Adrian to the door. "Oh, and about the girl ——"

Ballantine braced himself for yet another shock as he turned to stare at Falworth. "What about her?"

"It goes without saying, she is included in our arrangements. We've already . . . discussed it, and she seems quite amenable. After all, we wouldn't want to see any harm come to her."

"You've *discussed* it? When?"

Falworth grinned. "Are you annoyed that she prefers me to you?"

Ballantine kept his temper in check. "Frankly it doesn't surprise me at all. The two of you deserve one another."

"Of course, I didn't fall for her little story. The poor, kidnapped daughter of a Spanish Grandee? I knew what she was up to. I knew what she wanted from me. And I dare say, she's found out what I want from her."

Ballantine's head was spinning. Miranda Gold! Falworth was talking about Miranda Gold, not Courtney Farrow. Good God! He and Matt were worrying about the girl giving herself away and here he, Adrian Ballantine, agent for the American government, a man supposedly at the peak of his intelligence, cunning, and wit, nearly handed her over to Falworth on a platter.

"What you and Miranda do or don't do with each other is up to the two of you," Adrian said tersely. "And Jennings. It could take me a month, it could take me six months to get the proof I need to put *whoever* it is away. Until then, I'd be damned careful if I were you. Jennings isn't free with his sympathies, or his women."

"And the *Eagle*?"

"The decision is not mine."

"But you do have influence. And I'm sure there must be a paper lying around here somewhere . . . a document signed by the powers-that-be giving you absolute authority on board this ship in the event of an emergency?"

"Jennings is captain of the *Eagle*. While we are at sea, and while he continues to fly the Stars and Stripes and not the Tripolitan emblem, *his* authority is absolute."

"With exceptions."

"No exceptions."

Falworth pursed his lips. "Perhaps you're not as clever as I assumed you to be. You've placed yourself in a rather awkward position, haven't you? I mean, suppose he orders you flogged on a whim? Or has you shot for insubordination? As senior captain you do outrank him, don't you?"

"My rank has nothing to do with the chain of command on board this ship. The commodore was very clear on that point, and I'm afraid I have to agree with him."

Falworth sighed and tapped more ash onto the floor. "In that case, I should think you would want all the allies you could find. My offer still stands. And my terms. Think about it, Old Boy, and let me know."

He touched a finger to one silver streak in a mocking salute and exited the cabin without a further word.

Dressed in his seediest shirt and breeches, Ballantine made a brief appearance in the infirmary. He saw Courtney toiling indolently over a pile of cotton strips, rolling them into bandages.

"This woman, Miranda Gold — who is she?"

"Are you asking out of personal interest, Yankee?" Courtney sneered, briefly taken aback by the abruptness of the question.

"I'm asking because she had the same look on her face when she figured out who Curt Brown was as you did when her name was first mentioned. I want to know why."

A shadow flickered in the dark eyes. "Miranda knows I'm alive?"

"Is that a problem? If it is, dammit, I want to know about it."

"So you can plead ignorance and offer me to the wolves first?"

"Don't tempt me. And don't avoid the question. What will she do?"

"I don't know," she replied quietly. "If it suits her purposes to keep her mouth shut, she will. If she thinks she has more to gain by selling me out, she will."

Ballantine's face darkened like a thundercloud about to burst. "Is this an example of the loyalty you boasted of among your father's people?"

"Miranda was never one of my father's people," said Courtney harshly. "She was my father's whore. Her only loyalty is to herself." She stopped and seemed to collect herself, then added in a more restrained tone, "I tried to tell you this was a bad idea from the outset. I told you to send me back to the hold. Now you don't have a choice if you want to salvage your precious Yankee hides."

Matthew Rutger, who had been standing silently to one side, looked up at Courtney's words and studied the lieutenant's face. There was no hint as to what was going on behind the iron-gray eyes, no hint as to the cause of the tension lining Adrian's face.

"You'll stay with Matt until I say otherwise," Ballantine said firmly. "And your only hope of getting out of this in one piece is to keep your mouth shut and your eyes open from here on out. Matt — a word with you outside for a moment."

Courtney bunched her fists around a handful of cotton strips and glared at the two men as they stepped out into the companionway. She could not hear what was being said, but she noticed a worried frown on the doctor's brow and a quick glance in her direction before he gave a last curt nod.

Ballantine did not look at her again. He departed for the brig and Courtney was left to fume ineffectually at Dr. Rutger while he busied himself over his table of surgical instruments.

"The last of our men have been tended," he said after a lengthy, glowering silence. "If you'd care to stop scowling long enough, you can accompany me down the way, and I'll see what I can do to help patch up your friends."

"Seagram?" Court cried softly and dropped the roll of bandages. It unraveled, like a slithering white snake, but neither of them paid heed. "Oh please. Please, let me see him. Let me help him. I promise not to get in the way, or . . . or do anything to cause any trouble."

Matt was startled to feel his cheeks growing warm. Courtney Farrow was the most unfeminine creature he had met in a long time, and yet there she stood, appealing to him in a way that was both soft and sensual, and completely without guile.

"Doctor?"

"Of course," he stammered. "Of course you can help. I'll, er, just gather up a few tools here."

Courtney nearly overturned the bench she was working at in her haste to assist the doctor and follow him out the door. She needed no warning glance to tell her to lower her head when they passed crewmen in the companionway, or to stay close in the doctor's shadow as they walked past the armed marines posted outside the storeroom that served as a holding cell for Seagram and Nilsson. The room was small and airless, its closeness made worse by the presence of even more husky guards armed with muskets.

"All right, step aside," Matt ordered. "Give me some room and some more light so I can see what I'm doing. Curt — bring the lantern closer. Hold it above the cot."

The wall of guards shifted grudgingly as Courtney followed the doctor's command. At first she did not see Seagram, only Nilsson, and the sudden rush of panic caused the air to back up in her throat. But he was there, huddled in the corner, his massive arms weighted down beneath three heavy coils of chain. His ankles were manacled together, similarily weighted with chains, and the iron links were fed through a ring embedded in the wall. His face was shiny with sweat and blood. His shirt was in tatters; his flesh showed the scores of fresh bruises and kickmarks bestowed by his guards.

"Seagram," she whispered and started toward the corner. Matt's hand on her arm stopped her; there was a warning in his glance.

"We'll treat this one first, Curt. He seems to be the worst off."

Courtney looked down at the cot. Nilsson was lying motionless; his eyes were wide and fixed on the ceiling beams. His chest labored up and down to suck in badly needed air, each breath produced a rattle of bubbles from the crush of flesh and bone showing through his shirt. His hands were clutching the sides of the plank bed, the knuckles white and trembling through the waves of incredible agony.

"I'll need water," Matt said crisply. "And plenty of cloths."

Courtney's hands were shaking badly as she ladled water from a huge barrel in the corridor into a tin pan. Some of the contents splashed onto the boots and trouser legs of the guards as she dashed back to the cot, earning her muttered curses and deliberate jostlings with sharp, bent elbows. She ignored them in her concern for Nilsson and Seagram — especially Nilsson. His wound, reminiscent of Verart Farrow's, made it seem to her that she was reliving those last few horrible hours.

She could see the memories in Searam's eyes also as he watched the doctor's hand futilely attempting to staunch the flow of blood and somehow repair the gaping hole between Nilsson's ribs. All of them knew the task was a hopeless one and the best that could be gained would be an easing of his physical pain. Reverend Knobbs, droning tirelessly from his worn book of scriptures, had taken charge of his spirit.

Leaving Matthew with the pan of water, the cloths, the needle and thread, Courtney sidled toward Seagram as unobtrusively as possible. When no one remarked on her negligence, she knelt beside him and, conscious of the eyes boring into her back, she reached trembling fingers forward to probe the bloodied shreds of his shirt sleeve. Raw, bright pink flesh lay exposed in a strip from shoulder to elbow. The edges of his shirt were charred and stiff with congealed blood; his left hand was a sickly gray and was cradled limply in his right.

"Why did you do it, Seagram?" Courtney's lips barely moved, her voice audible only to Seagram. "Why?"

"I'm no lamb to go meek to the slaughter, lass. If I'm to die, I'll die fighting."

"Then why did you back down? You had the Yankees exactly where you wanted them."

The giant smiled briefly, even as he winced under Courtney's ministrations. "For you, lass. Duncan and Verart'd both curse me to hell and beyond if I'd spent ye'r life so freely."

"But it was my choice, too. And the only choice was to take our last chance to hurt them the way they hurt us."

"If I know ye, girl, ye'll find another way. Ye'll *make* another chance. And for that, I bought ye time."

"What makes you think the Yankee will honor the bond he made?"

"He'll honor it, lass. Ye come to know a man fast and well when ye stare at him across pistol barrels. He'll honor it."

Courtney heard the wall of guards shifting suspiciously behind her and she reached quickly for several rolls of bandages. There were tears stinging the rims of her eyes, and a tremor grew in her chin. A man who had always seemed to Courtney to be indestructible would be flogged to death in the morning and there was *nothing* she could do about it.

"We haven't much time, Court," he murmured, seeing the emotion riding high in her cheeks. "There are things ye have to know. Things ye must warn the O'Farrow about."

"Warn . . . ?" Courtney met the pain-filled black eyes. "Then you don't believe it either . . . what the Yankees said about his being hanged."

"There's no man been born who could place a noose

around Duncan Farrow's neck,'' he said, his whisper roaring in her ears. "Not Duncan's, not Verart's. Not *mine*, by God!"

"If he was dead, I would have felt it," she breathed. "I know I would have."

"Aye, and that's why ye've got to live, Court. Ye've got to find him. Warn him."

"Find him? But . . . how?"

"Verart told ye," Seagram hissed. "He gave ye the name o' the man to see, the place to go . . . I heard him tell ye. Do you remember it all?"

"I . . . think so."

"Ye're life depends on it, because that's where Duncan will go. That's where he'll be waiting on ye. *Tell no one else.* Not a friend or lover, not a man or woman, not a crack in the wall. *We've been betrayed.* D'ye understand me? Verart knew. He was on to the son of a whore, and it was only a matter of time before he would've nailed a face to the name."

"The name?"

"Aye. The filthy sneaking swine calls himself'' — Seagram's eyes flicked suddenly past Courtney's shoulder and the bearded jaw clamped firmly shut. Courtney continued to stare at him. She was aware of Matthew Rutger's presence by her side, but she longed to scream the burning questions: who? why? how?

Matthew glanced from the corsair to Courtney, uneasy with the tension he could feel between them.

"I've done all I can for the other man," he murmured. "It wasn't much, I'm afraid, but at least he's a little more comfortable. Let me have a look at this arm."

Neither Courtney nor Seagram moved.

"I told ye once to bugger off, Yankee," Seagram snarled, breaking the visual contact with Courtney. "I'm telling ye again. I'm not wanting ye're fancy medicines, and there's no point taking a saw to it when I won't be alive to see another sundown."

"No," Matt agreed quietly. "No point, I guess. But I

can bind it for you. I can stop the bleeding and maybe give it some measure of support."

The black beard parted to a slash of broken and neglected teeth, but before the rebuke could be put into words, Seagram felt the cool pressure of Courtney's hand on his.

"Let him help you," she said softly.

The curse was growled into silence, and the shaggy head leaned back against the bulkhead. His gaze remained locked to Courtney's while Rutger cut away the useless sleeve and wrapped several thicknesses of cotton tightly around the gaping wound.

"That's it then," Matt said when he was finished. "That's all we can do here."

"Please" — Courtney turned wide, imploring eyes up to his — "another minute . . . please."

"I'm sorry. We've already overstayed our visit. The guards" — he glanced over his shoulder — "have their orders from the captain. It was only by Adrian's intercession we were allowed to come at all."

"But ——"

Matt took her arm and firmly pulled her to her feet.

"*Seawolf!*" Seagram hissed, his hand grasping out for the cloth of Courtney's trousers. *"Find Seawolf!"*

Courtney whirled to look back at Seagram, but Matt had already pulled her insistently to the door. The black eyes seared into hers and were the last thing she saw before the door was slammed with finality behind them.

When Courtney was taken back to Ballantine's cabin at midnight, she was too exhausted, mentally and physically, to do more than sit numbly on the edge of the bed while Matthew lit the lantern and rummaged through the wardrobe to locate the hammock. She could not get the sight of Seagram's eyes out of her mind — the command in them, the warning in them, the *fear* in them. His order to "find Seawolf" echoed and reverberated within her brain, mingling with unshed tears, recoiling with the memories of cannonfire and crushed bodies. She stared at the thin pillow beside her, dreading sleep and the nightmares she was certain would crowd in upon her. Yet, she was so tired. . . .

"Found it," Matt announced, straightening. The expression on his face softened when he saw that Courtney had laid down diagonally on the cot, her feet still dangling over the side, and was fast asleep. He looked at the hammock in his hand, and with a sigh put it back into the cupboard, and a rueful smile gentled some of his own weariness as he lifted Courtney's feet onto the cot and tucked the blanket around her shoulders. His hand lingered a moment at the nape of her neck, his fingers teased by the soft auburn curls. In sleep she looked so innocent. So damned innocent. What hellish circumstances had led her to this end?

Matt's hand dropped away and he took one last look around the cabin before dimming the lantern and departing quietly for his own quarters.

It was well past four o'clock in the morning before Ballantine had satisfied himself that the bulkheads in the brig were sufficiently reinforced to stand off an assault from a battering ram. He was filthy with sweat and grime. His shirt, once white, was blackened and torn open over the breadth of his chest. He felt completely drained, but the hard work had helped to expend some of the rage and frustration the day's events had brought. Falworth's subtle attempt at extortion had come as a shock, no question about it. What was it about the best-laid plans . . . ? So much for Commodore Preble's assurances of secrecy. So much for the whole damned operation, for that matter. If one man could fit the pieces of the puzzle together, a dozen could, and since it was not certain that Jennings was the man selling information to the Arabs, it could mean a knife in the back in a shadowy companionway from any one of a dozen sources.

Compounding his troubles, there was the girl, and the prisoners' revolt. MacDonald's disclosure that someone had smuggled guns into the brig worried him more than he cared to think about. It could have been the same man he was after who was responsible, or it could be a totally unrelated incident. Some of the ordinary seamen — those who had found themselves on the receiving end of Jennings' sense of justice and godliness — might have succumbed to the lure of pirate's gold in exchange for a few guns. Discounting the wounded and those whose presence on the lower deck would have instantly roused comment, there were at least two hundred possibilities. Two hundred suspects. Two hundred more knives in shadowy corners whose owners were frightened of being discovered.

Ballantine wiped the back of his hand across his brow, angered by the film of sweat gleaming from the fine hairs on his wrist. As much as he'd needed hard physical labor earlier, he needed sleep now. Sleep and a chance to sort out the tangle of thoughts spinning round and round in his mind. Sleep might help brace him for a worse morning ahead, for the floggings, for the inevitable confrontation with Captain Jennings.

Ballantine stood on the threshold of his cabin and stared at the curled form sleeping blissfully unaware on his bed. His anger, barely contained, surged into his cheeks; his urge was to rip the blanket from the slim body and toss her into a broken heap in the corner. He had a hand oustretched for Courtney's shoulder and the taste of a harsh curse on his tongue when a single flicker of lamplight stopped him.

The sudden bath of light revealed a face twisted in the throes of torment. Her cheeks were awash with tears; the dark crescents of her lashes were squeezed tight against some dreamed horror. Her arms were clasped around the crushed pillow and her fingers dug into the thin ticking. Her whole body was rigid, wracked by convulsive shudders that accompanied the disjointed gasps and whispers.

Adrian's hand, still outstretched, inched toward the slender shoulder. The effect of the gentle contact was immediate, and Courtney's distress was shocked into silence.

Like a blind man groping for security, she flayed her arms at the empty air until she touched the solid wall of his chest. A sob sent her upward into his embrace — an embrace that was stiff and guarded at first, slow to accept, reluctant to open wide so that the frantic, groping hands would have something real to grasp onto. He winced as her nails dug into his back and shoulders. He sat on the edge of the bed and felt her tears run hotly down his flesh to form a tiny puddle in the crease of his belly. Haltingly, he smoothed his fingers along the arch of her shoulder and cradled the taut muscles of her neck. The breath left his lungs on a soft curse, and he stroked the silky auburn curls. He held her close and rocked her gently until the terrible tension left her body and the last of the bitter agonies were sobbed free.

He tilted her chin and studied the pale features in the lantern glow. His fingers lightly brushed her cheek, and he stared at the tears that clung, like diamonds, to his fingertips. Without thinking, he bent his lips to hers, covering the trembling mouth, kissing it with more tenderness and longing than he had felt a need to express in a very long time.

The softness, the vulnerability he discovered startled him. Earlier he had kissed a willful, defiant creature who had asked for a lesson in gamesmanship and had won one. Then it had been her spirit and energy that had challenged him; now he found himself kissing a warm, accessible woman who was tempting his body with exactly the kind of release it craved — a blinding, tumultuous release that would give him the escape he longed for. He wanted to forget and to be forgotten for as long as the darkness and the softness would allow.

He felt her lips quiver and begin to move beneath his. Hands that had grasped him for comfort moments before now clung to him with a new urgency and sent a chill rippling through his body.

What was he doing? What insanity had gripped him? Adrian started to pull away but the softness followed him and this time his flesh met a greater temptation: the bold firmness of a breast found its way into his hand, the crown thrusting eagerly to fill his palm. He lifted his mouth from hers, his lips bathed by the sweet tang of her tears. His hand cupped her flesh and even though there was a layer of cotton obstructing his way, the velvet softness branded its imprint onto his skin. The ache grew, robbing him of the ability to think clearly or to move. His breathing labored; blood pounded into his senses, drowning them, drenching them with need. He knew he had to fight the weakness in his arms and the hunger flowing into his loins. God, the hunger!

"No," he muttered hoarsely. "No, dammit . . ."

He eased Courtney quickly back onto the bed and drew the blanket high under her chin. He backed slowly away from the bed, but his eyes continued to devour her, to want her against all reason. His hands burned; his mouth tasted of tears and of innocence and of woman. He edged farther away . . . until he felt the hard planks of the door at his back, and then he turned and hurried out into the darkened companionway.

Courtney's eyes were startled open. She remained perfectly still, not knowing what had wakened her. Her body was tingling, her heart was beating against her ribs, her mouth felt cool and curiously expectant. Propping herself upright, she took a cautious look around the cabin; nothing seemed amiss. She was alone with the shadows and the solitary flicker of the spirit lamp. Her fingertips came away from her temples damp, and she surmised it must have been the nightmare that had frightened her awake. It had been so real. So ugly. So terrifying . . . until the end. And then a shadow had blocked out the horror. A cool, soothing shadow that had no name, no shape, no substance.

Her body continued to throb and for some time after she had nestled back beneath her covers, she could not dispel the ghostly image of warm hands, searching lips, and eager, straining bodies.

# Chapter Seven

Morning was announced by the clanging of the ship's bell. Sailors thudded across the decks, waking their mates, hastily folding, tying, and stowing their sleeping hammocks. On this day, like every other, there were duties that had to be completed before the breakfast bell tolled at eight. Decks had to be scraped free of splinters; rigging had to be inspected for damage; rails had to be varnished and cracks puttied.

Courtney registered the commotion through a dull mist of pain and confusion. Her muscles had stiffened overnight; the sores on her wrists stung; her throat was raw and tasted bitterly of her fear for Seagram. He was strong but no one could survive three hundred strokes. And it would be an ignoble death for a man who had breathed life and fire at every turn.

Something cool and hard intruded on Courtney's senses, and she looked down to see that she was clutching the small gold locket she wore as if it was a talisman, an icon to give her the strength she needed to carry on through the day. With trembling fingers she snapped the tiny clasp open and fanned the two halves apart. In one oval was a miniature of her mother, Servanne de Villiers. Pale blue eyes were set in a delicately regal, flawlessly beautiful face that had won the heart and devotion of a wild Irish adventurer. Duncan Farrow's boldly sculpted features were crowded into the second oval. The portrait did not do him justice aside from the mane of thick auburn hair and the square, stocky jaw, but she could picture the rakishness of his smile and the ever-present gleam in the dark, brooding eyes.

Servanne de Villiers had been the daughter of Valery Gaston de Villiers, financier and confidant to Louis XVI. She had eloped with Duncan Farrow against the express wishes of family and friends and her father, in retaliation, had sent a score of hunters to track the lovers down. He had found them within the week, only hours before they would have reached the coast and freedom. Duncan had been attacked and left for dead; Servanne had been carried back to her father's chateau, where her child had been born eight months later.

Within a few short years, the Revolution came into full bloody form. The king was imprisoned; the great estates of the aristocrats were confiscated, their owners herded into small, cramped prisons to await the impersonal judgement of the guillotine. By some miracle, Servanne de Villiers and her young daughter were smuggled to the city of Toulon, an important port that had been seized by anti-revolutionary forces and turned over to the British to defend. For the next few years Servanne aided countless fleeing aristocrats, but refused to leave herself, especially after hearing rumours of a wild Irish mercenary who was fighting on the side of the British. It took further months of delay to confirm his identity as Duncan Farrow, and yet more wasted time to send word to him that she had not been executed with the rest of the de Villiers.

By then it was too late.

A brilliant young artillery captain named Napoleon Bonaparte had been placed in command of the bombardment of Toulon. Servanne was once again forced to flee for her life, this time to the countryside where she and her child were kept safely hidden by loyal ex-servants. Attempts to re-establish communications with Duncan took another full year, but by then the strain of running and hiding had taken its toll on her health. Betrayed by greedy peasants and too weakened by fever to fight the overwhelming odds, in a last gesture of defiance Servanne arranged Courtney's safe delivery to the rendezvous with Farrow's ship while she lured the military troups to a village many miles away. For her bravery, Servanne had been presented to the guillotine by a cheering crowd.

Courtney snapped the locket shut and held it tightly in her clenched fist. The courage of a selfless mother flowed in her veins, as did the cunning and resourcefulness of the man who had vowed he would not rest until the sea had turned red with French blood. Duncan Farrow's war had not been against the Americans, until they had chosen to interfere, and in such a way as to not be easily ignored or forgiven. If Duncan was still alive — and Courtney believed it to be so with all her heart — she had to find a way to reach him. She had to be strong and determined enough to do whatever was necessary to survive so that she and her father, together, could bring vengeance down on those who had sought to destroy them.

"They haven't beaten us," she murmured. "They haven't beaten *me*, by God. I'll let them *think* they've broken me. I'll be meek and dutiful and —" She stopped, her gaze caught by her shimmering reflection in the small square mirror that hung over the washbowl. And what? she asked herself. You'll even let the Yankee lieutenant think he's won?

"If I have to," she whispered. "If I can find some way to make him believe it. Just long enough for him to lower his guard."

With the strength of new resolves, Courtney forced aside

her aches and pains and quickly vacated Ballantine's bed. She retrieved the linen neckcloth from the floor and carefully wound it around her breasts. She brushed her hair smooth, then washed with the ice-cold water from the pitcher. As an afterthought, she carried the jug out into the companionway and refilled it from the huge barrel of fresh water, taking the opportunity to take a thorough inventory of stairwells, storerooms, and hatchways.

Ballantine descended the steps as she hurried back from taking a quick peek forward to the gun deck.

He said nothing to her, did not acknowledge her presence in the outer hall except to cast a brief glance at her clothing. He was unshaven, and his hair was loose and windblown about his face. His clothes were grimy and rumpled and smelled strongly of the canvas he had made do with for a bed.

In the cabin, he kept his back to her as he stripped off his shirt and flung it with the rest of his soiled linens on the floor of his wardrobe. He leaned over the washstand and scrubbed his face, leaving a thick lather of soap across his jaw. A small ivory-handled straight razor was taken from a locked compartment beneath the table, and he began scraping the stubble from his chin. His gray eyes adamantly ignored the green ones that studied him so closely.

His chest, she noted, was armored in hard muscle; his waist was trim, his belly flat. The pelt of coppery fur began high on the curve of his breastbone and narrowed to a hand's width where it snaked into the waistband of his breeches. A finer version darkened his forearms and — she guessed — his long, powerful legs. Courtney calmly studied the breadth of his back and shoulders, envisioning the fine work she could have done had the razor found its way into her hands first.

The chipped mirror seemed to fill with the blue-gray of his eyes, and she felt them probing for her in the shadows.

"It is the ship's policy for all hands to witness punishments," he said matter-of-factly. "I had hoped to be able to spare you it, but unfortunately the captain has heard about 'Curt Brown' and will be expecting to see him on deck.''

"Curt Brown?"

"It was the best I could come up with on short notice," he said dryly. He straightened and rubbed the flecks of lather from his jaw with a rough towel, then took a brush to his tawny hair and smoothed it into a clubbed tail at the nape of his neck. His eyes found hers again as he tied and bowed the black silk ribbon.

"While we're discussing procedures, you might note that I like my coffee black and waiting for me when I waken. I like my biscuits to arrive hot and my porridge to arrive without a scum on top. The cabin will want a thorough scrubbing once a week, as will my laundry. I enjoy a hot bath every second day . . . you can make use of the water for yourself when I've finished. From here on out, you'll rise a half-hour before me. I hope you had a good night's sleep because if I ever catch you in my bed again, I'll blister you. Is all of that understood?''

Courtney reined in her temper. "Understood."

"That should take care of your mornings and keep you out of trouble. The afternoons you'll spend with Dr. Rutger in the surgery. Your lack of squeamishness could come in handy there. Dinners you'll take in here alone, until I'm satisfied that you know how to behave yourself, at which time you can join Dickie Little and the rest of the boys for scraps in the wardroom when the officers have finished their meal. Any pilfering or hoarding or fighting with the other boys will be dealt with harshly. Any lying, cheating, or stealing will earn the lash. Is all of *that* understood?''

"I understand," she said smoothly, "that you can go straight to hell."

The gray eyes flicked to hers as he half turned. "There will also be an end to the profanity. Use it again in my presence and you risk feeling the flat of my sword across your fanny."

Courtney narrowed her eyes and braced her hands on

her hips. "You wouldn't dare, you damned Yankee coward."

Ballantine took a deep breath. He had spent a sleepless night in the open air, mentally listing every excuse he could think of for sending the girl back down into the hold and cursing aloud every reason why he could not. His patience was at a low ebb.

"I'll warn you one last time —"

Courtney's eyes issued a blatant challenge as a stream of ripe Irish curses found their way from her memory to her lips. Ballantine did not wait to hear them through. His scabbard hung from a peg on the inside of the wardrobe door; he was within reach of it in two strides and had the blade hissing free of the sheath and carving the air before Courtney's heart had taken an extra beat. The flat of steel caught the tender flesh of her upper thigh with a loud slap, causing her to yelp inelegantly as she scrambled in retreat.

"You bastard! You self-righteous, yellow-bellied —" She gasped as a second, equally biting lash found its mark. The air exploded from her lungs, and she rubbed her stinging flesh with a frantic palm.

Ballantine's expression showed nothing beyond a grim promise in the set of his jaw. Still stripped to the waist, his mahogany skin glowing in rich contrast with his soiled white breeches, he resembled a raging warlord, sword poised, eyes blazing.

"You bloody bastard," she cried. "You damned, contemptible, Yankee bas ——"

The sword flashed brilliantly two more times, and twice her flesh jumped. The agony centered on her left thigh, and she looked in vain for a path to safety. He had backed her into the corner; there was nowhere to dodge to, nowhere to hide from the cold determination in his eyes. She was close to tears, but she willed away the sour knot at the back of her throat. Tears were a woman's weapon and she refused to use them.

"Does this make you feel big and powerful, Yankee?" she cried softly. "First your fists, now your sword. Does it make you feel good to beat a defenseless woman?"

"It's your time we're wasting," he cautioned her, unmoved by the accusation. "And your backside. I doubt that Duncan Farrow would consider this a fitting display of his daughter's intelligence."

A spark flared in the depths of the sea green eyes. "You're not fit to mention his name, Yankee!"

*"Lieutenant Ballantine,"* he said, raising the saber threateningly.

Her chin quivered and a tear crowded the corner of her eye. "Tell me something, *Lieutenant Yankee:* At the end of a long, hard day beating women and flogging wounded men, do you sleep well?"

The saber shimmered. His face was still a mask of anger, his stare cold and unrelenting, but a shadow moved behind his eyes — a shadow hidden from Courtney by her film of tears.

"Does nothing affect you, Yankee?" she asked in a disbelieving whisper. "Does your conscience never trouble you?"

"It troubles me as much as yours does you."

She shook her head slowly. "I have never ordered a mortally wounded man to die under the lash — a brave man whose only crime was wanting to die with dignity and honor. Tell me, Yankee, would you have been content to lie like a dog in your own filth and do nothing to try to free yourself and your men? Are you content now to hide behind your fancy gold braid and your arrogance and pass judgment on everyone else but yourself?"

"The incident sickens me," he said, quietly. "A great many incidents on board this ship sicken me."

"And yet you do nothing? How brave of you, Lieutenant."

The saber dropped to his side. Adrian's face flushed. "This is a warship, Miss Farrow, and we are at war. There are rules and regulations that must be obeyed whether I agree with them or not. The captain's power is absolute at sea; surely you, of all people, know that. Sometimes it rankles and sometimes it sickens, but were any one of us to challenge the chain of command, our own chaos would defeat us. The navy is no place for individual vanities. Not a one of us can survive without the support of a hundred others."

"Seagram won't survive at all," she said bleakly, and her slender shoulders sagged.

"The fighting is over for Seagram. He knew it the moment he decided to break out of the brig. It's over for your father and your uncle, for Garrett Shaw . . . for all your people. When will you understand that?"

"When there's no one left to fight," she replied quietly. "When there is no one to hate and nowhere to run. When will *you* understand *that*, Yankee?"

Ballantine stared at her for a long minute, then shook his head and walked back to the wardrobe. He resheathed the saber and drew a clean shirt from a neatly folded stack. He did not know if she believed what she said. He hoped not. If all she lived for was hate and vengeance, there would be no future for her, no hope, no happiness.

"You have one hour before breakfast," he said shortly. "All hands will be piped topside at eleven o'clock. You'll be stationed with the other boys, and since both Matthew and myself will be busy elsewhere, I'd advise you to stay close to Dickie and do exactly as he does."

"Advise? Don't you mean *command*?"

Ballantine glared at her. "Madam, if you want to kill yourself, that's up to you. If you want to share the lash alongside Seagram and his friend, or if you have an insatiable desire to spend time in the company of Captain Jennings — that too is your prerogative. To be honest, you aren't my biggest concern right now."

Adrian quickly stripped out of the soiled breeches and stepped into a pair of clean navy blue trousers. Tall white stockings were snapped to his garters, and his feet were stamped into high polished black boots. He thrust his arms into a white linen waistcoat and impatiently dealt with each of its ten small pearl buttons. His double-breasted tunic was dark blue and had a white standing collar and cuffs trimmed liberally with gold embroidery. His belt was strapped on and his saber slung about his lean waist. He took his bicorne down from the shelf of the wardrobe, relocked the compartment that held his shaving gear, then paused long enough at his desk to separate a leather journal and a chart from the clutter.

When he walked to the door, his eyes were hard and uncompromising again. "If you decide you want to live, Dickie Little will be by at 10:45 sharp. Don't keep him waiting."

Lieutenant Adrian Ballantine stood on the bridge of the *Eagle*, slightly ahead of and to the left of Second Lieutenant Otis Falworth. Sergeant Rowntree and Third Lieutenant Les Loftus completed the front row of officers; behind them were a double rank of midshipmen, eyes straight ahead, shoulders ramrod stiff, mouths set and grim. They were all in dress uniform, their swords burnished and gleaming, their crisp white collars and gold trim flashing smartly in the bright sunlight. Below them, flanking either side of the main deck, were the columns of marines in crisp blue and white, the able seamen in striped jerseys and black leather round hats, the landsmen in clean shirts and canvas trousers. All stood in the heat and silence with nothing to alleviate the tension apart from the gentle creaking of yards and tackle overhead.

The *Eagle*'s sails were loosely reefed, and she rocked effortlessly in the water. High on the mizzenmast, the Stars and Stripes wavered in the breeze, while on the mainmast the long trailing pennant of Captain Willard Leach Jennings fought to remain untangled from the slack rigging.

Courtney tipped her chin up so she could see out from beneath the brim of her black hat. Jennings' colors were red and black — oddly enough, the same as her fathers, although Duncan Farrow's red lion on a black field was far more impressive than Jennings' narrow black stripe on a red background. As for the Stars and Stripes, the flag conjured only disdain in Courtney's mind, unlike the bold green and white that accompanied the Farrow pennant.

She had never been to Ireland, but her father's stories had brought to life his glorious fighting ancestors, the beauty of the mists rising off the river Shannon, and the musky scent of peat fires crackling on the hearth. Duncan Farrow may have been exiled from the land he loved, but he had made it real for Courtney and, like the wild geese of Irish legend, he was convinced that even though he might die on a foreign battlefield, his heart would return to haunt the skies of his beloved homeland.

Dreams, Courtney thought, and her gaze descended from the mast to the bridge, to settle on the tall blond officer whose eyes smoldered directly into hers. She felt a thrill course along her spine, and a small part of her seemed to break away and float above the crowded deck, studying the strikingly handsome features with unabashed admiration. With the vibrant blue of the sky behind him and the stiff white collar supporting the stern, sunbronzed jaw, he was stunning enough to take any woman's breath away. Unbidden images of oakhard muscles and tautly leashed power sent a flush creeping into Courtney's cheeks, bringing reality crushing back down around her. They were waiting to witness the execution of Seagram and Nilsson. Ballantine was indirectly responsible. For that he deserved only her contempt.

The boatswain's pipe shrilled, breaking their contact as both of them looked toward the stern. Captain Jennings strutted into view, tipping his cockaded bicorne belligerently to the ranks of saluting officers.

Courtney Farrow had to rise surreptitiously onto her toes to catch a glimpse of the man as he moved toward the forecastle. Her memory of his face had not dulled in the week since the battle for Snake Island; her hatred, if anything, had increased twofold. She had been told that the man he had ordered gutted on the beach had later died from infection in the hold. Her father's men were being slowly starved into submission; many were fevered, most would not survive the long trip to Norfolk. Courtney's eyes grew inky with loathing as she watched the captain's progress to the bridge.

She saw the mottled, split-veined face cast an imperious glance around the deck of the ship, and she thought of a finely honed cutlass cleaving the bloated trunk in two. She watched the fleshy lips move as he exchanged a curt salutation with his officers, and she conjured a crimson fountain of blood in place of the words.

Dickie Little, a head shorter than Courtney and as slim as a reed, looked up at her, his dark eyes widened with alarm. He tugged furtively on her sleeve to catch her attention, then with more vigor when it seemed that she had not felt the warning.

Courtney glanced beside her, frowning in annoyance. The mute boy made an eloquent plea with his eyes. The other eight boys in their group were standing tense and silent, heads bowed, eyes lowered, not daring to call attention to themselves from any quarter. Landsman and sailor alike were also prudently keeping their eyes averted, and she realized she was expected to do the same. With a quick smile of gratitude for Dickie, she lowered her head in reluctant compliance — too quickly to notice another pair of gloweringly expressive eyes staring at her across the width of the deck.

Miranda Gold stood in the shadow of the mainmast; her posture of boredom sharpened suddenly to rigid incredulity. It was true! It *was* her! Courtney Farrow, alive, disguised as a cabin boy! What few curves the wench boasted were concealed beneath the baggy trousers and loose shirt. The ratty auburn hair was scraped into a queue and covered by a narrow-brimmed hat, one that shadowed her features and kept her as anonymous and nondescript as the other ragged boys. Had Miranda not been forewarned of Farrow's presence on the *Eagle*, she could have stood within ten feet of the hated form and not recognized her.

Courtney Farrow, *alive*! Good God, could nothing kill the bitch? She had been brought on board bloody and in chains, had spent a week in a rat-infested hold — *How had she managed to survive*? How had she escaped the indignities and degradation she deserved? And how, by all the saints, had she managed to worm her way into the protection of the arrogant and despicable lieutenant? Did he know who she was? *Did he know he was harboring Duncan Farrow's daughter?*

Miranda's amber eyes narrowed speculatively as she saw the skinny lad standing beside Farrow tweak the girl's arm savagely.

No. Farrow would never have admitted to anyone who she was. She probably won him over with . . . .

With what? Miranda scoffed. The chit wouldn't know what to do with a man if she had pictures drawn for her!

As for Ballantine, the more Miranda studied him, the more she despised him. She knew the type: aloof and guarded. Filled with scorn for anyone who failed to meet his strict, upright standards. Undoubtedly rich, a man who had never had to struggle or compromise himself for anything. Heaven forbid he should admit to a weakness or a desire he could not control!

Now, there was a picture worth savoring for the sheer absurdity of it: Courtney Farrow, thighs clamped and mouth screaming obscenities; Adrian Ballantine, his proud weapon shriveled beyond all possibility of bringing her to womanhood.

Miranda almost laughed aloud.

"Is the entire ship's company present, Mister Beddoes?" the captain asked in a loud voice.

The quartermaster stepped out of line and saluted. "All present, sir, or accounted for."

Jennings nodded pompously. "Very well. Have the prisoners brought forward to hear the charges and the declaration of punishment."

"Aye, sir!"

A drummer commenced rapping out a steady, staccato as the ten marine guards — including Corporal Angus MacDonald — were led through a narrow channel in the ranks of men toward the main deck. All were dressed in breeches and plain white cotton shirts; all were bareheaded, barefooted, and held their hands clasped into fists by their sides. MacDonald, the tallest by far, and the beefiest, was the only one to glance up at the forecastle bridge, and then only to make eye contact with Lieutenant Ballantine for the length of a brief nod.

"For dereliction of duty," the quartermaster announced in a tight voice. "Three dozen lashes apiece."

The drummer struck up another tattoo, and all eyes turned to watch the two corsairs as they were brought forward through the mass of angry men. Seagram seemed to stoop under the weight of filth and crusted blood. His arms were bound with the spirals of heavily rusted chain; his leg irons restricted his movement to small, scraping footsteps. His shirt and doublet hung in tatters from the brawny shoulders, and Courtney could plainly see the wide bands of blood-soaked cotton that held his arm rigid.

Nilsson was barely alive. He was half carried, half dragged by the escort of guards. From the blankness in his eyes and the grayness of his complexion, he did not appear to be aware of the proceedings. His head lolled on his chest, and a thread of pink-tinged spittle hung from the corner of his mouth.

Bringing up the rear, dressed in a long flowing robe, was Chaplain Knobbs. His head was bowed, his lips moving in feverish prayer over his open missal. Matthew Rutger walked by the chaplain's side, his plain black frock coat and fawn breeches looking somehow out of place amid the sea of uniforms and striped jerseys. His face seemed to have aged overnight. It was no longer boyish, but wan and haggard in the harsh sunlight, and his eyes were clouded with apprehension.

"Attempted escape," Beddoes droned. "Inciting to riot, perpetrating a hostile act against a vessel of the United States Navy. Taken in the act, they plead guilty. Three hundred lashes apiece."

Even though there was hardly a man aboard the *Eagle* who had not already heard the terms of punishment, scores of shocked faces were upturned toward the bridge. The prisoners themselves remained unmoved. Seagram's deepset eyes were fastened to Courtney's, as they had been from the moment he had spotted her in the blur of faces. He did not acknowledge the reading of the charges or the fact that he had been tried and sentenced without an opportunity to defend himself.

"Have the prisoners any last words to say?" Jennings asked blithely.

MacDonald stiffened and thrust his chest out on a deep breath. "Ma men accept their sentence, sar."

Jennings smiled and sucked in a pinch of air through his teeth as his pale eyes settled on Seagram.

An insolent grin split the wiry black beard. "Get on with it, ye damned jackanapes. And may ye rot in hell for yer trouble."

Jennings arched a brow. "Bravely said. And yet I think the sting will be mine to deliver over the next hour or so."

Adrian Ballantine, standing to the right of the captain, heard a grumble from the body of prisoners who were collected together at the rear of the assembly. They were blinking in the raw sunlight, hunched with cramps from eight days in the brig. All of them knew what was about to happen and that there was nothing they could do to prevent it. Ballantine felt their hatred washing over the deck in waves, and he silently cursed Jennings for insisting that the prisoners witness the proceedings. One shout, one surge against the guards, and they could have the makings of a bloodbath.

"Seize up the first prisoner," Jennings ordered and twined his fingers together behind his back.

One by one the ten marines were led to an iron grating that had been set against the shrouds. They were ordered to unfasten their shirts and remove them, then they were bound spread-eagled to the iron bars. None of the marines balked or uttered a sound. Each took his strokes with clenched teeth and streaming brow, accepting each hiss and bark of the leather cat-o'-nines as a personal triumph over pain. The lashes were dealt by a new man each time, the captain having decided early in his command that, after two dozen strokes, even the strongest man's arm loses some of its effectiveness.

Angus MacDonald was the final marine to be flogged. He shook off the hands of the man who sought to strap him to the irons and, instead, grasped the bars himself and stood braced for the kiss of the cat. The great slabs of muscle across his back barely rippled beneath the stinging lashes, and when it was done, he turned toward the bridge and tugged a forelock in a mocking gesture of respect for the helm.

Only the two corsairs remained. The hush that engulfed those assembled on deck was stifling; it pricked the skin and caused shudders of revulsion in men long hardened to the cruelties of life at sea.

When the quartermaster signaled to the men holding Seagram, the captain raised his ivory walking stick and wagged the end.

"No, no, Mister Beddoes. The other fellow first. Let anticipation be part of the punishment."

Nilsson was carried to the platform and thrust up against the iron grating. His shirt was torn open across his shoulders and stripped down so that it hung from the waist of his breeches. His arms were jerked apart and bound to the iron bars, as were his ankles.

"Seized up, sir," Beddoes reported.

The chaplain stepped forward and raised a shaky voice to the bridge. "In the name of mercy, sir, I implore you to reconsider the severity of the sentences you have ordered. As you can plainly see, neither man is capable of withstanding ——"

"Reverend Knobbs," Jennings interrupted, "what I plainly see is that you are interfering with naval disciplinary measures. If you favor keeping the skin on your own back, I suggest you return to your prayer-making and say nothing more to me."

Jennings gestured impatiently to the drummer and turned his back to the chaplain. The officers and sailors removed their hats, as they had for each previous flogging, and tucked them beneath their arms as the boatswain's mate moved onto the break of the deck. He shook the coiled length of whip, letting the four-foot tails slither free on the planking. He glanced askance at the captain, who nodded and drawled, "Do your duty, sir."

The mate braced himself against the roll of the ship. He swung the lash back and over his head, putting the full force of his weight into the swing as the nine tails cracked sharply across Nilsson's back. The prisoner jerked on impact, and his hands gripped the iron grate as if welding to it. His eyes bulged, and his lips drew back in a scream of agony that had not finished echoing across the deck before the hiss and crack came again . . . and again. The wounds to his ribs and thigh began to pour blood through the bandages. His fevered flesh shivered; his muscles went into spasms. The knotted tips of each leather tail tore into flesh that was already contused, drawing out splatters of blood on each stroke.

At the end of twenty-four lashes the mate stopped, his face and arms bathed in sweat. He ran the whip through his fingers, squeezing out the blood, then handed the lash to the next mate in line. Dr. Rutger had gone to Nilsson's side, but there was nothing he could do to ease the man's pain, nothing he could say to halt the debacle. His soft hazel eyes reflected a mixture of anguish and contempt as he looked to Adrian for support, but the lieutenant's face was impassive.

At the end of the second set of strokes, the prisoner fell silent; by the third he was limp and unmoving. A ring of blood surrounded him and marked the lash's path to and from the grating. Matthew rushed to Nilsson's side when the fourth set finished; one look was all he needed to turn bitter, outraged eyes to the bridge.

"This man is dead, Captain."

"Thank you, Doctor. Continue the punishment, Mister Beddoes."

Matthew leaped forward. "I said, the man is dead! The sentence is complete — you have your pound of flesh!"

Jennings leaned on the deck rail, his eyes narrowed to slits. "And I have ordered the quartermaster to have his men continue the punishment. Three hundred strokes were called for, three hundred he shall have."

The doctor was stunned, as was everyone within hearing. "That is . . . barbaric!"

"Dr. Rutger, you will stand aside at once!" the captain ordered.

"Be damned, sir! I will not!"

Silence washed over the deck. The company froze, not daring to breathe or to move so much as an eyelash. The creaking of clews and tackle overhead seemed deafening in the silence; even the wind contributed to the tension by plucking at a loose rope and vibrating it on the mast like a snare drum.

"I beg your pardon, Doctor?" Jennings said in an ominously smooth voice. "I don't believe I heard what you said."

Matthew ignored the warning on Adrian's face and stepped toward the bridge. "You heard me. You all heard me," he said and whirled accusingly to confront the ranks of men. "I'm sick of the needless bloodshed we tolerate on board this ship. The prisoner is dead; there is nothing to be gained or lost by continuing his punishment. For Gods' sake, cut him down and let his soul rest in some semblance of peace!"

Jennings frowned and turned to Ballantine. "Lieutenant. We seem to have a minor revolt brewing. Since you are the one most familiar with the consequences of such an action, perhaps you could explain to the doctor —"

"There is nothing to explain," Matthew retorted, his face flushing an angry red. "Adrian, for pity's sake —"

"Pity?" Jennings mused. "Yes, indeed, I would pity any man who condones such blatant disrespect for his commanding officer."

Adrian spoke through clenched teeth. "The prisoner is dead, Captain. What more can be gained by seeing the flogging through?"

"An example can be gained, Lieutenant," Jennings said, eagerly watching the conflict in Ballantine's face. "An example of authority and of respect for the discipline we *will* enforce aboard my ship!"

"Humane treatment of the prisoners would not be construed as a sign of weakness," Ballantine insisted. "Nor would respect for their dead in any way detract from your authority. The man attempted a reckless act and has paid with his life. What greater price do we dare ask?"

"I ask nothing," Jennings said evenly. "I have, however, given a direct order. One that will be carried out regardless of who attempts to stand in the way."

Ballantine tried another tack. "If you martyr a dead man, you may find yourself with sixty more equally determined rebels."

"Are you presuming to question my order, Lieutenant?"

"I question the consequences," Adrian replied tautly.

"Duly noted. I shall face them if and when they arise. Mister Beddoes" — he turned to the quartermaster — "have your next man take his place. The sentence will be completed as ordered.

"*No*!" Matthew roared, placing himself between the bloody corpse and the man holding the lash. "If you insist on seeing this travesty through, you will have to cut through me first!"

"*Matt*!" Ballantine stepped to the rail, and Jennings' ivory walking stick came smashing down on the oak rail beside him.

"If the doctor wishes to stand in the way of justice, then he shall have the pleasure. Beddoes! Have the flogging resume. *Anyone* standing in the path of the lash does so by his own choosing. *Now*, by God!" He smashed the cane down on the rail again. "And you'll put your back into the work or there will be more flesh stripped here today!"

The new mate coiled the lash back and sent it snaking toward the grate. Matthew turned and shielded Nilsson's body with his own, gasping as the leather strips were laid across his shoulders. With the second stroke, welts were raised on his neck above his collar as two of the nine tails found bare skin. His frock coat was thick enough to absorb most of the shock in the beginning, but after a dozen strokes, the cloth began to shred, and patches of white cotton shirt showed through the crisscrosses.

As the first splashes of blood seeped through Matthew's clothing, the numbing rage that had immobilized Adrian exploded. Fury blinded him to his own precarious position as he lunged past the grouped officers. He was halted, as was every other man on deck, by a blood-curdling roar that shattered the horrified silence.

Seagram had thrown his massive body forward, jerking the three men who had been restraining him off their feet and into a heap of arms and legs on the planking. He plowed into the ranks of midshipmen and crew, swinging himself like a dervish so that the ends of his chains spun out and flayed at the men like a scythe. The chain linking his leg irons snapped under the tremendous pressure, and Seagram was up the ladder and then shoving aside the marine stationed at the top before anyone could move to block him.

The captain, seeing the ferocity in the depths of the black eyes, shouted for protection and scrambled back to the far side of the bridge. A shocked marine found himself thrust into the giant's path, and without thinking, he raised his musket and fired point blank.

The force of the blast carried the corsair back against the rail. The rail gave way under the sudden strain, offering no support as Seagram's arms flailed wildly for balance. His hands folded over the gaping hole in his chest, and he pitched onto the deck, his body sending another wave of sailors scrabbling out of range. Only one figure darted toward the confusion rather than away from it. Courtney bent over Seagram in time to catch a few gasped words before the glitter faded from the sunken eyes.

Ballantine pushed his way past the guard that had formed around Jennings. The soldier who had fired the shot was still aiming the barrel of the musket at the sprawled body as if expecting the corsair to come to life again. Courtney was on her knees beside the body, her face bloodless, her eyes wide and haunting as they sought Ballantine's.

"Get away from the body," he murmured urgently. "Go below and lock yourself in the cabin and stay put."

"Seagram —"

"Did you hear me?" Adrian snarled, conscious of the men venturing closer now that the danger was apparently over.

"Please." She reached out a hand to his arm. "Please don't let them do anything to Seagram!"

"*Dammit, do as I tell you!*" He grabbed her roughly by the arm and spun her away from the body. She stumbled back into the crowd of sailors, but her eyes stayed locked to his, her lips trembling in a soundless plea.

Ballantine looked away and saw Matthew still protecting Nilsson's body with his own, although his head drooped and his fingers were frozen to the iron grate. Beside him, Dickie Little plucked frantically at the doctor's frock coat, his mouth contorted in anguish, his eyes streaming. The prisoners in the stern were shouting and surging against the line of marines — they were only a spark away from erupting across the deck. Whirling around, Ballantine saw the top of the captain's feathered cockade; the man himself was a bodiless babble of orders coming from within a wall of thick-chested marines.

"You!" Adrian shouted to the quartermaster. "Beddoes, quickly, cut that man down."

"But, Lieutenant —"

"*I said cut him down!*"

Beddoes recoiled from the savagery in Ballantine's voice; Sergeant Andrew Rowntree stepped to the grate and shouted, "Ay, sir!"

Adrian turned back to Seagram's body and found himself staring into the crisp blue eyes of Angus MacDonald.

"If ye'll nae mind, sar, I'll just be helpin' ye mysel'."

"Good man," said Adrian. Together they lifted the corsair and carried him to the rail. Two of the other guards who had been lashed helped Rowntree bring Nilsson's body from the grating, and the two corpses were gently shipped over the side. Then crew and prisoners alike fell silent, turning row by row to see what the reaction would be from the bridge.

Only Adrian ignored the hushed cluster of officers. He crossed the main deck to where Dickie Little was helping Matt to a seat on a capstan. The doctor's face was contorted with pain; his shoulders were slumped beneath the bloodied tatters of his coat. He glanced up as Adrian approached, but he could not force the words through his chewed, puffed lips.

"You damned fool," Adrian muttered. "What the hell were you trying to prove?"

"The same . . . the same thing you just did," Matt gasped and gave a weak smile. The smile turned brittle as he focused on the florid face looming up behind the lieutenant.

"Mister Ballantine?"

Adrian straightened slowly.

"You have at last overstepped your authority on this ship, Lieutenant. You have not only countermanded a direct order, you have encouraged the men to join in a demonstration of your contempt for my command. You leave me no option but to order you, and Dr. Rutger, confined to quarters, pending my decision as to whether your court-martial will be held here, on board the *Eagle*, or whether I should share the pleasure with my fellow captains in Gibraltar."

Adrian stared down at Jennings with unconcealed loathing.

The captain took a precautionary step back. "Mister Falworth!"

The Second Lieutenant moved forward eagerly. "Aye, sir?"

"Have these men — the lot of them — confined to their quarters. They may consider themselves under arrest and without rank as of this moment."

"Under arrest?" Falworth could hardly believe his ears.

"Do you have an objection, Lieutenant?" Jennings

demanded, directing a portion of his wrath toward Falworth.

"No sir. No, I ——"

Jennings cut him off and redirected his venom at Ballantine. "Your saber, if you please, Mister Ballantine."

Adrian's fists flexed. Reading the flinty contempt in his eyes, Jennings signaled furiously to a nearby marine.

"Soldier, if this officer does not relinquish his saber *at once* you are ordered to draw your pistol and *shoot to kill!*"

The marine was visibly shaken by the command, and more visibly relieved when Adrian's hands moved slowly to his belt buckle. He unstrapped the scabbard from around his waist and presented it to Jennings with a mocking flourish. The captain accepted the polished steel and leather, his face splotched crimson.

"Now get out of my sight," he hissed. "Take yourself and this worthless, yellow-bellied leech and get out of my sight."

"With pleasure," Adrian murmured and turned his back on the two officers. He supported Matthew as the doctor struggled to his feet, and with the sound of their bootsteps echoing in the taut silence on deck, he and Dickie Little steered the wounded man below to his cramped cabin.

There, they eased him onto his bunk and gingerly peeled away the layers of coat and shirt until his back was bared for inspection. Welts rose in a crisscross pattern, red and angry, across most of Matthew's back and shoulders. Few had split, but they were weeping copiously into the cloths Dickie pressed against them. Adrian fetched a crock of rum from the sideboard and poured a healthy draught into a tin mug.

"Here, drink this."

"No . . . don't need it."

"You'll need it when I rub the salt and turpentine in," Adrian advised him dryly.

Matthew swallowed hard and nodded as he took the

mug. "You're probably right. I never was one for heroics."

A grin trembled on Adrian's mouth, then broadened, and in moments both men were laughing at the absurdity of the statement.

"I guess we've done it this time," Matt said, sobering.

"I guess we have, old friend."

"Then why don't you look worried? You can't seriously be thinking you'll walk away from another court-martial."

"Drink," Adrian commanded. "And if it's any consolation, I *am* worried."

# Chapter Eight

Otis Falworth was ecstatic. Overjoyed. Incredibly pleased with the morning's turn of events. He had counted on Ballantine and Jennings going for the jugular at some point during the Mediterranean duty — the challenge to Jennings to have Ballantine break his probation was just too great to ignore, whereas the inbred codes of honor and ethics Ballantine wore around his shoulders like a mantle were simply too vast a weight. Falworth had watched and waited. He had played out the cards in his hand slowly and carefully, wanting to be assured, regardless of who emerged the victor, that he, Otis Claymore Falworth, would be on the winning side.

Until an hour ago the odds seemed to be heavily weighted in favor of Ballantine. Falworth had even volunteered to help nail the other bastard, for God's sake! Jennings was a prig, a blowhard who belonged to a dying breed of naval officers — those who purchased their power rather than earned it. It was only a matter of time before the Prebles of the world would take over — the Prebles and the Ballantines and the whole merry band of marching patriots who had scrabbled to the top on blood and sweat and skill. Falworth would give anything to belong to the elite club. He wanted his name to be remembered along with the Decaturs and the Lawrences, the Porters and the Stewarts — *Preble's Boys.*

Ballantine's little mission on board the *Eagle* had opened a realm of possibilities. Catch the spy, become an instant hero. The rewards would be limitless. Captain Falworth, Commodore Falworth, Rear Admiral Falworth . . . why, even the President would hear of his exploits. And wouldn't *that* set the family patriarchs back on their smug haunches! The years of snide abuse he had suffered would be over, once and for all. There would be an end to the railing comments: Otis had the poorest grades in school; Otis was worth the expense of sending him to college or abroad; Otis was sent into the navy in the hopes it could shape him into a man; Otis will never be more than a third-rate mariner. . . .

Well, he would prove them wrong. Thanks to cousin Charles in Gibraltar, he had been alerted to the nature of Ballantine's "probation" on board the *Eagle.* A few drinks, a few earnest avowals of patriotism, and Charles had spilled the entire story of the hoax with Sutcliffe. All of his "elaboration" had been in strictest confidence, naturally. And the poor boy was too dense to connect the information he shared with Otis with the kind of information that was finding its way into enemy hands.

The initial steps had been taken two years back, well before cousin Charles had appeared on the scene. A gaming debt had prompted Otis to "sell" his obdurate fellow officer to a British press gang in lieu of payment. When the British sergeant had heard he was from the American warship *Eagle,* a few more coins had painlessly crossed Falworth's palm in exchange for the ship's itinerary. Both nations spied on one another. Quite innocent. Quite harmless. And not nearly as profitable as it could be.

It was also at this time that Falworth had been promoted to fill the vacant position of Third Lieutenant. It was Falworth's first step up the ladder of power since he had graduated without distinction from the rank of junior midshipman. Discrediting Second Lieutenant James Wallace had been the next logical step, and it had been during the ribald celebrations over his second promotion that the broader scope of possibilities had presented itself. By then Charles had arrived in Gibraltar, the naval base shared by both the British and the Americans through the former's generosity. Charles had been assigned to the Commodore's clerical staff and had access to all correspondence between Preble and his lieutenants. A normally shy, mousey lad, Charles became quite boastful of his position and his responsibilities when under the influence of alcohol — even more so, Otis discovered, when he was in the company of other shy young men.

Finding buyers for this new line of information had been easy. The staggering sums of gold he demanded and received excited him. The danger and the intrigue fascinated him. The realization that such an important man as Adrian Ballantine had been despatched specifically to run him to ground all but took his breath away!

Another source of pride was that he *had* outsmarted the Admiralty for two years. Outsmarted, outfoxed, outmaneuvered the navy, his family, even his own commanding officer who watched the comings and goings on the *Eagle* like a hungry panther. And there was the real coup — convincing Ballantine that Jennings was the man he sought. A simple admission of greed, a feeble attempt at blackmail, and he had managed to get Ballantine to turn all of his guns on Jennings.

It was a pity they hadn't killed each other on deck this morning and removed the need for a formal hearing and a long, drawn-out court case. Falworth could have assumed his rightful place at the helm of the *Eagle*, immediately, and there would have been no need to share the credit with Ballantine for unearthing the "spy." Falworth could have had it all in one sweep: the accolades, the hero's welcome, the *Eagle* . . . Miranda.

The thought of Miranda made him sigh aloud. The very notion of possessing her openly made his heart palpitate. It sent blood rushing into his extremities, prickling into his fingers and toes, sliding deliciously into his groin. Twice now he had managed time alone with the wench — furtive and hurried to be sure, but Lord, the things that woman could do with her hands and mouth! The tricks she knew! The idea of having hours, days, weeks to spend undisturbed with her produced such an ache in his body that he groaned.

"Sir? Are you all right?"

"Wh-what?" Falworth spun around, startled by the armed marine behind him.

"Didn't mean to startle you, sir, but you sounded as if you were in some kind of pain."

Falworth flushed angrily. "I'm perfectly well, Corporal. You may go about your business. Why are you on the main deck? Is this your posting?"

"No, sir. I was just on my way to the captain's cabin to, er, escort Miss Miranda on deck while he works on his log."

Falworth glanced at the hatchway. The noon meal was being served to the crew. Half the bloody officers were confined to their quarters. Jennings' fetish for scribbling could keep him occupied for the better part of an hour at least. It was indeed a day for miracles!

Falworth moistened his lips and steeled himself against the pounding in his chest. "See here, Corporal er . . ."

"Spencer, sir."

"Yes, well, Spencer, I myself have been summoned to the captain's cabin — expressly to take the wench below so that she might spend some time with the other female prisoners. I'm told she has a . . . a sister among them and whines constantly to see her." He fixed a smile on his lips and added generously, "Since we appear to be at cross purposes, one can only assume Captain Jennings changed his orders at the last moment. Either way, I shall see to it. You may return to your regular duties."

The marine hesitated. "Sir, I appreciate the offer, but —"

"I'll accept the responsibility, if that's what is worrying you. Obviously there's been a mix-up of some sort. Rank may have its privileges, but the Old Man would have my hide if I were the one who chose to shirk my duties."

"Aye, sir. I see what you mean, sir." Corporal Spencer took a step back and saluted smartly. "Thank you, sir."

"You're most welcome." Falworth watched the marine hasten in the direction of the crew's mess. "Most welcome indeed."


Adrian communicated orders as best he could to Dickie Little to send for him if Matthew needed him for any reason. The doctor had consumed most of the jug of rum and had slipped into welcome unconsciousness. Adrian returned to his own cabin, scowling at the guard who accompanied him along the companionway and then stood at armed attention outside the lieutenant's door.

Adrian's body ached as if he had shared the lash with Matthew — or perhaps because he had not. Either way, he felt a need, and his first act, after locking the cabin door, was to go directly to his sea chest and search out another full jug of rum. His tunic was flung aside onto the bed. The collar of his shirt loosened as an angry finger thrust its way between cloth and throat. Several of the small pearl buttons on his waistcoat were violently parted from the fabric and scattered across the floor, followed instantly by the crush of the garment itself.

"What the devil are you staring at?" he demanded coarsely. Courtney pressed farther into the shadowy corner. He sucked thirstily at the mouth of the bottle and glared at her over the curved surface.

Her eyes were red and swollen from crying. Her lashes blinked fiercely to contain the brightness that stole into the emerald pools.

*You can beat me until your knuckles bleed, Yankee, and you'll not make me cry again. . . .*

A muscle in Ballantine's cheek quivered, and he splashed some rum into a cup and set it down with a thud on the desk.

"Go ahead. You look as if you need it."

He pulled greedily at the bottle, letting the liquor burn the sound of Willard Jennings' gloating from his mind. He drank until his eyes watered and he had to stop for equal gulps of air.

"Lieutenant?"

He leaned against the headrest and stared at a spider working dexterously to spin a web from the ceiling beam to the swaying lantern. He raised the jug and drank again before acknowledging the tentative whisper.

"You don't want to talk to me right now," he muttered gruffly. "No one should talk to me right now."

"But I have to know if . . . if Seagram . . ."

Ballantine inhaled sharply and closed his eyes as the rush of alcohol and oxygen clashed in his blood. His vision swam a moment before he was able to shake it clear and focus on Courtney. All he could see were dark eyes in a pale, frightened face.

Dangerous eyes, he thought. Eyes that a father never warned you about. Eyes that no mother had, nor sister, nor even a whore who could portray whatever emotion you asked of her. Eyes like that could make you forget everything you knew about yourself; they could make you *want* to forget.

"Seagram is dead. His body was" — the words were enunciated carefully around his thickening tongue — "committed to the deep. Are you going to drink that?"

Courtney saw that his finger pointed to the mug of rum. Her throat was parched from crying; her stomach was tied in a gigantic knot. She stepped haltingly into the light, and the steely eyes watched as she reached for the rum.

"He said something to you at the end. What was it?"

"Nothing."

"A man doesn't say *nothing* when he's about to die."

Courtney looked calmly at the Yankee, startled by her own audacity, and retorted, "Nor does he say anything that his murderers could want to hear."

The barb found its mark, and after a moment the jug was raised, tilted, and lowered again. Courtney sipped from the mug. The rum was sweet and cool, and the afterbite of it boiled into her stomach like a loaded fist. Ballantine barely flinched after each swallow, but she noted the fine sheen of sweat beading on his forehead and she could see that the strong fingers seemed to be losing their ability to hold the jug steady.

"You're getting drunk, Yankee," she said quietly.

"Indeed I am, Irish. You can join me if you like, or you can" — he waved a hand absently in the air — "not."

She was silent for a long moment. "How is the doctor?"

"Quite a bit drunker."

"I mean," she repeated patiently, "how is his back?"

"Blistered and hurting like hell, I should imagine."

"Why did he do it?"

"Why?" Ballantine arched a brow and smiled crookedly. "Because he isn't one for heroics. That's what he says, at any rate. Not one for heroics. Not like the rest of us."

Ballantine reached forward, missed the humidor on his desk by several inches, and frowned as he tried again. The lid refused to open under his clumsy fingers.

Courtney sighed and took the tin from his hands. "I'll do it, before you break the thing."

"You smoke cigars, too, eh? I should have known . . . you should have told me, I would have offered you one. Hell, you fight like a man, you drink rum and swear louder — and better — than I do; you dress like a man and cut your hair like a man . . . I guess it shouldn't surprise me to learn you smoke and spit like a man."

Courtney's hand froze halfway to her lips. Her father had taught her how to cut, moisten, and light a cigar, but she had always considered it a private moment that gave him great pleasure. Ballantine's scorn sullied the memory somehow. It made her feel cheap and tawdry.

She threw the cigar down in disgust and turned away from his mockery. The slow, fat tears were gliding from her eyes to her chin, dropping onto the front of her pale blue shirt, soaking through the fabric instantly, smearing and swelling and darkening.

"What do you know about me, Yankee? What can you possibly know about me or my father that would allow you to pass judgment so easily?"

"I know what I see," he snorted. "And what I hear."

Courtney glanced down at the baggy trousers and cotton shirt.

"He used to keep me dressed in silks and satins," she whispered. "In ruffles and bows and dainty little slippers. My hair — he used to love my hair. It was long and shiny . . ."

Courtney looked into the mug of rum before she held it to her lips, and this time it came away empty. She shuddered as the fireball sent a flood of color into her cheeks.

"I knew that as long as he kept thinking of me as his little princess, I would never completely share in his life. So I learned how to use a sword and a musket, how to throw a knife as good as any boy my age, how to splice rope and shimmy up a bowline, and" — she dashed the back of her hand across her wet cheeks — "and then I cut off my hair and tore up the silks and satins. I told him I didn't want to be his princess anymore, I just wanted to be his flesh and blood. At first he laughed and patted my head and told me it was a grand gesture, but I shouldn't have wasted my hair or his time. Then I took a sword and slashed off every single button on his doublet and breeches before he could make a move to defend himself."

Courtney smiled through her tears, recalling the startled look on the legendary Duncan Farrow's face as he grabbed for a sword with one hand and tried to maintain a hold on his dignity with the other.

"He took me out on the *Wild Goose*, and I proved to him I was as capable as any son he might have had. As loyal. As determined. After that he never called me his princess again. And if I had to do it all over, if I had to make the choice between being soft and feminine and pampered and being the daughter of Duncan Farrow, I'd" — she spun around to confront Ballantine — "I'd . . ."

His blond head was lying cradled in the crook of his arm. His eyes were closed, and his mouth was slack. The jug of rum was tilted at a precarious angle. She leaned over and caught the jug before the contents were dumped on the floor. Ballantine only sighed and buried his head deeper into his sleeve. The empty hand groped empty air for a moment then gave up and dropped flat on the desk.

"Yankee?"

She prodded his arm tentatively with a forefinger.

"Yankee, are you awake?"

She walked slowly around the side of the desk and stood behind him, studying his sleeping form with a curious detachment. She could see the hard outline of muscle beneath the linen shirt, the well-defined contours of his arms and shoulders. An elongated oval of dampness was making the cloth stick to his skin at the small of his back, and the warm, musky scent of masculine sweat sent a queer tingle through her veins. His mouth was not nearly as foreboding or austere when his guard was down, nor were the lines around his eyes and across his brow quite so prominent. His hair looked soft and thick enough to tempt her fingers closer, but she halted just shy of touching it.

"What were you before you became a bastard, Lieutenant?" she mused, reaching for the knife that was hidden in the waist of her trousers. She let the handle warm in the palm of her hand, and she angled the blade this way and that to reflect the glow from the lantern.

"I swore I would kill you, Yankee. I swore it for my uncle, for every man who died on Snake Island . . . for Seagram."

Courtney blinked away the fresh tears that welled in her eyes, and she gripped the knife with both hands. Her gaze marked the vulnerable indent just below his ear, just below the inflexible ridge of his jaw. Her fingers tightened around the hilt and the tip of her tongue slid across her lips.

"No one asked you to help me. No one asked you to hide me or to take on the responsibility of seeing me reach Norfolk alive. I didn't ask Seagram to exact any promise from you . . . In fact, I released you from your bond. I release you again . . . now. . . ."

Her hands began to shake, and she tore her eyes away from his throat to stare at the quivering blade. One quick plunge would end it. One slash would fulfill her obligation to Verart. . . .

But her hands refused to obey. She knew she might never have the chance again, that it had to be now or . . . or . . .

Her breath escaped as a sob. She felt the pressure dragging her arms down to her sides. Last night she could have killed him. This morning she could have killed him without a qualm — but now, in this moment of shared pain, she could not do it.

Her fingers opened, and the knife clattered loudly onto the floor. The noise startled Ballantine out of his stupor; the gray eyes snapped open, and his head jerked up off his arm.

"What the — ?"

Looking around quickly, he saw Courtney shrink back against the wall. He saw the knife, and he misread the sudden fear in her eyes. He scraped the chair away from the desk and lurched to his feet.

"So that's it, eh, Irish? Talk to me sweetly and as soon as my back is turned —" He glanced pointedly at the knife.

"N-no," she gasped. "No, I —"

"You what?" he demanded, advancing a step. "You weren't planning to use that on me? You simply stole it and walked around with it hidden in your clothes so you could throw it on the floor? Dammit, I warned you what would happen the next time you tried something."

His arm shot out, but Courtney anticipated the blow and was able to avoid it. Ballantine's reflexes were dulled considerably by the alcohol he had consumed, and by the time his anger had redirected his fist, she was darting past him, hoping to place the width of the desk between them. But his fingers managed to curl into the folds of her shirt as she fled past and the sudden yank not only threw her off balance, but it tore her shirt open as she spun, laying her bare from collarbone to waist.

Ballantine held fast to the cloth and used it to pin her to the wall. The ice-gray eyes blazed down at her with such fury that Courtney was too shocked to make an attempt to break free. She braced herself to feel his hand stinging across her face, and when it did not come, she peered up through the burning hot liquid in her eyes and saw that his gaze had moved lower, had fastened on the exposed breadth of her chest.

"My God," he murmured hoarsely, and the hand that was not bunched around her shirt advanced hesitantly until the soft white flesh was reverently cupped in his palm. His eyes lifted to hers, to the emerald drowning pools that had widened almost to the limit of their bounds.

Courtney could not move, could not think, could not breathe. She felt her flesh constrict beneath his hand, and she did not know how to fight the tiny shivers that emanated outward from his palm.

"Damn you," he whispered. "Damn you. . . ."

His mouth crushed down over hers, smothering her cry before it was fully formed. She was jarred into action, but it was too late; his hands were as determined as his body to hold her in place. His fingers twined into her hair; his thighs and chest crowded her against the wall. His tongue lashed hungrily into the recesses of her mouth; his breath came hot and insistent against her cheek. Courtney's fists hammered repeatedly at his shoulders, at his back, but her efforts to push him away failed. Her head began to reel, and the walls of the cabin seemed to shrink closer around them.

She felt him shift to gain access to the belt holding her trousers. She squirmed and struggled to bar the intrusion but failed. Her limbs were bared to his greedy hands and the cool air, her pleas were reduced to moans, then to tiny, choked gasps as he feverishly caressed the smoothness of her inner thighs. He found and stroked an urgent spark. The spark flared, and a buttery weakness spiraled through her body. She tried to remember that she hated him, that she had come close to killing him only minutes ago, but it was too late. Too late. Her body betrayed her as it had before, welcoming his searching hands with hushed, ragged cries. It pulled a moan from his throat by curling and undulating against him, by sending arms up and around the column of his neck, by pillowing breasts against his chest and teasing him to a blind, desperate need.

Adrian pushed the torn halves of her shirt from her shoulders, and with a tortured sigh, bowed his head, searing her flesh with a molten path of caresses. Her breasts were white as cream, rose-tipped, and as he took them hostage beneath his lips, Courtney's fingers crawled into the thick mane of golden hair, holding him to her for dear life, her mouth gaping open, her eyes filling with tears of disbelief. Her body pulsed with fire. Her legs lost their strength, and she closed her eyes to one exquisite spasm after another. His mouth on her breasts, his hands between her thighs . . . no one had prepared her for such as assault on her senses!

She caught her breath, feeling his eyes upon her. His hunger was mirrored in their depths; his desire was as brazen as the fiery ache that consumed her flesh. The floor dropped away, and she was in his arms being carried to the bed. His clothes were shed like leaves in a raging storm, and with the same wild, lashing urgency, he was pressing between her thighs, and his hands were guiding Courtney upward to meet him, to shatter her innocence on the first vaunted thrust of his flesh. The pain was a fleeting thing, gasped away on a startled breath, not like the other — the raw stretching presence that filled her again and again, searching, probing, tearing at her senses with each damp clash of their bodies. She groaned for the warm friction of his thighs chafing hers, for the bold rise and fall of his smoothly muscled buttocks, for the hoarse grating breaths that echoed her own. Deep inside she felt the expanding heat of his passion, and her gasps shivered into cries. She strained upward without awaiting the commands of his hands. Her entire body tautened on his, and she heard his sharp intake of air as he erupted within her.

Adrian's body shuddered into hers, and the darkness flared with a million brilliant lights; hot, searing lights that sent a new flush of exhilaration thundering into her veins. Like a powder keg touched by a spark, she exploded. She writhed and cried out soundlessly. Waves of ecstasy flooded through her, sending her nails clawing into his shoulders, her head thrashing side to side with astonished pleasure.

The sweet, stunning odyssey ended with a sob as she collapsed on the tangle of bedding, her senses reeling, her limbs quaking and drained of all strength. Her skin was drenched and tingling. The blinding tension of moments before had been released and had melted into an equally exquisite sensation: the lingering warmth of him still filling her, still bound to her with a disbelieving wonder.

It simply wasn't possible for such a thing to have happened to her. And yet it had. A single touch had obliterated her defenses. His hand on her breast, the torment of passion in his eyes — the *promise* of passion in his eyes, and in his hard, straining body. Ballantine was her sworn enemy, the man who had destroyed her home, her family. How could he also be the giver of such pleasure, such solace, such tender fury? It was wrong of her to have succumbed. They were both wrong to have surrendered to the weaknesses of their bodies.

Courtney curled her lower lip between her teeth and pushed gingerly against Ballantine's shoulder. With a reluctant sigh, he rolled beside her onto the mattress but kept an arm draped possessively across her breasts and shoulder. Courtney closed her eyes and fought the pleasant ache of desire, and only opened them again when the deep, even breathing assured her he was asleep.

She swallowed hard but the lump in her throat would

not go away. They were enemies before this thing happened, and in the morning they would be enemies again. It could not possibly be any other way. It could not.

Otis Falworth hiked his breeches up over his buttocks, wincing as the fabric chafed the more tenderly abused parts of his body. He fumbled with the row of brass buttons at the waist and snapped the braces up onto his shoulders. An anxious glance into the mirror resulted in a wry smile. His hair stood out like a washmop, the disheveled streaks at his temples making him look slightly maniacal. His face was flushed, although his skin was cool and clammy. His mouth looked as if it had been savaged — indeed, he swore it had been chewed in the throes of passion! He heard a deep, throaty laugh behind him and half turned toward the bed.

"We certainly do look like we have taken more than a casual stroll around the ship, my lieutenant."

Falworth grinned, and his sly brown eyes regarded the glorious curves and contours of the body that had nearly driven him mad this past hour. Her flesh seemed to glow, the shadowy valleys and clefts luring his gaze like winking jewels.

"More, my lieutenant?" she purred huskily.

"What?" His eyes flicked up from the raven thatch of curls that still glistened from their expended energies. An uncertain laugh, and his complexion shaded darker. "I doubt if there is any more in me, my love, much as I would like to believe there was."

Rising to her knees, like a sea nymph from an enchanted pool, Miranda crooked a finger and, dutifully, Falworth crossed to stand by the cot. The seductive amber eyes lifted to his; her hands slid up his shoulders and twined together at the nape of his neck. She leaned forward so her breasts swayed hypnotically as she angled her mouth up to his.

"Miranda can always find more," she breathed. "She can coax and tease. She has the patience of a thousand courtesans when it comes to treating her man with care.

And such a man! Such a bull, my lieutenant! Never," she moaned, "never have I felt this full of love before."

Falworth surrendered to the plundering lips. It was a dream come true! The most beautiful, most sensitive, most *sensual* woman in the world — and she wanted *him*! Damn Adrian Ballantine and his sly innuendoes; the righteous sod was jealous. Yes, that was it — Ballantine was jealous that he had not won Miranda's attention first!

A groan sent Falworth's hands to his waist, to reluctantly stop Miranda's efforts to unfasten his clothes.

"We've been here too long as it is," he muttered. "Jennings has probably sent someone out to look for us."

"Let them look," she declared fiercely and shrugged off his restraint. "Or do you not think I am worth a tiny risk, my lieutenant?"

Falworth's fists clenched in the flowing raven tresses, and he held her head firmly uptilted to him. "I'm willing to risk far more than you know, but not just for a few stolen moments here and there. I mean to have you, Miranda. All day, every day. And every night. . . ."

His mouth decended in a bruising kiss, one which nudged Miranda's estimation of Falworth's value up yet another notch. Winning his cooperation had been child's play and had actually helped alleviate some of the boredom of captivity; but she hoped she had beguiled him enough to remove another glaring obstacle to her future happiness.

"Oh how I wish I didn't have to return to that great sweating pig," she cried. "How I wish I could remain here with you!"

Tears spilled from the huge amber eyes and smeared wetly on Falworth's shoulder. His jaw tensed, and his nostrils flared until they were rimmed white.

"Soon, my love, soon," he soothed. "You must be patient."

"How can I be patient when I know there is no hope? We will be in Gibraltar in two days. Even if I am sent on to America, it will be as the slave of that . . . that *monster*!"

"No," Falworth insisted, and the temptation to reveal his plans was almost more than he could bear. "Everything will change in Gibraltar; you must believe me. Jennings will be gone, the *Eagle* will be mine; and no one, *nothing* will stand between us."

"But" — her lip trembled convincingly, and the tears continued to splash down her cheeks — "how can that be? Forgive me, my lieutenant, but how can you say with such surety that the ship will be yours? How?"

"Hush," he commanded and laid a finger across her lips. "It will be as I say; that's all you have to know."

"Never," she whispered frantically. "It will never happen. Not as long as *she* is still alive to torture me with her lies and threats."

"*She*? Who?"

Miranda lowered her head quickly. "No," she gasped. "I mustn't. They'll find out and . . . and no matter where I hide, they'll find me . . . and kill me."

"*Who* will find you? Why will they kill you?" Falworth tightened his fists in her hair and forced her to look up at him. "Who are you so afraid of? Someone on this ship? You said *she* . . . is it one of the prisoners?"

"Prisoner?" Miranda laughed sardonically. "She's no prisoner. She sits clean and well fed in a fine cabin. She walks the deck freely, not like a dog on a chain. She has no animal crawling on top of her day and night, no ——"

"*Miranda!*" Falworth's harsh snarl broke through her hysteria. "*What are you talking about*? *Who* are you talking about?"

"I'm talking about *her*," Miranda hissed. "Courtney Farrow. Duncan's daughter . . . your fine Lieutenant Ballantine's new cabin boy!"

Falworth's eyes widened, registering his shock. Ballantine's cabin boy was a *girl*! She was *Duncan Farrow's daughter*?

Miranda's heart thudded so loudly she feared it might be heard in the sudden silence. She had made the right choice — she could see it in the burning eyes.

"Yes," she cried. "Farrow's daughter. And she hates me. She *hates* me and would stop at nothing to see me dead!"

Falworth's mind reeled with the power of the weapon he had just been handed. Fired correctly, it could not only remove Jennings, but also discredit Ballantine, and he could claim full honors for trapping the spy. Ballantine would never be able to talk his way out of the charges: Concealing an enemy. Aiding and abetting. . . .

"But does he know who she is?" he wondered aloud, the excitement stirring his blood again. "If he knows and if he's keeping her deliberately hidden —"

Miranda wanted to laugh, but she restrained the urge to a smile. "Have I said something to help you, my lieutenant?"

"Help?" Falworth's eyes focused on hers, and she could read the malevolent gleam of triumph in them. She could also feel his exuberance rising hard and lusty against her belly. "You've just stamped the articles of my captaincy, my love. Nothing can stop me now."

"Nothing can stop *us*," she softly corrected him, and her hands ran determindly beneath his bulging codpiece.

"Us," he agreed, forcing her down onto the bed. "Two more days, and it will all be ours."

# Chapter Nine

Courtney opened her eyes slowly. The high, narrow slit in the wall that provided ventilation allowed just enough light to filter into the cabin for her to see where her clothing and Ballantine's littered the floor, the desktop, the overturned chair. The smell of extinguished whale oil and energetic bodies clung heavily to the stale air, and she wished desperately for somewhere to hide, some way to avoid the confrontation she knew must come. Would he remember? Would he blame it on the amount of rum he had consumed? Would he blame it on her?

She was lying on her side. One of Ballantine's arms was draped with familiarity around her waist; the other was beneath her head and served as a pillow. She could feel the feathering of his breath at the back of her neck and the accompanying rise and fall of his chest where the coppery fur brushed against her back.

Carefully, moving inches at a time so as not to disturb the sleeping Yankee, Courtney extricated herself from his

174

arms and slipped out of the berth. The aches and stiffness she half expected did not materialize immediately, and she straightened slowly, flexing her arms and legs to loosen the lingering sleepiness. Her slender body had borne the weight of a man roughly double her size — it was a wonder she could stand at all. Her breasts had been kissed and nuzzled and fondled so much she expected them to be black and blue. And her mouth! It was impossible to believe anything of its original shape and color remained.

But amazingly enough, there was a lightness to her step as she padded quietly over to stand in front of the square mirror. Braced for what she assumed would be the reflection of a puffed, distorted face, she was mildly astonished to see a dewy-eyed, radiant young woman she scarcely recognized. Her eyes were luminous, the green centers as clear and sparkling as gemstones; her skin seemed to glow warm and rosy without a hint of strain or sleeplessness. Her gaze dropped lower, searching out the source of the intriguing tingle in her chest, and she saw that her breasts were not swollen or bruised or grossly misshapen. Rather, they were round and firm, the nipples flushed proudly with new-found awareness.

Bewildered, she touched her fingertips to her lips, wondering why they too felt different. More sensitive — as if they could never again be used to form a harsh word. She could almost feel them pressed to his, parted and eager, hungering for unknown pleasures.

Courtney stared past the shoulder of her reflection to the sprawled, sleeping form of Adrian Ballantine. The cover was askew, and his body was boldly displayed. She had seen naked men before, dozens of them, accidentally and intentionally, yet none had made her blush. None had slowed the blood in her veins, or brought her heart to a sluggish standstill. Certainly none had caused her to stare long and hard at that which lay so limp and selfless now, yet which, when roused, could wreak such havoc on her confidence.

As she watched, an arm shifted, a hand skimmed absently

over the chest to scratch diffidently in the cloud of copper hair. A yawn was begun but ended on a sharp, strangled groan as the sudden movement startled the drums awake in his head.

Courtney did not wait for the bleary eyes to open and seek her out. She collected her breeches and belt from the floor and hastily pulled them on. She held up torn halves of her shirt and studied them with some dismay before she paid any attention to the sounds emmanating from the bunk.

"Good God," Adrian bit off a further curse as he struggled to sit upright. "How much did I drink? How long have I slept?"

"What's wrong, Yankee? Don't they teach you golden-haired bastards how to hold your liquor?"

"Irish, I —" He ground his teeth together and squeezed his fingers against his temples. His head was being crushed by giant hammers, and his stomach was sending threatening messages up into his throat. The coating was an inch thick on his tongue and as sour as cheap wine; his eyes itched as if they contained the sands of the Sahara. "I am not in the mood for verbal jousting. If you will kindly hand me my ——"

He stopped and took two shallow breaths. Then his eyes widened, and he seemed to notice for the first time that he was naked, that the cabin looked as if it had housed a small tornado, that Courtney made no move to cover her bare breasts or cloak the disdain in her eyes.

"I'm afraid I shall need a new shirt," she announced calmly. "You were in such a hurry yesterday to rid me of this one that I doubt it can be repaired."

Ballantine stared at the remnants of the shirt, then at his own nakedness, and his eyes seemed to drift out of focus.

"Of course, I'm assuming you have finished with me. After last night, I cannot imagine you wanting for more, but . . ." She shrugged and left the sentence dangling.

"Dear God," he muttered in horror, cradling his head in his hands. "Did I — ?"

"You certainly did. And with enough enthusiasm for me to pity your *betrothed* if she has a frail constitution."

Ballantine's complexion deepened to scarlet. The muscles in his jaw worked furiously, searching for some way to deny the obvious. He remembered leaving Matthew's cabin, he remembered the jugs of rum, and he remembered listening to the girl's voice as if it was coming through a long tunnel . . . but he could recall nothing after that. Nothing but . . .

He looked up and saw the slim, delicate waist, the plump breasts and the rosy aureoles that his tongue seemed to recall intimately.

"In the sea chest," he croaked, "there are spare shirts. Find one, for God's sake, and put it on."

Courtney arched a brow. "A pity you don't keep spare maidenheads there too, for situations like this."

Ballantine's head jerked up at her words, and the blood drained from his face in a dizzying rush. What the devil was she saying now? What was she accusing him of doing?

His hand bunched around the folds of the blanket, and he involuntarily followed her gaze to the smear of dried blood on the mattress cover.

"And you did it with such finesse," she said quietly. "I can hardly wait for the next animal to *rape* me."

The wracking pain within his skull spread down to engulf the rest of Adrian's body. "I . . . I was drunk," he began lamely.

"You were blind, stinking drunk," she countered evenly. "And you took it out on me, just as I said you would when you first suggested this arrangement."

Ballantine swallowed the sarcasm with a pointed lack of grace. He glared at her through a fog of self-disgust, followed her every move as she rummaged for a clean shirt, shook the folds from it, and drew it over her head. It was several sizes too large and made her look younger and even more the hapless victim.

Ballantine groaned and stumbled from the bed to the washstand. He slopped water from the pitcher into the basin then took a deep breath and plunged his face into the icy contents. When he came up, dripping and gasping from the shock, he saw Courtney perched on the side of the bed, casually studying his bare flanks.

"Look out in the corridor," he said, snatching at his breeches. "Tell me if the guard is still there."

Courtney sighed, but she did as she was told. She opened the door a crack and peered out into the darkened companionway, and when she turned back to Ballantine, he was in his breeches and bending over the sea chest for a shirt.

"There is a guard, but he's near the stairwell."

Adrian avoided meeting her embarrassingly direct gaze and shrugged into the cambric shirt. He glanced in the mirror and rubbed a hand over the stubble on his chin, frowning again as he realized he must have slept through the afternoon and night. A quick glance at his pocketwatch told him it was 7:35; the light through the ventilation shaft told him it was morning.

Still avoiding Courtney's mocking eyes, he found his keys and unlocked the cupboard that held his shaving gear.

"Always the proper officer," she mused sardonically. "How unfortunate your behavior as a gentleman is lacking."

Adrian's hand shook visibly as he unfolded the blade from its sheath. He knew what she was doing and why she was doing it, but for the life of him he could not think of a retort to stop her. He held his head through a particularly savage bout of throbbing before he bent over the washstand again.

"Would you like me to do that for you?"

He glared at her reflection. "I'm not in the habit of offering my throat for sacrifice, thank you."

"It isn't your throat that would give me the greatest pleasure to take a razor to," she said dryly, moving away from the door.

Ballantine located the emerald eyes in the mirror and glowered ineffectually. She only smiled and plucked the razor out of his hand.

"Sit down, Yankee, before you fall down. If I was going

to offer a sacrifice, believe me, I would have done so last night . . . or this morning while you were asleep.''

He hesitated, watching her through narrowed eyes. The fingers of one hand closed around her wrist while the others extricated the sharp blade from her grasp. ''All the same, we'll pass on this little display of domestic fealty, if you don't mind. You seem to be just a tad too eager to be of help.''

Courtney shrugged but made no move to pull her hand away. Ballantine continued to stare at her, frowning as if there was some subtle point he was missing, something he should see. But whatever it was eluded him, and he released her wrist and turned back to the mirror. Several nicks and a badly scraped chin later, he rinsed his face and toweled it dry.

''You'd better finish dressing,'' he said. ''I want to look in on Matt before I do anything else.''

''What else is there to do? You're under arrest, aren't you?''

When there was no immediate comment or denial, Courtney volunteered her own deductions.

''Why else would there be a guard out in the passage? Why the rum yesterday, and why the rambling self-pity?'' She paused and watched him fold the blade of the razor shut. When he noted her interest in it, he tucked it into the waistband of his breeches rather than trust it to the cupboard again. She merely smiled. ''You don't look too concerned. About the arrest, I mean.''

''I hide my emotions well,'' he said wryly.

''Not a difficult thing to do when you don't have any to begin with.''

Adrian sighed and closed his eyes for a moment. When they opened again, instead of the capitulation she hoped to see, Courtney found herself meeting a slate-gray threat.

''I'll accept the responsibility for what happened last night,'' he said evenly. ''I'll even go so far as to say: You win. You were right. I behaved like a ground slug, just like you said I would. But that's it. That's as far as it goes. Any more of your charming wit and sarcasm and I might start to reconsider. I might start to think: hell, the damage is done, why stop now? She must have enjoyed it or she wouldn't be pushing for more."

Courtney's cheeks flooded warmly, and she stumbled back, nearly tripping over the sea chest in her haste to retreat.

"I gather this means we understand one another?" Adrian asked. He waited for her grudging nod, then snatched up the linen neckcloth and tossed it to her. "Bind yourself," he ordered crisply. "And do something with your hair so it doesn't look so . . ." — he waved a hand, unable to bring himself to say any of the words that came readily to mind: pretty, attractive, sensual. The soft curls were shiny and tousled and stirred yet another memory of the night past; one of drenching oblivion, of burying his lips in the silky fragrance and feeling the lithe body arch eagerly beneath him.

The image shocked him, and for a moment he stared into the dark emerald eyes. She had called it rape, and he had no cause to doubt her . . . yet the images persisted. Eagerness. Intense, recoiling pleasure. Or was it simply his guilt struggling desperately for a means to justify his actions?

It was Courtney who moved first. She lowered her head and concentrated on wrapping the hated linen around her breasts. When she was finished, she had regained a measure of composure.

"Your captain — he looks like the type who thrives on court-martials."

"He thrives on intimidation."

She raised her head. "And does he intimidate you?"

"What he represents intimidates me, yes. Cruelty, injustice, demagoguery."

"Dema — ?"

Adrian smiled faintly. "Power through fear. The British navy mastered the art of using tactics like floggings and starvation to win obedience from its crews. I had hopes of improving our lot, by example if nothing else."

"My father was taken on board a British ship once by a

press gang," Courtney murmured. "It took him three years to escape, and he'll carry the scars for the rest of his life." Her voice toughened and she added, "He doesn't think any more highly of American ships or the way they treat their crews or prisoners. And when he sees what you've done to Snake Island . . . Well, you'd better warn your look-outs to keep a sharp eye over their shoulders."

"For ghosts?" he asked coldly.

"For whatever it takes to repay you, Yankee."

Adrian felt his temper rising and saw no benefit in continuing the argument. If she wanted to believe her father was still alive, so be it. If she wanted to cling to the ludicrous idea that a band of renegade pirates could be any match for a warship like the *Eagle*, he was not about to dignify her boasting with a rebuttal.

He cast a final, cursory glance around the cabin interior, then strode to the door. Courtney followed him out into the companionway and kept her head lowered as he barked out his intended destination with enough wrath to keep the marine a respectful distance behind them.

Almost immediately they were assailed by the strong scents of hot coffee and a coal fire coming from the forward galley. Courtney's stomach grumbled audibly, and she was reminded that she had not eaten since breakfast of the previous day. Her mouth flooded as she caught a whiff of the morning burgoo — the sludgey porridge the Yankees downed with such enthusiasm to start the day. She could understand Ballantine's reluctance to think of food at the moment, but there was no reason why she should be forced to starve along with him.

She was about to broach the subject when they arrived at Matthew Rutger's door. A second guard was posted outside the cabin, and Ballantine brushed past him with as much ceremony as he had dismissed the first.

The air inside the windowless cabin was rancid from the smoking lantern and the turpentine-based unguent that had been spread on Matthew's back. Adrian's throat worked frantically for a few hard swallows before he could acknowledge the nervous smile from Dickie Little. The boy had obviously remained at the doctor's bedside all night. His skin was pale, his hair crumpled and matted into cowlicks, his eyes heavy-lidded and underscored by dark shadows.

"Did he waken at all last night?" Adrian asked, cursing himself for forgetting the boy's handicap. He knew the lad was frightened of him to begin with, frightened of anyone tall and imposing who could only frown and snarl at his inadequacies.

Courtney stepped in front of Ballantine and reached out a hand to gently touch Dickie's arm. She smiled and asked in a series of rudimentary gestures if the doctor had been asleep since the lieutenant's departure.

Dickie nodded and returned her smile, and pointed to the empty jug of rum.

She threw a glance in Adrian's direction, but his only rejoinder was to scowl and drag a chair over to the side of the bed.

Matt's back was swollen and shiny with a laticework of red welts. Some were raw, with the beginnings of soft scabs forming under the coating of unguent. His eyes slitted open at the sound of the scraping chair; they were glassy from the pain and from a hangover that was no less devastating than Ballantine's. He was lying on his stomach, a hand and arm draped limply over the side of the cot.

"How do you feel?" was the first inadequate question.

"Not as bad as you look," Matthew murmured. "How many jugs did you pour down my throat?"

"I lost count," Adrian grinned. He signaled for Dickie to tend to the lamp and to fetch clean water for the basin. "And it wasn't your head I was inquiring about."

"You mean there is something else I should be able to feel?" Matt groaned and rolled his eyes. "My head and my stomach — which, by the way has already deserted me half a dozen times — are all I am aware of at the moment."

"A fine pair we make. Naples all over again? As I recall you spent three days leaning over the rails like a landlubber."

"You didn't fare much better." He smiled at the recollection. The officers from the *Revenge*, the ship Ballantine and Rutger had been serving on at the time, had forwarded a challenge to the officers of the *Cerberus* to pit Yankee holding-power against British. "As victors, you and Sutcliffe claimed the right to try to bed every wench within a league's radius. I may have spent three days at the rail, but at least I could stand."

Matthew noted the dull red flush that crept slowly up beneath Adrian's tan, and his eyes flicked past the broad shoulders to where Courtney was standing in the shadows.

"Of course, er, that was in your younger years. We were both, er, young and foolish." His fumbling made no impression on either of his visitors, and Matt frowned, changing the subject with a harsh clearing of his throat. "Have you seen him yet?"

"Jennings? No. Should I have?"

"I don't know. Any idea what the excitement is all about?"

"What excitement?"

"I have a very thin wall beside me. For the past hour or so, I've been hearing a lot of noise. Voices. I gather from the conversations that the morning watch has discovered another ship out there."

"Another ship . . . ?"

"It must be friendly. I've heard no alert. At any rate, if Jennings hasn't sent for you then he must think Falworth can handle it."

"Now *that* worries me." Adrian willed away the fog that persisted in dulling his thinking. They were a day's sail out of Gibraltar, by his reckoning. There were bound to be a number of vessels in the area — French or Spanish using the sea lanes to the Atlantic; an American escort sent to meet the *Eagle*; a patroling scout guarding the approach to the Moroccan coast. Any or all were possibilities. And yet one by one the hairs at the nape of his neck were standing to attention. "I wonder . . . ?"

A tentative knock on the open door interrupted what Adrian was about to say, and both men craned around to see the junior lieutenant, Loftus, standing in the entrance. He looked plainly ill at ease and kept glancing over his shoulder as if he expected to see trouble loom up behind him.

"Sorry to disturb you, sirs, but you weren't in your cabin, Mister Ballantine, and well . . . I mean, some of the men thought you should know. . . ."

"What is it, man? Spit it out, although if it's something to do with the ship, I'm afraid you'll have to take your complaints elsewhere."

"It's about the ship, sir, but not the *Eagle*. There is another set of sails on the horizon, sir, and closing in fast. A schooner maybe, or a cat. There's a squall approaching from the same direction, so she might just be trying to outrun it."

"Then I don't understand the problem. What colors is she flying?"

The midshipman shifted his weight uncomfortably. "Well, that's the problem, sir. She isn't. She isn't showing any identification, even though we've requested it."

"Who has the helm?"

"Mister Falworth, sir. But he doesn't seem to be the least bit concerned that our signals are being ignored."

"And you are?"

Again, the midshipman shifted, foot to foot. "Well, sir, according to regulations, in time of war any ship not immediately replying to a demand for identification is to be treated as a hostile."

"Has anyone pointed this out to Mister Falworth?" Adrian said dryly. "I would have thought he'd be eager to play with the guns."

"Sir" — another shift, another worried glance over his shoulder — "we haven't been called to alert. The decks haven't even been cleared for action."

"*What*?" Adrian was on his feet in an instant.

"No, sir. He and Captain Jennings are just standing there watching the other ship come up on us and discussing the weather as if nothing is wrong."

Adrian hissed out a breath through his teeth. Now, at least, he knew why the alarms were jangling at the back of his head.

"Very well, Mister Loftus. I'll go topside and have a look. Not that I'll be able to do much either way."

"That's all right, sir. We understand." He looked greatly relieved, and said so. "It's just that the men trust you, sir. You've taken us in and out of a few bad spots and we'd feel better knowing you were there."

Adrian started for the door but halted when he saw Matthew making a feeble effort to push himself up with his elbows.

"What the hell do you think you're doing?" he demanded, returning to lend a steadying hand.

"Getting on my feet," Matt grunted. "What does it look like? If there's going to be trouble, I'd as soon hear the news on my feet as on my" — he glanced at Courtney and checked himself — "belly. Curt, hand me a clean towel, will you? I'll need to have this muck wiped off my back or I'll ruin a perfectly good shirt."

"You'll do nothing of the kind," Adrian said to Courtney. To Matt, he added, "And you're going to stay right where you are. You can hardly sit up straight, let alone stand."

"I can stand," Matthew gasped. "I can stand."

"And I can fly. Curt, I'm giving you a direct order. If the doctor attempts to get up out of this bed, you have my permission to knock him flat down again. And take my word for it" — he said to Matt, conscious of the midshipman's startled expression — "the lad's in the mood for a good fight this morning. Don't tempt him."

Ballantine left with the midshipman, and Dickie Little closed the door behind them. The pang of excitement Courtney had felt upon hearing the news of another ship had dwindled rapidly when she'd heard the midshipman's estimation of the size of the vessel. She knew of no associates of her father's plying their trade so close to Gibraltar. Undoubtably it was a Yankee patroller.

Courtney's thoughts were drawn away from the sea by a movement on the cot. Dickie had an arm beneath Dr. Rutger's shoulders, and the older man was straining unsuccessfully to use the boy as a lever to sit upright.

"What are you doing? Didn't you hear what Ballantine said?"

"I heard him," Matt grimaced. "And if you have any ideas about taking advantage of Adrian's generous suggestion, think again. Damnation — !" His hand brushed across his forehead to remove the sweat. The motion of his arm brought a fresh shiver of pain from the lacerations on his back, and he groaned.

"He's right, you know," Courtney said quietly. "You're in no condition to be getting up."

"I'll be the judge of that. Now are you two going to help me, or do I disgrace myself here on the bedding?"

With Dickie on the one side and Courtney on the other, they were able to swing Rutger to an upright position. He wavered with the initial agony — both from his head and from his back — and had to clench his teeth hard to keep them from chattering.

"You're only making it harder on yourself."

"Give me a minute," he said stubbornly. "I'll be fine."

Dickie's hands moved in a frantic blur of concern, but the doctor only smiled and shook his head. Courtney watched a further exchange, surprising herself by almost understanding the jist of what passed between them. She was loathe to admit it, but she liked Matthew Rutger. He was honest and genuine in his dedication to his profession; not many ship's doctors were. Most were butchers, preferring to saw off arms and legs rather than waste the time repairing them. Many had been unceremoniously promoted from the rank of barber, since both jobs dealt with some degree of bloodletting.

He was not as broad in the shoulder as Adrian Ballantine, nor as athletically built. Nevertheless, there was no extra flesh on his frame. His belly was flat, his chest sculpted with hard muscle; his thighs were solid, and there was more power in the wiry arms than his deceptively soft appearance suggested. He was clad only in thin cotton drawers, and Courtney's inspection came to an abrupt halt at the scarred knee and calf of his left leg. A shiny ridge of fresh, misshapen tissue chewed its way from just above the kneecap to several inches below, forming an ugly twist of crippling flesh.

"It isn't very pretty, is it?" he murmured.

"Not many scars are," she replied calmly. "How did it happen?"

"The perils of being a ship's surgeon," he explained, seeing her eyes move over the other evidence of past injuries. "A canister shell exploded beside me. Luckily enough, I was already flat on my back from a previous shell or I would have lost the whole leg. As it was, they wanted to take a saw to me. Adrian stepped in just in time. Saved the leg, saved me . . ." Matt paused and his eyes clouded. "Then he lost his brother the very next night, when the fighting was over."

Steadier now, the doctor smiled reassuringly at Dickie Little and waved the boy's anxious hands aside. But the youthful face held his gaze, seeming to draw him back to the memory of another, similarly vulnerable face.

"Alan Ballantine," Matt mused. "He'd barely turned ten when he stowed away on the *Eagle*. He kept himself hidden until we were too far out in the Atlantic to do anything about it. Naturally Adrian was furious. You'd have to know a little about his family circumstances to appreciate the situation, but —"

"Tell me."

Matt glanced over, startled.

"Please. I . . . I truly would like to know something more about him. He's very . . . set in his ways, isn't he?"

"You mean stubborn? Arrogant? Opinionated and

nearly impossible to reason with?'' He grinned. ''Yes, he is. But a better friend than Adrian Ballantine, I'll never have. Besides, a good deal of his bluster is for show. He comes from very wealthy, very socially upright stock. He can't be entirely held to blame if some of the blue blood leaks through now and then even though he goes out of his way to staunch it. He joined the navy as an ordinary seaman and worked his way up the ranks with sweat and blood instead of simply paying for a commission. He didn't knuckle under either when the Ballantines put pressure on him to give up the adventurous life and assume his preordained position in the family business. He and his father had a bad falling out as a result of his independent streak, and they didn't speak to one another for almost five years.

''Then Adrian's mother died. He didn't hear about it until six months after the funeral, and when he finally did manage a furlough home, he was met with all the guns, so to speak. His father claimed illness — Samuel Ballantine hasn't been sick a day in his life. He also claimed Adrian's brother, Rory, had squandered most of his personal fortune and was starting on the Ballantine company profits. His two sisters had supposedly both married dandies whose primary concerns were gambling and drinking.''

Matt stopped and snorted. ''Before Adrian left to resume his duties in the Mediterranean, his father had won a promise out of him to seriously consider serving out his term and going home to Virginia permanently. Somewhere along the line he also managed to get himself engaged to his father's business partner's daughter. Adrian wasn't particularly pleased with either commitment, so you can imagine his frame of mind when he woke up one morning and saw young Alan's grinning face by the side of his berth.''

The hazel eyes lost their liquid softness and became cold and distant. ''It was about that same time he walked headlong into the trouble with Sutcliffe.''

''Sutcliffe?''

"Captain of the *Revenge*, and Adrian's commanding officer."

"And?" she prompted.

"And —" He frowned as if realizing he had said far too much already. "And if you add everything together: duty, guilt, honor . . ."

"A fiancée," she supplied dryly.

"Yes. That too. Perhaps that most of all . . . Deborah." Matt shook his head slowly, his expression altered perceptibly to one of awe. "Deborah Longworth Edgecombe is rich; she's beautiful; she has an elegance and grace that take your breath away."

Courtney bristled. "They sound like the perfect couple."

"If you saw them together, you'd think they were. And in time he might be able to convince himself the sedentary life is what he wants."

"You sound as if you don't think it is."

"I don't think he knows what he wants. I know what he doesn't *need* and that's another court-martial."

Courtney's curiosity raged. "*Another* court-martial?"

Matt grimaced again and his frown deepened. He waited for a particularly loud scramble of footsteps on the deck overhead to pass before he posed the question, "Are there any lawyers in your family?"

Courtney was taken aback. "No. Why?"

"Because you certainly have the instinct for it. You've got me spouting off like a fishmonger's wife at market. If you want to know anything else about Adrian, you're going to have to ask him. I happen to value my neck."

More running footsteps pounded on the deck, and both Matthew and Courtney tilted their heads up.

"Right," he said. "That hangs it. Help me stand up, I think I can make it this time."

"But you're not —"

"Either you help me, or you get out of my way!"

Courtney swore mildly and grasped him under an arm, wrestling with the limited space beside the bunk to help him stand clear. Dickie Little raced to assist, but Matthew gestured instead to the sea chest.

"A shirt," he gasped and mimed with his hands. "And my breeches."

"You won't make it as far as the door," Courtney predicted — accurately so, if for very different reasons. Matt had not taken a single step away from the bed before the ship lurched suddenly. A loud crunching roar burst into the space surrounding them, and the four walls seemed to explode inward, hurling all three occupants of the cabin to the floor in a shower of splinters.

# Chapter Ten

The captain and Falworth were studying the horizon through long brass telescopes when Ballantine emerged alone from the hatch directly below the bridge. The wind had a sharp, biting edge, and the ship's motion was choppy as she rode out the tall swells. The waves were flecked with whitecaps, and the sky above was a smoldering gray smudgepot, churning with thunderclouds. It was easy to pick up the curl of straining white sails off the port side; the sky behind the approaching ship was an ominous, lightning-cracked black.

Second Lieutenant Falworth was the first to notice Ballantine's arrival on deck. The junior officer was in full uniform: white breeches, navy broadcloth tunic, high black kneeboots. His brown eyes raked disdainfully down Adrian's open-throated, rumpled shirt.

"You're looking a little rough for wear this morning, old boy. Restless night?"

Adrian was not afforded an opportunity to reply as Jennings lowered his glass and stared down at him. "I believe you were confined to quarters, were you not, sir?"

Adrian refused the bait. "I was in the beakhead and heard the commotion. I was merely curious."

"Curious?" Falworth bristled. "Or envious?"

"Tut tut." Jennings held up a hand. "Perhaps we should permit the lieutenant an opinion. One hopes it will be his last. Come along then, Mister Ballantine. Dazzle us with your wisdom."

Adrian mounted the brief flight of steps to the raised bridge and took the proffered spyglass, noting the quick tightening of Falworth's jaw. Jennings was an insufferable bastard, but he wasn't stupid. He knew Ballantine's instincts and skills were valuable.

Adrian raised the glass to his eye, and the distant line of the horizon came abruptly forward, as did the sleek form of the advancing ship. Bow straight on, she was running with the wind behind her, making any but the most rudimentary identification impracticable. She was, however, bigger than a schooner and far bigger than a twin-masted cat. She carried fore-, main-, and mizzenmasts and rode the swells with the ease of a light frigate. She showed only one row of gunports — although the black paint on her hull made it difficult to be certain. She was fully rigged for speed, and there were no flags, no pennants visible on her tops.

Adrian swept the glass across the seascape to either side of the stranger, but he could see nothing other than roiling seas and sporadic flickers of lightning.

He lowered the glass slowly.

"Well?" Jennings snapped impatiently. "What do you make of her?"

"It's hard to tell anything at this distance. Has she replied to our signals?"

Falworth pursed his lips. "We have raised the accepted hailing codes, as well as a request for identification, but as yet she has chosen to ignore us. Of course, it is possible that she doesn't see us yet, what with the land at our back."

"Unless her crew is dead or stone blind —" Ballantine began and raised the glass again, this time to starboard. What he saw caused him to stiffen and lower the telescope with a gasp of disbelief.

They were hugging the Moroccan coastline, but instead of the usual four to five leagues of clear water between the *Eagle* and shore, there was less than one. And the gap was closing as rapidly as the wind could push them.

"Who the bloody hell ordered the course change?" he asked harshly, with no deference to Jennings.

Falworth's lips pressed into a thin line. "I did. I thought it was a prudent decision in light of the approaching squall."

"*Prudent*! There are hidden shoals and unpredictable currents all along this section of coastline. And as soon as that land mass sucks up the draft, we'll lose half of our maneuvering power."

"Maneuvering power," Falworth scoffed. "For what?"

Ballantine swung the glass around to open sea. He was alarmed to see how the stranger had gained on them.

"Have the decks been cleared for action?" he demanded. "Have the gun crews been alerted?"

Jennings looked from Ballantine to Falworth, "Gun crews?" then back to Ballantine, "You believe it to be a hostile vessel?"

"I don't know what to believe, and I won't until I see some form of identification."

"Mister Falworth is of the opinion she is one of ours."

"Mister Falworth," Adrian said through his teeth, "has taken the liberty of placing us in an untenable position. We're too damned close to land. We've forfeited the weather gauge even before we've begun. We don't have room to turn, and we don't have nearly the speed to make a run for it. On the other hand, our visitor not only has the wind, but also the choice of how to use it."

Jennings frowned and turned to the sub-lieutenant. "Mister Falworth, have you any reason to reconsider your strategy?"

Falworth reddened. "I am perfectly content with my decision. The lieutenant is, as usual, being overly dramatic. We have our backs protected in the event the ship turns out to be a hostile — *which I strongly doubt*! She hasn't the look of a Frenchman, or a Spaniard, and she's definitely not one of the seagoing deathtraps the local wogs seem to prefer. And what commander in his right mind would attempt to engage another ship with heavy weather closing in? The poor bastard is probably running hellbent for shelter, just as we are."

"A reasonable deduction," Jennings nodded and glanced askance at Ballantine. "And one with which I must concur. Good heavens, we are a day's sail out of the straits. No one would dare attack an American ship this close to the base."

*"Colors!"* A man called from the crow's nest. "She's running up her colors, sir!"

"Ahh," Jennings craned his neck to look up. "Now we'll find out."

*"Stars and Stripes, sir!"*

Jennings grabbed the glass out of Ballantine's hand and leaned over the rail as if the stance would help the magnification. Falworth's eyes locked with Adrian's and his mouth curved sardonically.

"All this fuss, Lieutenant," he murmured. "As I said, a compatriot seeking company to ride out the storm."

"Has she replied to our code?" Adrian asked urgently.

"Thursday is five and six," Jennings mused. "A solid red and a red on white triangle. The reply should be . . . *ha*! There are the ensigns: solid white, white on red. Is that correct, Mister Beddoes?"

"Aye, sir," the quartermaster replied after consulting with the code book. "Solid white, white on red. She's one of ours."

Jennings lowered the glass and rubbed his hands

together in the morning chill. "Good. Then perhaps she'll have news of how this bloody war is going. And fresh meat. Some lunatic took it upon himself to throw the livestock overboard yesterday in all the panic, and I had to make do with salted beef last evening. Well, Mister Ballantine? Have you nothing to say? Would you still prefer to fire a warning shot across her bows?"

Ballantine gazed out over the water. The speed of the other ship was easily twice that of the *Eagle*. She was giving no indication of taking in sail, even though she was safely within reach of shore. She was also coming into range for any heavy armaments she might be carrying.

"I don't like it," he murmured aloud, despite the derision in Jennings' voice. "Why did she wait so long to identify herself? And why hasn't she taken in sail?"

"Why can't you accept what your eyes plainly tell you," Falworth countered. "She's an American."

"She's flying an American flag," Adrian corrected him. "That's one of the oldest ploys on the sea — especially in this arena."

"She has also responded correctly to our codes," Jennings interjected with some annoyance.

Ballantine refrained from remarking on the confidentiality of the so-called secret codes, and instead turned to Beddoes. "Have the decks cleared for action and pipe the gun captains to the bridge."

"Aye, sir."

"Hold up there!" Jennings moved away from the rail. "How dare you countermand my orders. The helm is no longer yours to command, nor are the officers obliged to obey ——"

"*Tacking to port!*" came the same excited voice from above. "She's assuming a parallel course . . . there's . . . *there's men on the guns, sir! Ports are opening . . . They're running out —*"

The rest of the warning was lost to the horror of seeing the stranger present her starboard battery to the stunned observers on board the *Eagle*. Without any preliminaries the guns erupted with clouds of white smoke and blazing tongues of orange fire. Being less than a mile away, it took only seconds for the shots to find their marks. Spouts of white water rose alongside the *Eagle*. Shots slashed through sail and rigging, plowed into her decks and rails, and left the men in panic as they scrambled clear of the flying, flaming debris.

Ballantine was thrown heavily into the deck rail, and his breath was knocked from his lungs. Beside him, Beddoes raised a bloodied stump where his right hand and arm should have been and screamed in agony. Adrian tore the bandanna from the quartermaster's neck and used it to tie off the stump, then he hastened over to where the captain and Otis Falworth were sprawled near a gaping hole in the rail. Jennings' face was sliced on one side from a flying splinter; Falworth bore a gash on his thigh. Both appeared to be more dazed than hurt.

Adrian shouted for assistance before he went in search of Danby, the chief gunnery officer.

A second broadside struck with deadly precision. Chunks of spars and planking exploded through the air, raining down on the unprotected heads of the soldiers and sailors. Ropes twanged apart as chain shot and bar shot ripped through them; sails collapsed and the vessel reeled under the staggering impact of the bombardment.

"Helmsman!" Adrian ran to the stern, one eye on the men rushing frantically to arm the *Eagle*'s guns, the other on the sleek, graceful marauder. "Helmsman — hard to port! Get those topmen aloft! I want all the sail on that she'll hold! Move on those guns! Move! Move! Move!"

His shouts were drowned out in the roar of another broadside. He saw two crewmen blasted into crimson fragments as he vaulted up to the helm. He trained his glass on the enemy ship, aware that the *Eagle* was responding sluggishly to his command. The rough sea was making it difficult to hold a course or to execute any kind of swift, evasive move. But she was spirited and willing to try. A great hollow groan along the beam heaved the bow skyward, and the frigate hung for a sickening moment over the crest of a wave. Spray burst above the rail as she slewed sideways and seemed on the verge of careening. The wind grasped at her sails and filled them, hurling her forward into the trough. The sea rose in a wall and spewed a foaming cascade of water down upon her decks, but the *Eagle* shook herself free and thundered steadfastly into the next wave.

Hoping to have bought some badly needed breathing space, Ballantine was astounded to see that the raider had backed her topsails and had drawn to a near standstill in the water. She tacked nimbly across the *Eagle*'s stern, and Adrian watched helplessly — and admittedly in awe of the daring maneuver — as she came within hailing distance and caused the American warship's sails to gasp for breath and flounder long enough to absorb the shock of several cannonades down her exposed length. The forecastle was blown to eternity; the bridge disappeared in a fountain of bloodied splinters. Spars were torn from their braces, carrying lines, canvas, and men to their fiery death as shot after shot exploded on deck. A wildly snaking cable swept the boatswain overboard. The wheel spun against the opposing thrust of the wind and sea, and the *Eagle* found herself back in line with the hungry guns of the raider.

The enemy ship was now within pistol shot — fifty yards — and her gunners unleashed obliterating rounds of grape and canister shot into the *Eagle*'s masts and rigging. When the wind had fanned the smoke clear, there were pieces of the dead scattered everywhere. The decks were slippery with blood, and even the faces of the seasoned veterans paled at the extent of the carnage.

Adrian felt the madness surging through him like a fever. Blinded with rage and heedless of the danger, he threw himself at one of the nine-pounder bow guns. With superhuman effort, he single-handedly trained the gun on the looming enemy; he loaded it with double shot and fired, loaded and fired again and again, until his hands were blistered raw. The stench of smoke and blood coated his nostrils. Waves of superheated air swirled inboard after each salvo, stinging his eyes, choking into his throat, but he had thoughts only for the raider and the murderously brilliant tactician at her helm. The ship was close enough for Adrian to see onto the deck, to see the half-naked gunners firing coolly, continuously, seeming to take the time to fire each salvo in tune with the roll of the ship so that few rounds went wild or splashed harmlessly into the sea.

In one breath, Adrian cursed Otis Falworth like he had cursed no other living human being before. They were boxed in flush against the land with no room to tack away or to avoid the deadly assault. In the next breath, he conceded a small gasp of thanks that because of their proximity to the land, the enemy was equally hampered. He could not maneuver his ship between the *Eagle* and shore and would need to turn and tack against the approaching squall in order to make a second pass.

As if the marauder was privy to Ballantine's thoughts, the gleaming bow sheered away, having passed beyond the effective angle of fire. To his disgust, Adrian saw that she was barely scraped, that few of her sails were being hauled in for replacements, that none of her guns appeared to be smoking wrecks. He uttered a violent curse when he saw that a second tier of gun ports had indeed been cleverly concealed by the black paint on the hull. His earlier, hasty estimate of eighteen guns he now adjusted upward to thirty-eight, possibly more. And judging by the damage suffered to the *Eagle*'s hull, a good number of those guns were carronades — squat, ugly smashers that could crush a three-foot-thick hull as if it was tinder.

Flags broke out suddenly, replacing the Stars and Stripes. Riding proudly atop an ingratiating demand for surrender was a pennant bearing a charging scarlet lion on a black field.

Ballantine's mouth went dry, and the blood drained from his face. He backed away from the smoking bow gun and stumbled aft, passing several ashen-faced gunners' mates who looked to him wordlessly for some sign of en-

couragement. A ship of the American navy had never surrendered to a Barbary pirate, certainly never under such
humiliating circumstances.

In the sudden lull, all that could be heard on the *Eagle*
were the cries and groans of the wounded, the slosh of
water pouring through her riddled hull, the creaking of a
dangerously unstable topmast. Fires hissed and crackled
along the main deck. Men spoke in curses, uttering streams
of obscenities instead of intelligible sentences. Bodies were
everywhere — draped on spars, crumpled against guns
and masts, sprawled bloodily on the glistening planks.

"What the deuce is happening?" croaked a cold, harsh
voice from the quarter-deck. Jennings had moved there,
aided by Falworth. "Why are we being attacked without
provocation? Who is commanding that ship?"

Ballantine, stunned by the devastation he saw around
him, could not offer an immediate answer.

"Beddoes!" Jennings screamed. "Damn the man,
where is he? Who can identify those colors?"

"I don't know who is in command," Ballantine said
slowly, "but those are Farrow colors."

"*Farrow*! Duncan Farrow? But that's not possible!"

"No, it isn't!" Falworth declared, slightly shaken. "We
were assured that both of Farrow's ships had been taken.
We were dispatched to Snake Island *because* both ships
were taken!"

"Obviously they missed one," said Adrian, dragging a
trembling hand across his brow. It came away with a slick
smear of blood. His shirt was soaked with sweat, spattered
with blood; he stank of cordite and gunpowder, and the
unfamiliar, galling taste of defeat was rising sourly in his
gorge.

"You don't think Farrow himself is in command,"
Falworth gasped. He was —"

"He was hanged," Adrian snarled. "And the *Wild
Goose* was destroyed. So then you tell me, Lieutenant,
who the hell is out there now?"

"We'll have to haul down the colors," Jennings rasped.

"I see no other way out of this predicament. We have no choice but to surrender and hope for clemency."

"Surrender?" Ballantine wiped savagely at the blood that trickled into his eyes. "You can't be serious!"

Jennings flushed. "I assure you I am very serious, sir. Half of our guns are useless; the men are being slaughtered where they stand. We won't survive another assault like the last one."

"It doesn't mean we surrender!" Adrian exclaimed, shocked at Jennings' apparent disregard for the pride of the *Eagle* and her crew, not to mention the flag she flew under. An American warship had never surrendered to a corsair!

Ballantine fought to control his temper and his contempt as he thrust a finger in the direction of the squall. "We can double back and run for the heavy weather. Farrow — or whoever — won't be expecting it. Hell, no one would expect it with the seas as rough as they are, and if we can reach the curtain of rain before he realizes what we're about, we might just be able to lose him."

"And lose ourselves in the process," Jennings shrieked. "We have no steerage, no speed. We'd be overtaken before we'd covered half the distance!"

"Not if we move *now*! While he's gathering headway to make his turn. If we sit here and wait, we're inviting disaster. The men have heart and guts, but I agree we can't hope to withstand another raking."

"That is why we must surrender," Jennings insisted. "At once! Before it's too late!"

Ballantine took a step toward Jennings, his fists clenched by his side. "We will not surrender, you damned coward!"

"I gave you a direct order!" Jennings railed. "I order you to bring down the colors!"

Fury and disgust fought for control on Adrian's face, and his knuckles glowed white with the desire to sink into the corpulent flesh.

"We will not surrender," he repeated, his eyes savagely

bright. "We will stand and fight and die to the last man if need be, but by God, we'll not surrender."

"This is mutiny," Jennings gasped. "Mutiny you're calling for!"

"So be it," Adrian snarled and whirled around to face the gathered crew. "Are you with me, men? Do we bring in the colors or do we show these damned pirates how to fight a battle?"

There was a deafening cheer from the surrounding ring of officers and seamen. Shouts of *"Fight! Fight! Fight!"* rang through the air, echoing as high as the men on the topmost yards.

"No! I order you to haul in the colors!" Jennings screamed. "I order you! I order you!"

No one paid heed. The men were already in motion, wheeling the guns into new positions, calling for fresh shot, helping the wounded clear of the decks.

Jennings lunged for a cutlass held loosely in the hands of a nearby marine. Ballantine saw the move, and his fist caught the rounded jaw, low and hard. Jennings' head snapped back under the impact; his body was sent crashing against the base of the mast, then sank, like whale blubber, to the oak deck.

Adrian's steely gaze flicked up from Jennings and fixed on the astounded features of Otis Falworth. "Well, sir, you wanted your moment of glory. Here it is. Take the helm and watch for my signals, and by God, if you foul up one of them —"

Falworth shook his head and backed up toward the huge wheel. Adrian turned on his heel and pushed through the piles of smoking debris. He stripped off his shirt and tore a length of cambric from the bottom edge, using it as a bandanna to staunch the flow of blood from the cut above his eye. He strode the length of the quarter-deck and stopped by one of the massive long guns that had been buried under a tangle of broken spars and cables. The gun crew exchanged a fleeting, nervous glance among themselves, but when they heard the confident roar of his voice issuing orders they soon gave a rousing cheer and joined him in freeing the cannon.

With the same superb seamanship that the *Wild Goose* had shown in running her prey to ground, she bore down on the crippled *Eagle* once again. On board the Yankee warship, the cannon were primed and run out. A silence enveloped the decks that amplified the hiss of the spluttering fuses held aloft in readiness. Ballantine could feel the fear in the men around him; he could smell it and taste it with each breath he pumped into his lungs. And like so many of the others, he unabashedly moved his lips in a silent prayer and laid his hand on the cold, rough comfort of the black-iron monster that would decide if he lived or died.

The *Wild Goose* came at them fast. Her topgallants disappeared as she shortened sail to fighting trim; a moment later, the forks of orange flame and boiling, billowing clouds of acrid smoke spewed from both tiers of guns. The battle was on again. Hot grapeshot smashed through what little protection remained on the *Eagle*'s deck, exploding their projectiles of razor-sharp metal, nails, and musketballs, slicing through flesh and bone, canvas and cordage alike. Yards cracked overhead and twisted as the whipping shots carved them away. Sails slatted over, and the remains of the mizzen topmast crashed to the sea, dragging streamers of tangled shrouds behind. Marksmen from the *Wild Goose* concentrated their musketfire on the few courageous topmen who held to their posts, and the American marines began dropping one after another with ghastly precision. Fires broke out, and there were not enough brigades to control them. A flaming scrap of canvas drifted lazily through a gaping hatch and landed on a stack of flannel-encased powder cartridges. The explosion lifted ten square feet of decking and destroyed three vital thirty-eight-pounders on the lower gun deck.

The two ships closed to within one hundred yards, and to the Yankee's credit, there were signs of damage beginning to appear on the *Wild Goose*. Her sails became pockmarked with holes; her deck was cloaked beneath a cloud of smoke and flying debris. But within fifty yards, her carronades were brought thundering into action again, hurling forty-two pounds of destruction through the *Eagle*'s meager defenses. Cannon were unseated and whole crews were crushed beneath the weight. Men were driven screaming back from their positions and, finding nowhere to turn to escape the inferno of heat and blood and flame, they fled below into the passageways — already congested with the wounded — or above, where they were picked off with glee by the hungry corsairs.

Water bled through gouges in the hull. Smoke and steam clogged the airways, the companionways, the storerooms, the cabins, and drove choking hot fumes into every crack and crevice that harbored life.

Ballantine kept his gun crew firing steadily, scarcely able to see past the smoke that creamed from the muzzle between rounds. He loaded and fired without bothering to adjust the aim of the heavy gun — the *Wild Goose* was so close, it would have been a waste of precious time. Each round seemed to bring the Farrow ship nearer, and with her the threat of boarding planks and grappling hooks. Men were already lining her rails in readiness. Even more were sent high on the yards to spray the *Eagle*'s deck with musketfire. The choppy sea and gusting winds were no more of a deterrent than the cannonades that rocketed between the two vessels, causing each to buckle and roll in the turbulence.

Adrian felt the enemy's iron smashing through the gun deck below his feet as the *Wild Goose* trained a final raking broadside along her hull. The cables to the rudder were severed, and the Yankee warship heeled sideways in a lurch that sent her bow crumpling against the *Wild Goose*.

Ballantine hauled himself to his knees. He was blinded by the smoke and the pain, and his head seemed suddenly to be too heavy for his neck to support. He crawled several feet in agony before he was able to find something solid to brace himself against. He shook the blood out of his eyes and looked around the deck, searching for the source of the rapid thuds that were hooking into the rails and planks of the *Eagle*.

"Prepare . . . to repel boarders," he screamed and groped for one of the barbed handspikes strapped to the mast. He could not tell if anyone had heard the warning, or if anyone was alive in the carnage that spread out before him. His ears bled from the concussion of the guns; exhaustion and nausea dulled his senses to everything but the insult of seeing the men swarming across the planks to attack his ship. All of the repressed violence and anger erupted in a blood-curdling roar as Adrian hurled himself toward the oncoming threat. Beside him, equally wide-eyed and determined, was the cut and bleeding figure of the chaplain, John Knobbs. On hearing Adrian's call to arms, he grabbed a pistol from the hands of the dead sailor he had been praying over and staunchly took his place at the lieutenant's side. Together the unlikely pair led the charge to meet the wall of shrieking corsairs.

John Knobbs was grazed on the neck by a musketball. It slowed him, but he aimed and fired his pistol point blank, blowing away a portion of his assailant's shoulder. He threw the smoking pistol aside and scooped up the corsair's broadsword, dealing with two more attackers before several shots fired simultaneously halted him, and he fell forward in a plume of blood.

Ballantine slashed his way into the phalanx of men, dodging and ducking the cutlass blades that sought to stop him. A tall, black-haired corsair bellowed for the privilege of ending Ballantine's charge and lunged toward the wildly swinging handspike. Adrian saw the flash of crimson-stained steel too late to avoid it completely. The blade glanced off his temple, and he staggered back. His foot twisted over a pile of wreckage, and he stumbled back into a hatch — a hatch that was nothing more than a gaping black hole. He plunged through the gap and landed hard on the shattered deck below.

The black-haired corsair stood a moment and stared

down at the splayed body. When there was no sign of movement, he threw his shaggy head back, and with a blood-curdling cry of triumph, leaped for the mizzenmast. There, he raised a tattooed arm and brought his sword hacking down across the cable that held the American colors aloft.

# Chapter Eleven

Matthew Rutger forcibly blocked out the pain of his lacerated shoulders and groped his way back to consciousness. He was huddled with other wounded members of the crew — at first glance they appeared to number in the scores — lying on the *Eagle*'s quarter-deck, exposed to the teeming rain. The storm had struck in its full fury, drenching the fires and creating huge rolling clouds of acrid steam. The oak planking ran with rivulets of pink; men were groaning in agony; and the few who were able to move wept for their own inadequacies as they tried to help others less fortunate.

Matthew commanded his bruised limbs to function and began crawling over and between the rows of wounded men. Some were already dead, having bled out their lives in quiet desperation. Some were unconscious, their heads cradled by others who were not much better off. Most were nursing burns and shrapnel wounds, cuts and punctures, saber slashes, and bleeding welts dealt out by eagerly wielded truncheons. There was no sign of Captain Jennings, and Matt had not seen Adrian since their brief conversation in the cabin. He did not know how he, himself, had come to be on the deck in the pouring rain; his last memory was of being slammed into something hard and of hearing the girl scream.

Matthew straightened on his knees a moment and searched the sea of battered, anguished faces. He saw two of the younger powder boys, wounded and crouched together for warmth and comfort, but there was no sign of Courtney Farrow or Dickie Little. Matt's chest constricted with fear and he broadened his search. He dragged himself upright and shook the rain out of his eyes, squinting to see through the haze and swirling mists to where men were crowded beneath anything that afforded protection from the elements.

Surely these were not the only survivors of the battle! Surely there had to be more men than this pitiable lot!

"Dear God!" he exclaimed and scrabbled forward, ignoring the moans of men nearby. He moved the body gently, easing it over to lift the face out of the pool of filthy rainwater and sodden ashes. "Adrian? Adrian, can you hear me?"

He tore a scrap from the lieutenant's shirt and cleared the blood and grime away from his eyes and around his mouth.

"Adrian?"

This time he was rewarded by a stifled groan.

"Thank God," Matthew muttered. The doctoring instincts took over, and he inspected the cut over Adrian's brow, then probed gently for any sign of broken bones or internal injuries. By the time he had finished, a bleary, blood-shot eye had opened a slit. It focused on Matt's face with effort, then slowly panned around the deck.

"What . . . what happened?" came the croaked whisper.

"I'm only guessing, but I'd say from the looks of it, you tried to take on the entire enemy single-handedly. Wait. Don't sit up yet, give your head a chance —"

Adrian pushed aside the restraining hand and struggled up onto his elbows. He looked around at the drenched, suffering casualties, and he blanched beneath the grime.

"Good God . . . the ship," he gasped. "Is she . . . ?"

"I don't know," said Matt. "She feels as if she's holding her own. We aren't listing, or not so as I can see at any rate, and they've made no move to transfer the wounded."

Adrian craned his neck painfully. The *Eagle* was still bound to the enemy ship by dozens of grappling lines. A steady stream of corsairs were swarming back and forth across the planks, laden with crates and casks and supplies from the *Eagle*'s holds.

"They appear to have their priorities well in hand," Matt grumbled under his breath.

"Jennings?"

Matt shook his head. "I haven't seen him. As far as I can tell, they've grouped the wounded apart from the others. At least I'm hoping there are others. This cannot be all the crew." His voice faltered, and it took a moment to bring it back under control. "Beddoes is gone, Millar, Coop, Spencer, Danby . . . those are just the few I've been told about."

"The chaplain is dead," Adrian murmured. "Falworth was wounded, but not too badly. Jennings was alive and spouting at the mouth the last I saw."

"Who were we fighting? And why?"

The question was echoed on the faces of some of the men lying within hearing distance, but Ballantine did not answer. His gaze had strayed to the rubble that was once the forecastle and had locked on the figure standing in its midst. The man, like the ship he had commanded, had emerged from the battle remarkably unscathed. Six feet of lean, black-haired pirate stared down at the progress of his crew with eyes that burned as viciously as the fires that had raged around him earlier. He was naked from the waist up, save for the double leather straps crossed over his chest, which held three muskets apiece. A wide belt around his waist carried an assortment of dirks and a pair of long steel cutlasses. There was no question he was the leader. His shouts were met with immediate replies; a constant stream of messengers were sent to him from all points of the ship to report progress and wait for orders.

"Garrett Shaw," Adrian murmured, half in awe, half in disbelief.

"Who?"

"Garrett Shaw. Duncan Farrow's senior captain and commander of the *Falconer*."

"But . . . wasn't he supposed to have been captured with Farrow?" Matt turned and stared at the pirate, who was obviously in excellent health. "How can you be sure it's him?"

"The tattoos," Adrian said, directing Matt's eye to the corsair's muscular forearms. From elbow to wrist he wore coiled, hissing snakes that looked so realistic, they seemed to be writhing. "Verart Farrow had the boar; Duncan had a brace of crossed swords; and Garrett Shaw has snakes. He's known affectionately in some circles as 'the Cobra' because of them."

"Dear God. How did he find us?"

"Sheer killer instinct, I wouldn't doubt," Adrian grunted. Matt looked up in time to see the lieutenant straining to haul himself to his feet.

"What do you think you're doing? *Where are you going*?"

"I want to talk to that bastard," Adrian replied.

"Are you insane? He'd as soon kill you as look at you!"

Adrian shrugged off the doctor's hands and stood swaying against a broken section of rail, his chest laboring to keep the air flowing into his lungs and the blackness from enveloping him again. The motion was detected almost instantly, and the glittering blue eyes that Adrian had last viewed over the blur of a slashing cutlass drilled into him, nailing him where he stood.

Shaw grinned and barked out a curt order. A moment later, two burly pirates had Adrian's arms locked painfully behind his back as they propelled him forward.

Shaw's chest rumbled with amusement. "So you lived, eh, Yankee? Your skull must be damned near as hard as mine not to have split apart twelve ways to Sunday." The bulging arms crossed over his chest. "You have the look and smell of an officer about you."

"First Lieutenant Adrian Ballantine," Adrian rasped. "Of the United States warship *Eagle*."

The corsair studied him for a moment. "I've heard about you. And your ship. I was warned we couldn't afford to give you any advantage, and certainly not the courtesy of a polite challenge. Still," he paused and a flash of white teeth slowly appeared. "I didn't expect quite so much help."

He was referring to the disastrous course change that had backed the *Eagle* flush against the land, and more humiliating, the Yankees' complete lack of battle readiness. Adrian bore the man's mockery in silence.

"My ship —" he began.

"A fine vessel. A pity we had to put so many holes in her. You should have hove to when the *Falconer* suggested it the first time."

"The *Falconer*? But I thought —" Adrian blinked through the drizzle, peering at the tall mainmast and the pennant bearing the charging red lion.

"You thought we were the *Wild Goose*? Aye, we fly her colors." Garrett Shaw's voice took on a gravel-sharp edge. "And we'll continue to fly them until the lives of our comrades are avenged."

"Farrow?" Ballantine gasped, bracing himself as a wave of dizziness rippled gently through him.

"Taken in a trap that reeked of Yankee treachery — treachery we could not believe the depths of until we set foot ashore Snake Island."

Shaw shifted his gaze to a point past Adrian's shoulder where the line of newly freed captives were being led up through a damaged hatchway of the *Eagle* into the rain. Despite the battering they had suffered while trapped below during the battle, the men all wore grins on their gaunt faces. They laughed and howled greetings to their fellow corsairs, who waited on the deck of the *Falconer* with full pannikins of rum and chunks of fresh meat and cheese.

"I had a hard time convincing my gunners not to hull your toy warship to kindling," Shaw said tonelessly. "I told them it would be far more satisfying to see her towed like a dog into an Arab port and sold to Pasha Karamanli to be displayed as a trophy. You and your men will look good in chains and loincloths, Mister First Lieutenant Bloody Ballantine."

"We'll not be slaves to any man," Adrian snarled. "Of that you may be sure."

"I'm sure of nothing in this world, Yankee," Shaw laughed, "except the mortality of others. To that end, we'll try our damndest to meet your standards of hospitality."

"We have wounded."

"Your wounded will be transferred aboard the *Falconer*. We've a barber who does a fair turn with splints and bandages, and when he's finished with our lads — and if he stays sober long enough — he'll have a go at yours. As for the others. . . ."

Ballantine was having difficulty catching a breath. A loud hum in his ears muffled the voices around him. "The others . . . how many? Where are they?"

"You've a hundred and a half or so still able to haul a rope without spilling their guts all over the deck. We'll be putting them to good use in keeping this hulk afloat until we can tow her to port."

A hundred and fifty men! Adrian's shoulders sagged and his stomach gave a queasy lurch. Add to that an estimated thirty seriously wounded — one hundred and eighty men out of two hundred and seventy!

"The captain?" he gasped. "Where is Captain Jennings? I demand to be taken to him."

"You demand nothing, Yankee."

Adrian swallowed hard. The rain felt suddenly hot and

slick on his face. He shuddered and felt the hands grasp his arms tighter.

The corsair took a deep breath and bellowed into the air, "*Davey*!"

"Aye!" came the return shout from somewhere aft. "Comin'!"

Moments later, one of Shaw's fellow corsairs vaulted over a pile of rubbish and ambled to a halt beside the captain. He was short, broad, and villainous in appearance; his wiry chestnut beard was separated from a frizz of reddish hair by the brilliance of two deep-set blue eyes. He was shy of six feet tall by eleven inches, but what he lacked in height, he made up for in muscle-packed belligerence.

"Nay need to shout. I were right behind ye."

Shaw ignored the grumble. "Are the tow lines rigged, Davey?"

"Aye. Rigged and ready as she'll ever be. We moved extry pumps aboard, but the bitch is swallowin' water almost faster'n we can turn it out. I dunno if she'll wear the trip."

"She'll wear it. The lieutenant here has kindly offered the backs of his crew to ensure that she does."

"The lieutenant," Ballantine spat, "has offered no such thing."

"But he will," Shaw said with a cruel smile. He signaled an order to Davey Dunn, who grinned and leaped onto the lower deck. He walked to the first American prisoner he saw and hauled the wounded man to his feet as if he were a sack of fodder. A shove between the shoulder blades sent the man stumbling forward to the ladder. Shaw, standing at the top, did not take his eyes from Ballantine's face as he calmly unsheathed one of his pistols, took careless aim, and fired.

Adrian was in motion the instant he realized the corsair's intent, but it was too late. The crewman staggered back with the impact of the shot, staring in horror and disbelief as a broad crimson stain spread on his shirt front. The few seconds of life remaining to him were spent in raising bewildered eyes to the lieutenant. Adrian was halted mid-stride by a hammer-like blow to his midsection from one of the guards he had bolted from.

Shaw replaced the pistol in its sheath and coolly regarded Ballantine's struggle to remain on his feet.

"Davey, have the wounded Yankees moved onto the *Falconer*. Put them in full view of the healthy bucks we leave behind and, at the first show of stubbornness, have the weakest tossed over the side. Each order afterwards that these dogs choose to disobey, toss over another."

"Bastard," Adrian whispered fiercely, his hands folded across his belly, trying to contain the agony. "You're enjoying this immensely, aren't you?"

"Having an American warship crawling at my feet? Who wouldn't?"

"What I want to know," Adrian gasped and straightened awkwardly, "is how the hell you escaped when Farrow was caught."

Both Shaw and Davey Dunn stared at Adrian.

"For added incentive," Shaw said slowly, "we'll see that your life is the first to be expended. Your men seem to admire you. Half the Yankees we cut down were only on their feet because they saw the foolhardy charge you made. We'll see if they work as hard for you now."

The nausea grew overpowering in Ballantine's stomach; the taste of it was in his throat. He longed for the stamina for just one lunge at the corsair — just one chance to tear out the pirate's black heart with his bare hands.

Shaw read the desire in the lieutenant's eyes and bent his head back and laughed.

"God's blood, Davey, get this bastard out of my sight before I'm tempted to finish the job here and now. Fit him with a comely pair of bracelets and see that he has a prime location on the shrouds."

Davey Dunn nodded to the two men holding Ballantine. They dragged him roughly toward one of the boarding planks that bridged the gap between the *Falconer* and the *Eagle*. Out of the corner of his eye, Adrian saw Matthew grope his way past the wall of wounded who had gathered silently to watch the proceedings and shout a demand at Captain Shaw. Two heavy-handed pirates clubbed the doctor back and sent him reeling onto the planks.

Adrian snarled and jerked his arms free from his guards. He pivoted on his heel and smashed his fist into the one startled man's face, feeling the gratifying crunch of teeth and flesh beneath his knuckles. The second guard reached for Adrian's shoulders, but his hands slipped on the wet shirt and he was pushed off balance, crashing head first into the choppy swirl of water between the two ships.

Adrian's surge of energy carried him around to meet Davey Dunn. A threat was there, but although the wry-faced buccaneer rose no taller than Ballantine's armpit, the flint-lock musket he held aimed unwaveringly at the lieutenant's heart gave him added stature.

"Yer life ain't worth a pinch of fly dung if ye try it, Yankee," he said evenly. "But ye're welcome to larn it the hard way."

Adrian's blazing eyes surveyed the possibilities. There was no way out. Dunn was more than four paces away; Adrian knew he would be dead before he took a step.

The wiry chestnut beard shifted as the corner of Dunn's mouth slanted down in disappointment. He sucked in a mouthful of air and clicked it out between his teeth.

"Fer my part, I'd as soon carve youse all into shark bait and be done with it. Now move. And if I see ye so much as twitch a finger wrong, ye'll piss blood fer a month."

Adrian stumbled across the plank. Three more corsairs seized and pinioned him when he reached the other side and rough-housed him to the stern of the *Falconer*. The wound over his eye was pouring blood; it mingled with the rain to tint his soaked shirt pink. Cold iron manacles were clamped to his wrists, and he was shoved against the rat lines while each arm was forced high and fettered by the chains to cables.

His position on the shrouds gave him an unobstructed view of the length of the *Eagle*. His horror at seeing the full extent of her damages was compounded by the sight of the ragged survivors huddled opposite him in the stern. Unlike the wounded men, they still wore expressions of defiance on their faces. Sergeant Rowntree was among them; he shot to his feet upon seeing the lieutenant pushed and prodded to the stern of the *Falconer*. One side of his anxious young face was blackened beneath a bruise. His blue jacket and white cross-straps were torn and bloodied but he did not appear to be otherwise injured. Falworth was standing by the deck rail, his face pale with shock. He looked neither right nor left; each blink seemed calculated to conserve energy. Angus MacDonald, the stalwart marine corporal, was towering beside Sergeant Rowntree, his expression equally grim, but his hands wisely restrained the younger man from taking any foolish action.

Loftus, Crook, Prescott . . . three midshipmen out of twenty that Adrian could see at a hasty, blurred glance. No sign of the captain. No sign of —

The chains on Adrian's wrists were yanked tight and he concentrated on choking back the cry of pain. His ankles were shackled to the cables, and he could hear the corsairs laughing and spitting their contempt on him before they abandoned him to the raw wind and rain. The hum grew louder in his ears, drowning out the shouts that buzzed and whistled aboard both ships. He closed his eyes to the sight of his men being issued the ultimatum to work; he ground his teeth against the urge to shout out in fury and pain.

From the deck of the *Eagle*, Garrett Shaw stared thoughtfully at the diminished figure of the lieutenant. He recognized him to be a dangerous adversary; even now, when he was weakened from the fighting and the shock of defeat, the icy promise of revenge shone wildly in his slate-gray eyes. Ballantine was smart and he was not afraid to die. It was a dangerous combination and one Shaw had learned to respect over the years. As soon as the lieutenant's usefulness was at an end, so, too, was his miserable life.

Shaw watched Davey Dunn return across the planks to

the *Eagle*. Dunn was Farrow's man, his first mate, his chief gunner. He could be counted upon to see that the Yankee frigate was made seaworthy and that her crew cooperated fully. Dunn would also consider it a finer reward than any portion of the loot scavenged from the *Eagle* to be given the golden-haired lieutenant as a personal vent for his rage and frustration.

Shaw turned his attention to the progress of the wounded Yankees as they were kicked and prodded to their feet. The stronger among them supported the weak and limbless, helping them across to the *Falconer*. The most badly wounded would be dead within a day or two; Shaw had no medicine or sympathy to spare. The others would survive if they had the strength or will to do so.

Shaw issued some last-minute instructions and returned to the *Falconer* himself, remaining on deck long enough to ensure that her own repairs were well underway. There was no time to waste replacing sails and jury-rigging the damaged spars and yards. They were too close to the Gibraltar sea lanes for his liking. Much too close. The squall was showing signs of building again and that was the best cover he could hope for. With luck they would be underway within a few hours, and by nightfall, be tucked away in a safe cove where they could undertake the lengthier repairs.

A shame, he thought as he descended the aft hatchway, to have decided so late in the battle to try to salvage the Yankee ship. A few dozen less holes and she could have brought a better price from the Pasha. Who would have thought the Yankees would have been so ill-prepared? From what he'd heard of Lieutenant Bloody Ballantine, the man was as cunning and deadly in battle as . . . as Shaw himself, by God!

Shaw chuckled as he opened the door to his greatcabin. It was smaller than its counterpart on the *Eagle*, more compact, but more extravagantly furnished from the plunder of rich merchant trade ships. Since neither Garrett Shaw nor Duncan Farrow was in the habit of clearing the cabin during a battle, as the British sea captains did, it was frequently destroyed and the furnishings replaced.

Garrett looked about the shambles of his cabin with a scowl. Oak, mahogany, and teak splinters were scattered among gleaming gold tableware and jeweled goblets. A Yankee shell had burst against the hull, shattering one of the gallery windows and reducing the ornately carved sideboard to kindling.

He barely had time to splutter an exasperated curse over the Yankee's aim when there was a spurt of movement from one of the shadowed corners. He caught a flash of crimson, a glimpse of olive-warm thighs and shoulders, and in the next instant found himself smothered under the caresses of a sobbing, dileriously thankful Miranda Gold.

"Oh, Garrett," she gasped. "Garrett, it was so dreadful! So . . . so . . . ."

Shaw's dark blue eyes glinted speculatively a moment before the rakish smile reappeared. Not one to miss an opportunity, he tucked a hand beneath Miranda's chin, another beneath the ripe swell of her buttocks, and pulled her close, his mouth demanding a more wanton show of gratitude.

Miranda tensed, but only for a second. With a stifled sob, she flung her arms up and around his shoulders, ignoring the bite of the leather belts and weapons in her eagerness to show just how thankful she was.

When the kiss ended, Shaw released her with a hearty laugh.

"Ah, Miranda. Golden Miranda. You, alone, out of the lot, were the one I had no doubt would survive."

Miranda's breasts heaved upward against the low swoop of her neckline before her breath exploded on a curse.

"Damn your rakehell soul, Garrett Shaw. Is that any way to greet someone who has endured pure hell at the hands of a sow-bellied, mush-lipped peacock for over a week? I've suffered all manner of abuse, and —"

Garrett threw his shaggy head back and laughed harder. "If there was ever a man you couldn't tame, Miranda, I'd exalt him to sainthood myself. Come here, you lusty wench, and I'll give you such a fine abusing you'll not walk upright for a week!''

Miranda squealed in mock horror as Shaw's calloused hands tore away the thin layer of cotton to free her breasts. The token resistance ended on a gasp as he lowered his head with a growl and buried his head between them. Her hands went around his bare shoulders; her pelvis ground against his; his response was so immediate, so intense, she scarcely paid heed to the slim figure who moved from the gallery balcony to stand in the doorway of the cabin. The half-closed amber eyes met the dark emerald ones, and Miranda could not resist a smile. The tip of her tongue appeared and played across the full lower lip, which went slack again on a delicious shudder as Garrett's hands began searching beneath the crimson skirt.

Just as quickly, her nails clawed against the bulging muscles, and Miranda pushed herself free. She scrambled to place herself behind the solid shield Garrett's bulk afforded, and in answer to his startled gaze, stabbed a finger toward the door.

The gun Courtney had withdrawn from her waistband was aimed steadily at the flushed pair.

"Courtney!" Garrett exclaimed. "I thought you'd gone below!"

"Obviously."

Shaw forced a smile. "Why the gun? We're all friends here."

"I thought it might be needed to catch your attention."

"And so it has." The blue eyes flicked along the gleaming iron barrel to the grip of white knuckles. He walked forward slowly, halting only when the cold metal was pressing to his flesh. His hand rose and he slipped a finger between the wheel-lock and the firing pin to prevent an accidental discharge as he pried the gun gently from Courtney's grasp.

"You have my undivided attention," he said quietly.

Courtney's eyes lost some of their hardness. "I want to

know about my father. I want to know what happened."

Garrett's smile faded, and he looked down at the gun in his hand.

"He was my friend, Court. We lived and sailed together, almost like brothers. The three of us: Verart, Duncan, and me. Their loss cuts me as deeply as it does you."

"*Tell me.*"

"We were sold to the Yankees," he said bluntly and raised his head. "For a promise of gold, we were sold along with the *Wild Goose* and the *Falconer.*"

"*Sold*? By whom?"

"Ahh, when I find that out, girl" — the blue eyes filmed over with an unholy glow — "there'll be no easy death for the bastard. The O'Farrow was a good man. A good leader. He treated one and all fairly. I'll not rest until I've found out which of his men was a Judas."

"Then it is true," she whispered. "One of Duncan's own men betrayed him. . . ."

"Aye, and not for the first time, I'll warrant. There have been too many accidents, too many close calls, too many . . . coincidences over the past few months for my liking. Someone was selling us out, girl, at almost every turn. And he damned near succeeded in getting us all this time."

Courtney's shoulders slumped. She had refused to believe Ballantine when he'd hinted at a turncoat; she hadn't wanted to believe Seagram when he warned her about the same thing. Now Garrett was insisting that she believe him, and she knew he would have been the last to credit such deceit.

"What happened?" she asked softly.

Garrett sighed and began to unstrap the various belts and sheaths that held his personal arsenal. "We were supposed to meet Karamanli's envoy in a small bay near Moknine. When we arrived, the beach was suddenly crowded with gold braid and muskets, and the mouth of the bay was blocked off by three gunboats. Duncan and I went ashore, blind as an owl's asshole, and walked straight into the trap. We were held apart from the rest of the men and slated for a quick hanging as soon as the blue-bellies had finished drinking our rum and patting themselves on the backs.

"Somehow Davey — bless his warty hide — managed to escape into the bush with a dozen stout men. They waited until it was dark and crept back into the camp to break us out. We collected what guns we could, slit as many throats, brown and white, as we could lay a knife to, then swam out to the *Falconer* and the *Wild Goose*. The sentries were drunk, but not enough to keep them from giving us a bit of a fight, and by the time we could get the ships underway, the cove was alive with gunfire and soldiers.

"We cut anchor and ran for the mouth of the bay. The O'Farrow signaled he would go right while I was to lead the *Falconer* left and catch the three gunboats in a crossfire."

Shaw stopped and stared down at his hands. They were shaking with sudden violence, and he tightened them around a steel belt buckle.

"Damn me if I didn't order up too much sail too fast. A bloody downdraft took us, and we lost our studding boom before we were able to tack to port. Her bow swung wide, and before we knew it, we were ass-end-up on a sandbar. By the time we kedged ourselves free — and by God, there were some flayed backs in the offing for that one — the *Wild Goose* was surrounded and under heavy fire. She was aflame from stern to snout, and she was being hulled like a wooden decoy in a duck pond.

"We had a clear route past them," he added in a harsh whisper. "The O'Farrow had led them away from the entrance of the bay so that we could break free. The boom was still down and I had no steerage to speak of —" He stopped and looked at Courtney, his eyes dark with self-loathing. "I had no choice, don't you see? I would have lost the *Falconer* too if we hadn't run for it. When the sails were fully rigged, we came back. But it was over. We fished out a few survivors, picked a few more off the beach, and managed to chase down one of the gunboats and blow it to kingdom come . . . but the other two ran with the wind in their teeth.''

"And Duncan?" Courtney asked in a strained voice.

"Duncan wasn't among those we found. No one remembered seeing him after the fighting commenced.''

"Then no one actually saw him die?''

Garrett glanced up sharply. "We searched the bay; we searched the shore. No one saw him alive.''

"He could have been unconscious. He could have been taken on one of the Yankee gunboats.''

"Then he's dead for sure," Shaw said coldly. "What are you trying to do to yourself, girl?''

"*It's possible, isn't it*?''

"No! It isn't! If he was recaptured, do you think he would have been allowed to cheat the hangman a second time? They would have strung him to the nearest yardarm before he'd had a chance to cough the salt water out of his lungs. He's dead, Court. You have to accept it!''

"I can't accept it, Garrett," she said bitterly. "I can't explain it, but I just . . . I would *know* if he was dead. I would *feel* it. And if I felt it, I could accept it. But it just isn't so.''

Garrett turned away in exasperation. He snatched a dry shirt from a tumbled pile on the floor of the wardrobe and shrugged his broad shoulders into it.

"We went directly to Snake Island," he said tautly. "A few women and children had hidden in the dunes and were able to tell us what had happened. We stayed only long enough to bury the dead and salvage what little we could from the buried stores. I know what you mean by a *feeling*. I had it about you; I knew you were still alive." The piercing blue eyes glanced back at her. "I hold no such hope for Duncan.''

Courtney blinked back the sting of hot tears. Why couldn't she make him understand? Why couldn't she make anyone understand? Didn't they *want* to believe Duncan was alive?

"Seagram felt it," she persisted. "He told me he believed Duncan was still alive."

Miranda laughed suddenly, dryly, the first time she had drawn attention to herself. She was standing by the desk, holding her torn blouse with one hand, and Courtney noticed, with amazement, that she had somehow, from somewhere, acquired brilliant red paint for her nails. They looked like claws, the talons blood-dipped and sharpened for the next victim.

"You always did put too much faith in that ape," she mused, "though heaven only knows why. As for him knowing if Duncan was alive or dead — good Lord, he barely knew if he was alive himself at the end."

"Don't you dare say anything against Seagram," Courtney hissed. "He died trying to buy freedom for the rest of us."

"I knew he died," Shaw said loudly, hoping to avoid a cat fight. "But not the how of it."

"He organized an escape from the brig," said Courtney, her eyes locked on Miranda with loathing. "He and Nilsson were charged with being the leaders and were sentenced to a flogging. Nilsson died after only a few minutes in the shrouds, and Seagram —" There was anguish on her face as she turned to Shaw. "He had been wounded in the escape. Badly. He watched Nilsson die and he . . . he must have thought he had nothing to lose . . . so he tried to break free again on deck. In the confusion, he was shot."

"He was a good man," Shaw nodded. "A good fighter. He would have wanted to go that way."

Miranda's gaze slanted from Shaw to Courtney. The little bitch seemed to know exactly how to play on Garrett's sense of duty and loyalty to garner attention. Well, two could play at that. With a deliberate sigh, the hand holding the edges of her blouse dropped away, allowing her breasts to gape through the opening. The desired effect was instant. Shaw's eyes flicked over for the briefest of moments then deserted Courtney altogether as he waited to see if the cotton would slip farther.

Miranda took in Courtney's startled glance and the blush that crept into her cheeks as she was forced to raise her voice to break Garrett's distraction.

"What will you do with the *Eagle* now?" Courtney asked, seething over her father's whore's lack of conscience.

Shaw pulled his eyes away from the temptingly ripe flesh and frowned with the effort to realign his thoughts. "The *Eagle*? Aye, well, I had thought of keeping her to replace the *Goose*, but that was before Davey and the lads took it into their heads to crack her spine a good one. She'll take too much money and time to make seaworthy, and I plan to be basking under the Caribbean sun come Michaelmas Day. I warrant our old friend Yusef Karamanli will gladly take her off our hands."

"What would the Pasha do with a broken ship?"

"Display her for all the heathen world to see, of course. An American warship surrendered into pirate's hands! By the saints, he'd pay me a king's ransom for the privilege . . . and thrice as much again for possession of her righteous crew."

"Then you plan to sell them into slavery?" Courtney asked slowly.

"I'm not about to sail the bloody Mediterranean with them, that's a certainty. And don't go twisting your face all up with disapproval, wench. Where do you think you and the others would have ended up? If you weren't hanged outright, you'd've been indentured on some stinking Mississippi plantation bending your back by day and your knees by night. Nay, Court, they deserve it to a man, to be bound in chains and to lick Berber feet for the next twenty years. All of them save a few, naturally." His swarthy face broke into a cold smile. "The captain, for one. He'll make a prime bouncer for *la strappado*."

Courtney flinched inwardly. A particularly cruel death: the victim was hoisted to a yardarm by his wrists. The rope was sprung loose, allowing the body to fall to within a few feet of the deck. The jolt dislocated nearly every joint above the waist. A stalwart man could survive one such fall, but never more than two, and never in silence.

"Bless old Black Henry Morgan for his inventiveness," Miranda purred delightedly. "But I doubt whether the fat pig will survive the first trip up to the yard."

"I'll not spoil your entertainment," Shaw said with a grin. "We've a number of possible dance partners for him. The pretty lieutenant, for one."

Courtney's head jerked up. "Ballantine?"

"Aye, that was the name he gave. You had dealings with him?"

Miranda smiled slyly. "She had *something* with him."

Shaw glanced over sharply. "Meaning?"

Courtney stared, at a loss for words. It was Miranda's sultry tinkle of laughter that finally broke the silence.

"Didn't you know, Garrett? Dear Courtney was the golden-haired stallion's personal captive for the time we were on board the Yankee ship."

Shaw stiffened, and the dark blue eyes screwed down into slits. "*Personal captive* . . . is this true?"

Courtney felt a spray of gooseflesh rise along her arms. If she said a simple yes, Garrett would immediately assume the worst and Ballantine's life would be forfeit — and in such a way as to make the strappado look merciful. She had wanted to take her revenge on Ballantine, for Snake Island, for her uncle, for Seagram. She had almost killed him herself, but for her moment of irrational weakness. The price of that moment, it seemed, was never going to be paid.

"It's true," she said calmly. "He took me out of the

hold and disguised me as a cabin boy — he and another Yankee, the doctor. They led the crew to believe I was being paroled from the brig to work as the doctor's assistant.'' She shrugged noncommittally. ''I resented it at the time, but I suppose they saved my life.''

''Saved it for themselves, no doubt.'' Miranda added, not wanting to lose the advantage.

Courtney flashed the raven-haired harlot a murderous glance, only too aware of Miranda's intent. But, instead of giving way to her temper — a display which Garrett would have interpreted as a defense of Ballantine for the wrong reasons — Courtney laughed sardonically. ''Those two peacocks? They had hotter eyes for each other than they did for me. They were more interested in the reward they could demand from their commodore when they delivered me to Gibraltar.''

Miranda, hands on her hips, leveled an accusing stare at Courtney. ''I don't believe that. Not for one minute.''

''I don't really care what you believe. The fact is, the doctor is a cripple — in more ways than one — and the lieutenant is so taken up with himself, he'd sooner bed a mirror than a wench. Surely you must have found that out for yourself, *dear* Miranda, when he didn't sniff after the bait you offered to every warm-blooded two- or four-legged creature on the *Eagle*.''

Miranda's mouth sagged open. ''Why you lying little bitch! I was as much a prisoner as anyone in that filthy hold! More so, considering what I had to endure.''

''Yes, I can imagine what you endured. I can see how many bruises you suffered in the comfort of the captain's cabin, how many meals you did without, how many times you were flogged for your lack of cooperation.''

Miranda sucked in a lungful of air and hissed it free. ''Just because the bruises I earned are in places *you'll* never know about, it doesn't mean they're any less painful. Oh, I can believe the Yankee lieutenant never touched you. I can believe he would never have *dreamed* of using you for anything more than a boot*boy*. You're cold-hearted and foul-mouthed; you've as much appeal as a pineknot and you're as likely to tear the skin off any man fool enough to try you!''

"That's enough!'' Shaw growled, and Miranda whirled on him, hair flying and breasts heaving.

"You'd defend her? You'd take her side against mine — like the rest of them?''

"I take no one's *side* in such a petty battle. You both endured more than you should have and less than you might have, and if you don't stop your mouths here and now I'll be tempted to stop them for you.''

Miranda checked her urge to snarl a retort when she saw the ominous gleam of anticipation in Shaw's eyes. Her breath spluttered free on an explosive curse, and she brushed past him toward the cabin door.

"Davey Dunn has kindly given up his quarters for your pleasure,'' Shaw called after her. "I suggest you make use of them and cool down, my Spanish hellion.''

Miranda halted and spun to face him. "Dunn's quarters! To smell of offal and old sweat?'' The amber eyes slashed into Courtney's. "And where is *she* staying?''

"Where else but right here?'' Shaw said casually, spreading his hands and grinning.

The blood-red lips moved with a final barrage of muttered Castillian oaths, then Miranda was gone in a storm of crimson silk.

"Here?'' Courtney asked hesitantly, waiting for the echo of the slamming door to fade.

"Where else would you have me put you? You're still the O'Farrow's daughter. I can't have you swinging in a hammock with the rest of the crew. And besides'' — he moved closer and his powerful arms curled around her waist, drawing her into a firm embrace — "the bed is plenty big enough for two.''

Courtney stared into the dark blue eyes, startled yet not surprised by the suggestive offer. For several years, since she had turned fifteen and ripened out of childhood, Garrett Shaw had been proposing a physical union to strengthen the partnership between himself and Duncan Farrow. Love had never entered into the discussions; Garrett's appetites for wenching and drinking were too ingrained for him to consider a monogamous relationship. He desired possessions, however, and the harder they were to obtain, the more desperate he was to have them. Courtney had resisted his attentions so far, and Duncan's insistence that the choice be hers alone was the only thing that prevented Garrett from taking what he wanted by force.

Duncan was gone now. His ship and his crew were Shaw's. Would Garrett naturally include Courtney among the inherited properties?

She placed her hands flat on his chest and pushed gently. "Thank you, but no," she said coolly. "If that is the kind of arrangement you want, you'd best call Miranda back. I'm sure she'd be only too eager to oblige."

His arms tightened, the implied threat was barely masked by the faintly lustful chuckle with which he countered her resistance. "You've no need to play the shy virgin with me, Court Farrow. You are your father's daughter. You know the benefit of a strong alliance. And if it's your virginity you're fearing after" — he lowered his shaggy head suddenly, his mouth moving seductively along the curve of her throat — "I promise you'll not mourn it long."

Courtney felt a shiver of panic spiral through her body. He was in a winning mood, a conquering mood, and, she suspected, he would accept her refusal only as a challenge.

She took a deep breath and pushed with all her strength. His arms sprang open, and she twisted free, but instead of trying to run for the door, she faced him squarely, her green eyes blazing with anger, and assumed the boldly confident stance of a woman laying claim to her status as a legend's daughter.

"I said, I'm not interested. Not *yet*, Garrett. And certainly not this way."

His hands dropped down to his sides, and his smile took

on a hard edge. "You've put me off four long years, Court, and I'm not a patient man."

"I haven't noticed your lacking in bed partners," she snapped.

"In truth, would you want a fumbling innocent?"

"Perhaps. If he treated me with some manner of respect." The rejection was cold and dark in her eyes, and after a moment, Shaw shrugged the tension out of his shoulders.

"I've more respect for you than a man ought to have for a wench, Court. But perhaps you're right. Perhaps I want too much, too fast." He frowned and moved closer; this time his hands skimmed up her arms with gentle affection. "But I'll not stop trying. And I'll not accept defeat. Here — what's this . . . ?"

His hand had rubbed over the newly healed wound on her arm, and Courtney had flinched involuntarily.

"It's nothing. It's almost healed."

Garrett eased her shirt sleeve higher, frowning when he saw the raw pink seam in her flesh.

"It happened in the fighting on the beach," she explained. "I hardly feel it. The Yankee doctor cleaned it properly and stitched it well. In fact he . . . he risked a great deal for me. For Nilsson and Seagram as well."

Shaw's eyes narrowed. "Don't tell me he and the fancy lieutenant paroled Nilsson and Seagram as cabin boys along with you?"

"They did more than that," said Courtney, ignoring his sarcasm. "They intervened during the floggings. The captain had ordered three hundred strokes apiece for Seagram and Nilsson, despite the wounds they had received during the escape attempt. Nilsson was placed on the shrouds first and even though he died after only a few dozen lashes, the captain ordered the full count. The doctor protested and, in the end, placed himself in front of Nilsson and took the lashes himself."

"Aye," Garrett said with a slow nod. "I did notice several raw backs among them."

"As for the lieutenant, he was arrested and confined to quarters for countermanding the captain's orders. He . . . he had the two bodies dropped overboard before the captain could insist on seeing the punishment carried through."

"From the sound of it, girl, you're asking me to spare their lives."

"I'm merely suggesting that if we act like barbarians we'll be hunted down and dealt with like barbarians. The Yankees are strong, Garrett. You heard Father say he thought they would eventually win this war against the Tripolitans."

"You want me to set them *all* free?" he demanded incredulously.

"*No!* It's not their liberty I'm asking for, only their lives. Sell the crew to Karamanli, by all means. The humiliation and degradation of being sold into slavery is a suitable reward for what they've done to us — a fate more dreaded by them than any manner of torture or death you could devise. But if you take the captain's life — or the lives of his officers — in a brutal way, you'll be condemning us as surely as if you put a lead ball between their President's eyes. They wouldn't rest until they'd run us to ground. Until we know for certain who among us is the Judas, the Yankees still pose a formidable threat."

Shaw's chest swelled with anger. "We'll not be sold out again, Court Farrow. That much I promise you."

"In the meantime, you say the Pasha will pay handsomely for the *Eagle*. What about the Yankee Admiralty? They'd sell their souls to ransom back one of their own! Especially" — her voice took on a sly intimacy — "since I heard one of the crew mention that Jennings was related to Thomas Jefferson in some way. If that's true. . . ."

She did not need to elaborate; greed already flared in his eyes.

"Aye," he said and walked thoughtfully to the desk. He brushed aside a mound of dust and set two salvaged goblets in the cleared space. "Aye, you've a head on your shoulders, Court. As cunning and devious a one as your father's. Very well, I'll delay stretching the ropes on the yardarms until I've given the matter some hard thought. In the meantime —"

"In the meantime, I want the Yankee lieutenant."

"Eh?" The wine he was pouring from a flagon splashed onto the desk. "What's this you say?"

"I want to *personally* introduce him to the joys of slavery," she said with a convincingly malicious smile. "Even though his righteously honorable conscience may have prompted him to step in where Nilsson and Seagram were concerned, I still owe him for several days' worth of humiliation. I may even put him in skirts and have him serve me as a cabin *girl*! What say you to that, Garrett? A little entertainment to put us all in an easier frame of mind?"

She glanced casually at the bed to underline her meaning. Garrett's frown disolved to a grin and he nodded.

"He's yours. The doctor, too, if you've a mind to train two whimpering curs. Furthermore, when we arrive in Tripoli, whatever profit they bring is yours as well. You deserve a cut of the prize."

Courtney acknowledged the generous offer with a smile as she accepted the goblet of wine.

"To victory, Court. And revenge. 'Tis sweet as nectar when properly won, and by God, today's was sweet."

"To revenge," she murmured. "Now and in the future."

# Chapter Twelve

The weather continued to unleash foul, gusting winds and rain until well after midnight. The *Eagle* was given her slack and towed laboriously behind the *Falconer* to a deep-water inlet protected on three sides by tall palm trees and craggy, weed-covered slopes. Work on repairs began in earnest, despite the periods of downpour, thunder, and lightning. The crew of the *Falconer* had never been known to waste muscle on clean decks and spotless brasswork, but the ship's sails were refitted to within a degree of perfection, the guns were serviced and made ready for any emergency that might arise, and the racks of cutlasses and spikes were refastened to the base of each mast and cleaned and sharpened to a gleaming deadliness.

On board the *Eagle*, the American crew, under Sergeant Rowntree's supervision, worked grudgingly to patch and repair the damages. The best that could be hoped for was to plug the holes and keep her from floundering; any number of high waves had threatened to swamp her during the short tow. She was fitted with two large mainsails from the *Falconer*'s spares, but all three masts were either cracked or completely blown away from the topgallants up and there were no replacements available.

The women captives from Snake Island, newly released from the *Eagle*'s hold, were pleased to rummage through the small mountains of looted belongings and reclaim many of their own possessions. The bulk of the clothing was water-and-smoke-damaged, but still in better condition than what they had been forced to work and sleep in for the past ten days. Courtney had shown only mild curiosity about the bickering and haggling that took place over sorting the looted goods. She had not owned any fine clothes and had no interest in them now; she chose a long, hot bath instead, twelve undisturbed hours of sleep, and a feast of roast mutton, cheese, freshly baked biscuits, and a duff pudding thick with eggs and sugar. At Garrett Shaw's insistence, she occupied the *Falconer*'s greatcabin — alone — and on her own initiative, she had most of the garish furnishings removed and a few simple pieces brought in to replace the cleaned-out rubble.

The work kept her mind occupied. During the lapses, however, her thoughts continually wandered topside. She knew Adrian Ballantine had spent an endless, miserable night lashed to the ship's rigging, but there had been nothing she could do to intercede. She dared not show too much concern for his welfare lest Shaw, who had a violent and unpredictable temper, changed his mind and revoked her "ownership." She had ventured out at first light and had seen Dr. Rutger, but she had not singled him out or spoken to him. The appalling conditions in which the wounded were being kept — exposed to the elements and without medicines of any kind — deterred her from wanting to contact him; she knew what recriminations she would see in the soft brown eyes.

She had stolen a glimpse at the stern rigging, but the sight of Ballantine — his head lolled forward in the dripping morning mist, his arms spread and stretched beyond endurance in having to support his weight, his shirt and trousers torn over bruised and scraped flesh — disturbed her more than she cared to admit, even to herself.

Only after breakfast had come and gone did she find the courage to seek out the short, wiry first mate, Davey Dunn. He was just emerging from the beakhead, his face rumpled in a frown as he searched arduously for a louse that was on the prowl somewhere beneath his trousers.

"Ye want *what*?"

Her cheeks flamed. Davey was a good man, a skilled and fearsome fighter who had been with Duncan Farrow at least ten years. He had no use for subtleties, had probably never spoken in a whisper since childhood, and did not seem to care whose attention he drew to any conversation, private or otherwise.

"I said," she repeated, lowering her voice pointedly, "I would like to have one of the prisoners brought to my cabin."

"Yer cabin? What fer?"

"To talk. I have some questions —"

"Capt'n Shaw know anything about this?"

"He knows all about it," Courtney replied evenly. "We spoke yesterday and —"

"Capt'n Shaw's over to the Yankee ship," he said and spat a stream of oily yellow spittle out of the corner of his mouth. And as if that was the signal to end the conversation, he turned and started to walk away from her.

"When will he be back?"

"Eh? Dunno."

"Well, if he isn't here, I guess you'll just have to take my word for it and cut the prisoner down and deliver him into my care."

He considered the request for a moment and worked the large cud of tobacco from one cheek to the other.

*Phfit!* "Nope. Not without the Capt'n's sayso. And 'specially not if ye're talkin' about who I think ye're talkin' about."

Courtney placed her hands on her hips. "And just who do you think I'm talking about?"

"Fancy Britches. The one we got strung up in the shrouds." He paused and flashed an ocher grin. "The one Capt'n Shaw says can hang there till his parts shrivel and blow away in the wind."

Courtney could see she was getting nowhere fast.

"Very well, I see I'll have to have someone row me across to the *Eagle* so that I can speak to the captain."

"Nope."

"And why not?"

Dunn's head was bent as he resumed the search for the recalcitrant louse. At the sound of the irritation in her voice, his eyes flicked up to hers. " 'Cause he left orders he weren't to be disturbed — by anyone. He ain't slept since two days gone and he were lyin' there, out like a sot, last time I saw. An' sure as I can spit" — *phfit!* — "he'd raise all hell if'n he was woke for some yellow-bellied boot-lickin' son of a whore like Fancy Britches. Ahh, got the mangy bastard!" He held up the glutted louse and squash-ed it between thumb and forefinger, then wiped away the blot on his shirtfront.

Courtney ground her teeth. "Then the choice seems rather clear to me. Either you cut the lieutenant down on my orders, or I swim across to the *Eagle* and make sure the captain knows it was your stubbornness that drove me to do it!"

"Seems like ye're willin' to go to a peck o' trouble jest to ask some *questions*. What kind o' questions are ye askin'?"

*Trust no one, Seagram had warned. Not a friend or lover, not a man or woman, not even a crack in the wall.* Courtney knew, *she knew* she could trust Davey Dunn, of all people, and yet something kept her from revealing any more to him than she had to for the time being. Her answer was delayed, and delivered with enough frost to stir Dunn's suspicion further.

"The questions are personal. If the answers concern you, I'll let you know."

They glared at one another for a full minute, to the amusement of the crewmen within hearing distance.

Dunn's low opinion of most women was well known and to see him squaring off with Courtney Farrow — and apparently losing — was a sight to be savored.

"Well?" She demanded. "Will you have him cut down and brought to my cabin, or —"

*Phfit!*

"I'll cut him," Dunn scowled unpleasantly. "No need to flap yer nostrils, I'll cut him. I'll even bring him to you *personal*, but if'n I find out these *questions* have anythin' to do with what's *in* his fancy britches, I'll take the lash to ye meself!"

Having neatly shifted the brunt of the joke to Courtney, Dunn strode away and left her standing open-mouthed by the deck rail. She realized it was a mistake to avoid his questions. Why hadn't she taken Davey into her confidence? Why hadn't she told Shaw about Seagram's warning? *And why was she continually lying to protect Ballantine?*

Courtney hurried back to the greatcabin. Cleared of battle damage, the floor afforded a wide area in which to pace and she worked herself into such a state that she was all but ready to cancel the request for an audience with Ballantine when she heard the dragging footsteps out in the companionway.

She yanked the door open and was met by a ragged, soaked shadow of a man.

"Here he be," Dunn announced unnecessarily and shoved Ballantine through the door without waiting for a nod from Courtney. "A prime proud specimen of Yankee know-how, if'n I ever saw one."

Ballantine's clothing was in shreds, drenched and clinging to muscles that twitched in the sudden warmth. His hair was plastered to his brow and neck; his wrists were raw and bled fresh pink onto the ropes that bound them together. A second length of rope was stretched from his wrists to his ankle chains, making it impossible for him to raise his hands more than an inch from his body, or to take anything but small shuffling footsteps. He kept his eyes lowered although she sensed it was an attempt to control his fury rather than to signal defeat.

How does it feel, Yankee? she wanted to ask. Forced to stand in your own filth and humiliation while someone clean and well-fed gloats victoriously over you?

"Thank you, Davey," she said quietly. "You can leave us."

"Alone?" The grizzled brows shot up to his hairline.

"Yes, *alone*! You can stand outside and keep your ear pressed to the door, if you like, but I will speak to him alone!"

Dunn chewed fiercely for a moment and screwed up the corner of his mouth for an explosion of juice. A particular sharpness in Courtney's stare made him stop, and he swallowed noisily before peering up at Ballantine.

"Damn right, I'll be outside the door. And if'n I so much as hear ye cough funny, I'll be after yer bowels like a hungry shark."

Ballantine did not look up.

Dunn shuffled grudgingly to the door and muttered a curse as he slammed it behind him.

Courtney exhaled slowly. Ballantine's gaze lifted to hers for the first time, and she could see that her assessment had been correct. His eyes were red-rimmed from pain and fatigue, underscored with plum-colored smudges, but their centers flashed with a surfeit of rage.

She had not realized the extent of his injuries. Aside from the copious bruising and scratches, he had a cut over his eye, an ugly furrow deep to the bone that must have been throbbing devilishly. His complexion was flushed, whether from anger or fever she did not know, and she had to fight the instinctive urge to untie his hands, help him to a chair, and tend his wounds.

"We seem to have found different ways to spend the night, Yankee," she said quietly, forcing smugness into her voice. He did not react; only the briefest of quivers in the ropes binding his wrists told her he'd heard what she said.

"Apparently you fail to see the humor in all of this," she continued and crossed over to stand beside the broken gallery window. She wished a breeze would carry in some cooling air. Her cheeks were warm and her blood was hot, but she'd be damned if she'd show any signs of weakness to the Yankee. "I find it infinitely amusing that our positions are the exact reverse to what they were a few short days ago. Me, the victor; you, the vanquished. Have you nothing at all to say? No urge to plead for quarter from the desperate cutthroat pirates you so recently scorned? I warned you not to underestimate us, Yankee. I warned you that no matter what it took, we would have our revenge."

His voice was so low, his response was almost inaudible. "I'm glad to see you were not hurt in the fighting."

Courtney stared up at the smoldering gray eyes, uncertain whether the tautness in his voice was bitterness or sarcasm.

"I find it difficult to believe you were worried one way or the other."

"*Worried* is probably too strong a word," he agreed easily. "Curious is more like it . . . although I've always heard that cats land on their feet. You have the temperament, and the instinct to have nine lives. No, I guess it doesn't surprise me you lived through this."

A deeper flush leaked into her cheeks, and her voice cracked despite her determination to remain impassive. "Your own survival is quite amazing in light of the chances you take. I heard about your confrontation with Captain Shaw yesterday on deck. I'm astonished it wasn't you he shot instead of the other sailor."

Adrian could taste the hot, metallic sourness of fever at the back of his throat. He wished he could free a hand to wipe away the beads of sweat crawling down his temples, or free his pride to ask for a single mouthful of cold, clean water . . . but he could do neither.

"Where is Matt?" he asked in a strained whisper.

"Here. On board the *Falconer* with the rest of the wounded."

"And their condition?"

"How should I know?" she snapped. "I'm not a doctor, not even an interested observer. I could care less if they all rotted of corruption to the last man."

"Somehow I don't believe that," he mused wryly.

"No?" The green eyes flashed as she paced away from the window. "Surely you can't be thinking I feel any sympathy for their plight? I would only have to think back on how my uncle's men were treated to stifle any such charitable notions!"

She stopped by the sideboard, and after a moment of thought, poured herself a mug of water. "Captain Shaw had his heart set on killing you before I stepped in. I can easily step out again, with a clear conscience, having made the offer and having had the offer refused."

"What offer?"

"Your life. The same offer you made me as I recall."

Adrian closed his eyes briefly, wearily. Did she think this was a game? Or was he simply going mad.

"I'll not play anyone's fool," he said quietly.

"Then you'll not live to see Tripoli."

"Tripoli?" A start jolted his eyes open again. "Is that where we're bound?"

"Eventually. We'll remain in this cove until the temporary repairs on both ships are finished, then we sail for Algiers."

Adrian held his breath; her disclosure was too horrible to be a nightmare. Courtney watched his expression change, watched apprehension grow in it. Was it just occuring to him that the horror could be only beginning? Had he truly never considered the possibility of capture? Of slavery? At least she had been warned from the outset of her days with Duncan Farrow that capture, imprisonment, even death were all real possibilities. Almost inevitabilities. They gave meaning and value to the word *freedom*, something the Yankees obviously took for granted in their arrogance.

The shadow Courtney saw, or imagined she saw, in

Ballantine's eyes was quickly brought under guard again.

"Jennings . . . is he still alive?"

"Are you worried about him?"

"He is the *Eagle*'s commanding officer."

"And a stalwart humanitarian," she snorted derisively. "Don't concern yourself about him, Yankee. He's receiving suitably hospitable treatment."

"Then he *is* alive?"

Courtney paused. "Yes. Although again, I can't predict for how long, or in what condition he'll arrive in Tripoli. As for yourself" — she set the mug of water down — "I think it only fitting I return the favors you so generously afforded me. You'll have the opportunity to earn an easier passage for yourself by acting as my steward. You can fetch my meals and tidy the cabin; scrub the floors, polish my boots . . . it will be good practice for when you receive your loincloth and iron-link anklets. Oh yes, and I think a bath should be among the first priorities. I've smelled better things in a Berber gutter."

The rope joining Ballantine's wrists to his ankles strained to its limit. "It will be a cold day in hell, madam, before I become anyone's bootboy — especially yours."

The emerald eyes glittered vindictively. "You would prefer to be chained to the rigging again?"

"I would prefer to take my chances out in the open with the rest of my crew. Matt is badly hurt; he can't be expected to cope with all of the wounded alone."

"And you want me to send you out to him?" she cried in amazement. "And just what, in all of your bloody arrogance, makes you think for one minute I would do so? Have you forgotten the number of times I asked — no, *pleaded* — to be sent back to my uncle's men? Have you also forgotten your answer to me — that I was no ordinary prisoner! Well, clear your ears for the news, Yankee: you are no ordinary prisoner either! I'll not be offering you one single consideration over and above what you offered me. I'll not tell you how your crew is faring! I'll not tell you how many of your wounded have died or how the others are being treated! I'll see them starved and flogged and forced to work until they drop dead on their feet! I'll deal you exactly the contempt you dealt me, and by God, if it's called for, you'll feel the same bite from the flat of my sword!''

Courtney's fists were clenched, and her chest heaved beneath the thin cambric shirt as if she had been running. She whirled away from Ballantine, not trusting herself to keep her nails from scoring his face, not wanting him to see the bright shine of tears in her eyes. *Tears*! What was happening to her! Where was her rage, her vengeance? Why was it that the simple act of his standing there and looking at her made her knees weak and her mouth dry? How could she fight the twenty different emotions clashing about inside her if all he had to do was look at her and she was lost?

''You will do exactly what I tell you to do, Yankee,'' she grated harshly, ''or your Dr. Rutger will find himself strapped to the rigging again, and this time there will be no shirt, no coat between him and the lash.''

Adrian swayed slightly. He blinked the sweat out of his eyes and steadfastly strained against the cords binding his wrists. He welcomed the searing pain as his already damaged flesh was smeared bloody. His only thought was to free his hands, to reach the narrow shoulders, the arch of her throat . . . to squeeze until the life was choked out of her.

''Matt helped you,'' he said evenly. ''He helped your uncle's men, too. I don't believe you would take your anger at me out on him.''

''You're doing it again, Yankee: guessing what I will and won't do.'' She shook her head slowly. ''And what I won't do is be any less the daughter my father expects me to be. There is more at stake here than merely appeasing my anger, more even than wanting to see you humiliated the way you humiliated me. There are deaths to be avenged, wrongs to be atoned for, betrayals to be exposed. But, then you must know all about betrayals, Yankee,'' she said, facing him with a toss of her auburn hair. ''Or haven't you wondered yet how Captain Shaw came to be in possession of your naval codes?"

Adrian took a measured breath. "I've wondered."

"And to what lengths would *you* be prepared to go in order to satisfy your curiosity?"

Ballantine could not think clearly. He could not see his way past the sudden swirl of dizziness that left this mouth even drier than before. Sweat drenched his face; the salt stung his scrapes and burned his eyes. Far more telling of his inadequacy to meet the girl's challenge — his hands trembled and his breathing was labored.

"Nothing to say, Yankee? No witty rebuttals?"

Ballantine swallowed with difficulty. The room lurched and took a slow revolution. He spread his feet farther apart to counteract the whirling pinwheels of light, but the chains caught him up, and a tremendous shudder made the pain inside his head explode throughout his body.

Courtney moved instinctively to catch him before he crashed forward onto the floor. His weight nearly staggered her, but she managed to pivot him so that he landed heavily in a chair. His eyes were closed, and his head rolled to one side in utter exhaustion.

Courtney stared down at him, at a loss what to do. She could call Davey Dunn — no doubt he *did* have his ear bolted to the door. But Davey was short on sympathy and downright barren when it came to compassion. He would sooner drag the lieutenant away by the heels than take the time to help him.

"Don't you dare pass out on me," she warned, her voice unsteady, as she ran to the washstand and splashed water into the china basin. She snatched a towel from a hook and carried both back to the desk and set them beside Adrian.

His teeth were locked against a shiver. The chill of the rain and wind had been dispelled by the heat of the cabin, but the strain of fighting the pain and weakness for twenty hours was proving to be more than even he could withstand.

Courtney hesitated a moment longer, then reluctantly brushed aside the fallen locks of sun-bleached hair that covered his brow. His skin was clammy to the touch, although the sweat ran in shiny streaks down his temples and throat. It was the first time she had intentionally touched him, and the shock of it spread through her body like ripples in a quiet pond. Something inside her churned hotly for the length of several shallow breaths, then, as if a knot had suddenly lost its tension, she felt the anger and the need to hurt him fade. In their stead rose up the instinct to hold him, to soothe him, to cradle his head to her breast and take away the pain.

As she held the cup of fresh water to his mouth, she curled her lower lip between her teeth and concentrated on the ugly gash over his temple. It was about five inches long, matted with hair and grime; if it was not cleaned and sewn properly, it would leave a brutish scar.

The wound in her upper arm throbbed — a sharp reminder: without Dr. Rutger's expert ministrations, her arm might have become infected, or gangrenous. At the very least she would have bled into a state of weakness. Ballantine was absolutely right, although there was no need for him to know it — she would not take her anger out on the doctor, even though the threat of doing so might be the only leverage she had for controlling the lieutenant.

With cool detachment she set about to find a needle and thread among the captain's toiletries and to clean the wound and stitch the ragged edges of skin together. She was tying a knot in a strip of cotton bandage when she realized the steely gray eyes were open and studying her.

"Your talents extend beyond removing splinters, I see. You should have told Matt; he could have put you to better use."

"You don't live the kind of life I have without learning a thing or two about treating wounds."

His eyes darkened slightly. "And yet half of it you spent dressed in silks and satins. Quite a reversal, I'd say, and one that took a great deal of courage and conviction to make."

The color in Courtney's cheeks ebbed, then returned a

deeper shade. She straightened and retreated a step, not trusting either the look in his eye or the proximity of his body to hers. She knew his hands were bound and immobile, his movements sorely restricted, and yet she felt more vulnerable than she ever had before.

Stabbing the needle into the shank of thread, she replaced it on the desk. She refused to look directly at him, but she could feel his eyes, like warm hands, running over her body.

"You say my fate lies in your hands . . . until Tripoli?"

"Yes. Until Tripoli."

"And Matt?"

"No harm will come to him — to any of your men as long as they obey orders."

"You haven't told me where Captain Jennings is being held."

"No," she replied tartly. "I haven't. We are still enemies, you know. You are my prisoner, not my keeper, and I fail to see what right you have to ask me questions, never mind to assume I will answer them!"

Ballantine's face remained impassive. "I'm sorry. It was presumptuous of me."

Courtney glanced up, expecting to read mockery behind the soft apology, but there was none and the lack of it completely disarmed her. Her cheeks burned crimson, and her breasts were suddenly so sensitive to the contact of the cambric shirt that she shivered.

Adrian watched her reaction, and his senses sharpened instantly. The apology had come from the depths of weariness; he had not consciously tried to undermine her composure, but he saw that he had touched a nerve. He had glimpsed her like this once before: in his cabin, the morning after he had supposedly raped her. He had detected a conflict in her emotions then, although he could not identify it. He saw it again now in the widening of the emerald eyes and it gave him further cause to wonder.

He had accepted the charge of rape because she had told him it was so and because he had only the dimmest of recollections to call upon for a defense. But what if he hadn't actually raped her, if she had gone to his bed willingly? It would mean there was a way through the barriers she had carefully erected around her emotions over the years.

She had asked him to what lengths he was prepared to go? Any lengths at all!

"You win again, Irish," he said quietly.

"What do you mean?"

"Exactly what I said. I'm tired, and I hurt like hell, and I don't want to see Matt put through any more than he's already suffered. You win. I'll be your dutiful servant." He saw the suspicion in her eyes and was careful to add, "But only until we arrive in Tripoli. After that, I have no intention of being your slave, or anyone else's."

"If you're thinking of trying to escape once you get your strength back —" Courtney stopped; the gleam in his eyes confirmed that that was indeed what he planned. It was precisely what she had planned had the *Eagle* docked in Gibraltar.

"Yes? You're going to help me?"

Courtney backed away, his obvious amusement driving her from him.

"Not likely, Yankee. And if you try it while you're in my presence, I'll stop you *dead*. Do we understand one another?"

"Perfectly."

Courtney strode to the cabin door. She flung it wide, and Davey Dunn came to an immediate, bristling attention.

"Eh? I didn't hear ye call."

Courtney's eyes were dark and unreadable as she glanced toward the lieutenant. "The smell of Yankee pride is becoming oppressive, Davey. Take the lieutenant topside. He's so desperate to know what is happening with his men, let him find out first hand. Let him haul away their slops and clean their festering wounds. Maybe he'll learn a little humility."

It was not the kind of punishment Dunn would have chosen, but he nodded and yanked on Adrian's ropes, bringing him to his feet with a grunt of pain.

"I 'ope ye have a strong gut, boy. From how I see it, there's enough work for ten healthy men and enough limbs partin' company with their owners to keep the eels happy for a week."

Adrian took the shove between his shoulder blades without balking. He paused beside Courtney, but she kept her eyes averted and her mouth pinched firmly shut.

# Chapter Thirteen

Matthew Rutger dragged a trembling hand across his forehead and sat back numbly on his heels. The man stretched in front of him was dead. He had made no sound, had not moved or wakened out of the coma that had set in after the transfer from the *Eagle* to the *Falconer*. The name was Peerce, and he and his shattered limbs would become one more pile of cleanly picked bones on the bottom of the bay.

Matt had been awake the night through, doing what he could for the wounded members of the *Eagle*'s crew. He had no medicines, no bandages other than what he could tear from clothing, no food, and only the rainwater they were able to trap in canvas pockets for drinking. He wanted to lay down and die himself. He was tired and discouraged. His back had progressed through every stage of agony imaginable and beyond to some that were not. He had managed to clothe himself with the pickings from men who no longer needed earthly comforts, and while his own lacerations no longer bled, there were stains from a dozen torn limbs soiling his sleeves and breeches. His face was pale, the skin drawn taut over his cheekbones. His eyes shared and reflected the pain of every man around him.

Matt sighed and covered Peerce's face with a scrap of sail. The rain had stopped and the sun was struggling to break free of the clouds, but the air was so dense with humidity and mosquitoes, it seemed they were only trading one hell for another.

"*You!*"

Matt looked up and blinked uncertainly. The corsairs had erected a barrier of crates and broken timbers around the prisoners, a pen which was shared by the goats and sheep and perfumed by them.

"You with the striped back! Pay a mind here!"

Matt followed the direction of the shout and recognized the wiry corsair who had led Adrian to the shrouds. He thought his mind was playing tricks on him when he saw the tall figure standing behind Dunn, but then he found his voice and staggered clumsily to his feet.

"Adrian!"

"I'm told ye been caterwaulin' fer help, Yankee," Dunn spat. "Well, here ye are."

Matthew's eyes communicated a silent greeting to Ballantine, but in the next instant flicked to Dunn to plead the urgency of their situation.

"These men need shelter. And food. For the love of God, can't you see they're dying? And more will die if they don't receive attention quickly. A cup of broth, some unguent for the burns —"

"Stow yer whinin', Yankee," Dunn growled. "Or I'll be doctorin' ye gut to gizzard for fishbait."

He shoved Adrian forward and spat once more onto the deck before he closed the gap in the barricade and strode away. Matt's shoulders sagged as if every muscle had been drained of blood.

"Are these all the men we have left?" Ballantine whispered, still trying to take in the horror of the pen.

"Twenty-three," Matt said grimly. "Six died through the night; Peerce went a few moments ago. Or it could have been an hour ago . . . two . . . I don't know anymore."

Adrian looked over at his friend. Matt was obviously nearing the limits of his endurance. They both were, but neither could afford the luxury of collapsing.

"We can sit over there," Matt said and led the way to an overturned crate. "Anything damaged besides your head?"

"Nothing important other than my pride. Can you get through these ropes somehow?"

Matt thumbed the thick cords with fingers that hadn't the strength to budge the tight knots. "It should only take me an hour or so to chew through them," he muttered disgustedly.

"In the pocket of my breeches . . . I put my razor there yesterday, before all hell broke loose. As far as I know —"

"It's still here," Matt cried and produced the slim, folded blade. He glanced around quickly, to see if they were being observed by any of the guards, then began to saw at the ropes. While he did, he peered curiously at the white bandage on Adrian's head. "You have a private source I don't know about?"

"The girl," Adrian commented. "She patched me up."

"Courtney? She's alive?"

"Unfortunately, yes. Ahh —" The bindings parted, and Ballantine rubbed gingerly at the chafed, torn flesh on his wrists. "She wouldn't have been for long if I could have wrapped my hands around her throat."

"This wasn't any of her doing."

"She wished for it hard enough. How many men do they have guarding this pen?"

"Four or five, why?"

"Armed, naturally."

"Like individual armadas."

"And the *Eagle*? Any word from her?"

"None. Did you really expect there to be?"

"I didn't expect them to be bowing their heads and shuffling around like beaten dogs!"

"You can't seriously be thinking —"

"They intend to sail us into Tripoli, Matt. They plan to tow the *Eagle* there and hand her over to Karamanli, along with a few score hostages — or slaves, depending on the mood his highness is in. Either way, do you know what that will do to Commodore Preble's plans for a swift end to the war?"

"He won't have too many left," Matt said quietly. "Unfortunately, I don't see how you can do anything to prevent it."

"Either do I at the moment, but we have to think of something." His gaze strayed to the battered hulk of the *Eagle*. It was moored less than fifty yards from the *Falconer*, and he could clearly see signs of activity both above and below decks. "If only we had some way of communicating with those men. . . ."

The *Eagle*'s marine sergeant-at-arms, Andrew Rowntree, stared out across the narrow gap of water that divided the two ships and stifled the urge to simply lean his face up to the shattered planks and shout across the distance. At twenty years of age, he was bristling at the indignity of being taken captive by a scurrilous crew of pirates. He had long since decided that he could give his life for no better service than his country, and his own safety was not a factor in controlling his urges. What did dampen his spirits was the knowledge that his crewmates were rudderless. They were well guarded, beaten for any sign of insubordination, and underfed and underwatered so that they could not regain any of the strength they had lost in the past twenty-four hours. The fact that the wounded were hostages to ensure the Americans' cooperation was another deterrent — possibly the biggest — as was the deliberate isolation of the *Eagle*'s senior officers. Lieutenant Ballantine was on board the *Falconer*, as was Jennings as far as they could determine. Second Lieutenant

Falworth had been removed at dawn and escorted across, which left two junior midshipmen, himself, and Angus MacDonald holding the only rank above private.

Without leadership, the men were floundering. Rowntree refused to accept the situation; there were one hundred and forty-six healthy survivors from one of the best damned warships afloat, and he was not going to give up until he had found some way of putting those resources to work. If he could only find a way of communicating with those on the *Falconer*. He had seen Lieutenant Ballantine cut down from the rigging earlier, and while he had looked more dead than alive, the fact that he still moved and breathed offered some hope.

Andrew felt a firm hand on his arm and looked up to see the Scot, Angus MacDonald, beside him. Rowntree was leaning against the bulwark; his face was bathed in the light that filtered through a hole in the outer skin of the hull. The rest of the storeroom was in darkness save for a single greasy oil lantern that cast more smoke than light. The air was pungent with the smell of crowded bodies. The brimming slop barrel had not been emptied since their incarceration, and it added its own cloying rankness to the shadows.

"Ye should gi' yersel' a chance at some sleep, laddie," MacDonald scolded gently. "Ye were awake all night, poundin' a hammer like the Devil himsel' was at yer heels. It wouldna' do tae ha' ye fallin' doon wi' the fever."

"I can't sleep, Angus. God knows, I've tried, but every time I close my eyes. . . ."

"Aye, Laddie. Aye, I ken how ye feel. I've seen the same man die in mine eyes a hundred times."

Andrew sighed. Angus had earned a burned forearm in the shelling of Snake Island, bruised ribs and a nasty cut on the side of his head from the beach fighting, a grazed shoulder during the attempted breakout on the *Eagle*, and a crisscross of raw pink weals on his back from the flogging. He had added a complement of bruises and scrapes during the sea battle with the *Falconer*, and as a final insult, had had his pride and glory — the full bushy moustache — singed from his upper lip while dousing a fire on deck.

"Angus, why aren't you flat on your back?" Rowntree asked in awe.

"Ach! It'd take more'n a few wee stings tae put a Mac-Donald under. Come along noo, the swine ha' brought us food. It's nae much by the smell o' it, but ye'd best eat it tae buy yersel' strength."

"Strength for what, Angus?" Rowntree sighed wearily. "Strength to rebuild our ship so these blackhearts can sail her into Tripoli as a prize? The Pasha will paint her with yellow and green frescoes and have paper lanterns hanging from her masts. If only . . ." He turned and gazed out the damaged hull again. "If only there was some way to get in touch with the others. Lieutenant Ballantine, for instance. If we could just speak to him, get to him somehow."

"Wi' these blacknecks crawlin' doon our gullets every two tairns? Ye'd have a better chance at postin' a letter and seein' it delivered by packet."

"I suppose you're right," Rowntree said and then frowned. "Why do you think they took Lieutenant Falworth across?"

The Scot took a deep breath, swelling his bare, barrel chest. He winced from a sharp pain in his damaged ribs, but it did not stop the fine Gaelic curse that he bestowed on Falworth's soul.

Andrew regarded him blankly a moment, then returned to his scrutiny of the corsair ship. "I assume you weren't telling me anything I didn't already know."

"The swine," Angus spat. "He's a shifty one and nae above sellin' his soul tae the Devil if he thought it'd buy him a clean pair o' britches and a night wi' the pirate wench."

Andrew dismissed the bitterness with a wave of his hand. He knew Angus MacDonald and Falworth had locked horns often in the past — that was why such an excellent soldier as Mac was normally assigned to guard duty in the stinking brig.

"The problem, as I see it," Rowntree muttered, "is that any method we use to attract the attention of our men on the *Falconer* will also be seen by their guards. That rules out lights, shouts, even hand signals or flags."

"Hand signals," the Scot grunted softly. "Normal hand signals, aye, but what o' the kind the doc uses tae talk wi' wee Dickie Little?"

Andrew Rowntree's eyes widened, and his head turned slowly from the slit. He stared at Angus, who grinned faintly.

"Dickie Little," Rowntree murmured. "Why the blazes didn't I think of that? Is he here? Is he with this shift of workers?"

"Aye, he's here, in yon corner."

Andrew pushed himself away from the bulwark, his eyes searching anxiously in the shadows for the small, huddled form of Dickie Little. He was where Angus had said, crouched in the corner of the storeroom, his eyes closed, his thin arms wrapped around his knees, hugging them close for comfort. His face was blackened by layers of soot; his hair was singed to the scalp on one side of his head.

Andrew hunkered down beside the boy, momentarily at a loss. With his eyes closed, Dickie had effectively escaped into his own private world. None of the other boys had ever had much to do with him; they preferred to tease and taunt him, to ape his deafness rather than to try to understand it. The men on board the *Eagle* had not been much better. They cuffed him if he got in the way, twisted an ear or boxed them if he mistook an order. Only Matthew Rutger had spared time for the boy.

Andrew reached out and gently touched Dickie's arm.

Enormous brown eyes flew open at once, bright with the kind of fear no one else on board would comprehend. Andrew immediately held up a grimy hand to assure the boy there was no need to be frightened. Dickie did not move, did not react other than to hug his arms and legs tighter against his chest.

"We need your help, lad," Andrew said, conscious of

the desperation in his voice. "Please, Dickie, how can I make you understand?"

"Let me try," said Angus, bending down beside the sergeant. Despite his Scots gruffness, he had a warm smile when the urge was upon him to use it; he used it now, at the same time crossing his massive arms over his chest. Dickie's eyes widened, and he looked from Angus to Rowntree and back.

"I seen him and the doc use this sign many a time," MacDonald murmured. "I ken it means 'friend'."

Andrew smiled hopefully and did likewise, folding his arms across his chest. Dickie continued to stare for several moments before he slowly, hesitantly, relinquished his grip on his bent knees and returned the gesture.

"Thank Christ," Andrew muttered. "What now? How do we tell him what we want him to do? And even if we manage to get a message to the *Falconer*, how in hell will we know what comes back?"

"Worry on it when it happens, laddie," Angus said, his eyes still focused on the young boy. He added a verbal plea, more for his own benefit. "Ye can trust me, lad. I gi' ye an oath on me mether's grave."

He stood and held out one of his hands. The other he used to point to the other side of the storeroom, to the small square of light.

"Come along, Dickie," he whispered. "We've a man's job for ye fair an' proper, an' ye're the only one o' us what can dae it."

Dickie's hand moved a fraction, as if a nerve had suddenly twitched. Angus saw it, and his smile became even more encouraging, the palm of his hand more welcoming.

"Good lad!" he cried fiercely when he felt the small, cold fingers slip into his. "Good! Noo . . . tae the window."

Angus helped the boy to his feet and slowly led the way through the silent, wary men who had turned their complete attention to the proceedings. When they arrived at the crack in the hull, Angus dragged an empty crate over for the boy to stand on to see out the slit. The haunted brown eyes studied the narrow view — the rim of trees, the calm waters of the cove, the anchored *Falconer* — then turned to Angus blankly.

"What would the sign for 'doctor' be?" Andrew wondered aloud.

Angus cast his piercing eyes around the hold. "Dae any o' ye blitherin' fools ken the sign for 'doctor'?"

A few scruffy heads had the wit to shake in the negative; others simply stared.

"What would be logical?" Andrew asked, with a shrug.

Angus started to spread his hands, then stopped midgesture. He brought them together again and mimed a needle and thread stitching into his wounded shoulder, then he pointed out the hole.

The sadness in the boy's face deepened, and he lowered his head, nodding slowly.

"He probably only thinks we're telling him the doctor is on the other ship."

"Aye, but at least he kens." Angus leaned forward and grasped Dickie's slender shoulders. He touched the quivering, bloodless lips with his finger, then touched his own . . . then pointed out the broken slats. He repeated the sequence, adding some haphazard hand movements to try to communicate the idea of conversation to the boy. And again, patiently: the needle and thread, the finger to his lips, the gestures out the shattered planks. His smile of encouragement became a grin, then a beaming triumph when Dickie suddenly grasped the meaning and grabbed Angus MacDonald's huge hands in his own.

"By God, he understands," Andrew gasped.

"Was there e'er a doot?" the Scot demanded, still grinning like a fool.

"Now we just have to figure out a way of attracting the doctor's attention . . . *if* he's still alive, and *if* he's been left topside with the wounded."

"He'll be wi' the wounded," Angus declared. "Or I'll pairsonally send all o' their bleedin' souls tae hellfire!"

Andrew peered anxiously through the hole even as Angus pried carefully and quietly at the loose splinters and chunks of wood to widen the gap.

Ten minutes passed. Twenty.

There was little sign of movement on the quarter-deck of the *Falconer* where the prisoners were being held. A slight commotion caused Andrew to clutch the corporal's arm in excitement, but nothing came of it. It was a further ten minutes of frustrating vigilance before a head popped into view and was lowered behind the barrier of crates and boards again.

Several sluggish heartbeats later and Andrew's fingers dug into MacDonald's arm. "Look! I can't be certain, but I think it's . . . *Lieutenant Ballantine!*"

"Aye, and the doctor! Noo, laddie," Angus hissed and touched the boy's arm. Dickie needed no further prompting. His eyes were shining with recognition; his mouth quivered into a smile; his hands moved in furious patterns — to the chest, the mouth; in circles and sweeps . . . and always back to the heart.

"Good God, it's Dickie!" Matthew whispered in disbelief.

"Can you make out what he's saying?" Adrian asked urgently, watchful of any guards who may have seen the boys' face appear between the planks of the hull.

"He's telling me he's happy to see me," Matt said. "That he was afraid I was dead — that all of us were dead."

"Who is with him?"

Matt's hands moved in short, brusque motions, and after a pause the answer came flashing across.

"They've been split into three work parties of about fifty each. Rowntree's with him, and MacDonald. . . ."

"By God, we may have a chance after all," Adrian murmured. "Is there someone over there who understands the boy?"

"I gather they're trying." Matt smiled proudly and added, "He'll *make* them understand if he has to."

"Good. First we have to know how they stand. You say

three shifts of fifty? When do they change, where do they go, how closely are they watched . . . *Have they any kind of weapons at all*?''

Matthew relayed the questions. The responses came almost fifteen minutes later, after an obviously lengthy struggle with interpretations for the two marines.

"A crowbar and two knives," Matt said, flatly disgusted. "A hell of a beginning for an armed revolt, if that's what you're after."

"Nevertheless, it *is* a beginning," Adrian insisted. "And by God, if I know anything at all about those men, it's the beginning of the end for Shaw and his people!"

At the precise moment Adrian Ballantine was envisioning Garrett Shaw's downfall, the captain was sprawled on the tester bed in the *Eagle*'s greatcabin. His teeth were bared, his face was bathed in sweat, the veins in his neck were strained into cords and each breath he managed to hold was a victory of will. His naked body glistened with a feverish urgency, an urgency that was transmitted to Miranda Gold through each of the ten fingers he had curled into her raven hair.

She had been rowed across to the *Eagle* an hour before, using the excuse of a "personal matter of grave importance" to argue her way past the guards. Once in the greatcabin, she had stood at the foot of the bed and stared down at Garrett Shaw's sleeping form for several minutes, admiring the smooth, hairless splendor of his muscular chest, the trim waist, the buttocks and thighs that seemed carved out of marble.

Soundlessly she had stripped out of her blouse and skirt and crept onto the bed beside him. The game had been decided by a faint stirring at his groin, a rise of flesh that had been hardened by the softest of teasing breaths.

Miranda was not exactly certain at what stage he had come fully awake, only that he responded to her hands and lips with an awe-inspiring virility. She had not waited for an invitation to straddle the beckoning hips; she had not attempted to stifle the gasp as he thrust his heat deep inside her. A single, expert maneuver of her pelvis set her entire body to tingling, and after that, she was only concerned with easing her own inner tensions. It had been so long since she had sought pleasure for herself, since she'd had a man capable of giving it to her. Jennings's efforts had been laughable, Falworth too greedy to worry about anything but his own satisfaction.

It was her turn to be greedy now. She sighed as she felt the animal come alive within her, felt it stretch and surge to unbelievable depths. She threw her head back and let her body govern her moves, moaning and shivering deliciously as the tension mounted higher and higher. Her hands grasped his waist; her knees tightened on his thighs to guide her, grind her closer. She gasped at each searing thrust of his flesh, and she strove to heighten her ecstasy, to manipulate the growing bursts of pleasure until she had created continuous, rhythmical waves. Five minutes . . . ten minutes . . . twenty . . . she did not know how long she rode her magnificent stallion. She only knew he was worthy of her best efforts — he had shuddered twice within her but showed no sign of weakening or hastening her to an end. The dark blue eyes were open and locked on her face. His body shone from his exertions, and his hands alternately clenched and relaxed with the motion of her hips.

The waves grew in intensity, and Miranda's head lolled as if in a drugged euphoria. Her lips went slack, and her hair tumbled over her breasts like a black cloud. Garrett pushed it aside, and his thumbs teased the taut peaks, and she shivered again, deeper this time, threatened by something she could not control much longer. His torso strained upward, and his mouth tormented the pebble-hard crowns of her breasts even as his hands skimmed down, slid between her thighs, and stroked her to a sweet madness.

A series of sharp cries came rapidly as the tumult of clashing sensations jolted along the length of Miranda's body. She plunged and writhed uncontrollably, relinquishing all but the feeblest ability to retain her composure as Garrett arched and drove into her. As one they tensed, his hands frozen to her hips, hers braced against his chest as the molten ecstasy swept through her body, recoiled through his, then doubled back in a spiraling, soaring rapture.

She clung to him until a faintness began to take hold, and then she could do little more than collapse in a weak bundle on his chest. Too hot to bear the contact, she rolled free with a groan, her hair remaining like a damp black web across the lower half of her face. Her mouth felt parched, and she moistened her lips enough to keep them from cracking as her smile bubbled into a husky laugh.

"My God," she gasped. "I'd almost forgotten what that felt like! No wonder you leave a trail of wenches hobbling behind you like poled cats."

"None of them hiss and scratch half so fine as you," Shaw grinned.

"Me?" She laughed again. "Then why is it you've never invited me to stay permanently in your bed?"

"I thought you liked it where you were. And besides, I've never wanted any woman badly enough to try my sword against Duncan Farrow."

"Ahh, so it was Duncan's wrath you feared."

Garrett propped himself on an elbow and let his eyes savor the planes and valleys of the body stretched alongside him. "Let's just say I had a healthy respect for his temper. I'm a patient man. I knew it was only a matter of time before you belonged to me."

As patient as a circling vulture, Miranda thought and felt her body begin to tingle under his gaze. And just as humble. He'd made no secret of the fact that he had wanted her, almost from the moment Duncan had led her ashore on Snake Island. But then, everything that was Duncan's, Garrett coveted. His ships, his island, his men, his reputation . . . his daughter.

His daughter! The thought brought a faint flush of annoyance to Miranda's cheeks.

"Yesterday, in your cabin, I had the distinct impression it was not me you were waiting patiently for, but someone else."

"Courtney?"

"Yes, Courtney," she retorted acidly. "Poor little Courtney. Sweet little Courtney. *Brave* little Courtney. And since you left the cabin shortly after I did, may I assume it is still *virginal* little Courtney?"

The black brows crushed together and a grin appeared. "My, my, such tender concern for your lover's daughter."

"My former lover's daughter," she corrected him archly. "And I'll warn you now, Garrett Shaw, I have no intention of sharing anyone with her again."

"Meaning me?" The grin broadened.

"If you think she has something so special, by all means rape the chit and get it out of your system. But if you want to keep me" — her eyes slid lower on his body — "and I *know* you do, you'll have to have your fling and be done with her."

He laughed softly, and his hand skimmed up her thigh to lightly fondle a breast. "I'm touched that you care about my . . . system. But I not only intend to bed her, I intend to take her as my wife. Unfortunately, however, I don't believe she would settle for anything less as proof of my ardor."

"Your ar ——" Miranda's mouth sagged open. She could not believe what she was hearing. "You plan to *marry* her? After we . . . after I. . . ."

"After you honored me with such a pleasant tumble? My pet, the one act has nothing to do with the other. You want me, you can have me; whenever, wherever —"

Miranda's anger exploded with a curse as she flung his hand away from her breast. She scrambled for the edge of the bed with the intentions of gathering her clothes and storming out of the cabin. A firm hand on her arm stopped her. A rougher tousle and a curse-laden struggle landed her on her back again with Shaw's weight pinning her flat.

"Let go of me!"

"No."

She gasped in outrage. "Let go of me — *now*!"

Garrett shifted his weight and with a laugh, stifled her protests beneath his mouth. He dragged her arms above her head and held both wrists trapped in one of his hands while his other moved down her writhing body.

"You should at least hear me out before you take it upon yourself to throw your future happiness away."

"Future happiness!" she cried. "As what? Your mistress? Your alternative on nights when sweet little Courtney clamps her thighs together and pouts! No thank you, Garrett Shaw. No thank you indeed."

"Ahhh, Miranda. . . ."

"Stop that!" she shrieked and squirmed violently to dislodge the hand that was stroking determinedly between her thighs. He only laughed and pressed his mouth into the curve of her throat.

"I can give you what you need," he murmured, "what you want."

"Bastard! My only needs are to get away from this ship. To get away from this pestilent country, these stinking people, this rotten life."

"Then we both want the same thing. And you shouldn't be so quick to throw away what I'm offering."

"You haven't offered anything yet," she spat.

He kept his eyes locked to hers as he planted a large, wet kiss on the crest of each heaving breast. "Shall I start with several hundreds of thousands of dollars in gold? Or would you prefer land as far as the eye can see? Jewels? Furs?"

"What are you talking about?" she demanded. "What gold? What jewels?"

"I'm talking about a fortune, my Spanish beauty. An empire. Wealth beyond your wildest imaginings."

"Oh Lord," she sighed derisively. "You aren't believing that old story about the chests of gold and gems that were smuggled out of France with Courtney?"

"I said empire, not fairy tale. Although I wouldn't be too hasty to discount the stories entirely. There were chests taken on board with the girl, and her grandfather was the financial advisor to Louis XVI. It's possible. Very possible."

Miranda's arms were still pinned even though she had

ceased her struggling. She craned her head forward, the better to see his face.

"Garrett?"

"Mmm?"

"If it wasn't the treasure you were talking about. . . ." She laid her head back down and took a deep breath. His tongue was creating distracting shivers of pleasure where it strayed to the soft indents of flesh around her naval. "What fortune, what empire *were* you talking about?"

"The one in America."

"America?"

"Aye, my beauty. Sitting there patiently, waiting to be claimed."

"Claimed . . . How? By whom?"

"By Courtney. It's her money, now that Duncan's gone. Her inheritance, you might call it."

"Inheritance?" The amber eyes narrowed. "What inheritance? Will you stop that. I can't think straight!"

Garrett chuckled and withdrew his hand. "It was Duncan's final joke on the world — or didn't you know he was planning to turn respectable? He's been converting all of his profits from his raiding ventures into gold. He's had it shipped to America for the past ten years or so, ever since he discovered the existence of a daughter. He's bought land, built a mansion, planted cotton fields . . . why he's founded a small dynasty and all under another name. Him and his blasted codes and passwords and ciphers — he has a fortune locked up in America, and as far as I have been able to determine, Court holds the key" — he tapped the side of his head — "in here. A simple rape wouldn't put her in the mood to hand it over to me, now would it?"

"You mean she's the only one who knows?"

"Duncan's dead. Verart's dead. Who is the sole surviving member of the family?"

"What about me? Didn't he make any provisions for me?"

"Apparently not," Garrett mused, watching yellow sparks of rage flare into her eyes. "Mind, you weren't the only one to be overlooked. I was his partner and yet he was about to sell both the *Wild Goose* and the *Falconer* to Karamanli and his navy of cutthroats. This was to have been his final run through the blockades. That is why he insisted that Courtney and Verart stay behind. He wanted to be sure they were safe. Ironic, wouldn't you agree?''

"Did she know?"

"About his plans? I think not." Garrett's handsome face darkened. "He didn't even deign to tell me until we were approaching the rendezvous at Moknine. He gave me the option of buying the *Falconer* myself or selling my services to Karamanli for a full captain's share of the profits."

"Why couldn't you buy both ships? You've wanted them long enough. Surely you must have acquired enough gold over the years to afford it."

"Acquired, aye. Several small fortunes that would have kept a prudent man happy for years to come. However" — the white teeth flashed in a smile — "prudence was never one of my virtues. I enjoy life's pleasures too much to take frugality seriously. Or retirement. Duncan did both."

He swung his long legs over the side of the bed and crossed to the desk. He took a thin black cigar out of an ornately carved humidor and regarded Miranda through a brief sputter of flame and smoke. Her brow was folded in an angry frown. Her long fingers were tapping on the rumpled bedding.

"Frugal," she snorted derisively. "He tossed the odd coin my way if I was lucky. The odd paltry trinket, a dress or two. . . ."

"Ahh, yes, well" — Shaw exhaled a stream of smoke and savored Miranda's golden nudity — "that was another way in which we differed. I've always had a soft spot in my heart for a pretty wench. Jewels and gold and silk always seemed to make them all the more pretty."

He approached the bed again and extended one of his tattooed arms. The snakes writhed with the movement of his muscles as he upturned his hand and uncurled the lean, suntanned fingers. Nestled in the callused palm was a ring — a huge square-cut emerald the size of his thumbnail, surrounded by diamonds each of a size to make a separate dazzling solitaire. The fire and brilliance of the gems took Miranda's breath away, and she rose slowly to her knees, gaping first at the ring, then at Garrett's watchful face.

"It's . . . exquisite," she murmured.

"It's yours, if you want it."

"Mine?" she gasped. She reached out trembling fingers for it, but before she could touch the ring, Garrett's fist curled shut again.

"This is, regrettably, the only trinket I have in my possession at the moment and I may need it a while longer to convince Court of my sincerity."

"Sincerity?" If she could believe him he was offering her all the wealth and comfort she had ever dreamed of. If he was lying, if he was toying with her or stalling for time . . . "Why do you have to convince her of anything? Why can't you simply pull out her fingernails one at a time until she tells you what you want to know?"

Garrett lowered the cigar. "My, what a cold-hearted vixen you can be."

"Don't be childish, Garrett. And don't tell me the thought hasn't occurred to you already."

He grinned, "Aye, it's occurred to me. It's also occurred to me that I'd have as much success 'pulling' the information I need out of her as I would had I tried to pull it out of Duncan."

"So much for loyalty," she said dryly. "But then we both know how loyal you've been over the years, don't we, Garrett? And I don't just mean between the sheets."

Garrett's expression assumed a slightly ominous coolness. "Perhaps you'd care to tell me what you do mean?"

"I mean, you've been cheating him for years — taking the choicest prizes for yourself before he even knew the tally. I know you've gone on raids when he thought you'd gone for supplies, and I know you had contacts with the slave market in Algiers where you've sold the prisoners you were supposedly setting free. He knew it too. Perhaps that was why he planned to be so generous with the disposition of the *Goose* and the *Falconer*. Now, now, don't go swelling up on me with your anger. What does it matter?'' She sidled closer to the edge of the bed, close enough to slide her hands up over the iron-hard surface of his chest and lace her fingers together behind his neck. ''Duncan's dead. Everything belongs to you, regardless of how you came by it. Regardless of what you did to get it.''

The dark eyes glittered strangely. ''Are you implying it was me who sold Duncan to the Americans?''

''Did you?''

She felt a sudden tension in his body, and she saw a shadow pass briefly through his eyes. She knew Duncan had never completely trusted Garrett, and she knew enough not to trust him herself, but greed did not make traitors. Not greed alone.

''No,'' she whispered with a slow shake of her head. ''No, you wouldn't have been that foolhardy. Not if you left Davey Dunn alive. But one has to wonder about studding booms that fell so conveniently and prevented you from running to Duncan's rescue in time to save the *Goose*?''

Garrett tossed aside the cigar with a snarl and twined his fingers around the skeins of raven hair. ''The booms *did* slip. The *Falconer was* crippled.''

''And I *do* believe you,'' she said evenly, her eyes glowing. ''But there are others who might not. Courtney has been asking questions all over the ship. She may start men thinking. She may start *Dunn* thinking. Can we afford to let that happen?''

Garrett eased his grip, but his hands remained wrapped around the shiny black hair. ''I'll handle Dunn if need be.''

''And Courtney?''

His eyes moved to the supple red lips, then to the equally intoxicating lushness of warm, silky flesh that pressed invitingly against his. His mouth was brutal as it crushed to hers; his answer was as plain as the sword of flesh he used to seal their silent pact.

She had won. Courtney Farrow had lost and she had won! She would have Garrett and everything that rightfully was her due.

With a shiver, Miranda cried out her triumph, a cry that was as feral and primitive as the man she was lashed to.

# Chapter Fourteen

Tentacles of mist rose from the dense green vegetation choking the cove and shrouded the two anchored ships in fine, clinging droplets of dew. A chorus of wails and creaks and shrieks of rustling creatures surrounded the *Falconer* and the *Eagle* as the second night of darkness descended upon them.

The crews of both ships had worked continuously throughout the daylight hours, through periods of muggy heat and baking sun. They patched and mended torn sails, cut new spars from the stands of trees that lined the shore, and rebuilt the rails and planking as best they could with the supplies at hand. Shaw's original estimate of four days' work looked to be fitting into three, which pleased him immensely. With the repairs well along, he began to think it wise to restrict the use of lanterns and cabin lights. He wanted to take no unnecessary risk of having a passing ship glimpse a stray light where no light should be. By day, the masts and rigging blended in with the tall trees, but by night, the coastline was a black velvet backdrop. Even the glow from an unguarded pipe could betray their presence.

Thus, the huge brass deck lanterns were to remain cold and dark throughout the night. There were to be no signal lamps in the rigging, no cracks of light splitting through the heavy canvas curtains tacked across the portholes and ventilation shafts. Late-night revelry had to be confined to the lower decks, and the men were instructed to convert an empty cargo bay into an area for drinking, gaming, and wenching — if they still had the strength for such things.

Courtney stood on the narrow balcony that ran the width of the greatcabin. It had been built more for decoration than practicality, but the strip of walkway afforded her easy access to fresh air without a loss of privacy. It was far cooler on the gallery than inside the cabin, especially with the heavy canvas sheets draped across the windows.

Her elbows rested casually on the oak rail and her chin was propped thoughtfully in her palms as she watched the last sliver of pink light melt out of the sky. The water in the cove was three fathoms or more — twenty feet deep — darkened during the day by the weeds that spiraled up from the sandy floor. At dusk it had become a rippling sheet of silver; now it was inky black. So calm. So soothing. She wished she could remain on the gallery all night intead of having to endure what would surely be a repetition of the previous night's fiasco.

Garrett Shaw, Miranda Gold, Davey Dunn, and she had shared the evening meal together in the wardroom, and it had been a disaster.

Davey Dunn had glowered and bristled at her throughout the meal. He did not agree, it seemed, with Shaw's decision to allow her equal say in the treatment of the Yankee prisoners. She had insisted on a tarpaulin to shield the wounded from the broiling sun — Dunn thought they should stew in their own misery. She had ordered bandages and surgical instruments to be made available for the Yankee doctor's use — Dunn declared she had gone soft in the head, that they should be left to lick their wounds and shiver in discomfort. She had ordered meat broth and fresh fruit to be taken to them, and water buckets for drinking and washing — Dunn spat in the buckets and kicked over the first soup tureen in disgust. He had flatly refused the first invitation from Shaw to join the dinner group, and it had taken a direct order and a veiled threat for him to appear.

Garrett Shaw had not been his usual ribald self. He had obviously dressed with care, arriving in the wardroom looking like the pirate king he aspired to be in a dark blue brocade jacket and white nankeen breeches. His shirt had been starched and ruffed to a foppish degree, yet somehow, on the powerful shoulders, with the contrast of the mahogany tan and the jet-black mane of hair, he had looked more roguish, more sensually regal than Courtney ever remembered seeing him.

He made her own tawdry appearance seem like a deliberate snub. She had forgotten how Shaw liked to flaunt his position and his possessions by following the naval custom of dining formally in the evening. It wasn't that she had forgotten, exactly; it was more that she had not considered it practical under their circumstances. But regally he had arrived, and angrily he had taken in her shabby canvas trousers and the same plain cambric shirt she had departed the *Eagle* wearing. Even Dunn had managed a clean vest and shirt; and, she suspected, put a bar of soap to good use on his face and hands.

Her mood did not improve when Miranda swept through the doorway dressed in a cloud of silvery-yellow satin. Her long raven hair had been piled into a crown of shiny curls that caught and reflected the candlelight in soft shimmers. The gown had no bodice to speak of, and what little satin there was, was molded skintight to the curves of her breasts. The suspense was palpable as the men watched, eyes wide and unblinking, to see whether or not the fabric could maintain its fragile placement. They hung off her every word, jumping to their feet each time her wine goblet needed replenishing. And without fail, the boldly seductive amber eyes were able to draw Garrett's into an embrace and hold them well into an uncomfortable silence.

When she did speak, her carefully modulated comments only served to make Courtney's one-word answers appear to stem more from jealousy than irritation.

Jealousy!

The word jarred a memory loose, of a conversation she'd had with Garrett earlier in the day, when he'd all but defended Miranda's actions on board the *Eagle*.

"Now Court, you can't go holding that against her. She isn't like you or me. And she certainly couldn't have hoped to hide what nature so generously bestowed on her."

"She saw to her own comforts, Garrett. She didn't shed a tear or spare a thought for the fate of the others. And you didn't see her on the beach. You didn't see the way she deliberately flaunted her 'unfortunate' endowments to earn the Yankee captain's attention."

Shaw'd had the beginnings of a grin on his face. "Better the captain than a score of lustful sailors. And how do you know for certain she had no intention of helping her fellow prisoners? How do you know what she did and didn't do?"

"I know Miranda."

"Aye, you know her like a father's daughter knows his mistress. And I warrant you have more jealousy over the wench in your little finger than a dozen hungry men would be having."

"*Jealousy!*"

"Aye, jealousy." The grin had broadened and the blue eyes had raked casually over the canvas trousers and shapeless shirt. "You resented every minute she spent with your father, and you envy her every hot-blooded stare she wins from a man. And don't try to tell me otherwise, Court Farrow, or I'll bend you over my knee on the spot."

Courtney's cheeks had flamed; her anger had swelled her throat shut against the words of rebuttal. She *had* resented Miranda's every moment with Duncan Farrow, but not out of jealousy — she had fought too long to overcome the disadvantages of her own femininity to covet someone else's. What she did resent, however, was that Duncan or any other man could be blinded so easily to

Miranda's duplicity. A loose blouse, a fluttered eyelash, a slightly breathless helplessness, and normally hard, cynical men like Duncan Farrow or Garrett Shaw were unable to see that she was just as hard, just as cynical, and far more cold-blooded in her manipulations than any lusting male could be.

Miranda had wanted Duncan solely for the prestige of being his mistress. And as heartlessly as she had stalked him to ground, she was apparently going after Garrett now.

Taking a final, deep lungful of the evening air, Courtney straightened from the rail and walked back inside the dark cabin, careful to close the narrow door and fix the canvas sheet in place before she lit the desk lantern.

The unopened trunk of clothing Garrett had sent down earlier caught the glow of the candle and seemed to beckon to Courtney as slyly as the smile on a hangman's face. She had fought hard, to ignore the memories that sometimes crowded in upon her until she thought she would smother from them. Memories of a softer time, a prettier time when dresses and laces and delicate ribbons and satins were the most important things in a little girl's life. The memories belonged to Courtney de Villiers Farrow, and she had no place for them now. Yet, Garrett and Miranda, even Adrian Ballantine, were forcing her to face the pain of recollection.

Adrian Ballantine. She did not want to think about *that* night or about how he had turned her world upside down. There was no denying he had changed her. She was still changing, with every passing hour and shifting mood. Because of him she felt vulnerable where she had felt strong and secure before. Because of him she felt softer. Angry one minute, sad the next, and constantly filled with an aching tension that had no definable source, no relief.

Perhaps she should fight Miranda for Garrett. Perhaps she should not refuse his offer of protection, regardless of its price. He was handsome, he was virile; she could think of worse ways to spend a lonely night.

Garrett Shaw . . . Adrian Ballantine.

She had found pleasure in the Yankee's arms; surely she could find it with Garrett. It was only a matter of flesh and blood, of how the flesh performed, not of who did the performing . . . or was it?

She poured herself a goblet of red wine and stood before the full-length cheval mirror. There was nothing coarse or ill-bred about her face. Her lashes were long and upswept, her cheekbones delicately sculpted, her eyes almond-shaped and quite capable (she was sure) of executing a flirtation. Her nose was ordinary, but straight and unobtrusive. It led to a mouth she had always considered unremarkable but, when she looked closely, there was a definite fullness to the lips, a suppleness that became more pronounced when she moistened them with the tip of her tongue. It was the same mouth that had held the Yankee lieutenant's attention far longer than she had thought possible — or necessary. And she distinctly recalled the pleasurable sensation of his tongue probing for hers, twining and thrusting, and finally winning her surrender.

She felt her cheeks grow warmer as her eyes slipped lower, to where her breasts pushed against the fabric of her shirt. They were not nearly as full or voluptuous as Miranda's, but there, too, Ballantine's attention had lingered. He had traced and retraced the distended crowns, plundering them with hands and lips and tongue until she had drowned in a flood of blinding pleasure. And then, when his thighs had come between hers, and the heat of his body was all she knew or wanted. . . .

Courtney turned abruptly away from the mirror and drained the wine from her goblet in three deep swallows.

It was ludicrous to keep thinking of Ballantine in that way. Ludicrous and unhealthy. Garrett had humored her request to keep him alive, and he had tolerated her interference with the wounded prisoners on deck. But he was not a stupid man, nor a man without jealousies of his own. If by word or deed he became suspicious in any way of her motives for wanting Ballantine spared, or if he thought for a single moment that the Yankee had already taken what he had so steadfastly sought these past years . . . the strappado would seem a merciful death indeed.

After refilling her goblet, Courtney crouched beside the ebony and brass sea chest and hesitantly reached for the shiny metal clasp. She lifted it and raised the lid slowly, as if whatever was waiting on the inside might leap out and devour her. Nothing leaped, however. And the only devouring done was by her eyes as they widened to take in the profusion of colored silks and laces that burst from the tightly packed chest. Dresses of muslin, silk, and lawn came tumbling out in her curious hands as did layers of lace and linen underpinnings, silk chemises, richly embroidered overdresses and mysterious garments the like of which she had never seen. She found a small ivory box containing exotic perfumes and cosmetics, bolts of gleaming brocade and satin, a dozen pair of silk stockings so sheer she could see her hand through the weave.

She sat back on her heels, her hands reverently cradling a sheer white muslin dress. It looked so fragile and delicate with its tiny bodice and short-capped sleeves, so softly feminine . . . She stroked the cloth against her cheek and smiled. She buried her nose in the crushed folds and breathed deeply of the sweet sandalwood scent.

But surely there had to be more to the dress than this! She was accustomed to seeing brightly colored taffeta skirts, voluminous layers of petticoats, and rigid whalebone stays from the cargoes of captured merchantmen. There had been no single style or fashion adhered to by the women of Snake Island, no trends to follow, no social world to dictate what should or shouldn't be worn, but . . . when had petticoats and modest, bulky velvets and cottons been replaced with feather-light gauze and dainty silk overdresses? If she had felt awkward dressing like a gypsy, how would she feel dressing like an empress? How would she look?

Courtney bit down on her lower lip and found herself staring at her reflection in the mirror that was attached to the inside of the trunk lid.

*. . . you dress like a man and you cut your hair like a man . . . an undernourished, ill-bred pirate urchin . . .*

She reached for her goblet of wine and drained it hastily. The mirror continued to hold her eye, and she moved the cup away from her lips slowly, while leaning closer to the trunk to inspect her image. A hand crept up to her nape and pulled the bit of twine she had used to bind her hair into a queue. The auburn curls sprang forward immediately to join the wisps that had already escaped, and Courtney could not contain the sigh that escaped her lips. For one brief moment she wished she had a waist-long cascade of hair, thick and glossy, spread around her shoulders in all its abundant glory. Like Miranda's hair. It always managed to look immodestly disheveled, as if she had just tumbled from bed and was eager to tumble back.

Courtney raked her fingers through the tousled curls and frowned at her reflection.

*. . . nineteen? You look ten years younger . . .*

Grimly determined to somehow improve her appearance, Courtney snatched up a silver-handled brush from the trunk and began stroking it furiously through her hair. She experimented with the assortment of combs and fillets she found in the cosmetics box and in the end was able to clear most of the curls up from the nape of her neck and push them into a frothy crown on top. The results were pleasing enough, and she leaned back to admire the change, turning her head this way and that to marvel at the graceful arch of her throat and the tiny, perfect lobes of her ears.

"Ill-bred and undernourished, indeed," she muttered and reached for the wine decanter.

Duly fortified for the next step, she sorted through the shimmery soft assortment of undergarments — or what she supposed were undergarments. Drawers, she knew, and a strange little contraption like a belt with long tapers that she suspected was used to hold up the silk stockings. She held up a long, sheer breath of ecru silk that had two thin shoulder straps of cream-colored ribbons and, after a fruitless search for anything resembling a corset or corset-cover, realized the shimmy was all that would be between the dress and her skin.

The dress itself was pure white muslin, with a high waistline and an alarmingly low neckline. In fact, there was no more than two or three inches of fabric rising above the green satin ribbon that divided the skirt from the bodice. Even worse, she discovered when she had donned the garments, the bodice was cut in such a way as to give support beneath her breasts, while at the same time mold them into an embarrassing plumpness. She wriggled and tugged at the muslin but there was simply no way to raise it to cover more of the exposed flesh.

Her lower lip was savaged again before she dared step in front of the cheval mirror to judge the finished product. Her first reaction was to gasp and raise her hands to cover her cleavage. Her second was to lower her hands slowly, to lift her eyes from the stunning neckline and meet the bold emerald sparkle staring back at her. There was a soft pink blush to the sun-kissed complexion, and an uncertain, trembling smile beginning to take shape.

It was the face in the locket. The face of a beautiful young woman. And she was not thin or gawky or boyish-looking; she was slender and fine-boned and perfectly suited to the cut and style of the gown. A slight adjustment — she reset the puff of the cap sleeves to cover the wound on her upper arm — and the creamy smoothness of her shoulders was bared even more; the bodice was made that much snugger; her breasts were made that much more prominent — not in a vulgar or brazen way, but in a way that made her lift her head higher and lend her smile the confident air befitting a true French aristocrat.

For the first time, she did not attempt to stifle the outpouring of memories — of fancy glittering ballrooms, of tall white wigs and sweeping brocaded gowns. Strains of a long-forgotten minuet echoed distantly in her mind, and she closed her eyes, the better to see the swirling, dizzying couples that bowed and pranced to the music. She was somewhere above them, staring through the railing of a balcony, her child's eyes wide and bedazzled by the rainbows of colors, the sparkle of a thousand candles reflected in the prisms of the crystal chandeliers. She could hear the tinkle of laughter and of champagne glasses. She could see her mother, so beautiful, so elegant, surrounded by a sea of handsome, smiling faces — looking up, searching out the large emerald eyes that stared at her so hungrily, smiling, touching pale white fingers to her lips in a secret, loving gesture. One day, she seemed to be saying. One day you will know all of this too.

Courtney opened her eyes, awakened to the present by the sound of a footstep. Her gaze flicked to the upper corner of the mirror, to the face that had appeared over her shoulder, to the pair of smoky-gray eyes that were locked on hers with equal astonishment.

She whirled around and came face to face with Adrian Ballantine. Neither of them moved, neither spoke. Only his eyes conveyed the depth of his shock as they took in the full sweep of her dress, her hair, the straining half-moons of flesh that swelled against the bodice.

"Wh-what are you doing here?" she finally managed to gasp. "How did you get past the guards?"

"I didn't," he said softly. "I was escorted here at the end of a musket."

Courtney glanced past his broad shoulder and noticed the ship's purser, Harry Pitt, standing in the open doorway. He was a short, balding man with skin like parchment and a smile that brought to mind a bleached skull. His eyes were popped almost out of their folds of crow's feet as he raked them up and down, taking in Courtney's altered appearance. With the candlelight glowing beside her, the white of her dress blurred like mist, one that clung provocatively to her curves and gave a shadowy hint of the slimness of her waist. Her hair trapped the golden light; the wisps at her cheeks and throat created a soft aura of firelight around her face.

Both men stared, and she fought an urge to shield herself from their gazes.

"Why have you brought the prisoner here?" she asked hotly.

"Ahr? Ye orther'd it, din't ye?"

"I certainly did not."

Pitt's eyes strayed to the dusky cleft between her breasts. "Well, I were told ye wanted to 'ave this 'ere dog brung to the cabin to see arfter yer chores. If ye've nay chores, I'll heigh 'im back to the kennel wi' the others."

Courtney glanced at Ballantine. Her instincts told her to send him away. She had deliberately *not* called for him all day, specifically to prevent the reappearance of the confused emotions that were already beginning to affect the way the blood flowed through her veins. But if he was a weakness, and if he was going to continue to exert this strange power over her, she had to know. She had to somehow overcome it. She had to overcome *him*.

"Thank you, Mister Pitt," she said coolly. "In truth, I do have need of the Yankee's skill with a holystone and bucket. You can leave him here."

"Yer want I should stay an' see 'e does 'is work proper?"

Courtney crossed to the desk and withdrew a long-snouted pistol from the top drawer.

"I think I'm quite capable of seeing he does the job well. You can go on about your business and return for him near the dinner hour."

"Dinner . . . aye."

"Oh, and Mister Pitt?"

The rheumy eyes flicked up from her bosom. "Aye?"

She cocked the pistol and aimed it casually in his direction. "In the future, you will knock on my door before you enter."

The implied threat was delivered so calmly, Pitt's cadaverous smile took a moment to fade. He looked down the barrel of the gun, then up into her dark, unscrutable stare, and he backed toward the door. "No call to take on airs," he muttered. "Yer father'd nay approve."

"My father isn't here, which is precisely why the gun is. You might want to pass the information on."

Pitt scowled and muttered something unintelligible before he hunched out into the gloomy companionway.

Courtney strode to the door in a swirl of white muslin, and after a moment of angry contemplation, she slammed it shut and slid the bolt across.

Ballantine had not moved. His eyes had followed her across the cabin, but as soon as she turned to face him, they were studiously averted.

"Having trouble with your own men?" he mused.

"Nothing I cannot handle."

The impression of a smile was on his lips, although his expression had not changed. Courtney's pride was pricked, and she raised the heavy gun and aimed it at the center of his chest.

"I'm not afraid to use this gun, Yankee. Don't tempt me."

The gray eyes met hers; the smile became distinctly mocking.

"I happen to be a very good shot."

"I don't doubt it."

"But am I going to have to prove it? If I am, if you're planning to try anything foolish, I'd as soon shoot you now and be done with it."

"What on earth could I be planning? You have the gun. You also have the ability to bring a dozen armed men crashing through the door if you scream. And, even assuming I could get my hands around your lovely throat, where could I go afterwards?"

The bland arrogance in his voice angered her. She was unable to form a retort, and so she simply stared at him, the gun steady and unwavering in her hand. His wounds were obviously mending well. He had replaced his torn shirt with another: a coarse homespun that exaggerated the bands of muscle in his arms and across his chest. The bandage around his temple was still remarkably white, though only partially visible beneath the unfettered locks of tawny gold hair. The long hours of exposure to the sun had not done him any harm either; his complexion had darkened to a rugged mahogany, which only emphasized the wolfish gleam of the teeth. His eyes were as cool and insolent as when he had been the one in command. She could almost see a glint of amusement in them — amusement at a pirate wench who was playing at being a lady!

She took a deep breath in an effort to cool her blood, and instantly regretted it. The bodice of her dress did not expand with her chest; it merely thrust her breasts into greater prominence, an effect that did not go unnoticed by Ballantine.

"Move over beside the brazier," she ordered brusquely, jerking the snout of the pistol to indicate the direction. "The air is becoming damp. You can light a fire while I finish dressing for dinner."

His smile took on a wry twist. "I certainly hope there is more to that dress somewhere."

"The brazier," she said from between clenched teeth.

When Ballantine reached the small iron stove in the corner of the cabin, he bent down on one knee and rattled coal from a tin bucket into the stove's black belly.

Courtney's wrist ached from the weight of the gun; she lowered it, careful to keep her finger in proximity to the trigger. Her mouth was terribly dry, her palms were cool and moist, and she could not keep from staring at the sinuous muscles rippling across his back and shoulders as he built a fire in the stove. How was it possible for him to look so healthy and roguish after two days in the hell she had banished him to on deck? He was with his men, yes, and his precious doctor friend, but most of the wounded had succumbed to fevers and dysentery, and that in combination with the stifling heat, the flies, the smell, and the suffering . . . he should at least have had the decency to look pale and haggard.

Ballantine straightened, startling Courtney alert again.

"Anything else, Miss Farrow?" he inquired with an air of servitude.

A faint wash of color rose in her cheeks. "You may refill my wine goblet," she commanded, pointing to the decanter and the cup. "And you may stop staring at me."

"Was I staring? Forgive me, it must be that the heat on

deck has affected my manners. But then, any woman who chooses to wear a gown like that should expect the odd glance to come her way."

"You were hardly glancing."

"You are hardly what I expected to see," he countered evenly.

"An ill-bred pirate urchin?"

He grinned again. "Did I call you that?"

"On several occasions."

His eyes traveled soberly down her body. "In that case, I'd have to say you are *very* good at disguises."

Courtney's flush deepened. Why was he doing this? Where was his bitterness, his defiance? She could respond to those emotions — easily. What she could not handle was compliance, or worse: flattery.

She moved away from the door and went behind the enormous desk. Placing the gun pointedly within reach, she sat in the deeply padded leather wing chair and tapped her fingers impatiently on the arm.

"My wine?"

Adrian had to step around the piles of discarded clothing that had been tossed from the sea chest. He picked up the decanter and filled her goblet to the brim with blood-red claret.

"Set it on the desk," she snapped. "Then you can . . . you can put all those things back into the trunk."

Adrian placed the goblet on the desk and glanced at the jumble of frilly trappings scattered at his feet. With undisguised bemusement, he held up a sheer wisp of silk that was much like the garment she wore beneath the muslin dress. Horrified, Courtney jumped up and snatched it out of his hands.

"Never mind the trunk. I'll do it myself."

"I'd be only too pleased —"

"I said, never mind!"

He shrugged and watched her drop back in the chair. She raised the goblet and sipped from it, but the dryness in her throat persisted and she ended up draining the cup. She set it down with a slightly unsteady hand and glared up at Ballantine as she saw his mouth flicker again.

"That's pretty strong wine if you're not accustomed to it," he said when she demanded he refill her goblet.

"You are hardly the one to give me advice on drinking. And who is to say I'm not accustomed to it?"

"Who indeed?" he murmured and eyed the tray of silver goblets. "Still, a young lady should never drink alone."

Courtney gaped at his audacity as he poured himself a goblet of wine before he refilled hers. Her fingers danced on the stock of the pistol and her eyes blazed.

"Have you ever wondered, Yankee, what would have happened had we both been fighting on the same side? Suppose my father had been fighting *against* the Pasha, instead of for him, and suppose we had met as allies. Would you be quite so unwilling to take me seriously?"

"I take you very seriously, Irish."

"No." She shook her head. "No, you don't, Yankee. You only treat me seriously when you think you have something to gain by it. On board your ship, for instance, when you knew I was the only thing standing between Seagram and eternity. Or yesterday, when you thought you could play on my sympathies. It was a convincing fainting spell. You deserved applause."

A spark of anger flared in his eyes, and she felt a rush of satisfaction.

"Perhaps you were even thinking I would help you escape? Is that it, Yankee? Did you honestly think one night in your bed, one drunken *rape* would leave me so besotted?"

Ballantine's voice was level. "I don't suppose you will believe me if I say I regret what happened that night as much as you do. Or that it has nothing to do with how I feel about you."

She regarded him slyly over the rim of her uptilted goblet. "How *do* you feel about me, Yankee? I know you enjoyed my body, even though you say you don't remember. Or perhaps you enjoyed it too much. Doesn't your *Deborah* please you the same way?''

A muscle clenched in Adrian's jaw. "My fianceé has nothing to do with this."

"No? Does that mean you won't be telling her about me? About how you tumbled from your lofty pillar of virtue? What was it you said?'' She pursed her lips thoughtfully, ignoring the hard light in his eyes. "Ahhh, yes. I believe you said it would take an enticement from the devil himself to make you dishonor your commitment to your sweet Deborah. Is that the excuse you will give her? That you were *enticed* by the devil?''

"Demon rum, most certainly," said Adrian, cuttingly blunt. "And I don't recall ever mentioning Deborah's name to you."

The wine was singing in her blood, bolstering her courage; she leaned back in the chair with a husky laugh. "You also claim not to recall tearing my clothes off, or forcing me into your bed. Or will your story be that *I* raped *you*?''

Adrian felt the blood hammering in his temples. His gaze was lured involuntarily to the unseating of muslin as she stretched her arm forward for the decanter. More than a hint of roseate flesh peeped into view and remained there, though she was blissfully unaware of the slippage. The memory of that soft, warm flesh had left an impression in his mind's eye that no amount of rum could have dulled. He remembered the feel of them, supple and honey-smooth one moment, straining eagerly beneath his lips the next . . . despite what she accused him of. *Despite what she wanted him to believe!*

He forced himself to concentrate on her hands, on watching her pour out the wine. God, how long did it take to fill two goblets?

Courtney leaned back, carrying her brimming goblet with her. "Go ahead, Yankee, drink up . . . unless you have reason to fear for your honor again?''

In an attempt to curb his anger, Adrian reached for the

wine and raised it to his lips. Courtney did likewise, and their eyes locked together over the silver rims.

Why, it isn't so difficult to find his temper and prod it, she mused. Prod it enough and he'll make mistakes just like any other mortal human. He's no threat to me; he has no mysterious powers. If anyone feels threatened, it's him — and how sweet a victory it would be to have him acknowledge that threat!

"A second stumble from the mighty pedestal of virtue," she murmured speculatively. "Now that would be difficult to explain, wouldn't it, Yankee? Even the *urge* to stumble would be extremely discomfitting to a man of your stolid convictions."

Adrian tensed visibly as she stood up and walked slowly around to the front of the desk. She stopped within an arm's length of him and let her gaze rake insolently up and down his rigid body. Much as he wanted to, he could not take his eyes off her face; he could not stop his senses from responding to the sharp clean fragrance of her skin. Soap and hot water seemed like sinful pleasures from some distant life to him, and her apparent recent enjoyment of both sent shivers racing through his flesh.

More than that, there was something new and disturbing in her eyes. Adrian wished he could scratch viciously at the wound on his temple — the pain would help clear his thinking and sharpen his wits. Her eyes were playing with his body, teasing him, swallowing him into a bright green whirlpool and throwing his instincts off balance; they could no longer be trusted.

*Take your opportunity now*, they told him. *Strike out! Lash out! Don't fall into any of her traps again. Think of home, think of Deborah, think of Seawolf . . . think of anything!*

Courtney set the goblet on the desk and stood completely still, lured onto more dangerous ground by the disdain she sensed in him. Her skin prickled from the heat of his eyes staring down at her, her heart pounded within her breast, and she knew he was daring her, challenging her . . . mocking her.

She raised her hands and laid them with deliberate tenderness on his chest. The shock of contact sent a chill along her spine, and she held her breath, wondering if she was imagining the fleeting tremors beneath her fingers. The thong joining the front edges of his shirt was loose enough to make parting the homespun an easy matter. She spread her fingers through the thick, coppery mat of hair, tracing them over the hard-surfaced flesh, over the bands of solid muscle that were almost hot to the touch. Her fingertips found his nipples; hard and waiting they belied the forced complacency in the granite jaw.

Her explorations ventured upward toward the strong pillar of his neck, her fingers lingering on the carved hollow at the top of his breastbone before they followed the curve of the brawny shoulders. Her eyes climbed to the sculpted set of his stubbled jaw, and her heart skipped erratically over several beats. His mouth had tightened to a grim line. A nerve leaped convulsively in his cheek, drawing her eyes higher . . . and even if his hands had not chosen that moment to bite into her shoulders, she would have gasped aloud at the naked fury blazing from his eyes. Like shards of light glittering off the blade of a sword, they slashed into her, pierced her, impaled her so that she could not have moved even if her limbs had the ability or the will to do so.

Before she could draw a breath, her wrists had been captured, twisted down behind her back, and she was being crushed ruthlessly against the wall of his chest.

"Is this what you want?" he snarled, and his head bent toward her. Courtney twisted back and away but he was not deterred. His mouth plundered the slender curve of her throat, searing her flesh. Courtney's senses reeled under the assault, and it was with the greatest difficulty that she was able to wriggle an arm free, to swing it hard and catch the arrogant jaw with a resounding slap, seconds before his mouth claimed possession of hers. He barely hesitated long enough to hiss a curse against her lips before he trapped both wrists at the small of her back again and angled them at such a painfully cruel slant, she gaped up at him in shock.

Her mouth trembled open. Her eyes widened, grew darker, then shimmered suddenly behind a veil of tears. Adrian stared at her. He watched her eyes brim and the tears etch a glistening path down each cheek. He was still pinning her close against his body and he could feel her breasts heaving against his chest, he could feel the quaking in her arms and legs; as much as he tried desperately not to yield to it, he could feel the burning response in his own body, too powerful to deny.

The anger drained from his expression as quickly as it had risen, and he cursed again, softly this time. Who was this woman, this half-child? How was it she could rouse him to a killing temper one minute, then touch a flame to his desires the next?

His hands slid up her arms to cradle her neck. His thumbs brushed across her cheeks to staunch the diamond-like sparkle of tears she had vowed never to show him again. He bowed his mouth to the shiny rivulets, then moved lower, smothering the gasp that tried ineffectually to halt him, then claimed and held the stunned, quivering lips beneath his.

Courtney's despairing sob was lost to a low moan. She pressed her body deeper into his, furrowing into his embrace, pressing her breasts against the exposed fur of his chest to wage a war — softness against hardness, passion against pride. She felt the tension in his body, the power in his arms as they tightened around her. Her fingers clawed into the flexing muscles of his shoulders, her lips parted beneath his and her tongue met his in a wild dance of thrust and counterthrust. The coarse rasp of his unshaven chin scored her flesh, causing shudders to quake throughout her body. There was violence drumming in his chest, violence that she could feel and taste, and it sent her emotions whirling and clashing within her.

Adrian's fingers raked into her hair, dislodging the combs and scattering them across the floor. He forced her head back, arching her neck at a painful angle while his mouth blazed a scorching trail of caresses down along the curve of her throat. Her bodice, barely clinging to her breasts, forfeited its hold and released the dusky pink nipples to greedy fingers and a demanding mouth. His tongue flicked repeatedly over and around the painfully swollen crowns; his lips skirted the creamy white softness and returned again and again to the straining peaks, swirling and suckling until there were fresh tears streaking into her temples. Courtney's knees buckled, but he did not attempt to support her or to stop her from slipping to the floor. Instead, he knelt down beside her, his mouth still fastened hungrily to her flesh, still feasting on the ripe bounty like a man possessed.

Her ragged cries sent his hands on a fiery mission and in a few brief strokes, the muslin gown, the silk shimmy, the stockings and drawers were tossed into the shadows like wind-blown clouds. The rough growth of stubble drifted lower, on the smooth plain of her belly. She was dizzyingly aware of the hot, swirling patterns his tongue was leaving in its wake, and she writhed in breathless anticipation as she felt the searching, stroking fingers between her thighs. The combined assault flooded her senses with a physical yearning so intense, so mindlessly urgent it frightened her.

Adrian felt it; he spread her limbs, bracing her as his lips descended inch by aggressive inch. Courtney gasped as she realized where his course would eventually take him, and she tried to twist away, to bar his passage. But Adrian's hands were firm on her thighs, and the first shocking incursion of his tongue was met with a groan — one that came from somewhere beyond her darkest fantasies. She began to thrash as the warm, wet insistence probed and plundered unmercifully. The waves of pleasure came hotter and faster; became searing jolts of ecstasy that stole the breath from her lungs and all thought of modesty from her mind. Her lips fell slack and her eyes turned luminous. Her brow dampened and her nails scored the bronzed shoulders with dozens of tiny scratches.

Adrian's mouth lifted from her body, and her harsh

groan of disappointment sent him kneeling above her. His chest was shiny with sweat, his muscles corded sensuously as his hands skimmed up to the satiny smoothness of her breasts, then down again, to the soft thatch at the junction of her thighs. The dark green eyes locked on his, and her lower lip curled between her teeth. She could feel his anger and his passion; she could see the agony of desire that burned in his eyes. Her hands clenched into fists and rode lightly on his shoulders, her fingers flexed spasmodically as she acknowledged his skillful manipulations. Cries trembled into her throat, and she knew she had to choke them back . . . but how . . . how?

Through a blur of numbing pleasure she saw him pause to strip away his clothes. She saw her own hands tearing frantically at the barriers that kept them apart, and when he rose above her again, she stared at his body: a gleaming statue in the candlelight, magnificently bold in its readiness.

She closed her eyes as the forest of coppery hairs brushed against her breasts, setting her body on fire, sending her mouth on a desperate search for his.

"No," he hissed, and his hands were twining in her hair again, forcing her head back, forcing her eyes to meet his. "Not until I hear you say it."

"S-say it?" she gasped, bewildered. "I don't underst —"

His fists tightened, cutting the protest short. "I didn't rape you that night, did I? You took what I had to offer as selfishly, as *willingly* as I took what I needed from you. I want to hear you say it, Irish. Say you wanted me then and you want me now."

"N-no. No. . . ."

"Yes," he whispered savagely, and his body thrust into hers without warning, the fierce joy of it driving her arms up and around his broad shoulders. His mouth descended to attack her pride, his tongue ravishing her, demanding more than she imagined it was possible to give. And below, the stretching, thrusting power of him drove deeper, faster; his passion grew and spread and stroked into her with a determined ferocity. There was no way to deny the hunger in his body, or the helpless, shameless way she welcomed each violent surge of pleasure.

"Say it," he commanded on a gasp. His hands plunged beneath her buttocks, yet they delayed in lifting her against him, delayed until the ache within her was whipped to a feverish crescendo.

"Yes," she cried softly. "Yes . . . oh, yes, I . . . I wanted you. I . . . *want* you!"

Their mouths locked together; his hands guided her as the frenzied motion of their bodies peaked and crested and soared simultaneously into a raging eruption of ecstasy. Courtney twined her long legs around him, crying out as he filled her. Not a single nerve ending escaped the wildfire of sweeping passion. She was totally inundated, hopelessly shattered and fragmented by the awesome reality that it was not merely flesh and blood she was responding to, but the man himself.

They collapsed in a breathless tumble of arms and legs, their skin slippery with each other's sweat, their pulses racing, their bodies still clenched and clinging as if neither wanted to be the first to let go. Courtney felt as if they must have become fused together in the heat of their consummation. She held him tightly; she ran her hands along the sleek muscles of his back, savoring the languid motion of his body as he coaxed the last of the minutest shivers free. Her heart swelled with pride, knowing she had given as she had received, knowing Adrian was as reluctant to leave the soft haven as she was to release him.

Adrian pressed a final, tender kiss into the damp nest of curls below her ear and gently levered himself free. He rolled beside her and without a word, gathered her determinedly close in his arms. She went willingly — a fact which only served to make his expression bleaker.

It was incredible to him that he had done this. His men were suffering, dying in the worst misery imaginable; they were facing an uncertain future of chains and slavery. He should have followed his first impulse and wrapped his hands around the slender throat — to squeeze it, not caress it. He should have wrested the gun from her and used it the way Seagram had used a match and powder keg to bargain for freedom. But he had done neither. Instead of fighting her, he had capitulated to the one mouth, the one body that defied him to go against his sense of duty, of honor — against all obligations to home, to family, to country. Instead of bargaining for his men, he had forced a wild, untamable creature into making an admission that made him ache inside.

And the rewards for such a victory? None but a few moments of splendid oblivion. What had he changed by having her admit she wanted him? What had he accomplished by surrendering to her surrender? Nothing. Nothing the cold voice of reason could not erase in a moment.

Courtney's head rested in the curve of his shoulder, her hand resting on his chest as if it had always belonged there. She could hear his heart thundering within the chamber of muscle and sinew; she could almost hear his mind churning with thoughts that surely had to be an echo of her own. She was alternately cold, then very warm. She blushed furiously one moment, blanched the next; felt a need to speak volumes at one turn of thought, fell helplessly shy of courage the next. What could she say? That she felt like a woman for the first time in her life? That she *wanted* to feel like a woman, with a woman's weaknesses, a woman's need to depend on the strength and mastery of a man?

How could she, when she knew what he was thinking. What he *must* be thinking of a woman who had enticed him into an act which he had tried desperately to avoid. Whores did that. Women like Miranda Gold did that to men like Duncan Farrow and did not think twice of their perfidy. Yet, despite the animal passion he released in her, Courtney did not feel like a whore. She felt warm and soft in Ballantine's arms. Comfortable in her vulnerability. *Safe.*

She pushed herself slowly up out of his arms, staring

around the cabin in absolute horror. Muslin and silk, breeches, stockings, combs and pins were scattered across the floor as if a storm had blown through the cabin.

With a shiver of panic, she snatched up the silk shimmy and clutched it over her nakedness while she collected the rest of her clothes. Suddenly foolish and frivolous, the clothes seemed to be mocking her even more than the cool gray eyes that followed her every move.

"You'd best get dressed, Yankee," she murmured, keeping her face averted. "The guard will be returning at any moment."

"Courtney. . . ."

"Did you hear what I said, Yankee?" She whirled on him angrily. "Do you have any idea what would happen — to both of us — if we were found like this?"

Adrian reached out a hand to her, but she jumped up and began shoving the gown and underpinnings into the trunk with careless haste. She grew increasingly impatient at Ballantine's slower, less frantic dressing, and was overcome with resentment when he stopped and frowned at the canvas trousers and cotton shirt she retrieved from the chest.

"He's probably spread the word throughout the ship that you were dressed for dinner," Adrian said quietly.

"What?"

"The guard," he reminded her. "He was nearly as shocked as I was when he saw you. Shaw is no doubt expecting a refined beauty to dine with him this evening."

"A pox on what he expects," she declared with false bravado.

"Nevertheless, if he's the kind of man I think he is" — Adrian stood and finished fastening his breeches — "you'll only be giving him reason to speculate on what changed your mind."

Courtney glanced at the locked door, and her skin paled noticeably. She looked back at the open trunk, at the brimming hillock of silk and muslin. A single tear spiked on her lashes as she raised huge, hauntingly dark eyes to Ballantine.

"I can't," she whispered.

"Of course you can," he said gently, and had to fight the urge to take her in his arms again. His voice toughened and he bent over the trunk. "I'll even help you, although I'm damned if I know why I should. If I wasn't able to keep my hands off you, neither will he be."

Courtney looked up, startled, but Adrian steadfastly ignored the fear in her eyes as he lifted her arms and dropped the silken shimmy over her head. It barely covered the pink crowns of her breasts, while molding to their shape and fullness like water flowing over smooth stones.

The slippery cloth seemed to fall like a curtain over his past perceptions of her. Dear God, how could he ever have thought of her as plain or ungainly? Her skin gleamed like rich cream in the candlelight; her hair shone with threads of gold, her eyes glowed in a face that seemed to become more radiant with each passing moment. And her body — legs that were long and lithe, a waist narrow enough to span with two hands, and breasts that filled his hands and tempted his mouth with their sweetness. What man would not find her irresistible? She wouldn't stand a chance with Shaw.

"Courtney —"

"That's the second time you've called me that," she interrupted, her voice sharp and brittle.

"It's your name, isn't it?"

"Yes, but I don't think you should be using it so freely."

He sighed. "We've just spent the better part of an hour doing things usually reserved for people who are on a first-name basis. How much freer does it have to be?"

"I —" Her strength failed her and she lowered her chin in dismay. "I just don't think —" Her voice faltered and she tried again. "What happened was wrong. You know that yourself: It was wrong."

"Right or wrong, it happened."

"But . . . it doesn't change anything. It can't possibly change anything."

Adrian took a deep breath before he tucked a finger beneath her chin and tilted her face up to his.

"No," he whispered. "It doesn't change anything. But maybe it makes whatever will happen over the next few days a little easier to bear."

A bit of color dawned in her cheeks, and she looked into his eyes without commenting, without moving. Adrian broke the silence as he had created it. He smiled gently and brushed the back of his fingers against her cheek. "Now finish getting dressed while I pick up the rest of these things. And be sure you put this where it belongs."

"This" was a length of frothy, delicate lace that he had plucked up from a pile of linens on the floor.

"What is it?" she asked, mystified.

"I believe they call it a tucking piece, my charming innocent. It goes . . . there" — his eyes dipped to the swell of her bosom — "to keep certain things safely in place."

Courtney blushed furiously and turned abruptly to the mirror. The tucking piece did indeed make a difference. She did not feel quite so naked, or quite so apt to fall out of the muslin bodice if she leaned forward. When she was fully dressed she took the brush to her hair again and attempted to repeat her earlier efforts with the combs and fillets. Once again, her hands faltered, and she leaned toward the reflection, her fingertips lightly tracing the shape of her mouth.

"It looks kissed," Adrian murmured from behind her. "Unfortunately, I haven't been able to shave for the past two days."

Courtney's gaze lingered on the pink-chafed skin of her cheeks and throat. After a further thought, she searched through the trunk and found the small ivory cosmetics box. A light covering of white dusting powder took away the angry red, and she snapped the lid of the box closed and faced Ballantine again.

"Better," he agreed, then frowned. "But there still seems to be something missing."

"My locket," she gasped, and a hand fluttered to her bare throat. A moment later and she had found it, as well as a length of green ribbon to replace the worn leather thong. She started to tie it in place around her neck, but Adrian's fingers assumed the task, his eyes fastened to hers in the mirror.

The knot tied, he could not resist laying his hands on the smooth, bare shoulders. Nor could he resist bending forward and pressing a kiss to the nape of her neck. He felt her tremble and saw the flush darken in her cheeks as her eyes closed with the pleasurable sensation.

"You'd better unbolt the door before your friend comes back," he murmured. "He looks like the type who would kick it in rather than trouble himself to knock."

She did as she was told, and none too soon. She was barely away from the door when they heard bootsteps in the outer corridor, followed by a coarse belch and a thump that could have been interpreted as a knock. The door was shoved open.

"Well, lass?" Harry Pitt belched a greeting and picked a morsel of food from between his teeth. " 'E do all yer chores wi' no squawkin'?"

"Well enough," she said coolly. "Is the captain at dinner?"

"Aye. Waitin' on ye. I tol' 'im 'e had a right-fine surprise in store. Right fine." The squinty, watery eyes slid up and down the muslin dress, and Courtney was silently grateful to Ballantine for insisting she wear it.

"You can take the prisoner back to the others now," she said.

"Will ye be wantin' 'im tomorry again?"

Pitt's choice of phrases sent a flood of warmth into her

cheeks, and she compounded her discomfort by glancing at Adrian. He had also read a double meaning into the words, and a gleam danced in the smoky eyes.

"I'll send for him if I do," she stammered and, with as much dignity as she could muster, she swept out of the cabin and hurried along the companionway toward the captain's wardroom.

# Chapter Fifteen

Courtney halted on the dimly lit threshold and paused to give her heartbeat a chance to return to normal. Her legs felt weak and loose in the joints, her stomach was churning, her cheeks and throat were burning like hot embers, and she was certain the thudding within her breasts would be heard throughout the cabin. Thankfully the wardroom was no less gloomy than the companionway. A single four-pronged candlestick was flickering on the dining table, the flames casting a dull glow on the rich white linen cloth and solid gold dinner service.

Garrett Shaw stood at the far side of the room. He was pouring wine into a crystal glass, one of four that matched the tall cut-glass decanter he had appropriated from an English merchantman. He seemed preoccupied — angry, almost — as he poured the wine, and he looked even more elegant than he had the previous evening. He was wearing a black cutaway coat, black breeches, and a striped maroon and white brocade waistcoat. His linen neckcloth was tied and bowed high under the stern jaw; his hair was shiny and fell in thick, shaggy waves over his collar. He looked as if he should be headed for a night at the opera, not dinner on the lower deck of a pirate ship.

"Good evening, Garrett," she said softly. "I hope I haven't kept you waiting long."

"Another ten minutes," he retorted angrily, "And I'd've —"

Courtney held her breath. The blue-black eyes had found her in the shadows and had taken an extra blink to scatter whatever troublesome thoughts had put a frown on his face. The crystal glass had halted mid-way to his lips, and his entire body, it seemed, had turned to stone. Courtney recognized the same look of astonishment in his eyes as had been in Adrian Ballantine's, and she experienced a fleeting, fervent wish that she had never ventured near the sea chest.

"I see I am not the only late arrival," she said coolly, glancing around the empty room. "But then one can always rely on Miranda to make a grand entrance." She stared directly into Garrett's eyes and smiled. "Aren't you going to offer me some wine?"

Shaw averted his eyes grudgingly, for as long as it took to splash some wine into another goblet. When he looked up again she was no longer standing in the doorway, but had moved nearer to the table. The fingers of light from the candles beckoned his gaze to the creamy curve of her neck, along her bared shoulders, over the gentle, soft swell of her breasts.

He slowly crossed the room, his mind still unable to fully take in what his eyes were showing him. Without a word, he extended a hand and cradled her cool fingers within his palm. A shiver skittered icily along Courtney's spine as he raised her hand to his lips and pressed a warm kiss against her skin.

"By God, Court Farrow, you've your father's gift for surprises. And damn my eyes if I've ever seen such a rare, fine beauty as yours."

Courtney flushed painfully beneath his penetrating stare and hastily reclaimed her hand. "All this fuss. Surely you've seen me in skirts before, Garrett."

"A baggy scruff of cotton ten times the size of you and shapeless enough to hide twenty." He grinned, "Aye, I've seen you in skirts before . . . out of them as well. It doesn't change what I'm seeing now."

She had the distinct impression the blue eyes were melting slowly but surely through the flimsy layers of muslin and silk and she cast a furtive glance downward in alarm. The expanse of flesh did little to reassure her. She took a tiny sip of wine to mask her discomfort but then remembered what effect the spirits had had on her earlier. Her flush deepened.

"Garrett, if you don't stop looking at me like that, I'm not going to have any clothes left on at all."

"Now there's a pleasant thought," he murmured and moved closer.

Courtney deftly sidestepped the advance and presented her back to him as she crossed to the opposite end of the table.

"I understand the repairs to both ships are progressing well."

"Aye. It is my fondest hope to be away from this accursed cove before the sun climbs high tomorrow."

"Tomorrow? But I thought you anticipated at least four or five days."

"Aye, I did. And I'd take as many if I could, but within a fortnight the approaches to Tripoli will be alive with Yankee gunboats."

"How do you know that?"

Shaw grinned easily. "The Yankee captain was quite talkative when he had a hot iron kissing his private parts."

She looked at Shaw with some surprise. "I thought you said you weren't going to touch Jennings."

He shrugged and toyed with the cuff of his frockcoat. "The men needed some diversion; I needed some information. I was hoping he knew something more about the trap at Moknine, but considering how eager he was to answer all my questions, I'd say he knew nothing about how the Yankees came by their information.''

"Was?" she said quietly. "You mean he's dead?"

Shaw shrugged again. "No stamina. No loss either, I warrant. And what of it? Are you telling me you had a soft spot in your heart for him as well?"

Courtney's temper was pricked by the sarcasm, but she refused to take the bait. Shaw refused to drop it so easily.

"Davey tells me you've been plaguing him for two days now, demanding this and that for your pet Yankees."

"They're wounded. It's inhuman to stand by and watch them suffer unnecessarily. They fought hard and they fought well — isn't their defeat enough degradation to force on them?"

"To my mind it isn't nearly enough."

"You'd like to torture them all, I suppose."

"One or two of them," he agreed, smiling. "At any rate, you've got Davey Dunn in enough of a rage to string the lot of them up by their toenails. I'd keep my notions of charity work to myself if I were you, or you might find yourself chained into one of Dunn's work gangs."

"*That's* another sore point," she argued. "He won't let me do anything on deck. He won't let me help with the repairs, he won't let me help with the stores belowdeck, and he flatly refuses to let me go over to the *Eagle*."

"Because there's nothing for you to do topside. Or below. Or on the *Eagle*. You've been a prisoner on board that blasted ship for over a week, and before that you fought in a hellish battle — you bear the wounds to prove it! Davey's only following my orders by refusing you. You deserve a rest."

"We *all* deserve a rest but, until we can all afford to take one, I see no reason why I should get any special treatment."

"You're the O'Farrow's daughter. There's reason enough."

"Dammit!" she exploded angrily. "If I hear that excuse

once more, I'll scream! I'm Duncan's daughter, yes. If anything, it means I should be proving his faith in me wasn't misplaced. I'm as good as any man you've got on deck, Garrett Shaw. I can patch a sail and splice a cable. I can saw and hammer and damn well ream out a cannon as well as I can aim and fire one! What I *can't* do — what I *won't* do — is languish in a cabin all day long eating figs and demanding to be waited on hand and foot as if I was queen of the Nile!"

The reference to Miranda's daytime activities broadened Garrett's grin, and Courtney held up a hand to stem any attempt he might make to excuse her behavior. "I know, I know. She isn't one of us. And you have no idea how relieved I am every time I am reminded of that. But it doesn't mean she should be able to snap her fingers and have a dozen men at her beck and call. Do you know what she demanded this afternoon?"

Garrett set his wine glass on the table and folded his arms across his chest. "No," he mused wryly, "but I have a feeling I'm about to find out."

"A sailmaker." Courtney spat the word out as if it was poison. "She asked Peter Cook to send a sailmaker to her cabin to alter one of her gowns! Where does she think she is? *Who* does she think she is? And don't you dare tell me I'm jealous, Garrett, or so help me I'll . . . I'll. . . ."

She stopped because her breasts were heaving painfully with the effort to gain a deep breath of air. She stopped because Garrett had laughed softly, had leaned forward and was pressing his lips into the curve of her shoulder.

"Garrett, please — this is serious!" She stumbled back, but he simply hesitated a moment then followed. A hand reached out, lean and bronzed, and plucked the dangerously tilting wine glass out of her hand.

"And I'm telling you in all seriousness," he murmured, "that you've absolutely nothing to be jealous of."

"Garrett, I —" Her back came up abruptly against the wall. The candlelight was behind him, and she could barely distinguish more than the dark slash of his brows as he sent his mouth searching through the wisps of hair at her temple. Courtney's hands were wedged against his chest but there was no way she could hope to push herself free, or stop his mouth from wandering lazily down her cheek, down past her earlobe to the rapid pulsebeat in her throat.

"Garrett," she gasped, "Not now, for heaven's sake."

"Not then, not now." His mouth sought to capture hers but only tasted a corner before she was able to twist away. "I'm a patient man, Courtney, but not a holy one."

His body shifted, and one of his hands molded itself to the shape of her rounded bottom, pulling her forward, introducing her to the hardness of his thighs. His other hand slid up her back and cupped around her neck, the pressure restricting her movements so she could not wrench away again.

"Why are you fighting it, girl?" he whispered huskily. "You know it's what you want."

"It isn't," she cried, and shivered as she felt his lips move hungrily down to the straining swells of her breasts.

"Aye. It isn't healthy for a woman to deny what her body craves." His laugh was a hot breath that seared through the muslin directly over her breast. "Nor is it healthy to tease a man the way you've teased me."

"I haven't teased you," she gasped. "I haven't! Please stop, Garrett . . . please!"

*"By all means, Garrett, do stop!"* Miranda's icy voice shot out of the gloom of the companionway like a bolt of lightning. "Unless of course you've planned a little show for our dinner entertainment?"

Garrett's arms dropped as he turned to face Miranda. Courtney sagged against the wall, the relief flooding through her limbs like cool water.

"Ahh, Miranda. What a pleasant surprise."

Miranda glared at Garrett's mocking greeting. "I can see what a surprise it is. I'm sorry, did I disturb your predinner tryst? Which of your hot little trollops couldn't wait until your food was digested?"

The amber eyes glittered scornfully in Courtney's direction and took several seconds to widen with recognition.

"The heat," she declared quietly. "It must be affecting my vision."

Garrett laughed and drew one of Courtney's resisting hands forward so that she had no choice but to step into the light.

"The heat of your blood, perhaps," he said. "Well, what do you think of our Courtney?"

"*Our* Courtney?"

"Surely some of the credit belongs to you, Miranda, for the change in her appearance. You did decide which clothes to send her."

"Yes, but I didn't think —" Miranda bit off the rest of her words when she saw Garrett's grin. He was enjoying himself: a cock between two hens. She *had* selected the clothes to send to the little bitch's cabin — on his orders. And she had deliberately chosen styles and fabrics she *knew* the girl would refuse to wear. She never dreamed the chit would challenge her so boldly, or be so obvious about her designs on Garrett Shaw.

Miranda forced the rage out of her expression and smiled tightly. "Naturally, I'm pleased to see she approves of my selections. It only proves what I said to Duncan years ago — that there is always hope, regardless of how futile things might seem."

Courtney pulled her wrist out of Garrett's grasp, her eyes flaring at Miranda as the woman approached the dining table. She was dressed in pale blue silk, the gown styled much along the same lines as Courtney's, with a high empire waist and a shockingly low décolletage. There was no tucking piece to attempt concealment or containment of the overflow of flesh and, as she passed in front of the light, it was obvious she had decided to go without the restrictions of any other undergarments.

Courtney snatched her wine glass off the table and quenched the dryness in her throat with the blood-red Madeira. Her own gown was tight and restrictive, the stockings were stifling her legs, the dainty green satin slippers were pinching her feet. What had felt beautiful and seductive for one man felt cheap and tawdry for the other, especially since it made it seem as if she was competing with Miranda for attention.

As if reading Courtney's mind, Miranda laughed huskily and ran her hands along the shimmering folds of silk.

"You should have stayed with your guns and sabers, my dear," she murmured in tones too low for Garrett to overhear. "I warrant you understand their usage far better than you understand the weapons nature provided you with . . . such as they are." And in a louder voice she added cheerily, "I trust your hairy little friend, Davey Dunn, will not keep us waiting too much longer. I'm positively famished."

"From a hard day's work, no doubt," Courtney grated between her teeth.

"Unfortunately Davey won't be joining us," Garrett said, handing a glass of wine to Miranda. "He spent most of the day underwater trying to rig new cables to the *Eagle*'s rudder."

Miranda crooked a finger at the fourth table setting. "Then who —"

Garrett smiled. "Someone you both know — one of you quite well, as I understand it. The other will, perhaps, find his presence more of an amusement than an annoyance."

"Now you do have me intrigued," Miranda said dryly. "I cannot think of a single amusing soul on board this ship."

"Did I say he was from this ship?"

"You don't mean you've invited a *Yankee* to dine with us."

"To dine, aye. And to satisfy my curiosity on a few matters."

Courtney looked up from her glass and found the dark blue eyes upon her.

"I find myself curious about a great many things that

went on aboard the Yankee frigate," he continued mildly. "Curious then, curious now."

Courtney's heart fluttered in her throat, like a sparrow caught in the talons of a hawk. *Not then, not now . . .* Was he deliberately reminding her of the kiss moments ago? Or was there an even crueler game of cat and mouse in store? She saw Garrett glance toward the door, and her own eyes made the leap in a rising panic. Standing in the entrance, grinning broadly and obviously present by arrangement, was Harry Pitt.

"Ye want the lieutenant now?"

"Now indeed, Mister Pitt," Garrett nodded.

"The lieutenant?" Miranda breathed, barely able to contain her excitement. There was only one Yankee Garrett was curious about, only one matter that scratched at his suspicions like a thorn. And judging by Courtney's reaction, his curiosity was warranted.

"This should be a highly entertaining evening, indeed, Garrett," she mused. "If you don't mind, I'll just take my seat. I wouldn't want to look too interested — or too eager."

She claimed the seat to Garrett's right without waiting for direction. Courtney hesitated, wondering if she could produce any excuse believable enough for Garrett to accept her departure.

"Court?"

Garrett's hand was on her arm, leading her firmly to a place at the table. She was conscious more than ever of his formidable size and strength, and of the danger she invited on each quick, guilt-ridden breath. Her concerns for Ballantine's safety came back in a flush of liquid fear: *if he knew, if he even suspected. . . .*

A cackle and shuffle of feet sent two pairs of eyes to the doorway. Only Miranda refrained from swiveling her head in the direction of the door. She was far more intrigued by Courtney's obvious discomfort. Whatever had gone on between the little bitch and her golden-haired lieutenant was still going on! Her reason for insisting that the lieutenant and the doctor be placed in her own personal care was now amazingly clear.

Garrett lowered his long frame into his chair and raised his wine glass in greeting. "Good evening, Lieutenant. I trust you have found your new accommodations to your liking?"

"The cabin is comfortable enough, although the stench of the orlop deck is not exactly what I would call inspiring."

Miranda gasped and sent her long raven hair flying over her shoulder as she turned toward the familiar voice. Lieutenant Otis Falworth stood at the cabin's entrance, affecting a suitably belligerent pose. He wore clean black breeches and a crisp white shirt opened to a deep vee over his chest. His hair was brushed into a tail at his neck, captured by a black velvet bow.

"I thank you again, Captain, for your kind invitation to join you this evening. And for the opportunity to bathe and change into more civilized clothes. Lice and sweat were never my adornments of choice."

Garrett Shaw grinned and pointed to the decanter of wine. "Help yourself, Lieutenant. Then join us in a hearty toast to our mutual interests: liberty and prosperity."

Falworth tipped the Madeira into a goblet and smiled at Miranda. "You're looking . . . ravishing, as usual."

Miranda swallowed hard and glanced at Garrett. "What is he doing here? Why have you brought him on board the *Falconer*?"

"It was by his request," Shaw said easily.

"*His* request?"

"And a small enough one at that, considering who he is and what he has done for us in the past."

"I still don't understand," Miranda snapped irritably.

"I think I do," Courtney said slowly. "He was our source in the American navy. He was the one who sold us the sea codes, the shipping schedules, the blockade routes. . . .'' She stared at Falworth expectantly as if she did not quite believe him capable of such deviousness.

"I don't believe I've had the pleasure," Falworth murmured, returning Courtney's stare.

"Court Farrow," Garrett said. "Duncan Farrow's daughter."

Falworth glanced sharply at Miranda before reverting his gaze to Courtney. "Duncan's daughter? Surely not the same one Lieutenant Ballantine attempted to keep disguised as a cabin boy?"

"The same," Garrett said with a chuckle and sipped his wine.

Falworth's dark eyes boldly inched over Courtney. "The man must have been mad. Where is he, by the way?"

"With the wounded, here on the *Falconer*." Shaw lowered his glass. "Where I can keep an eye on him."

"You mean he's still alive?" Falworth was shaken out of his bland good humor.

"Is that a problem?"

"It certainly could be. It may come as an unpleasant surprise to you to learn he isn't exactly what he appears to be."

"Meaning?"

"Meaning he was only temporarily posted as the *Eagle*'s first lieutenant. In reality he is a senior captain on Preble's personal staff. He was assigned to the *Eagle* with express orders to find the leak in naval security and seal it. Permanently." Falworth sighed. "Fortunately I was warned of his mission well in advance and was able to send him sniffing in ten different directions. Even so, his presence on the *Eagle* made it necessary for me to exercise extreme caution, as you can well imagine."

"Was that why we were given no advance warning of the trap waiting for Duncan and myself at Moknine?" Garrett asked silkily.

"My dear fellow, I didn't know of it myself until the captain held a private meeting in his quarters to reveal his orders *after we were under sail*." Falworth smiled tightly. "Believe me, if I could have warned you, I would have. I imagine Duncan Farrow's gratitude would have kept me in fresh linens for several years."

"And you've no idea who the Americans have as a contact within our camp?"

Falworth pursed his lips. "Only one man might know that: Adrian Ballantine. And you have about as much chance of prying the information out of him as you have of squeezing water from a stone."

"I've drunk from many a rock in my time," Shaw said easily.

"Not from this one, you won't. If he knows you want something from him" — Falworth shook his head — "he'd watch you flay his grandmother alive before he'd talk. Good heavens, he stood by and watched his best — and only — friend flogged bloody for no good reason."

"You're referring to the doctor?"

"Rutger, yes. A rather simple-minded, but equally patriotic lout."

"And yet I'm told he halted the flogging of Nilsson and Seagram. That doesn't sound like the act of a man without a conscience."

"His interference was for purely pretentious reasons. He and Jennings had a . . . thing . . . between them. Jennings was always pushing the lieutenant hard; Ballantine, in return, challenged Jennings' authority at every opportunity to try and draw him out into the open. You see, he believed Jennings to be the man he was after."

"And Court? Why would he help her?"

Falworth turned slowly to meet the emerald green eyes. "He obviously wanted something."

She met his gaze steadily, aware of Garrett's eyes boring into her also. "You obviously want something as well, Lieutenant," she said calmly. "Dare we guess what?"

"Oddly enough, I want nothing that should put undue strain on either you or your coffers. I should like to be taken to Tripoli, as planned, and to be handed over to

Karamanli to be held for ransom to the American government — again, as planned." He allowed the request to sink in as he savored more of the Madeira. "You see, I have no taste for the fugitive life. I prefer the pomp and ceremony accorded a hero on his return home. Heroes are so much in demand these days, you know. I could expect a promotion to an important position, perhaps even attract the attention of a rich heiress."

"Then why reveal yourself at all?" Shaw asked with a smile. "You could have had your hero's homecoming without taking the chance of your own men discovering your collaboration."

"True enough. However, in order to gain the right kind of notoriety, to gain a prominent place in the history books, I could do no better than to produce the spy the Admiralty craves so desperately."

"Dead, naturally."

"Naturally. And preferably without any witness to contest the claim."

"Ballantine?"

"He's far too dangerous to either one of us to allow him to live."

Shaw considered the statement a moment, then smiled as he steepled his fingers beneath his chin. "I presume you have something to offer in return? I mean, what is to stop me from selling you to the Americans myself? No doubt they would pay handsomely for the privilege of stretching your neck."

"They would indeed. But then you would have no intermediary to see you safely through the Straits of Gibraltar. You would have no guarantee that Preble wouldn't send half the fleet to hunt you down, and certainly no one willing to swear that you and your ship were blasted out of the water by the treacherous, double-crossing Yusef Karamanli. Unless, of course, the life of a fugitive appeals to *you*? Or to Miss Farrow? Or to Miss Gold?"

Shaw gave no outward response to the proposal. It was Miranda who leaned forward interestedly.

"You could guarantee us safe passage out of the Mediterranean? You could convince your American navy that the *Falconer* was destroyed and her captain killed?''

"I could even provide wreckage and bodies, if you desired it. And a simple change of names buys you anonymity once you're past the blockade of the Straits.''

Shaw's fingers parted. ''The Straits are blockaded? As of when?''

"As of the middle of June, when the *Eagle* left port en route to Snake Island. Preble has ordered every ship stopped and searched topgallants to timbers. He is an ambitious man, determined to win this war and cleanse the earth of all undesirables along the Barbary Coast — no offense intended. The *Falconer* would never break through to open water, assuming you mean to escape by sea. If by land, well, the journey is a long and perilous one through desert and hostile territory. And since anything other than wogs and camels tend to attract a great deal of attention in the area, my guess is, you'd be received by military arms wherever you tried to emerge. The third alternative, of course, is to remain here under Karamanli's protection. But long before he actually loses the war, you can be sure he will offer many sacrifices.''

"Garrett?'' Miranda turned her amber eyes to Shaw. "If what he says is true, then how —''

Shaw's hand warned her to silence. "And what guarantee do we have that you'll keep your word? That you won't do the exact opposite of what you say and send the *entire* fleet down my throat to add fuel to your blaze of glory?''

Falworth flicked absently at a mote of dust on his sleeve and smiled blandly. "Were I to do that, how would I collect the fifty thousand gold double-eagles I intend to be paid for my services?''

Shaw regarded him through hooded eyes before his even, white teeth flashed in a grin. "I admire your nerve, Yankee. So much so, I will even give your offer consideration.''

Falworth inclined his head slightly. "I shouldn't dally

too long in making a decision. As I said before, Ballantine is a dangerous man to keep alive any longer than is necessary. He knows the fate you have planned for his ship and crew. He won't swallow it peaceably, I can promise you."

"I should fear a single, unarmed man?" Shaw snorted derisively.

"Without the shackles of any military codes to bind him, he'll be acting on instincts alone, and in that respect, he's like a lit fuse looking for a powder keg."

"The obvious question here would be to ask why you haven't removed him long before now? An accident at sea, a misfired musket during battle? Either would have been simple enough to arrange."

"Unfortunately, I used those very methods in order to . . . improve my position on the ship's roster. Too many 'accidents' would have left a spoor a yard wide to my door. Besides, until two days ago I believed he could actually be of some use to me alive. Also I confess I found it infinitely more amusing to wear away at him bit by bit. Quite a fascinating subject, really. His recuperative powers, mental and physical, are extraordinary. Even the death of his young brother was taken in stride."

"Were you responsible for that too?" Courtney asked quietly.

"Not directly, no. It actually was an accident, by all accounts. The boy slipped and fell and bashed his head on a block and tackle. But it served my purposes to let the lieutenant *think* it was no accident, to foster the belief that the boy overheard something he shouldn't have." He turned back to Shaw with a frown of annoyance. "I repeat, it would be a fatal error on your part if you were to underestimate Ballantine, as Jennings did."

The pads of Shaw's fingertips traced a pattern around the rim of the crystal goblet, and he settled his glance on Courtney.

"You don't agree with the lieutenant?"

"I can't believe you're even listening to this pompous

fool," she retorted, the anger and contempt flaring in her eyes. "Of course he wants Ballantine dead — to ensure the safety of his own traitorous neck. As for his" — she paused, then spat the word — "*offer* . . . he's betrayed his own country, his own men! What on earth makes you think he won't betray us? His word? His demand for fifty thousand in gold?" She scoffed. "He'd earn twice as much selling us out to the Americans."

"My dear Miss Farrow," Falworth countered, "you're sadly misinformed if you think my government is lax with its purse strings. Karamanli's demand for a mere thirty thousand in tribute was the spark that ignited this war. Granted, you would be a valuable prize for them to capture, but to actually pay for the acquisition would be another matter entirely."

Courtney pushed to her feet with a loud scraping of the chair legs on the floor. "I have no intention of enduring the insults of this man's presence any longer. When you come to your senses, Garrett, I would be delighted to share a meal with you again. Until then —"

"Now Court —"

"Good night, Captain Shaw," she said frostily. A derisive glance toward Miranda and a scathing look at Falworth carried her furiously to the door. She heard Garrett shout her name angrily but she ignored it and hastened along the narrow companionway. When she had the thickness of the aftercabin door between her and the corridor, she released the pent-up air in her lungs. Her heart was pounding fiercely within her breast, her emotions were in a turmoil.

She closed her eyes and leaned her head back against the wooden door.

Would any of this have happened if she'd simply been locked in the hold of the *Eagle* with Seagram and the other prisoners from Snake Island? Would she be torn apart now if she'd never laid eyes on Ballantine, or spoken to him, or touched him? Would she have been able to sit and listen to Falworth's propositions with a cool, clear mind? Duncan would have. He would have heard the Yankee out, as Garrett was doing; he would have weighed the advantages and disadvantages carefully, *unemotionally*. He would have expected her to do the same, not to display such obvious distress. *Damn* Adrian Ballantine for doing this to her! She *should* have shot him earlier when she'd had the chance. At least then she would have been able to put him out of her mind once and for all! Damn him! Damn —

Courtney's eyes popped open, and she stared at the desk in sudden horror. It was, at first glance, as she had left it. A few papers, a quill and ink, the two empty silver goblets. A second sweep confirmed it: the gun was gone! The pistol she had placed there to keep Ballantine at arm's length was gone.

She ran quickly to the desk and yanked open the drawers, hoping against hope she had put the weapon away and forgotten. But she knew, as surely as she felt fear squeeze her heart, that Ballantine had been standing beside the desk when he sent her to unbolt the door. She had turned her back on him for *one minute*, and he had managed to slip the gun from the desk and conceal it in his clothes.

"The fool," she cried softly. "The bloody, arrogant fool!"

"I didn't know you felt so strongly, girl" — Courtney gasped and looked up as Garrett's voice intruded on her panic — "or I never would have had the Yankee join us."

"Garrett!"

He closed the door quietly and raised a hand to show a full bottle of red wine. "A peace offering? From an arrogant fool to a . . . a beautiful woman who I wouldn't have angry with me for all the gold double-eagles in the world."

"But" — she moistened her lips and stammered out a lame reply — "what about Miranda? And the Yankee? Surely you didn't leave the Yankee unguarded!"

"He isn't going anywhere." Shaw smiled. "And I've no doubt Miranda will keep a sharp eye on him. A shame to spoil the meal, however."

"I . . . Actually, I'm not very hungry."

"Good. Neither am I." His eyes flicked to the bed. "I'd much rather finish the conversation we began earlier."

Courtney glanced at the bed as well, but to wonder if the pistol she kept tucked behind the pillow was still there, or if it too had somehow found its way into Ballantine's hands.

Garrett set the wine bottle down and frowned at the two silver goblets. "Were you expecting company?"

Courtney clasped her hands together and took an involuntary step away from the desk. "N-no. No, of course not."

Shaw glanced up at her from beneath the slash of black brows. "Of course not," he murmured. "No man on this ship would dare try his hand at taking my place, unless he had a wish to see an early grave."

"Your place? You make it sound as if I've been declared your personal property."

"You have objections?"

"I object to any man telling me what I can or cannot do; where I can and cannot go; who I do or do not belong to. You should know that much about me by now, Garrett Shaw."

"Aye. I know you've a mind of your own. As stubborn and wild in spirit as your father, rest his soul. But you still need a strong hand to guide you, Court Farrow. Someone to protect you and look after you."

"I'm quite capable of looking after myself."

"Are you now?" A grin appeared slowly. "And if the word was to spread through the ship that I no longer sought any claim to you — how long do you think your bed would stay empty at night? How safe would you be walking the decks? Or venturing below?"

"You're referring to my father's men," she said coldly.

"Aye, and while he was in command, they were loyal to the death. But he isn't in command now, lass. I am. You know yourself corsairs are a fickle breed. They respect power and authority, not memories. They tolerated you in the past because of Duncan, and because you were more like a son to him than a daughter. They respect you with a cutlass or a dirk in your hand, not with questions and suspicions spouting from your mouth."

The retort forming on Courtney's lips froze as Garrett shook his head.

"You've been asking questions all over the ship, girl, and it's not healthy for you. Supposing the man we want is among us — and there's no reason to believe he isn't — and supposing you happen to ask him the wrong questions about where he was or what he saw during the fight with the American gunboats. And supposing he began to worry that you might figure out who he was — what the devil would stop him from sticking a knife between your shoulderblades and silencing you permanently?"

"I have to know who betrayed my father," she said with quiet vehemence.

"And you think I don't?"

"I don't see you asking any questions."

"There are ways and there are ways, girl. I've been asking and I've been listening, but not so as any traitor among us would know what we suspect."

"And have you learned anything?" she grated. "Are you any closer to finding out who the Judas is?"

"I'm finding out who he isn't," Garrett said evenly. "And who he isn't is damn near as important as who he is."

"In other words you're telling me to do nothing. To sit and wait and do absolutely bloody nothing!"

"Ahh, I can see the fire in your eyes, Court Farrow. Telling you to do nothing is like inviting you to do the opposite. Nay, I've given you free run of the ship. I'll not go back on it now."

"You *gave* me run?" she blurted hotly. "Should I be honored that you *gave* me run of my father's ship?"

He bent his head to the task of pouring out two goblets of wine, and when he lifted his eyes to hers again, they were gleaming with amusement. "Are you laying claim to it then?"

*Claim the Falconer for herself*? It was not a totally

outlandish idea. There were ships that sailed with women at the helm, and crews willing to follow a woman's orders if she proved herself cunning and ruthless enough.

Shaw laughed softly, reading her mind. "You're strong, aye, an I wouldn't deny you might find a man or three on board willing to follow your cutlass, but is that what you want? To divide the ship rather than join it together to make it stronger than it ever was? Is that what Duncan would have wanted you to do?"

As he spoke he came around the side of the desk, and Courtney could not help but be reminded of the other tall, bold man who had dared to play similar word games with her only a short while ago. She could almost swear Adrian's masculine scent was still in the cabin, on her skin. She could still feel the tender ache between her thighs and the warm abrasions on her skin from the chafing of his beard . . . his hands . . . his lips. She was confused, and Shaw's nearness was confusing her more.

"Have you given thought to your future, Court? Have you decided where you want to go when our business here is finished?"

"Go?" Her tongue slipped across her lips to moisten them, and she moved haltingly past him to stand near the canvas-draped gallery door.

"Surely you've no hunger to stay about these climes any longer than you've a need to? I myself have seen enough sand and camel dung to last a lifetime. I was thinking . . . of a new start somewhere. The Caribbean, maybe, or the Americas. Like the Yankee said, a change of names, a new past — who would know?" He paused, and his eyes were pulled to the solemn glitter of the oval locket and the cleft in which it nestled. "It was Duncan's dream as well: to live the life of a baron in America once he rid the earth of all sodding Frenchmen. It was his dream for you, too, born a lady, to return to the life of the gentry."

"I never asked him for dreams," she said quietly.

"You never asked him for anything. That was why he wanted to give you it all. It's a rich new life waiting in America . . . in Virginia."

"Virginia," she whispered. She felt a tiny shudder vibrate down her spine. Virginia was Ballantine's home. He was inescapable — in her present, in her future.

Shaw frowned at her apparent lack of attention. "Aye, Norfolk runs many a profitable merchant fleet in and out . . . or *was* it Norfolk?"

Courtney stared at the stub of the candle on the desk, her gaze transfixed by the single, pure yellow flame. "Norfolk? Yes . . . yes, the lawyer is in Norfolk, but after that. . . ."

"After that?" Courtney was startled by the eagerness in his voice, and Garrett covered the slip by tilting his goblet upward in a salute. "I'm glad to hear he wasn't foolhardy enough to plan to stay in Norfolk for any length of time. Not even Duncan could have hidden forever in the midst of a large Yankee naval base."

She smiled weakly. "No, I suppose not. But he never actually talked about his plans for the future. Only Verart did, and then only at the end, when he knew he was dying. I guess he wanted to be certain I knew . . . in case. . . ." She faltered and looked up into Garrett's dark eyes. "It was all so confusing those last few minutes. I wasn't really paying attention to what he was saying."

"But you do know how to go about claiming what your father left for you, don't you?"

"I know the name of the lawyer I'm to see; the name I'm to give him to . . . to. . . ." She stopped and Garrett smiled again. He had moved closer. There were not so many shadows between them, yet his face seemed masked. "You knew about it? You knew his plans?"

"Only what he told me: That he wanted a better life for you. He wanted to be sure you never had to scrape and scratch for anything, that you never had to be alone. Your father made us all rich men, Court, did you know that? Himself, Verart, and me. If there was no other reason, there'd still be that debt I owe him, a debt I'd see repaid by making certain his wishes for your future were honored." His hands closed around her wrists, and he lifted them tenderly to his lips. "But you know full well there are other reasons for my wanting you, Court. For my wanting to protect you, to have you by my side . . . to keep you warm at night and filled with pleasure."

Courtney heard what he was saying, but the blood throbbing loudly in her ears would not allow her to make sense of it. His lips were tracing the faint blue veins in her wrists, kissing her palms, kissing the tips of her fingers.

"If he were alive and on board this ship now, Duncan himself would give our marriage his blessing."

"Marriage!" She gasped and stumbled back, jerking her hands unceremoniously out of his.

"Aye," he chuckled. "You thought you'd never hear that word from these lips? I never would have thought it either. And frankly I've never wanted any one wench to keep my bed warm at night — not until now. You're the one to blame for my redemption, Court Farrow. There's never been a woman able to keep me at bay so long. But the time has come to put the games aside. I want there to be no doubt as to who you belong to, nor any doubt as to who has possession of my heart."

"Garrett, I — " She looked down as she felt his hand around hers again, raising it effortlessly even though she balked at his touch. Something cold and metallic was passed over her fingertip and pressed stubbornly over the resisting knuckle. When his hand shifted away, she was startled to see he had slotted a ring onto her finger. The enormous emerald center stone burned from the surrounding halo of diamonds, each of which caught the glow from the sputtering candle and split the beam into a million tiny fragments of light.

Garrett watched for the reaction on her face. It was a ring fit to melt any wench's heart — even one belonging to an ice maiden. He had counted on it to soften the last of Courtney's resistance, and it was apparently doing just that. Her cheeks had drained of color, and her eyes had grown as large and shimmering as the emerald itself.

His chest swelled, and he curled a hand around her

waist, drawing her forward. Courtney's gasp parted her lips as his mouth slanted over hers. Her arms were pinned against his chest, and she was powerless to fend off the hot, calloused hand that fondled its way up the muslin curves to fit itself boldly around her breast.

"Garrett!" She tore her mouth free and writhed within the iron hard circle of his arm. "What are you doing! Stop!"

"Not this time, my fiery little hellcat." He laughed huskily and squeezed his hand tighter around her flesh.

He tasted bitterly of strong wine and tobacco, and Courtney cried out in anger and revulsion as his mouth bound itself to hers like a gag. It was not a kiss of passion, but of dominance; no sweet flood of desire grew under the greedy, grasping fingers, only rage and a sense of violation.

She heard a tearing sound and realized neither the tucking piece nor the muslin bodice was able to withstand Garrett's ardor. She shoved at his shoulders to wriggle free; she kicked out with her feet and her knees, but her efforts only deepened his laughter and tightened his arm so that she was forced farther and farther back into a painful arch.

His finger plucked at the last threads of muslin, and her breasts popped free of their confinement, the nipples rosy and upthrust from the coarse abuse. Garrett's dark head bowed, first to one, then the other, his mouth defiling the memory of gentler lips. His teeth razed the quivering buds of flesh until Courtney was breathless from the pain.

A sob was wrenched from her throat as she felt her knees bump against the wooden side of the bed. She was folded forcefully down onto the mattress, his weight driving the remaining air from her lungs. More of the muslin tore, then the silk shimmy shredded and fanned out beneath her thrashing legs. Garrett's hands plunged beneath her bucking hips, and he began to shift her this way and that, to grind her against his bulging groin. His mouth smothered her cries, and he seemed not to feel or care that she was tearing at his hair, clawing and scratching at his face and neck.

Courtney was rapidly losing strength. Ballantine's lovemaking had exhausted her and left her weak — too weak to withstand Garrett's relentless assault. Her skin was inflamed from the friction of his clothes; her body ached from his roughness, from the brutality of one who was determined to brand her, whether she was willing or not.

A curse lifted his mouth temporarily as his overly eager hands fumbled with his own clothes. A stubborn button made him lever his torso up and away from hers, and Courtney seized the opportunity to strike out with both fists. It was the emerald ring that brought an end to his lust. The stone sliced through the tanned flesh of his cheek, opening a gash several inches long to the corner of his mouth.

"By the Christ . . . !" He reached down and grabbed a fistful of her hair, slamming her head back into the mattress while his free hand probed for the damage to his jaw. He stared at the blood on his fingers, then at the look of horror on Courtney's face.

"By the Christ," he rasped again, "it's time you found out who's in command of this ship and everyone on board. You're mine, dammit. I've bloody well earned you and everything that comes with you."

While he spoke, his fingers clamped around her throat and ruthlessly sealed off the passage of air to her lungs. She felt a new wave of panic spread like a chilling mist over her body. Her limbs writhed, and her fingers tore at the vise-like grip; her chest burned from the pressure; her lips parted to a soundless scream. Wavering blackness robbed the last of the strength from her arms and legs. She lost sight of his looming face; she could no longer hear his hot, heavy breathing. Even the pain seemed to seep away, leaving her empty, limp, and totally without feeling.

Garrett waited for the glazed green eyes to flutter closed

before he relaxed the killing grip. He delayed an extra moment, watching for any sign of further resistance, then he stood up from the bed and started peeling away his jacket, his waistcoat, and shirt. His lips pulled back in a snarl and he spat blood angrily onto the floor.

Courtney was aware of movement somewhere nearby; dimly aware of a black shadow crowding into the fog that clouded her eyes. She felt the slow return of sensation along the length of her body, a prickling heat that grew rapidly into a searing, overpowering agony. Her throat opened in a shocked gasp; her lungs gulped and coughed for air that came in stabs of white-hot pain. She rolled onto her side and with achingly slow swimming motions, tried to crawl to the edge of the bed. She had hardly managed to claw her way a few inches before her legs were pinned beneath a leaden weight.

The weight had hands and fingers, and they skimmed purposefully up the pearl-like sheen of her naked thighs. They probed the soft thatch of auburn curls and stroked up to the smooth, flat plane of her belly. Courtney scrambled farther away, her eyes locked in horror on the two hissing, coiled snakes that were on Shaw's forearms.

"I don't want to have to hurt you, Court," he murmured, his voice as silkily soft and seductive as the tongue that furrowed its way up from her navel to the sensitive underside of her breasts. "You're a woman, by God, and you're going to learn to appreciate the pleasure of being one if it takes me the whole night long."

A knee was forced between her thighs, and Courtney felt the thickness of him slide along her flesh. His mouth carried the assault up to her bruised throat and into the curly tousle of her hair; an arm went beneath her shoulders to brace her as he raised his hips and brought them into position over hers.

Courtney sucked in a great mouthful of air and rammed her knee hard and fast into his groin. She felt the gratifying crush of rigid flesh and pulpy tissue and was rewarded almost instantly by the sight of Shaw's body jackknifing to one side. His curse exploded in a roar, one that was cut short as the shock blossomed and shuddered into his arms and legs. His hands flew instinctively to cradle the damaged area; his body collapsed onto its side, and his knees folded up against his chest.

Courtney scrambled free, hampered by the shreds of her clothing. She shrugged off the silk and muslin streamers and dove her hands beneath the pillow. The pistol was still there! She primed and cocked the weapon and leaped to her feet, her hands holding and aiming the gun unwaveringly at Shaw's sweat-beaded brow. Her eyes burned with fury and disgust. Her face was ashen but for a crimson splash of Garrett's blood that had smeared on her chin.

"I should kill you for that," he hissed.

"Except that I have the gun," she said in a choked whisper, "And I have far more incentive at the moment to pull the trigger."

Garrett pressed his cheek into the covers and ground his teeth against a wave of nausea. His throat and chest were drenched in sweat; his arms and shoulders were shiny with the strain. He straightened his legs slowly, his hands gently massaging away the shooting barbs of pain.

"Put the damned gun away," he snarled. "You've made your point."

"Have I? Then get out of my sight, Garrett, before I use this."

The blue eyes glittered from her set face to the pistol. He closed his mind to the pulsating agony in his groin and sat slowly upright, and under Courtney's wary gaze, retrieved his breeches and carefully drew them on. The rest of his clothing he gathered into a bundle and tucked it under his arm.

Courtney moved hastily out of his range as he walked around the foot of the bed. She kept the gun clenched steadily in her two hands, kept the muzzle pointed unerringly at his chest as he moved toward the door.

A coldly ominous smile touched his lips as he glanced back at her; the promise was hard and malicious in his eyes as they took a long last look at her nakedness. Courtney held her breath, clutching the gun tighter as she stared at the thin trickle of blood beginning to streak its way down his throat and onto his chest.

"You belong to me, Court Farrow. Make no mistake. It's only a matter of time before you accept it . . . one way or another."

# Chapter Sixteen

Miranda Gold stared at Otis Falworth for a full minute after Garrett's hasty departure from the wardroom. He seemed unconcerned. The sly, dark brown eyes were hooded and pensive as he studied her in return.

"More wine?" he asked finally, the grooves on either side of his mouth deepening with mockery.

"Why didn't you say something to me? Why didn't you tell me who you were?"

Falworth laughed briefly. "My dear woman, I scarcely knew you well enough to place my life in your hands. Another day's sail would have put us in sight of Gibraltar and the naval courts. Information like that would have bought you your freedom ten times over, and I doubt very much if the few pleasurable moments we spent together would have outweighed the value of freedom."

Miranda smiled tightly. "Then you can understand why I find myself in the awkward position of having to agree with Courtney. I can't see you settling for a mere fifty thousand in gold and a hero's wreath."

Falworth leaned back in his chair, his fingers tapping the base of his empty glass. "If that's what you believe, why didn't you speak out when she did? Throw in your support, so to speak."

She shrugged. "Shaw will make his own mind up, regardless of who agrees or doesn't agree."

"And which do you think he will do?"

"Accept your offer or sell you to the Yankees?" Miranda leaned back also, her amber eyes speculative, her arms crossed beneath her breasts, plumping them to epic proportions. "In truth? I think he'll kill you."

"And risk the blockades and the vegeance of the American navy?"

"He's been hunted before. He's also broken through blockades before. He'll probably keep you alive as long as you continue to provide him with information — and as long as you continue to amuse him."

"What makes you so sure he won't sell me to the Admiralty, or even to Karamanli?"

"I'm not. Those are both possibilities. You asked me what *I* thought he would do and I told you."

Falworth considered the coolness of her statement and reached for the wine bottle. "So why tell me anything at all? Wouldn't it be more loyal of you to go along with the pretense and keep me happy and unsuspecting?"

"I'm sure it would. But then I'd never convince you to help me."

"Help you? How can I possibly help you?"

"Did you really mean it when you said you could get someone past the blockade to America?"

"Yourself, for example?"

"You said the ships were being stopped and searched. I presume that means anyone suspicious had best have papers, documents . . . something to prove they are who they say they are?"

"It would be wise."

"You neglected to mention it to Garrett."

"I neglected to mention several things. But as you say, so long as I keep providing him with tidbits of information. . . ." He smiled and crooked a forefinger in a mock salute.

"*Can* you provide safe papers?"

"I can provide a multitude of useful things — assuming I am sufficiently motivated to do so."

"And what, precisely, would motivate you, Lieutenant?"

His gaze dipped to the swells of her breasts. "What, *precisely* are you prepared to offer?"

"The most obvious answer would be: me. Whenever, however you want me — for as long as you want me."

Falworth felt a thrill of anticipation stir in his loins. He found it difficult, suddenly, to concentrate on anything more complicated than drawing the next breath.

"You still haven't told me why," he managed to say.

"Because I want to get off his ship. I want to get away from these animals. I want to get away from Garrett Shaw — alive. I can't do any of those things without someone's help. *Your* help."

"Again . . . *why*?"

"It's quite simple, Lieutenant. I have a . . . sixth sense, if you'd like to call it that. I've trusted it most of my life, and as you can see, it's kept me alive and reasonably healthy up to now."

Falworth took exaggerated stock of her body, her very healthy body. "Granted."

"My sixth sense is telling me" — she lowered her voice — "to get away from here. Quickly. Garrett is up to something, and I *don't* trust *him*."

Falworth glanced at Courtney's empty seat. "Something to do with her?"

"It *all* has to do with her. He is planning to woo her off her feet — in fact it wouldn't surprise me if they were rutting like boars right now — then he plans to wed the bitch and take her to America to claim her father's fortune."

"Duncan Farrow left his daughter a fortune?"

"As I understand it, a veritable empire. Founded years ago and built with the profits from his raiding ventures. He and Verart invested in land, cotton, slaves, ships . . . the little bitch is an heiress like no other heiress you're likely ever to come across again. At least . . . she will be, if she can get to America to lodge her claim.''

Falworth's eyes narrowed sharply. *"If?"*

Miranda leaned forward and slid her empty glass toward his end of the table. "If Garrett has his facts correct, and I have no reason to disbelieve him, all someone has to do to collect the inheritance is to contact a certain lawyer, who in turn introduces her to a banker, who then releases twelve extremely profitable years' worth of accumulated wealth.''

"You said *someone.* I take it you mean the girl has never actually been to America, never actually met this lawyer or this banker?"

"Never," Miranda said with a sly smile. "Furthermore, I seriously doubt if she is even aware of how vast the fortune is, or of what lengths a person might be willing to go to lay their hands on it.''

"Someone like Garrett Shaw?"

"Someone exactly like Garrett Shaw. I happen to know he's squandered most of his own profits, and the lure of a small empire is too much for him to simply sail away from. He knows about Duncan's fortune. Unfortunately he doesn't know the name of the lawyer to see, or the name Farrow used to set up the trust.''

Falworth filled the goblet and slid it back, his fingers coming into contact with Miranda's. "Are you implying you have the information he needs?"

"I might. Even though Duncan was a clever, closed-mouthed bastard, he *was* a man. Like most men, he considered women to be nothing but ornaments, barely worthy of notice. It could be I overheard some names, saw some notations on a map that meant nothing to me at the time, however —"

"However, with the correct assistance, you might be able to recall those names and notations?"

Miranda smiled, and her long, slender fingers caressed his.

"What about his daughter? What about Shaw? You said that *he* has plans to collect this fortune.''

Miranda's eyes sparkled. "Duncan obviously had no intention of including me in his future plans, and I already told you, I don't trust Garrett. For that, I feel no obligation whatsoever to play fair, especially not with Courtney Farrow." She paused and took a deep breath. "I've decided I've been used enough. I want it all from now on, not just the scraps and leavings. There's more than enough for the two of us to share; more than any handful of gold double-eagles could buy; more than any dowry a hero could hope to marry into, even if he was promoted to admiral."

Falworth looked down at his hand and watched the suggestive motions of Miranda's fingers stroking his. "Are you proposing we somehow make the first claim on the inheritance?"

"It could be done," she murmured confidently. "*I* could do it — but I need help. I need *you*, Lieutenant."

Falworth turned his hand so that the teasingly cool fingers were caught within his. "You're saying you think it would be different with me? A man who has — as your charming friend so graciously pointed out — sold his country and his men for profit?"

"It would be different with us, Lieutenant, because we understand each other. We would be entering into this agreement each knowing what the other wants." She drew his hand closer, letting the backs of his fingers rest against the warm curve of her breast. "And because we would be good for each other. You do enjoy my company, don't you?"

His fingers uncurled slowly, the tremor in them visible as he brushed over her rising nipple.

"Indeed," he murmured. "I do enjoy you, Miranda. More than I should. More, possibly, than it could be healthy or wise to do."

"As unhealthy and as unwise as it could be for me to trust you, Lieutenant. But if you're uncertain, perhaps there is someone else who would be willing to help me —"

"No!" Falworth captured her wrist before she could pull it away. "No, Miranda, I want what you want. And God knows, I've wanted you since the first moment I laid eyes on you." He gripped her wrist tightly. "But how in blazes am I supposed to help you get away from this ship when I may not even be alive to see Tripoli myself?"

"Leave it to me," she said. "I will see that you stay alive. Can you swim?"

"Not well enough to cross the Atlantic," he replied dryly.

She did not acknowledge the humor. "Enough to take you ashore once we've anchored in Tripoli? Garrett prefers the open sea at his back and rarely moors closer than five or six hundred yards to shore. A boat would be impossible; we would be seen and heard. But to swim ashore late at night . . . most of the guards would be placed aboard the *Eagle*. If we're clever enough and quick enough, we could talk our way onto a small fishing boat and be safely away from port before any alarm is sounded."

"And if we're taken ashore as soon as we drop anchor?"

"You won't be," she assured him. "Karamanli is an Arab. There are certain traditions to be upheld, certain rites of barter to go through before any trades take place. Your crew will sit on board ship at least a day or two before the terms are agreed to. And Garrett is not stupid. He knows as long as the Yankees remain on the ship and his guns remain aimed at the palace walls, he'll win every point he bargains for."

"It might work," Falworth conceded.

"It *will* work, my lieutenant. I will keep you alive until we leave Tripoli. From there on it will be your job to take us safely and speedily to America. Can you do it?"

"For you and the wealth you promise," he murmured with a smile, "I can do almost anything."

"I'm so pleased to hear you say that," she mused, "For there is one small favor I must ask of you. Not an unreasonable one, I'm sure you will agree, since its *execution* is necessary for our success."

"You want me to kill Garrett Shaw?" he asked, his resolve wavering for the first time.

"Good heavens, no," she laughed. "You'd never come within a prayer of killing a man like him. No, Lieutenant, it is the other one who must be silenced: Courtney Farrow.''

"Why? What harm could she do to us?"

"What harm?" Miranda leaned back, leaving his hand to grope empty air. "Should she somehow survive to make the crossing, despite the blockades and the searches, and should she appear one day in Norfolk and begin asking questions. . . ."

"I see your point," he nodded grimly.

"I'm so glad," she said derisively. "How is it a man can cold-bloodedly arrange the deaths of a hundred of his own crewmen, the betrayal of a hundred more, yet balk at the thought of killing a single worthless female? But never mind, Lieutenant, I have an alternative in mind — one that might just take care of both of our problems at the same time: the Farrow bitch and your hellhound, Adrian Ballantine."

"How —?"

"Shhh!" Miranda shot up a warning finger and glanced toward the door. Garrett Shaw's voice bellowed out again, clearer as his footsteps stormed past the wardroom door.

Miranda's eyes gleamed suddenly, as a smile tugged at the corners of her mouth.

"Well, well, well," she murmured. "So she's turned him out again. We *will* be perturbed at that!"

She stood up immediately and smoothed the flowing ripples of pale blue silk.

"Where are you going?" Falworth demanded.

"To take advantage of his acute frustrations, naturally," she said with a deep-throated chuckle. "How better to convince him of my loyalty and compliance?"

Falworth surged to his feet. "You're going to him now? You're going to . . . to. . . ."

Miranda regarded his flushed features with some amusement. "I'm going to — what is it the smithy's say — strike while the iron is hot? The good captain will be hot indeed, and extremely vulnerable to the odd whispered suggestion. You wouldn't want me to let such a golden opportunity pass by, would you?''

He grabbed at her arm and drew her hard against his chest.

"And if I said I needed you as much, if not more, at the moment?''

"I'd tell you you'd have to be patient," she said, staring directly into the infuriated brown eyes. "And I'd tell you the rewards for your patience would be . . . inestimable.''

The luscious red lips parted as she rose on tip-toe and pressed herself into his embrace. Her tongue displayed no shyness nor any lack of expertise as it darted into the well of his mouth. Falworth groaned, and his arms started to clench around her, but she twisted adeptly away and danced to the door in a swirl of watery silk. The amber eyes were smoldering with promises as she glanced back at him.

"Soon, my lieutenant. Soon I will be yours and yours alone. And soon we will have hours, days, weeks filled with pleasures — pleasures you will not have imagined in your wildest dreams.''

"Miranda — !''

Falworth's mouth clamped shut, even as the sound of her name echoed on the closing door. She was gone. She was going to *him*. The thought left Lieutenant Otis Claymore Falworth trembling like an impotent schoolboy.

Miranda shivered sensuously as she approached the door to Garrett's quarters — a meager, spartan cabin located in the forecastle. To get there she had to walk through the stuffy confines of the lower gun deck, past the ogling eyes of the off-watch crew members who paused in their wenching and drinking to follow her progress. She scarcely noticed them. Her thoughts were divided between Garrett Shaw and Otis Falworth. The former was a hard, lean animal with primitive instincts and totally self-centered goals. The latter was equally dangerous in his ambitions but not nearly so difficult to manipulate.

Falworth was nowhere near as appealing in appearance or performance, but one had to make certain allowances . . . at least until his usefulness was at an end. Virginia was rife with gallant, virile men. One of them would surely be willing to help rid her of a grasping nuisance.

Miranda tossed her raven hair back from her shoulders and adjusted the plunging neckline of her gown downward. She knew what Garrett appreciated. She knew what any man appreciated when his masculinity had been threatened or questioned.

Humming absently, she slowed her pace as she came abreast of his cabin door. It was slightly ajar; the spill of escaping light cut through the musty darkness of the companionway. She tilted her head and peeked inside while a finger pushed gingerly on the wooden panel to open it farther. Garrett's shirt, coat, and maroon-striped vest lay in a heap where they had been thrown. The captain stood naked to the waist, his back to the door, his feet braced wide apart. One arm was raised, holding a mug of rum to his lips; the other held the stoneware jug in readiness.

God, but he was a magnificent specimen, she thought. The slabs of muscle across his shoulders and back were enough to cause her bones to melt. The tight black breeches molded to his lean hips and thighs, emphasizing every carved and sculpted sinew. Even the sight of the tattooed snakes writhing on his forearms sent tingles up Miranda's spine. Why did he have to be so pig-headed? So bullish in his designs? Why couldn't he see that she, Miranda, could offer far more than Courtney Farrow ever could. Ever *would*!

"Garrett? I thought I heard someone walking past the wardroom."

"You heard me," he grunted, keeping his back to the door. "What of it?"

"Why, nothing. I just wondered . . . I mean, is everything all right? Would you like some company?"

"No, I wouldn't like any company," he snarled and splashed some more rum into his mug.

"My, my." Miranda pouted. "Did we have a lover's

spat? Wasn't she as eager to part her legs for you as you'd hoped she'd be?''

Garrett glared blackly over his shoulder. Miranda was leaning on the jamb of the door, her hands held casually behind her back, her breasts jutting against the silk, promising to burst free, like grapes out of their skins.

"Well, what did you expect?" she asked, bristling at the scowl on his face as he turned back to his rum. "After spending a week in the Yankee's bed, she probably thinks she's too good for the likes of you."

The mug descended untouched from his lips.

"Surely," she murmured slowly, "you didn't believe the nonsense she fed you about the Yankee lieutenant's carnal preferences? He's as much a fop as you are, Garrett Shaw. In fact, from what your charming dinner guest has been telling me, this Ballantine has enough of a reputation with the ladies to throw yours into shadow."

Garrett slammed the mug down on the rickety wooden shelf and rounded on Miranda. "What are you trying to tell me? Are you saying she lied about what went on aboard the *Eagle*?"

"I'm telling you nothing you shouldn't be able to see for yourself. If you'd care to look closely at your *virginal* bride-to-be, you'll see she has a certain lightness in her step — as if she no longer feels the need to walk with her thighs clamped together."

Garrett's jaw tensed, and the silence was stretched taut — as taut as the mask that suddenly over-stamped the powerful and ruthless set of his features.

"You knew about this. You knew all along about . . . *him*?"

She shrugged indifferently. "I'm a woman. I can tell these things with a single glance. I suppose it take a jealous man two or three."

"Why didn't you say something before now?"

"It wasn't up to me to open your eyes, Garrett. If they're so blinded that you can't see her making a complete and utter fool out of you —"

He was across the tiny cabin in two strides, his hands

gouging into her shoulders. "Shut up! Shut up, do you hear me?"

"Or what?" she demanded archly, her eyes alive with tiger-gold flecks. "Or you'll take your anger out on me, your *jealousy*? Did you honestly think she had something special, or was it just a burning need to be the first, the only, man in her bed?"

Garrett had no answer. His rage thundered through his veins, boiling the blood to a murderous degree. Miranda disregarded the pain where his fingers were all but crushing through to the bone and with a husky laugh, she pressed forward. Her breasts rubbed the smooth surface of his chest. Her hands slid along the rock-hard thighs and converged on the front of his breeches.

A curse and a quick flinch backward gave her a startling insight into the cause of his foul temper. Her eyes skimmed down his body, and she clapped a hand over her mouth to stifle her surprised giggle.

"My God . . . she didn't! She didn't actually stop you by —?"

Shaw shoved her roughly into the wall, but it was no use. Not even the pain of several jolts silenced her. She laughed until the tears filled her eyes.

He released her with a final thrust that sent her ebony hair flying across her face. He strode back for the jug of rum and drank the fiery liquid until the sound of laughter and the bruised fury in his groin ebbed.

He felt her presence behind him and braced himself as the feathery touch of her fingers traced their way across his back, down to the lean band of muscle around his waist and around to the smooth steel of his belly. Nimbly, the fingers worked to unfasten the black breeches. Teasingly they peeled the dark nankeen down over his bare flanks and with caresses as light and fleeting as a summer breeze, they massaged and nursed some warmth into his flesh.

"There now," she breathed soothingly, her lips and tongue moving with equal determination over the rigid muscles of his back. "We'll have everything back to normal in no time. Miranda can fix anything, didn't you know?"

Garrett ground his teeth together and inhaled slowly, deeply. The lids squeezed shut over his indigo blue eyes, and he pictured the scene in his mind's eye rather than watch it unfold: Miranda slipping down onto her knees before him; Miranda's hand sliding up his thighs, cupping his flesh gently, flattering him with fingertips and tongue, using her mouth with such expertise that he forgot where he was, who he was. He opened his eyes and looked down at the top of her languidly moving head. He blinked once. Twice. And it was Courtney he saw kneeling in reverence before him. Courtney's hands he felt, her lips and bold, saucy mouth seeking to pleasure him.

"I knew you'd come to me," he muttered under his breath. "I knew you wanted me. Yes . . . yes. . . ."

A groan curled his fingers into the raven tresses. His hips augmented her rhythm until the threatening surge began to mock the ability of his legs to hold him upright. The threat shuddered into reality, and he gasped, his hands unable, unwilling to drag the persistent mouth free. His teeth clenched. The veins in his neck stood out like blue snakes. The dark eyes rolled skyward.

Miranda refrained from venting her triumphant laughter, or even smiling with satisfaction, as she brought the mighty pirate king quavering to his knees. Instead she doubled her efforts, knowing each mindless groan was helping to seal the fate of Courtney Farrow.

# Chapter Seventeen

The night air raised goosebumps along Courtney's arms and legs as she crouched in the darkness of the bridge superstructure. Her breathing was shallow, but controlled. Her ears were tuned to catch the rush of the outlying surf, the eerie cries of the night creatures, the stealthy footsteps of patrolling guards.

She had been huddled motionless in the shadows for ten minutes waiting for her eyes and ears to adjust to the sounds of the ship at sleep. She was dressed in black breeches and a black silk shirt she had found among Garrett's possessions. Her feet were bare and noiseless, her vision as sharp as a cat's and twice as canny as she felt her instincts rising to the challenge. It was a game she had played often with Duncan Farrow; a game he had devised to test her prowling abilities as well as her reflexes in a dangerous situation. She had always excelled in the playing of it, often only losing to Duncan by mere seconds.

The object had been to get on the ship, search it for

something that had been hidden, then get off again without being detected or caught. In this case, the game was to move about on deck without being seen by any of the guards. The darkness was her best ally. The sky was moonless but its legion of stars were so bright and plentiful they cast their own light across the quiet cove. Crates, capstans, coils of cable all looked misshapen and out of proportion. The masts and yards loomed in silence overhead, like tall sentinels in a forest. The tarpaulin over the prisoners' pen was ridged with peaks and valleys like desert dunes.

Courtney pivoted on the balls of her feet and sidled closer to the outer barricade. She wriggled the last five feet on her belly, found a narrow gap, and slid beneath the ropes and between the crates without incident. Again she stopped and waited for her senses to adjust to the utter blackness. Most of the wounded Yankees were asleep. She could identify their positions by the snatches of labored breathing, the involuntary moans which came when a wound was jostled. She could not see where she crawled, and progress was slowed by the need to grope carefully in small circles before she moved in any direction. The stench of infection and unwashed bodies helped guide her away from the sprawled forms.

She worked her way slowly and painstakingly around the miserable confines of the pen, not knowing how she would identify Ballantine's from the other shapeless bodies, only trusting her instincts to do so. If he was as wide awake as she was, as wary of the guards, then more likely than not, he would be alert to an intruder beneath the canopy. She was counting heavily on it. If he was as clever as Falworth said — and she had no reason to doubt that — Ballantine should already know exactly where she was and be taking steps to intercept her.

Even so, the hand that snaked out and clamped over her mouth was as unexpected as the arm that curled around her waist and lifted her noiselessly into a pocket formed by two overlapped crates. A man's weight slammed down on top of her, an arm immediately locked against her throat cutting off both her air and her attempt to whisper who she was. She could not distinguish any of Ballantine's features but she thought she caught a brief glimpse of the stark white bandage around his forehead moments before the world started to spin and her vision pooled with swimming, nauseating lights.

"What the hell —" Ballantine's exclamation was hardly louder than a breath as he realized the body wriggling beneath his did not belong to one of the burly guards. He shifted his weight from her legs and relaxed the grip at her throat enough to allow her to take air, then he moved his lips next to her ear and breathed an ominous threat.

Courtney's eyes widened, and she jerked her head in a response. The hand clamped over her mouth was lifted, and she gasped gratefully as she pushed the steely fingers away from her throat. It took a few dizzy moments for her throat muscles to recover and her voice to regain the ability to give sound to the curses her lips were forming.

"—*of a bitch*! You're supposed to be tied up!"

"And you're supposed to be sound asleep in your cabin," Ballantine hissed. "What the hell are you doing wandering around here at two o'clock in the morning?"

Courtney swallowed with difficulty and massaged her aching throat. Ballantine sensed the reason for the pause, and she felt his hand on the curve of her shoulder, his fingers gently kneading the cruelly pinched nerves.

"What are you doing here?" he asked again.

"I came to cut you loose," she said with a frown.

"You what?"

"You heard me!" A gasp was smothered beneath his hand — gentler this time, but emphatic none the less. She sensed movement in the darkness next to the blot that was Adrian, and she saw him turn his head and mutter a few brief words.

"Dr. Rutger?" she breathed when the hand was removed from her mouth. He might have responded, but she couldn't hear past the low hum throbbing in her ears. But she saw him melt away into the shadows again, probably to stand guard.

"You were saying?" Adrian's voice was clearer, his mouth a scant inch from hers. *"Quietly."*

"The *Falconer* is ready to sail. Shaw is taking her out in the morning, along with the *Eagle*. This is your last — and only — chance to get off and get away before you're fitted for slave bracelets."

"You want to help me to escape?" There was an unmistakably mocking inflection in his voice. "Why would you want to do that?"

"Don't think it's because of anything that happened today. I could care less if Shaw sold you to Karamanli or Abhat Khan the Slaver."

"Then why are you doing it?"

"Does it matter?" she sighed with exasperation.

"It might."

She swatted the kneading fingers away from her bruised neck. "Are you worried it's a trap? Do you think that's why I'm out here risking my neck and my position on board this ship?"

"If that was the case, it wouldn't be so much of a risk, would it?"

Courtney's eyes burned. His voice was cool and remote. His hand had returned to her neck but she had the feeling the gentleness would turn to savagery at the first hint of treachery.

I want to help you, you fool! she wanted to shout. I'm trying to save your life, though God only knows why.

Aloud she said tersely, "Let's just say I pay my debts. You saved my life, and I'm returning the favor. Once you're off this ship, all debts are canceled. If I see you again, as my enemy, I'll kill you. Fair enough?"

"Fair," he mused calmly.

"How good are you at hiding in the desert, Yankee?"

"Passable."

"I believe you already have a gun?"

There was a slight pause, and she could swear she felt him smiling. "I have it."

"Then . . . if you and the doctor are ready?"

That won another pause. A startled pause, she thought, but he did not bother to question her sudden generosity.

"Matt!" The name was hissed into the blackness, and Rutger turned away from the barricade. He had not followed the muted exchange; their voices had been kept too low.

"Matt, come on. We're getting out of here."

"Out of here?" The doctor stared into the shadows. "How?"

"Over the side, I presume. Are you up to a swim?"

Matt hesitated, and Courtney detected sudden tension.

"I can't leave the men," he said finally. "I'm the only thing standing between them and a canvas sack. They barely get any manner of care as it is. If I leave, they'll get absolutely none."

"You can't do anything for them if you're in slave chains," Adrian said quietly, his voice flat, empty of conviction. Courtney frowned but she had no time to reflect on what she was hearing.

"We can't sit here arguing about it," she hissed urgently. "If you don't leave now, you don't leave."

"Then I guess I don't leave," Matt said easily.

Courtney looked to Adrian for some sign of support, but he remained a blank, silent shadow. She turned back to the doctor and, despite the danger that grew with each second's delay, she tried one last time to convince him to go. "Once the lieutenant is found missing, I can't answer for what manner of retaliation Shaw will consider appropriate, or who it will be directed at. *I can't guarantee he won't take out his anger on the wounded men . . . or on you!*"

"I guess I'll have to take the chance," said Matt slowly. "Adrian? Good luck. God speed."

"I'll be back," Ballantine murmured grimly and clasped a hand to his friend's shoulder to seal the promise.

Matt held his breath as he watched the two shadows crouch across the main pen and disappear through the barricades. He slumped against the crates and cursed softly as his back scraped on the rough wood. He would have been a liability, at any rate, he reasoned. With his crippled leg and his lacerated back he would not have lasted more than a couple of miles in such a mad dash. Adrian's plan was better . . . if it worked.

"There's a guard by the rail," Courtney whispered, crouched in the shadows beside Ballantine. "In a few moments he'll walk back to the other end of the deck. I'll distract him long enough for you to go over the side, shinny down the anchor cable, and swim to shore. You should be safe enough."

They were on the starboard side, facing the narrow mouth of the cove and the finger of land that curved around to form the bay. The *Eagle* was behind them. A swimmer could follow a straight line out to the peninsula and be relatively safe from prying eyes.

"Shaw keeps three men on the shore over there, as lookouts," she warned.

"I'll watch for them."

Courtney started to rise, but Ballantine's hand shot out and grabbed her wrist.

"What is it?" She stared at him through the shadows. His eyes were locked to hers and his mouth was a mere line, as if he wanted to say something, but could not quite formulate the words.

"Will you be all right?" he asked finally.

"I can take care of myself," she murmured, conscious of the hollow echo in her voice. She had said much the same thing to Garrett Shaw moments before he had overpowered her with ridiculous ease and almost raped her. But she was determined it would not happen again, regardless of the threat she had seen in the blue eyes.

"Jennings is dead," she said brusquely. "And the man you're after is Lieutenant Falworth."

Courtney felt the shock ripple along Ballantine's arm.

"What? *What did you say*?"

"Shaw knows all about you — from your Lieutenant Falworth. About how you were put on board the *Eagle* to search out the traitor who was selling us your secrets." She paused and he heard a soft, sardonic laugh. "It seems we have something in common after all."

"Are you absolutely certain? It's *Falworth*?"

"He joined us for dinner this evening. He told us everything, and I'm sure he's convinced Shaw you're a dangerous man to keep alive."

Her dark eyes probed his face, and she cursed the shadows for cloaking his expression. "I told you, Yankee, because I thought you had a right to know, after everything that's happened. There are things I have to know as well, and if you can tell me who betrayed my father? . . ."

A muscle jumped in Ballantine's cheek, the only outward sign of the rage that was growing within him, throbbing through his veins, infusing him with a strength of purpose that would have been terrible to see had she been able to read it in his eyes.

"Adrian . . ." she whispered, "Please. I have to know."

He shook himself to rid his mind of the pictures he was conjuring — pictures of Otis Falworth, prim and stiflingly proper in his tailored uniforms, Falworth smiling slyly, assuring Adrian of his assistance in trapping Willard Jennings as the spy. Was Falworth responsible for Alan's death as well?

"Where is he? Where is Falworth being held?"

"He mentioned something about the orlop deck. That's all I know. Adrian —"

The gray eyes cleared, chased away the cloying images. "I can only give you a code name, nothing more. No one ever saw him, no one ever talked to him face to face; it was all done through notes, left in prearranged locations, exchanged for gold —" A loud, scraping footstep nearby sent Adrian's hand around Courtney's shoulders to pull her hard against his chest. The guard was less than a dozen paces away, poised as he sifted the night sounds trying to detect whatever had spooked him away from his indolent patrol.

Two minutes . . . three passed without a sound, without the faintest motion from Courtney and Adrian. Her cheek was pressed against his shoulder, her senses flooded by the scent of his skin, his hair, the sweat of their mutual instincts to survive. The curve of his jaw was just above her brow; his hand was buried in her hair, holding her protectively, possessively against the shield of his body. Despite the danger she longed, suddenly, to fling her arms around him, to bury herself in his embrace one last time. In a few moments he would be gone and she would never see him again. Like a gust of wind, he would have blown into her life, toppled her defenses, and left, leaving nothing in his wake but a shambles. Her past, her present, her future held no meaning. Nothing mattered beyond the pounding, reverberating beat of her heart.

She became aware of the gray eyes staring down at her, and she knew the guard had moved on, the danger had passed. Yet he was in no hurry to release her. He must have sensed the blind desire quaking through her body, for his hand shifted to cradle her chin; his mouth tilted down and covered hers. The kiss was one of desperation and of need. He demanded the last shreds of her pride, her strength, her identity, and at the same time surrendered his own — willingly, knowingly. It was an admission, the closest he might ever come, she realized, and the knowledge made her cling fiercely to him, to prolong the moment until the ache in her breast became too strong to bear.

Uncaring of the consequences, unaware if he even heard, when they broke apart she gasped, ''God help me but . . . I still want you!''

She pushed out of his arms and darted swiftly along the deck, the tears blinding her to danger, real or imagined. She stumbled into a coil of rope, recovered, and dashed on until she arrived breathless and trembling at the guard's farthermost patrol.

She recognized the corsair at once. His short, wiry body swiveled in anticipation of an attack, and when he recognized Courtney, he finished swallowing the cud of tobacco he had partly inhaled down his throat, and the tension boiled over into a furious tirade.

"What the hell 're ye doin' up here, wench? Have ye no brains in yer head to charge on a man like that, in the middle o' the night, in the middle o' a watch?"

"I . . . I'm sorry, Davey," she gasped, her body shivering and numb, her mind reeling away from the man she had left twenty yards astern. She longed to turn around and search the shadows. She ached to watch him safely over the rail, into the bosom of the sea, to freedom. She wished desperately she could run back, run with him. . . .

"Ere, what's wrong, lass? Ye look like a ghost's after ye."

"Wh-what?"

A handful of short, square-tipped fingers gripped her upper arms and led her to a seat on an anchor capstan.

"Sit. Afore ye fall," he commanded, and she obeyed dumbly, like a mute, wounded animal.

"I'll kill 'im," Davey Dunn muttered. "I vow I will. If he's touched so much as a hair on ye're head, lass, tell me and I'll kill 'im. Slow, like, so's he knows he's a-dyin'."

Dunn's words broke through the turmoil of her emotions, and she stared up at the grizzled features.

"It's a small ship," he said gruffly. "There's no privat'cy on board, ner too many secrets. A body can't hardly take a piss without some wise ass peerin' at the color. Might be it's none o' my business, and if that's so, tell me. If ye want Garrett Shaw pawin' and stabbin' at ye, tell me an' I'll leave ye to him, even though yer father'd be rollin' in his grave and spittin' maggots."

Courtney swallowed hard, trying to take in Dunn's denouncement. He thought it was Shaw she was running from, and he was prepared to kill for her if she asked it of him.

"Oh Davey, Davey . . . I'm so confused." Fresh tears sprang hot and stinging into her eyes, forcing her to bow her head to keep such a blatant show of weakness from the blustery corsair.

"Confused?"

"Davey — I don't know who to turn to anymore. I don't know who or what I am. I can't think straight! Part of me wants to be strong and show Garrett and the others that nothing has changed . . . a part of me wants to just run away and hide. I'm . . . I'm so afraid of being alone."

The wiry fuzz around Davey Dunn's mouth worked furiously to find a way to respond to such a helpless entreaty. In the end, he sat down hard beside her and gripped her hand so tightly she feared her fingers would permanently mesh together.

"Ye're not alone, girl. Ye've never been alone. Ye've always had me, though I've never been one to put it into words 'r deeds. I owe more to Duncan Farrow than ye'll ever know, and I've a deal more respect for his daughter than she might believe. I know I were always tough and hard on ye, but it had to be so. Fact is, if ye was my own flesh and blood I'd've treated ye no different. Harder mayhap, aye. But ye're not alone. Ye'll never be alone, so long as I've a breath in my body."

Courtney stared wide-eyed at the man she had always feared, had always kept her distance from. She knew very little about Dunn's past, no more than anyone else except perhaps Duncan. He boasted no close friends, male or female, and while Courtney had never actually considered it for longer than a passing thought, she had regarded him with suspicion. *Trust no one*, Seagram had warned, and she had listened well.

"Davey," she whispered, feeling suddenly weary beyond all measure. "Davey, I don't know what to do. Someone betrayed Duncan. Someone sold him to the Yankees."

The red fuzz shifted. "Aye. I knew that."

"You" — she looked up — "*knew*?"

"Aye. Ain't pig's blood flowin' through these veins. I smell't sum'mit wrong ten month back. Told Duncan about it too, but 'e were slower to see it. Twice before someone were waitin' on us where no one had've ought to've been. Third time lucky, I guess."

"Do you know who it was?" she breathed, alert again.

"Someone real close to yer father, I warrant," he said, low and gutteral. "Someone he trusted. Someone who know'd 'is plans same time 'e did."

Courtney's fingers returned the vehemence in Davey's grip.

"*Garrett*?" she cried softly. "Oh no, Davey — *no!*"

"I've nay proof," Dunn said sharply. "But I've nay reason to think 'e's as pure as a saint neither. Ye ought to know yerself after tonight, what with 'im sniffin' out yer father's gold."

"*What?* What are you talking about?"

"Ye mean 'e were subt'ler than I thought 'e would be? 'E didn't outright ask ye 'bout Duncan's land . . . where it were, how to claim it, who to see in Virginny?"

Davey felt the shudder of recognition in her, and she heard a coarse, derisive laugh.

"Bastard. Yer father weren't even gone an hour and Shaw were through 'is papers like a locust. Why do ye think 'e tore hell fer leather to the Island, and then to chase after the *Eagle*? Mind, if 'e hadn't, I'd've taken the ship and hunted the Yankee meself, but 'e were near frantic thinkin' 'e'd lost a chance at the gold."

Courtney detached her hand from his and pressed her fingertips against her temples, trying to stem the sudden hammering in her head.

"Are you saying? . . ." She couldn't finish.

"I'm sayin', watch yerself, lass. I'm sayin' I wouldn't tell 'im nothin' . . . I wouldn't tell *no one* nothin' they don't need to know." He took a deep breath and added, "Unless'n o' course ye want to tell 'im."

Dunn was staring at the glitter of the emerald ring on her finger. After Shaw had left the cabin, Courtney had tugged and pried and tried to soap it free, but the knuckle was swollen and the ring refused to budge. She tried it again, under Davey Dunn's scrutiny, but the loathsome thing refused to leave her finger. With a sigh of resignation she looked up at Dunn, in time to see Adrian Ballantine step out of the shadows and bring his pistol down in an arc across the back of the corsair's thick neck.

With a grunt, Dunn slumped forward, his eyes popping, his jaw gaping in surprise and pain.

Courtney jumped to her feet, stunned. *"What are you doing? Why did you —?"*

"Sorry," Adrian said grimly. "And believe me, I'm sorry about this too, but there's no other way."

Courtney saw the blur of his fist too late to avoid it. It struck her jaw in a crosscut, snapping her head back and rendering her unconscious almost immediately. Adrian moved quickly to sweep her into his arms before she collapsed to the deck and, after a hasty glance behind him, he slung her over his shoulder and hastened to the rail. He swung a long leg over the oak and stole a precious moment to distribute her weight more securely before he slithered down the anchor cable to the water. She floated free until he was able to turn and tuck an arm across her chest. He kicked out strongly and swiftly, making very little noise or disturbance on the surface of the water as he towed her away from the looming hull of the *Falconer*.

Within ten feet of shore, his knees scraped the sandy bottom, and he was able to stand and lift Courtney's body in his arms as he stumbled ashore. He ducked into the long rushes and paused to catch his breath while he glanced warily back at the two moored ships.

Courtney moaned softly in his arms, and he looked down at her. The starlight was dusting her face, the wet clinging black silk shirt had parted to reveal a deep cleft between the paleness of her breasts. He did not want to stop and think about what he had done or why he had done it. He hadn't even consciously thought the action through. He only knew he wanted her off the ship and safe — whether she thanked him or hated him for it later.

Gathering the slender body close to his chest, he hunched over and ran with her through the dense brush, his footsteps carrying them toward the thicker curtain of trees.

Sergeant Andrew Rowntree and Corporal Angus Mac-Donald sat by the torn planks of the hull, their faces anxious as they peered out into the darkness. Andrew chewed nervously on his lower lip, his eyes darting frequently to the Scot's face.

"He should have been here by now. Do you suppose something has gone wrong?"

Angus sighed expressively. "Ye're an impatient pup, Andrew m'boy. He said he'll be here. He'll be here."

Rowntree licked his lips again and nodded. His palms were filmed with the dampness they always had before a battle; his mouth tasted sour. His teeth were coated and gritty, and he wondered if a decent time had lapsed since the last trip he had made to the slops barrel. He loathed the waiting. Once the fighting was underway he knew he would push all these petty discomforts to the back of his mind . . . but it was the waiting!

To distract himself, he let his attention wander from the smashed planks to the small, pale shadow crouched alongside Angus's massive bulk. No one had wakened the boy. No one had insisted that Dickie Little take any part in the coming activities, and yet the boy was there. Immovable. The dark brown eyes rarely flicked away from the indistinct outline of the prisoner's pen on board the *Falconer*.

The Scot's lips moved quietly in a curse.

"What is it?" Andrew demanded, craning forward.

"We're losing the darkness."

"What?"

"The moon. She's risin' up like a virgin's tit."

Sure enough, Andrew did not need to follow the disgusted thrust of Angus's finger to see where the glistening white curve of the moon was peeping through the sway of palm trees. Ten minutes at most and it would be clear of the obstructing slope and trees, and the cove would no longer be under a protective cloak of blackness.

"Damnation," Andrew muttered. "A little luck would have been nice for a change."

When Ballantine was confident the strips torn from his shirt would hold Courtney securely, he retraced the steps he had taken from the cove and made his way around the semicircle of brush until he was crouched opposite the *Eagle*. From his vantage point, the *Falconer* was hidden from his view, but something else was amiss. It took several minutes for him to detect the subtle change. The sky was becoming distinctly lighter and showing a pale wash of hazy moonlight behind the crest of trees.

Ballantine melted quickly into the shallow water and threaded his way through the undulating weeds until he was waist deep, breast deep, neck deep in the chilling water. With the same care as he had taken on his flight with Courtney, he approached the hull of the *Eagle*, his arms making only the tiniest of wavering ripples on the glass-smooth surface. He had taken the folding razor from his breeches pocket and clamped it between his teeth, but otherwise, he was unarmed. The gun he had stolen from Courtney's cabin, he had left with her. The powder was wet and useless, and he did not have any to replace it. He would have to rely on Andrew Rowntree's initiative to have supplied some manner of weaponry to the men on the *Eagle*.

It was unthinkable for the American frigate to be towed ignobly into Tripoli at the stern of a pirate ship. Ballantine would rather blow her apart at the seams and send her to a fiery death in this hellhole of a cove than subject a great lady to such a fate. His men agreed. With the help of Rowntree and MacDonald, a raiding party of handpicked men were willing to die to spare the frigate such an end.

Ballantine cut through the silvered inkiness of the water, swimming noiselessly to the side of his ship. He treaded water at the baseline and listened for any sign of a wary guard on patrol on her upper deck. He was still unable to see the *Falconer*, but he could see that the starboard side of the *Eagle* was already awash in moonlight, and once he rounded the bow, he would be in direct view of anyone glancing toward the frigate.

He adjusted the handle of the razor more securely between his teeth and followed the protective shadow as far as he could. There was no sign of activity on board the *Falconer*. No guards' heads were to be seen as they paced the decks. He had taken care of the one in the bow who had nearly discovered him and Courtney, and he had struck Dunn hard enough to ensure a full night's sleep. There were at least two others he knew about but he had not had time to deal with them; not and see Courtney safely on shore at the same time.

Again he refused to consider his motives for such a foolhardy act and instead pulled himself hand over hand along the side of the ship, stopping when he had the gaping hole directly above him. There were no footholds, no convenient cables to use to climb to the ravaged opening. He could not risk a shout, however quiet, nor could he afford to simply hang in the water and hope someone would look out.

Aiming carefully, he leaned away from the hull and tossed the folded razor in a gentle arc through the blackened gap in the planks. A few seconds later a rope made of torn and knotted shirts slithered out the opening and plopped into the water.

"Thank God, sir," Andrew Rowntree said as he and MacDonald grasped hold of Adrian and hoisted him through the hole. "You were so late in coming, we thought. . . ."

"*You* thought," Angus interjected gruffly. "And what did I tell ye?"

The moon touched the old soldier's face, highlighting the bushy frown and the grim, craggy set to his mouth. A new bandage had been added to his collection — this one around his forehead.

Adrian grinned, "Angus, you old warhorse, you look like hell."

The Scot arched a brow. "I wouldna' be throwin' stones, ifn' I were you."

Still grinning, Adrian searched the ring of tense faces until he found one that was paler, more apprehensive than the others. Matt had given him a few quick lessons and Adrian held up his hands to Dickie Little in the manner of a friend greeting a friend, then quickly reassured the fawn-like eyes that Matt was alive and healthy, that he and the men on board the *Falconer* were behind the night's mission one hundred percent.

"Our timing couldn't have been better," Adrian said aloud. "Shaw intends to take both ships out of the bay in the morning. It's just as well we planned for tonight; we wouldn't have had another chance."

"We don't have much of a one now, all things considered," Andrew murmured.

"Weapons?"

"We managed to come up with a few. Knives mostly. Clubs, truncheons . . . not exactly prime weaponry to go up against muskets and pistols."

"We have surprise on our side and that counts for a great deal. Guards on the door?"

"A brace o' drunken sots," Angus provided. "As well as a wooden bar."

Adrian raked the wet locks of tawny hair back from his brow and frowned when the uselessly sodden bandage came away from his wounded temple. "Then we'll all be leaving the way I came in. Angus — you'll take your party of men to the stern and gain the upper deck by way of the achor cables."

"Aye, sar! An' eager to do it we are!"

A chorus of quiet, intense "ayes" swelled from the shadows, and Adrian felt a perceptible easing of the burden from his broad shoulders. "Good. Damn good.

I'm counting on you to take command of the decks long enough to allow the rest of the men to get out and get to shore. If you can't get to the armory to use gunpowder for the charges, start fires. We'll burn her into the water if we can't blow her.''

"Aye.''

"Sir?'' It was Andrew Rowntree, looking puzzled and a little hurt that he had been passed over as commander of the raid.

"When I left the *Falconer* there were at least two more sentries awake and breathing. I'll need a handful of good men to come back with me, perferably those who are the strongest swimmers. With that blasted moon so bright we'll have to do the distance underwater.''

"Count on me, sir,'' Rowntree volunteered immediately. "Loftus and Kelly are good swimmers. Kowalski bellyaches, but he's got the best lungs on board.''

"Good, because once they get there, they'll have to help Matt evacuate the wounded. If it's at all possible we're going to move every last man off. We have to expect to lose some of them, but not without a damn good fight.''

Another wave of murmured support rippled through the crowd of men before they were hissed to silence.

"I won't order any man to go,'' Adrian nodded. "And I don't have to tell you of the danger.''

Rowntree grinned boyishly. "Hell, sir, if Angus does his job properly the corsairs will be too busy over here to look under their own noses.''

"I'll dae my job, ye young whip,'' Angus scowled. "Ye just make prime cartain ye get Archibald MacGregor off that Barbary sow. He's nae too fond o' water and wi' a torn leg he'll be like as to squeal like the clarty Glaswegian he is, so mind ye tap him good on the brain afore he kens what ye're aboot.''

"Noise will be our prime enemy,'' Adrian agreed. "If this plan has any hope for success, it has to be completed in absolute silence. The slightest sound could cost a life." He let the warning sink in for a moment then asked if there were any questions.

"Any word on the captain, sar?" Angus wondered.

"He's dead."

"And Lieutenant Falworth?" Rowntree asked.

Ballantine turned without answering. "Angus — all we really need is one large hole below the waterline. She's so low now she'll go down like a stone. Make sure you give yourself and your men ample time to get clear. You're a cantankerous old coot, but I've grown kind of fond of you."

MacDonald beamed under the praise. "Ye can count on me, sar."

"Everyone else" — Ballantine directed his orders to the silent crew — "I want you off as quickly and as quietly as you can go. Hug the *Eagle*'s bow until you're into her shadow. There's a twenty-yard swim to the cover of the weeds, then a clear run into the bushes. Head for the rise at the west end of the cove and we'll all rendezvous a mile down the coast. Don't stop for anything. Don't wait. My hope is the corsairs won't think we're worth the time or energy to chase. When the *Eagle* burns, her fires will attract company from land and from sea — the latter especially — and I'm counting on one of our own patrols to show the most curiosity. That's it then, unless there are any questions? Angus, pick your men and distribute whatever weapons you have to them. Andrew?"

"Ready, sir," said the young sergeant. He had removed his boots and stripped down to his breeches, as had the eight burly men he had selected from the crush of willing volunteers. Each had a knife tucked in his waistband and an oddly shaped object clutched in his hands.

"Angus's idea," Rowntree explained, seeing Adrian's inquisitive look. "A stocking filled with nails and bolts and scraps of iron. We had to literally take up the floorboards to fill them, but we've made four dozen of the bastards, and I for one wouldn't want to be on the receiving end."

Adrian tested the weight of it and agreed.

"Lieutenant!" An excited voice called from his watch by the gap in the planks. "Cloud, sir, banks of 'em comin' in fast."

"That's it then," Adrian said urgently. "We go now, while there's some chance of cover. Good luck, men."

"Luck, sirs," the men replied but Adrian was already through the hull and shimmying down the cloth rope. When his group was in the water, Adrian gave a signal and one by one they filled their lungs, and their heads dipped below the surface. With the watery, moon-etched clouds as a guide, the ten men kicked off from the side of the *Eagle* and swam to the *Falconer*, all but one making the crossing without the need to surface. The single head that broke the surface did so quickly and with such a soft *splop*, the half-dozing sentry on the stern rail of the *Falconer* barely troubled himself to gaze over the side.

Adrian cursed away the fatigue he felt in his arms and legs as the men huddled behind him at the base of the pirate frigate. One by one they swam for the anchor cable, climbing hand over hand to the row of deadeyes that jutted out from the side of the ship. They crabwalked sideways along the rail, careful to keep their heads low and their ears alert to any sound of movement on deck.

The moon shook itself free of the cloud bank and bathed the ship in a shimmery soft glow. Adrian craned his neck above the rail to scan the length of the quarter-deck and ducked back down as he saw the heads and shoulders of two corsairs standing so close to the rail he could have reached out and touched them.

He raised two fingers in a mute warning to Andrew Rowntree, who was crouched in the rigging lines beside him. Andrew nodded and unfastened the spiked sap from his belt. On a count of three they vaulted simultaneously over the rail, Adrian's knife slicing through the tissue and cartilege of one guard's neck before the corsair was even aware of him. Andrew brought the sap down hard and fast on the second man's neck, tearing away both the startled cry and half the bloodied tissue of his throat in the process. The corsair was dead before he struck the planking, and Andrew stared first at the blood gushing over his feet, then at the nail-filled cosset.

"Damn," he muttered. "It really works."

"You had doubts?"

"I doubt everything Mac does when it's blessed with a Gaelic oath."

Adrian bent over the body of the guard he had killed and searched him for weapons before dragging the corpse to the huge anchor capstan. Andrew was directly behind him and they hastily covered the two bodies with a sheet of canvas. Adrian waved the other waiting men aboard and led them in a running crouch along the quarter-deck to the prisoner's pen. Adrian stood watch at the same spot where Courtney Farrow had breached the barricade, while one after another, the men ducked between the crates.

"Shall I check for more guards for'ard, sir?" Andrew whispered.

"While you're about it, close and tie off the hatches. It won't stop them for long if they really want to get out, but it might delay them. When the men are ready, move them off — and remember: *quietly*!"

"Aye, sir. Will you be along, then?"

"I have some unfinished business below, Mister Rowntree. Don't wait for me. Get the men off, get yourself off, and get away from this cove before all hell breaks loose."

With the speed and silence of a panther, Adrian melted into the shadows and was gone before the sergeant could protest. Andrew watched and listened a moment, then he too followed the outer barricade until he was alongside the forecastle bridge. The hatchway was open. It took less than ten seconds to pull the heavy panel closed, loop some cable around the wooden latch and anchor it to the decorative rail.

# Chapter Eighteen

Miranda made her way quietly back through the rows of sleeping corsairs toward her own quarters. She had taken one of Garrett's shirts to replace the torn blue silk frock and had any of the men happened to grumble awake, he would have been treated to the vision of a pair of long, shapely legs gliding past his hammock. She did not care if they wakened, or if they saw her. She was furious, bristling with a rekindled loathing for all men, especially Garrett Shaw.

The bastard had called out *her* name. In the middle of the most glorious demonstration of erotic skill he was ever likely to experience, the bastard had groaned out a rum-soaked declaration for Courtney Farrow! It had taken every last ounce of Miranda's willpower not to grab his most prized possession and twist until she had broken it off at the root! Instead, she had lain there, fuming, seething, boiling until he had dropped off into a fitful sleep, then she had gingerly pried herself loose, snatched up the first garment she could lay a hand to, and departed, tossing a scathingly obscene gesture at the sleeping form.

Her anger was no less virulent when she arrived at her own cabin. She tore the shirt from her back as if the very scent it carried had scalded her skin. Not satisfied with merely removing it, she clamped her teeth to the hem and savaged the linen, continuing the destruction until all that remained was a small pile of shredded strips. Those she kicked, and in her fury, her toe slammed into the side of the wooden bed. Her mouth formed a perfect oval of pain, and the amber eyes smarted behind a film of tears.

"Bastard!" she cried when the pain subsided and she could speak. "Swine! Filthy, lecherous pig! You want the little bitch that badly, you can have her! Take her! Do whatever you want with her if she'll let you. You deserve each other!"

Muttering and swearing, she yanked her sea chest open and found a clean blouse and skirt. She took a narrow leather strap and buckled it around her upper thigh, then fit a razor-sharp dirk into the empty sheath. A second pearl-handled dirk went into the waistband of her skirt, and a second, even more obscene gesture was hurled at the mirror in farewell.

With a toss of her raven hair she left the cabin and moved stealthily toward the stairwell that led below. She wasn't exactly certain which storeroom Falworth was being held in, but she was not daunted. The most logical place would be where the water barrels were stored — every other compartment was crammed with booty from the *Eagle*.

The main danger was the locker set aside for the crew's use at night, where the lights could be used freely without fear of detection. She could already hear the buzz of voices and the odd laugh and cackle that signified that a few stalwart revellers were still awake. The door to the locker was partially closed to muffle the sounds from the rest of the ship, and a broad swath of light cut into the passage. She tiptoed up to the very edge of it and peered into the interior, but the men inside were watching intently as one of the women stained a newly pricked tattoo of a naked dancer on a crewman's forearm.

Curs, she thought. Low-lifes. Dogs. I don't need any of you, including Garrett Shaw, to get what I want — what I *deserve*.

Miranda darted past the door and headed swiftly toward the storage holds. The air was dank, rancid with mold and rat droppings. She could hear the scurrying of small furred feet ahead of her and as she rounded a corner, she saw a guard seated on a cask between the doors to the two sternmost holds. He was awake, engrossed in picking the maggots out of a stale biscuit. A single candle flickered in a wall sconce, the flame throwing off a weak circle of yellow light.

She patted the dirk at her waist, and as an afterthought, loosened the thong over her breasts so that the cloth gaped. She moved forward, the swish of her skirt causing the guard to glance up in surprise.

Harry Pitt's mouth went slack as he looked into the gaping cotton blouse. A partially swallowed crumb of biscuit took three bobs of his adam's apple to clear his throat.

Miranda stepped confidently into the light. "I want to see the prisoner."

Pitt wiped the back of his hand across his mouth to remove a shiny layer of grease. He stared at her dumbly as if he did not recognize the language she spoke.

With a deep breath, Miranda repeated the request. "I need to see the Yankee lieutenant, the one you brought to the wardroom earlier this evening."

Pitt's eyes flicked beside him to the door on the left.

"Ye do, do ye?" The ugly, pockmarked face screwed up suspiciously. "What fer?"

"That's my business," she said coolly.

"Capt'n Shaw know ye're here?" The yellowed eyes were stripping her naked as his hand wiped slowly across his mouth again.

"The captain has his business with the prisoner; I have mine."

"That so?" Pitt grinned. "Still, he might be right peeved if I was to let jest anyone wander in and out as they pleased."

Miranda sidled closer. "And rightfully so, I suppose. But that's only because he doesn't want everyone to know."

"Know what?"

Miranda widened her eyes innocently. "Why, about the gold, naturally. If everyone on board knew the Yankee was paying for his comforts with a chest of gold . . . well, the captain would have to share it, wouldn't he?"

Pitt's eyes jerked up from the shifting cotton. "Gold? Gold ye say?"

Miranda held a finger to her lips. "A thousand ingots, hidden somewhere on the Yankee frigate — or so he says."

" 'Ow do ye know about it?"

She indicated the door with a conspiratorial roll of her eyes.

"He told me. He tried to use it to bribe me into helping him escape."

"Capt'n know that?"

Miranda shook her head slowly, her eyes gleaming in the candlelight. "I was hoping I could . . . persuade the lieutenant to tell *me* where the chest was. I mean, if Garrett was planning to take it and keep it for himself . . . why shouldn't someone else, equally enterprising, do the same thing?"

Pitt licked his thin, parchment-like lips. "Man's caught stealin' or hidin' prize money, 'e's keel-hauled."

She smiled and placed her hands on the sweat-stained chest. "The man who helps me," she murmured huskily, "will *feel* as if he has been keel-hauled, but believe me, he'll live to swim another day."

Pitt swallowed hard. He felt her hands trail lazily down, and he groaned.

"What's wrong, Mister Pitt? Don't you believe I would reward a man who helped me?"

His mouth gaped as the nimble fingers searched for the loop of his belt. His eyes rolled down; his hands came forward to grasp the creamy olive shoulders. Her hand jerked and he gasped. She stepped quickly back before the claw-like fingers could clench into her shoulders again, then watched impassively as his bony fingers curled around the pearl handle of the dirk and tried in vain to dislodge it from where it protruded from his belly. The groan of surprise was low and drawn out as he crumpled to his knees. He teetered a moment, his eyes wide and staring at the blood-spattered hem of Miranda's skirt. Then he pitched forward onto the floor.

Miranda waited until the hideous twitching stopped before she leaned over and retrieved her knife, calmly wiping the blade on his shirt sleeve before she tucked it back into her waistband. She searched his pockets and found a ring of brass keys, one of which fit the door on the left.

Otis Falworth was already on his feet, and judging by his expression, she guessed he had overheard the proceedings in the hall.

"Good God," he murmured, staring at the body and the growing puddle of blood.

"Never mind God," she said archly. "Drag him in here out of the way."

"Are you mad? Someone's bound to find him."

She straightened from her search of the guardpost, a long-snouted pistol to add to her collection of weapons in her hand.

"I don't intend to be here long enough to worry about anyone finding him. I'm . . . _we're_ getting off this ship tonight."

Falworth stared at her blankly. "Tonight?"

"There's a lower gangway hatch we can use. It's a twenty-yard swim to shore and once there we'll be well hidden by weeds and brush. Garrett's taking the _Falconer_ out of the bay tomorrow. This is our only chance."

"Chance to do what? Go where? We're in the middle of nowhere."

"*Nowhere* has villages and ports. I know enough of the language to get us by."

"But . . . there are nomads, and Berbers. . . ."

"And I haven't time to argue about it," she snapped, planting her hands on her hips. "I'm leaving this ship. Are you coming with me or not?"

As she turned on her heel and started to walk away, his hand shot out and grabbed her by the arm.

"All right, all right. I'll go. Wait until I pull the body into the cabin and cover it."

Shortly thereafter they were hurrying along the darkened passageway. At the foot of the aft stairwell, Miranda held a finger to her lips to warn him to silence. They were directly below the gangway hatch, a small rectangular door on the starboard side, cut into the planks between two thirty-two-pound long guns. On either side of the hatch, strung between the remaining eighteen cannon on the lower deck, were the hammocks of the sleeping crew. The likelihood of one of the men waking was inestimable, but the door was left open for ventilation and was the only unguarded way off the ship.

"You *are* mad," Falworth declared in a whisper after he had poked his head above the top step. "There's ten feet of open deck to cross, and the moon is lighting the path like a beacon."

Miranda smiled, her eyes gleaming with excitement. "You once told me you were willing to risk anything to have me, my lieutenant. Were those just the words of a lustful man, spoken in heat?"

Falworth studied her face, faintly visible in the waxy half light that spilled down the stairwell. Her lips were slightly parted, moist and dark. Her breasts pushed at the cloth of her blouse, the distended nipples reminding him of everything she was offering.

"I'll even go first, my brave lieutenant," she breathed. "You can follow, or you can remain here."

With a swirl of her skirt, Miranda darted up the steep ladderway, hesitating at the top for a moment before the slender calves climbed out of sight. Falworth stared up the ladder, his tongue sliding desperately across his lips to try to moisten them. He rubbed his palms slowly on his breeches to try to dry them. He had not bargained on this.

"Damn," he murmured and moved forward, his hands on the guide lines, his foot lifting to the first rung. But a movement in the shadow behind the stairwell distracted him and his foot missed the step, falling heavily to the deck.

"What the —"

Adrian Ballantine, half-naked, dripping wet, caused him to flinch back from the steps altogether.

"Don't," Adrian warned, his voice an ominous slash in the darkness. "Stay in the light. Keep your hands where I can see them."

"Adrian! Where did you come from? How did you get away from the others?"

"The *how* isn't important," Adrian murmured. "The *why* might interest you, however."

Falworth glanced up the ladderway but there was no sign of Miranda. "Good God, man, nothing matters now except that we're both free and we have a chance to escape. Come with us. I've bribed the girl to help me get ashore —"

"No," Adrian snarled quietly, one hand reaching for the scruff of Falworth's neck while the other pressed the cold edge of a knife into the arched throat. "*You're* going to come with *me*."

Falworth resisted only until the knife kissed deeper. "Yes! Yes! I'll go with you wherever you say."

Adrian directed him back into the darkness of the companionway, and Falworth heard a soft creak, as if a door was being pushed open. It was the sail locker, empty of most of its spare canvas, but not completely unoccupied. The stub of a candle was sitting in a lump of wax on a shelf, the light too weak to do more than define the shadows. One of them was the sprawled body of a corsair, his limbs askew, his head bent at an odd angle to his shoulders.

Falworth licked his lips again. "Are you planning to tell me what this is all about? We're on the same side, for God's sake!"

The knife moved, and Falworth felt the sweet, sharp slice of the blade into his flesh.

"Which side is that, Lieutenant?" Adrian sneered harshly. "Whichever side happens to pay the most?"

Falworth gasped and tried to swallow the panic rising in his chest. He was aware of something warm and wet sliding down his neck, soaking the collar of his shirt.

"Please," he croaked, "let me explain."

"That's what I'm here for — explanations. Starting with *why*."

"Why?" Falworth stammered; shortness of breath caused beads of sweat to rise across his brow. It would do no earthly good to stall or to lie. He should have known this would happen sooner or later. Damn Shaw for not —

*"I'm waiting, Lieutenant!"*

"Debts!" Falworth gasped. "I had debts I couldn't meet. Debts I had no hope of ever repaying."

"So you sold out your country and your crew?"

"No!" The knife bit deeper; the blood began a steady trickle. "At least . . . not at first. Please — I'll tell you everything . . . everything! Only don't kill me. Not here. Not like this."

"Your cousin at the Admiralty office — was he your source?"

"Yes, but —"

"The *name*," Adrian spat, his eyes as cold and flat as steel.

"W-Winthrop. Charles Winthrop! But he didn't know anything about it, I swear. His only crime was that he liked to brag and he thought . . . he thought I was only interested in his position."

"Go on."

"Wh-what else do you want to know?"

"How you made contact with the enemy."

"A tavern. I . . . I met an Englishman there —"

"An *Englishman*! You mean you never dealt with Farrow directly?"

"If you'd just let me explain," Falworth said through his teeth, his jaw clenched against the threat of the knife.

Adrian adjusted his position so that Falworth was pressed flush against the wall and had no option but to watch his fate being decided in the cold depths of Adrian's eyes. The steel blade eased slightly.

"Explain," Adrian commanded.

"I only dealt with the Englishman. That's what he called himself — 'the Englishman.' I don't know who he was. I never knew what he looked like. I only ever heard his voice. He was always careful never to let me see him. It could have been you for all I know."

"How did you meet this . . . Englishman?"

"I . . . a debt I owed a senior lieutenant on the *Eagle*. I couldn't pay it. He threatened to expose me as a cheat and a liar. We were in Gibraltar at the time and . . . and I approached a press gang with a few coins and a time and location where they could intercept the lieutenant."

"You bastard —"

Falworth swallowed hard, fighting the pressure on his throat. "The next time we were in port, I was approached by another man. Someone who . . . who. . . ."

"Someone who offered you a great deal of money for an insignificant piece of information?"

Falworth nodded through the drenching film of sweat. "Y-yes. How did you know?"

"I didn't," Ballantine said scornfully. "But it had to be something like that. It's the way it usually starts — a little bit of blackmail, then more, then they've got you and it's too late to pull out."

"Yes. Yes, that's it. It was too late —"

"How did the information get into Duncan Farrow's hands?"

"I don't know. I didn't know it *was* going to Farrow, I swear it. I mean . . . I wouldn't have sold them anything if I thought it was going outside Gibraltar. I mean . . . we spy on them, they spy on us. He was an Englishman, for God's sake. He had an accent!"

"Anyone can fake an accent, you fool!" Adrian snarled.

Falworth's hands splayed against the wall. His fingers brushed something round and solid, and he grasped it in desperation. "Y-you're going to kill me, aren't you?"

"You've just confessed to treason. Can you think of any reason why I shouldn't kill you?"

"I can get you off this ship," Falworth gasped with a trace of hysteria in his voice. "I have Shaw convinced I can see him safely through the Straits and into open water. Of course I had no intention of letting him escape. I would have turned him over to the navy as soon as we reached Gibraltar —"

"Of course you would have," Adrian agreed dryly.

Falworth blinked the sweat out of his eyes. It was pouring from his brow and temples and it flowed between his shoulder blades like a stream. Adrian leaned ever closer and lowered his voice.

"Tell me about Alan."

"Alan?"

"You implied you knew something about his death . . . that it was more than an accident."

Falworth's eyes bulged from their sockets. "I was lying! I only said it to earn your confidence, to get you to believe it was Jennings. I . . . I swear it!" His hand tightened around the pike. "I don't know anything more about your brother's death than what you know. It was an accident! A cleat swung loose and —"

"And crushed his skull; yes . . . after it put a neat little puncture mark through his chest, through his heart."

"A puncture?" Falworth cried. "You mean he was stabbed?"

"You tell me."

"I don't know! I swear I don't! And I'm not taking the

blame for it!'' The pike came up; too late, Falworth saw the gleam in Adrian's eyes and realized that Ballantine had been waiting for him to commit that fatal error. The ball of Adrian's knee drove into Falworth's wrist and forearm, the force of the blow snapping the bone and causing the pike to fly out of his grip. At the same time, the knife was pressed deep into his throat and drawn slickly through cartilege, sinew, and tendons, severing the jugular and the windpipe before Falworth could gasp either surprise or pain. A sickening gurgle and hiss of air were the only sounds in the small compartment.

Falworth's mouth worked convulsively, and his eyes bulged at Adrian in horror and disbelief, but Adrian had already stepped away. Without the support of Ballantine's arm, Falworth's body slipped slowly down the wall, his head jerking with the thick spurts of blood.

Adrian's face showed no reaction, but his fists were trembling by his sides, and his belly muscles ached with the tension. After several moments, the urge was still great within him to slash the knife again and again until there was nothing left but pulp, but a few deep breaths brought him back under control. He had no idea how long he and Falworth had been in the sail locker. Surely the men would have nearly all been evacuated and, knowing Andrew Rowntree, the young sergeant would come looking for Adrian despite his orders to the contrary.

Ballantine's eyes flicked to the stub of the candle, then to the body of the corsair sprawled on the canvas. There had been a strong odor of rum on the clothes and breath of the man as he had stumbled out into the passageway — with the intention, no doubt, of fetching a wench to share the coziness of the locker. As a trysting ground, the compartment was private and secluded. It was also — if the designs of the *Falconer* and the *Eagle* were basically alike — directly above the powder magazine.

Adrian located the jug of rum beside the makeshift canvas bed; he drizzled the contents onto the folded sails, the dead corsair's clothes, Falworth's clothes. He unstuck the candle stub from the shelf, unmindful of the hot tallow dripping down his fingers, and after a cautious glance out into the companionway, he threw the candle onto the soaked canvas. The rum caught instantly with a quiet *whoosh*. The thirsty yellow and orange flames raced from canvas to shirtsleeves, then dribbled to the leg of Falworth's breeches.

Adrian closed the door and started to retrace the route he had taken from the upper deck. He got no farther than two steps when a shadow detatched itself from a niche and blocked his path. The shadow held a cocked pistol aimed squarely between his eyes.

# Chapter Nineteen

Courtney's eyes slitted open, and she groaned softly. She was lying on something that smelled of damp earth and rotting vegetation. Her clothes were wet and clammy against her skin. Her hair was soaked, and matted with bits of mud and clinging weed. Trees were swaying gently overhead, and she wondered why she could see them so clearly. An attempt to sit upright brought another discovery: her hands and ankles were bound securely, and a wadding of cotton was stuffed in her mouth. The ache in her jaw forced her to remember the last fleeting moments on the *Falconer*. She had been talking to Davey Dunn, talking about the man who had betrayed Duncan . . . then something about gold . . . and then Ballantine had loomed up out of nowhere, knocked Davey unconscious, and punched her in the jaw!

It was the last thing she remembered — a ball of rock-hard knuckles. She had no idea where she was or how she had got there. She had to assume that, in his lunacy, Ballantine had kidnapped her from the *Falconer*, had tied her and gagged her and deposited her in the bushes. But why? Was he hoping to use her as a hostage? As leverage to persuade Shaw to release his men?

With a surge of fury, Courtney tried to scream but produced only a deep, strangled wail that caused more pain to her nose and throat from the vibration than the paltry whistle was worth. She squirmed and thrashed to test the strength of her bonds, but there, too, accomplished little more than an increased throbbing in her shoulders and legs.

She lay back, panting. Was it her imagination or did the hollow thrum of the pounding surf sound closer? Had Ballantine carried her over the crest of the slope that surrounded the cove? The ground cover was too dense to see through, the trees too close to determine if the ships were visible or even within shouting distance.

She would kill him. If she ever broke free and if she ever had an opportunity, she would kill him for using her like this! How could she have been so blind or so stupid to think that he *wouldn't* make use of her?

Another frantic burst of energy caused her arm to rub painfully against the protruding root of a tree. When she grunted away the frustrating pain, she became aware of the thin band of leather strapped to her forearm, concealed by the black silk sleeve. Holding her breath, Courtney strained awkwardly to work two fingers beneath the cuff, to coax and prod the slim handle of the dirk free of the sheath. She found it hard to believe Ballantine had failed to search her for a weapon, but she was grateful for *his* stupidity.

It took a few minutes of awkward maneuvering for her to saw through the cotton strips around her wrists; another moment of quick but gentle prying to remove the gag and massage her aching mouth shut again. Her fingers found a swelling on the left side of her jaw; her tongue found a ragged edge where a tooth at the back of her mouth had been broken off by the blow.

A swift slash severed the strips at her ankles, and she sprang to her feet, a bitterness settling around her shoulders like an icy cloak. It was welcomed. It cleared her mind of all soft and foolhardy thoughts, and brutally forced her to face the truth.

Ballantine had used her again, had heartlessly and cold-bloodedly used her all along. On the *Eagle* to assuage a physical discomfort and as a means of stopping Seagram. After the battle to earn sympathetic treatment for his men. In the cabin this evening to prove his mastery over her body, to mock her, to distract her while he stole the gun and God only knew what else from the cabin. And then he had let her make a fool of herself by helping him to escape, by prying out the name of the man he had been sent to find, by providing him with the means to hold Garrett to ransom. No doubt he was standing, at that very moment, cocky and arrogant in Garrett's cabin demanding the release of his men in exchange for Courtney Farrow's life.

*Garrett!*

The name shocked yet another memory free — of the conversation with Davey prior to Ballantine's intervention. Dunn suspected Garrett of being the traitor!

The thought brought Courtney up sharply, her bare feet skidding on a tangle of weeds as she halted on the crest of the slope. Below her, awash in shiny iridescence, lay the cove and the two sleeping ships. As she stared at the silhouettes of yards and rigging, her mind rejected the notion that Garrett Shaw had betrayed Duncan Farrow. Shaw was ambitious and ruthless. He was cunning and conniving and dangerous in every sense — but he was no Judas.

And yet, in a terrible way it made sense. Garrett was close to Duncan. He knew the plans for the raids well in advance. Designing an elaborate trap at the bay of Moknine would have been easy . . . as easy as telling the Americans when to attack Snake Island. Ballantine had said the traitor was known only by a code name. They had all devised code names years ago when they were fighting the French — Duncan, Verart . . . Garrett. Garrett had been known as "the Cobra." Was that the name the Yankees had come to rely on?

God, she was tired of it all. She should take Seagram's advice and find her own way to America. If Duncan was alive, he would go there. And if Duncan was alive he would know how to deal with the Garretts and the Ballantines. She would no longer feel lost and alone. She would feel safe again.

Find Duncan, Seagram had commanded. The burly giant had known, as Courtney knew, that a fleet of Yankee ships would not have been able to capture and hold Duncan Farrow. And certainly would never have been able to hang him.

Courtney took a deep breath and turned to look behind her. From her position she could see the glittering swath of the coastline stretching westward. Tangier lay in the west. Casablanca. Marrakech. Her father was well known in all three ports; she would have no trouble booking passage across the Atlantic; merchant ships made the crossing practically every day, and once in America she could —

A sudden roar shattered the tranquility of the night air. As she whirled and gaped, the deck of the Yankee frigate seemed to tremble; the spars and yards began to shake like the arms of a palsied old man . . . and then the planks of the deck swelled and lifted. They burst apart at the seams, scattering wood and canvas skyward in a shower of flames. A brilliant yellow fireball exploded upward and out, shooting burning debris into the moon-washed sky. The roar sent Courtney's hands up over her ears; the wave of hot dry air made her briefly avert her face from the blast. Screams and shouts and the sound of gunfire split the remaining silence wide apart, and like magic, the deck was alive with running men. They leaped overboard and swam frantically for shore. They dove into the cooling waters to douse the flames that were tearing eagerly at their clothes and skin. Many swan for the *Falconer*, and there too there were shouts and the sound of gunfire.

Hardly aware of what she was doing, Courtney stumbled down the slope. She heard voices in the trees beside her, men running in the opposite direction, and she recognized them as fleeing Americans. They came so close she had to swerve and duck around a thicket of weeds to avoid being seen. Her heart was racing so fast and her veins were stinging with so much adrenalin, it took a full minute for her to realize that the danger was not only from the Americans. Less than ten feet away, one of the crewmen from the *Falconer* was running a boy to ground. With horror, she recognized Dickie Little, his thin legs faltering as he fought to escape.

Courtney darted from the cover of the bushes and ran to intercept the corsair. She reached them just as a hairy hand grabbed Dickie's arm and yanked him to a painful halt. The pistol the boy had been carrying flew out of his hand and landed in the dirt at Courtney's feet.

"Wait!" she cried. "Don't hurt him!"

The corsair's fist was raised; the blade of the knife he held glinted coldly. He recognized Courtney with a scowl.

"Eh? Not hurt 'im? The little bastard shot me. Look 'ere!"

He pointed to a graze on his ribs, hardly more than a scratch.

"He's only a boy. Let him go. You've a score of grown men to choose from if you have a need to prove your manhood."

"Eh?" The corsair's eyes slitted from the insult, and his hand tightened on the boy's arm until the wide brown eyes rolled upward and he shivered from the pain. The corsair's gaze raked along Courtney's body, and with an evil sneer, he shrugged Dickie aside and took a purposeful step toward her. "Aye, so it's proof of my manhood ye're wantin', is it? Mayhap it's a lesson ye're long overdue in takin', li'l mistruss Farrow."

Courtney bent over and quickly snatched up the pistol Dickie had dropped. It was double barreled, double shotted, but the boy had fired at least one of the charges. Was the other still in the chamber?

The corsair's grin widened as he watched her fumble with the steel pin to set the hammer in full-cock position.

He was obviously confident. Did he already know two shots had been fired?

The corsair's hands stretched out toward her. A twig snapped in the bushes behind them, and his eyes flicked briefly past her shoulder, giving her just enough time to force the tremor from her hands, raise the pistol, and pull the trigger.

Miranda's head jerked around at the sound of the nearby explosions, giving Ballantine the opening he sought. His hand flashed out and grabbed the muzzle of the pistol, twisting it out of her hand.

She had stopped him outside the sail locker, the surprise on her face matching that on his.

"Well, well," she murmured. "If it isn't Lieutenant Ballantine. Out for an evening stroll, are you? Without an escort?"

"I thought I'd take a tour of the ship," he said dryly.

Miranda's eyes did not waver from his face, yet she could see his entire body. The faint light in the passage outlined his broad shoulders, the damp dishevelment of his hair, the arms that hung loosely at his sides.

"Where is Falworth?" she demanded.

"Dead."

She sucked in a breath. "You killed him?"

It was a question that needed no answer, and she took a cautious step back, out of range of the long, too casually held arms.

"He said you were dangerous. He told Shaw he couldn't afford to let you live."

"Shaw should have taken his advice."

"Perhaps I'll do him the favor," she said evenly, tightening her grip on the pistol. "How did you get down here?"

"The forward hatch. It's the only one open. My men have sealed all the others."

"Your —" She paused and her finger curled against the

trigger. "A nice try, Lieutenant, but I'm not buying it. Shaw has guards posted all around the ship."

"Only four, surprisingly enough," Ballantine said matter-of-factly. "And three of them are dead. Not very smart of Shaw to post such a light watch."

"Apparently not. This will, however, inspire him to kill all wounded prisoners in the future, especially if you attempt to organize any kind of a foolhardy escape."

"Past tense. They're gone."

"All except you?"

"I had some unfinished business — but then you must know all about it."

"About Falworth? Yes, I know."

"And you were willing to take a chance with a man who admittedly planned to doublecross you as soon as you were away from Shaw?"

Miranda's eyes narrowed. "Assuming, of course, the fine lieutenant wasn't doublecrossed first."

"Of course," Adrian murmured, conscious of the strong smell of smoke in the companionway. In no time at all the locker would be an inferno, the passageway a death trap.

"I would have thought any unfinished business you had would have taken you to the aftercabin. Or have you had your fill of her?" Miranda added sweetly.

"I'm surprised you care what happens to Courtney."

"Oh, I care. I care enough to want her out of my life — permanently."

"Is that why you were trying to leave the ship with Falworth?"

"One of the reasons." She paused, and her finger slipped out of the trigger guard. "I figured there wasn't much point in staying, now that Shaw has made his choice clear . . . or didn't you know he had moved into the aftercabin with her? He was a trifle disappointed to discover she was no longer a virgin, but I gather she's managed to convince him of her . . . preferences?"

Ballantine was given no time to react to the statement. A

sudden volcanic blast from the *Eagle*'s powder magazine stunned them both momentarily, and Miranda long enough for him to wrest the gun from her hands. He grabbed a wrist and pinned her arm behind her back before she could dodge to avoid him. She would have screamed, or at the very least struggled to break free, but when he twisted her around, she was given a clear view of the bright tongues of fire lapping out from beneath the door of the sail locker. Ballantine wasted no time in pulling her back along the companionway toward the afterhatch.

"You'll never get off this ship alive," she hissed angrily.

"Another word, madam, and I'll make certain one of us doesn't."

"Lieutenant Ballantine?"

"Rowntree! What the devil are you doing down here?"

The sergeant stepped out of the shadows. "This was the only hatch left open. I figured you had to be down here somewhere."

"I ordered you —" Ballantine melted against a recess in the wall, his hand clamped brutally over Miranda's mouth as the sound of running feet, pounding fists, shouts and curses warned them of the aroused corsairs. "Are the men safely off?"

"Aye, sir. Every last one of them. MacDonald's on board —"

"*What*?"

"He thought we might need help, so after he set the charges he led his men across —"

"The bloody fools!"

"— and frankly, sir, they were eager for it. These bastards were wanting a good fight for what they've done to us, to the *Eagle*. To the credit of the men, sir, after the wounded were helped ashore, not a single man-jack of them obeyed the order to run. They've all come back, either here or to the *Eagle*."

"Well we'd better get topside and put an end to it, because the *Falconer* is about to blow."

Rowntree glanced back over Adrian's shoulder to where

the screams and shouts had taken on a new urgency stoked by the throbbing yellow glow at the end of the companionway.

"Yes, *sir*!" he said and vaulted toward the ladderway.

"Move, if you value your life," Ballantine hissed into Miranda's ear, and he half carried, half dragged her up the ladder behind Rowntree. Men from the *Eagle* were positioned at the top, holding captured cutlasses and boarding pikes, in a defensive ring around the two emerging officers. A surge of screaming corsairs came out of the darkness, swords slashing, muskets spitting spark and shot, knives hacking and slicing at the valiant corps of marines.

Miranda was more terrified of a wayward cutlass finding its way to her throat than she was of the fires or the continuous volley of explosions. She groped frantically for the pearl-handled knife at her waist, but it was gone. She kicked her skirt high and reached for the dirk strapped to her thigh, and was rewarded by the warm press of the handle against her palm. She swung it up and slashed at the ironhard vise around her waist. She stabbed and slashed again and heard Ballantine grunt. The hand over her mouth jerked away and tried to capture her flailing arm but she felt the knife strike solid flesh again, and this time, the arm went limp and released her.

She spun away from Ballantine and screamed for a clear path through the swarming corsairs. She burst free of the fighting, miraculously untouched, and ran along the smoke-filled gun deck toward the forecastle. There she found more slashing cutlasses, more sweating, straining, bleeding bodies fighting to the death in front of, and blocking, the starboard gangway. She barely paused to curse before whirling and running for the ladderway that led to the upper deck.

Ballantine was surrounded by a crush of Americans and corsairs. He was vaguely aware of pain in his left forearm, but he felt a naval cutlass pressed into his hand and his thoughts were for nothing else but to use it effectively against the swelling ranks of pirates.

With Rowntree by his side, he fought his way to the forward hatch, and together the pair defended the retreat as the handful of Americans climbed to the upper deck. The *Eagle* was ablaze. The glare from the exploding magazine was lighting the deck of the *Falconer*; the air was fogged with smoke and drifting ash; cinders rained down on the heads of the men as they carried the battle to the deck rails.

Ballantine was shouting for his men to abandon the *Falconer* when he caught the sound of a familiar bellow behind him. Garrett Shaw, dressed in breeches and leather crossbelts, was charging along the deck, a cutlass raised in one hand, a pistol in the other. The gun was discharged point blank into the swarm of Yankees and the empty weapon thrown onto the deck. A second was drawn from the crossbelts and aimed and fired before Adrian could fight his way through the wall of men to confront the Barbary captain. One of the armed corsairs stepped in front of Shaw and pointed a musket at Ballantine's chest.

"Shaw!" Adrian shouted.

The shaggy black head swiveled to find the source of the shout and with a snarl, he shoved the man with the musket aside.

"Come on, Shaw," Adrian growled. "We're evenly matched — or don't you think you can win in a *fair* fight?"

Shaw threw the empty pistol aside and shrugged the crossbelt from his shoulders. He tore a barbed pike from a rack on the mainmast as a backup for his sword and advanced slowly.

"No one touches this one!" he roared. "The golden-haired bastard is mine!"

Adrian deflected the first two wild swings of the cutlass with an ease that deepened the scowl on Shaw's face. He darted in on a quick thrust, which Shaw countered with a deadly sweep of the pike. Adrian flinched as the iron hooks gouged a deep, splintered gash out of the rail where his arm had been. He barely avoided the return sweep as the pike whistled past his ear to shatter a crate to fragments.

Grasping his sword in both hands, Adrian cut a swath across Shaw's ribs before he could regain his balance from the previous lunge. A wide stripe of red appeared diagonnally across the bronzed flesh; the blood beaded from it in a crimson necklace before the red pearls broke and spurted down his skin. The pike returned the insult, glanced off Adrian's shoulder as it screeched into a metal cleat and showered both their heads with sparks.

Shaw backed away a pace and shook a spray of sweat from the ragged black mane. He surveyed the damage to his adversary, noting the bloodied shoulder, the hanging, almost useless left arm. Ballantine's chest was gleaming with sweat and blood, yet there was a cool determination in the flinty gray eyes that set a grin on Shaw's face.

"I'm going to enjoy cutting your heart out, Yankee. And I'm going to enjoy carving it in tiny pieces to feed to the gulls."

A roar of laughter sent the handpike carving across the planking at the level of Adrian's knees. Ballantine chopped at the violent arc and managed to jar the pike from Shaw's hand. In the same motion he slid the blade upward, peeling skin from the corsair's hand and arm. Shaw spun away, avoiding a follow-through that would have pierced his belly.

Shaw took a deep breath and lunged. He feigned a dive to the right, and when he saw Adrian brace himself to ward off the expected blow, he swung low and fast to the left. Adrian felt the cold steel punch through his thigh, and he staggered back against the rail. Shaw threw the bloodied sword aside and clawed his hands around Adrian's throat, squeezing until the muscles bulged in his arms. Adrian's hands had flown up in a reflex defense, but only his right hand had any strength remaining. His sword had clattered to the deck. His back was being nearly broken in two over the oak rail, and he was separated from the rest of the men by at least five long paces.

Shaw's smile was ferocious, his breath as hot as a dragon's as he pressed his advantage. Adrian's face flushed from the strain of the deadlock, his legs trembling with the effort to counter the backwards push.

Andrew Rowntree dragged his sword from the belly of the corsair who had fallen at his feet and took a hasty glance around at the carnage. There were bodies and blood everywhere, smoke, sweat, cinders . . . He gasped and unsheathed the knife from his waistband just as Garrett Shaw was removing one hand from around Adrian's throat, bunching it into a fist, drawing it back to deal the final blow that would break the lieutenant's back, snap his neck — or both. Andrew threw the knife and heard the shocked scream as the blade split the back of the clenched fist.

Adrian grunted air into his lungs as the pressure at his throat was startled loose. He drove his fist into Shaw's jaw and knocked the corsair away, then staggered unsteadily to where his sword had fallen. He heard a faint rumble from somewhere beneath his feet and was thrown heavily against the rail. He heard splashes and saw men flinging themselves from the shrouds and rigging. He vaguely noted that the trees were moving — no, the *Falconer* was moving! Someone had cut through the anchor cables, and she was drifting toward the mouth of the cove.

But that was all he noticed. Another tremendous explosion shattered the air beside his ear, and his senses reeled with the stinging burn of cordite and gunpowder. Ballantine could not see who had fired the musket; he could see nothing at all beyond the frozen tableau of men fighting, men dying. The *Eagle* burned magnificently behind them. Falworth was dead. Courtney was safe . . . He closed his eyes and gave himself to the sensation of falling, of tumbling over and over through space, of plunging into a cold, soundless void. He thought he groaned a name, but he couldn't be sure.

# Chapter Twenty

Courtney heard the click of the mainspring as it released the steel pin. There was a delay while the flint sparked and ignited the powder, then an explosion sent the lead ball out the barrel and plowing into its mark, dead center of the corsair's furrowed brow. The force of the shot stopped him in mid stride, the shock of it caused him to stagger back, dead before he hit the ground.

Courtney's arm ached from the recoil, and her eyes smarted from the bite of the powder flash. She stared at the dead corsair in a kind of numb disbelief, then sought out the cringing form of Dickie Little.

"It's all right," she murmured. "He can't hurt you now."

He trembled to his feet, his eyes and nose running wetly as he sobbed into Courtney's arms. She dropped the heavy pistol and gathered him close to her breast, knowing how frightened he must be, locked in his world of silence. She remembered Matthew Rutger telling her the boy had lost everything — his family, his hearing — when the ship he had been a passenger on had exploded. No doubt he relived that awful moment with each fresh eruption that buckled and ripped across the *Eagle*'s deck.

She glanced toward the cove and shivered. The recently jury-rigged masts and yards were collapsing under fountains of flame and sparks. The cables were snapping from their tackle and writhing through the air like burning snakes. Men were leaping overboard, their shouts drowned out by the thunderous roar. They swam toward the *Falconer* and scrambled for the lines and netting only to find the second ship belching smoke as well, the upper decks alive with fighting men.

Bodies floated on the surface of the churning water, some American, some corsairs, illuminated in grizzly detail by the fires. Someone had managed to axe through the anchor cable, and the departing tide was luring the *Falconer* closer to the mouth of the cove, leaving thrashing men in her wake; men too weak to swim after her.

Courtney knew the glow in the sky would be visible for miles. Any patrolling ships — Yankee or otherwise — would be attracted to it like moths. Shaw could not afford to let the *Falconer* founder. He would have to cut his losses, regain control of his ship and run her into open water. Even in the confusion on deck someone had noticed the drift and had ordered men into the yards to loosen sail and steer her clear of the curved finger of land. The Yankees caught on board were fighting to the rail, taking a last flurry of slashes, then turning and jumping for the safety of the water.

Courtney had only seconds to make a decision: to stay ashore or to leave with Garrett Shaw and the *Falconer*. She was a strong swimmer; she could make up the distance well before the ship passed through the mouth of the cove.

"Dickie" — she grasped his shoulders and held him at arm's length — "Dickie, I have to go now. You have to stay. You have to run as far and as fast as you can. Garrett will be furious; he'll come after you if it's at all possible —"

"B-but the doctor? . . ."

Was it a trick of the wind, or had the pale lips moved in a whisper?

"Dickie? Dickie, can you hear what I'm saying?"

The boy blinked and a grimy hand smeared the tears across his cheeks. "Y-yes, miss."

Courtney was momentarily at a loss for words. "Dickie, I . . . I'm happy for you, but . . . you have to leave this place. You have to get away, quickly."

The boy shook his head determinedly, then flinched as another explosion tore through the night. Courtney opened her arms and he leaned into them willingly, burying his face against her shoulder until the noise and flare had died down. There were more voices on the slope — angry, vengeful voices raised in triumph.

Courtney searched for the ghostly shadow of the *Falconer*, but the ship was almost hidden behind a swirling wall of smoke.

"Dickie, I have to go now. I have to leave you. I can't be taken prisoner again. Can you understand me?"

The small, oval face lifted to hers. "Yes, miss. I understand."

"Then you must run up the hill now. Go with the others. You'll be safe with them."

"The doctor —"

"Doctor Rutger can't be too far behind. He'll find you, I know he will. But I also know he would want you to be safe."

"Please, miss," he pleaded softly, his scraped hands plucking at her sleeve. "Stay with me. Stay with us."

"Oh Dickie, I can't. I can't! I don't belong in your world, in their world. I don't —" She bit off her words. What good would it do to explain it? The Yankees would be picked up and transported to Gibraltar and from there, home to a hero's welcome. She was still Courtney Farrow, daughter of Duncan Farrow. If she wasn't hanged outright in Gibraltar, she would surely face indefinite imprisonment in whatever hellhole they chose to put her in.

"I can't," she said quietly and on impulse, leaned forward and brushed his cheek with a kiss. Then she tore herself from his embrace and ran the rest of the way down the slope to the thickest patch of weed and rushes.

She waded knee deep into the water and ducked into the protective cover of the shoulder-high reeds. She was aware of the bitter warmth of tears streaming down her cheeks, but she did not know when they had begun or why they persisted. She knew she had no choice. She had to get to the *Falconer* and get away before it was too late.

She flinched as a red-hot splinter of wood arced over her head and plunged hissing into the water. She stumbled in her haste, and a weed tangled around her foot and ankle, throwing her forward into the water. She choked and gasped, staggering upright again, and was preparing to dive into the open stretch beyond the reeds when she saw something floating face-down several yards away.

There was no mistaking the broad, muscled shoulders, the torn white breeches, or the shock of sun-bleached hair. It was Adrian Ballantine. His arm seemed to move, seemed to be grasping forward in a last feeble attempt to push the water behind him, but the hand sank beneath him and he rolled slowly, spiraling into the inky depths.

Courtney dove into the bed of weeds that were sucking Ballantine down. She felt them reach slippery tentacles around her wrists and ankles, but she fought them off and stroked determinedly for the faint white blur beneath her. She grabbed at a shank of blond hair and kicked as hard as she could for the surface, but he was too heavy and her fingers slithered free. Her face broke clear of the water, and she swallowed another mouthful of air, then jack-knifed straight down. This time she hooked an arm beneath his and dragged him, weeds and all, to the oily bright surface. She kicked and stroked one-armed into shallower water, until her feet scraped bottom. Only then did she stop to angle his face, to pound him sharply, viciously between the shoulders, to wrench his arms and slap his face . . . anything to start him breathing again.

"Adrian! Damn you, breathe! *Breathe*!"

There was no response. Frantic now, Courtney placed her mouth over his cold lips and forced the air from her lungs into his. She was rewarded by a rush of seawater and by what might have been a faint spasm in his chest. She tightened her arms around him and breathed into his mouth again and again until she felt another spasm, stronger this time, echo throughout his body. Another breath brought forth a gurgled cough, and he retched, ejecting the water he had swallowed. Courtney kept a hand beneath his chin and an arm around his waist to keep him from slipping back into the water.

A loud volley of explosions made her glance quickly over her shoulder, in time to see the *Eagle* buckle one last time. The water was too shallow to completely cover the burning hulk, but as the main body of timber sank gracefully below the surface, it forced great boiling clouds of steam skyward. What little remained of her superstructure continued to burn through the rising, hissing steam, making the clouds throb with an eerie inner light.

The *Falconer* was passing through the mouth of the cove. Courtney looked down at Ballantine; he was barely conscious. The retching had passed, and he was gasping fitfully at clean air, but he was weak and trembling.

"Stand up, Yankee," she commanded harshly. "You've got to stand on your own now. You're strong enough. You can do it!"

There were shouts coming from the dense brush along the shoreline — Yankees searching for stragglers!

She heard a familiar voice shout in her direction. "There's someone in the water. Sergeant, can you see who it is?"

"No, Doc . . . Wait! Yes, there's two of them. Hey there! You!"

Courtney felt the panic rise in her, and she attempted to

push Ballantine toward the shore. His eyes fluttered open and he peered closely at her face. His mouth opened and his lips moved, but there was no sound other than a painful rasp of air.

Courtney turned and splashed into deeper water. Behind her, Adrian's hand clawed at the loose folds of her shirt and held fast, even though she kicked and flailed and lashed out to be free. More shouts indicated someone splashing into the reeds nearby, and she reached frantically for the knife strapped to her wrist.

Andrew Rowntree pushed aside a handful of weeds and saw the boy that the lieutenant had paroled from the *Eagle*'s brig. He had a knife raised and was about to bring it down where the lieutenant's hand was twisted into his clothing. Rowntree lunged the final few steps and knocked the blade off target, then dove for the boy's midsection even as he shouted for Rutger. He plunged with Courtney into the tangled bed of weeds and grappled furiously for control of the knife.

Ballantine swayed unsteadily on his feet, his body being pushed and pulled by the action of the water. A blinding pain in his chest and head prevented him from speaking and from comprehending what was happening.

Matthew slogged through the water and took in the scene in a single glance. The wound on Adrian's head had reopened and blood poured down the side of his face. His left arm hung limply at his side. He was standing at an odd angle, as if barely able to keep balance, but his eyes were burning fiercely as he stared at the two bodies churning the water white beside him. Rowntree was fighting hand to hand with one of the corsairs and, from their positions, appeared to be winning. Arms and legs were flailing; the bodies rolled over and over, sending water spouting for yards on either side. A fist caught Rowntree squarely on the temple, and he redoubled his efforts, managing to catch the corsair's wrist and yank it around and up into the small of his back.

The pain caused Courtney to gasp in a mouthful of

muddy water. The pressure increased, and she felt her knees wobble, then fold as they were kicked out from under her. She was pushed face down into the slimy silt of the bottom. She coughed out the water that was already burning in her throat, but there was nothing but mud to replace it. Her attempts to unseat the powerful weight on her back ceased. The pain in her arm blossomed and spread until her whole body was seared with agony.

Matt had an arm beneath Adrian's shoulder to support his weight as he helped him toward solid ground, but the lieutenant resisted and instead floundered toward the crouched-over Rowntree.

"No," he croaked dryly. "No . . ."

"Adrian, for God's sake —"

"Courtney!" Ballantine's voice was a harsh scrape in his throat. "She pulled me out!"

"Courtney?" Matt frowned, then whirled to stare at Rowntree. "Sergeant! No! Wait . . . the lieutenant wants the girl alive! Sergeant, do you hear me? *Let her go*!"

Rowntree responded to the doctor's command and stood up at once, his hands dragging the weakly struggling boy to the surface. As soon as Courtney felt air on her face, she swung around hard, coughing as she flayed blindly at the shadow beside her. Instinct sent her hand groping for the second dirk she had strapped to her calf, and it was in her fist before the sergeant could blink, slashing out at him before either Matt or Ballantine could intervene.

Rowntree released her shoulder with a yelp as the blade scratched through the tender flesh of his breast.

"Get away from me," she warned. "Stay back, or so help me —"

Rowntree cursed and took an angry step toward her, but a shout from Matt stopped him.

"Don't try it, Sergeant! She'll have you carved into fillets before you can raise a hand."

Rowntree began a question, but it was answered amply as his eyes fell to Courtney's gaping shirt front.

"Good God, she *is* a woman!"

Matthew exchanged an urgent glance with Adrian.

"Allow us to introduce you to . . . er, Courtney Brown, Sergeant," Matthew said, "And as the lieutenant once cautioned me, she has a fondness for sharp objects. In the future you'd be wise to search her if she's out of your sight for more than ten seconds."

Ballantine's eyes had not left Courtney's face. "Give the knife to Rowntree," he ordered in a dry rasp.

"No," she said and twisted so that the weapon was pointed threateningly at him.

"How far do you think you'd get, even if you used it on one of us?"

Courtney's dark eyes slid past his shoulder, to the hazy, smoke-filled mouth of the cove. The *Falconer* was gone. Only the swirling mists of smoke remained.

With a cry she ran for the deeper water. She got no more than four swimming strokes away when she felt a hand grasp her ankle and haul her back. She fought without the strength or energy to do so, and Rowntree had no trouble slipping a hand around her waist and carrying her back to the shallows.

"He'll come after you!" she screamed. "Garrett will come after you if you don't let me go!"

"He'll find an eager welcoming committee if he does," Ballantine said evenly and indicated the ring of silent, watchful men collected along the edge of the brush.

Courtney stopped struggling and sagged against Rowntree's arm.

"Please." Her dark eyes held Ballantine's in a desperate plea. "Let me go."

"I can't do that," Ballantine murmured. To Rowntree he added, "Bring her up on shore, Andrew. And if you value your hide you won't turn your back on her."

"Aye, sir," Rowntree said grimly.

"Bastard," Courtney hissed with quiet vehemence. "I hate you. I wish I had let you drown!"

Adrian stared at her intently. "Maybe both of us made a bad mistake tonight."

Matt tightened his hold on Ballantine's arm. "Come on. Let's get you on solid ground and see what's left to salvage."

Two men from shore waded into the knee-deep water to assist Rutger in leading Ballantine onto dry land and lowering him gently at the base of a thick palm. The bleeding at his temple had slowed to a trickle and needed only a cursory inspection. His left arm bore three deep gashes which Matt frowned over at length before directing his concerns to the dark, ominous stain spreading on his upper thigh.

"Good God," he muttered, stripping off what was left of his shirt. "Between you and Angus MacDonald. . . ." He let the sentence hang as he tore the wet cotton into strips.

"Where is the corporal?" Adrian asked with a grimace.

"I don't know. I haven't seen him."

"Andrew?"

"No, sir." Rowntree shook his head. "The last I saw, he was on the *Falconer*, wielding an axe like a bloody great windmill."

"Dickie?" Matt looked up anxiously. "Has anyone seen young Dickie?"

Courtney looked steadily at the doctor but kept resolutely silent. She had no intention of speaking to any of them, ever, if she could possibly avoid it. And especially not to give them any good news!

Her gaze shifted away from the doctor, and she found herself staring into a pair of cool gray eyes. She held them a moment, then disdainfully turned her head away.

The rebuff was not lost on Adrian, nor was her obvious desire to disassociate herself from them. Or was it from him? Miranda's words rang in his head — Courtney and Garrett Shaw choosing to share the aftercabin . . . the bed. . . .

He forced himself to focus on the crisply burning masts

of the *Eagle*, on the bodies floating on the surface of the water, on the tall column of black, twisting smoke. He hoped with all his heart that the *Falconer* was burning itself into a fiery hell; it was no less than she or her captain deserved. The fact that there had been no explosions yet was of no concern. The blaze alone would take hours to bring under control, and hours of manning buckets and pumps meant a shortage of crew to guide the ship to safety. One small, feisty gunboat across her bows, and Shaw was finished.

"This cove will be attracting scavengers by the droves," he murmured aloud, noting the dawn was no more than an hour or so away. He winced as Matt tied off a thick pad of cotton around his thigh, the pain reminding him there were other wounded men to be considered. "How many did we lose? Any idea?"

"We won't know until morning," Rowntree said grimly. "But the price was a steep one."

"The price of freedom always is." Adrian took a deep breath to try to steady the pounding in his chest and the remaining vestiges of nausea. "Andrew, you'd best get the others organized and moving. I want to put a couple of miles between us and this place by morning."

"Aye, sir."

"And take a rough tally of what weapons we have. Surely the men came away with more than a handful of socks."

Matt looked puzzled, and Rowntree held up one of the saps by way of explanation.

"The men took everything they could lay a hand to," the sergeant said to Adrian. "Muskets, pistols, pikes. I'd say Shaw would think twice before tacking about and coming after us."

"At this point it isn't Shaw who worries me the most." Adrian struggled to his feet with the help of Rowntree and the doctor. "Just because we've foiled Shaw's attempt to lock us in chains doesn't mean there aren't a hundred Berbers waiting over the next rise, eager to oblige."

"Aye, sir." The dangers of being run aground on Barbary soil were impressed vividly in the minds of all seamen. The prospect of slavery ranked well behind the horror stories of being staked out under the broiling sun, painstakingly skinned inch by inch, or being used for live target practice by hostile nomads. As soon as the *Eagle* was discovered and identified, her crew would be considered prize game and hunted accordingly.

"I'll post rear and front guards," Rowntree said. "And if I can find Mac —"

"Ye're lookin' in the wrong places, ye young snap," came a hoarse croak from the bushes. Angus MacDonald, torn and bloodied in a score of new places, swaggered into the little clearing, his face split in a grin. "An' I brung ye another wayward soul. . . ."

Dickie Little detatched himself from the Scot's massive shadow and hurled himself into Matt's outstretched arms.

"Doctor, doctor! You're alive!"

"Dickie, thank God, I was —" Matt stopped. He stared down at the boy, a look of astonishment on his face. "What did you say?"

Dickie grinned shyly. "I said I was happy to see you're alive, sir."

Matt caught a shallow breath and held it while his hands lifted from the boy's shoulders to cradle either side of his head. His soft hazel eyes were swimming as he carefully asked the question, "Dickie, can you hear me?"

"Yes, sir. Not very well, not very clearly, but yes, sir. I can hear you."

Matt looked up at Angus MacDonald, then Adrian. "I don't know how . . . or why. The explosions, perhaps."

Dickie had been content to beam up at the doctor, but a slight movement off to the side made him glance at a slim, huddled figure.

"You stayed, Miss! You stayed with us!"

Courtney made no comment, no move to welcome the boy into her arms.

"Miss?" The boy looked bewildered, and a little angry as he glared accusingly at Matthew and Adrian. "Have you hurt her? You have no reason to treat her like an enemy. She was very brave. She saved my life."

"Saved your life?" Adrian's voice was low, his eyes locked on Courtney's. Dickie misread his expression as doubt, and he reached out a hand and touched the lieutenant's arm imploringly.

"Yes, sir, she saved my life. She shot one of the pirates. He was chasing me through the trees, and she shouted at him to stop. When he wouldn't, she picked up a gun and shot him clean through the head. And then she made me hide in the bushes. She told me to run but I couldn't. I just hid until the corporal found me and . . . and . . ." He groped desperately for a way to soften the harsh frowns on the faces of the tall, wary officers. "Please, you must believe me."

Rowntree, MacDonald, and Rutger were staring at Courtney but she refused to acknowledge any of them. She dug her nails into the palms of her hands and used the pain to help her control the waves of emotion building within her. She didn't want their gratitude; she didn't want their admiration or respect — or their pity. Most of all she did not want to have to look into the cool gray eyes and see the distance there. He did not need her anymore. He was once again in command, in control, and she was once again an unwanted responsibility.

It was Rowntree who eventually broke the strained silence. "We should be moving, sirs. The dawn. . . ."

"Yes," Adrian agreed, his voice sounding sharp and cold. "See to the others, then. We'll be along directly."

"Can you manage?"

"Of course I can manage," he grunted and pushed away from the support of the tree. His leg trembled under him; if not for Rowntree's quick hands, Adrian would have pitched forward onto the ground.

"Thank you, Sergeant," he gasped. "I just need another minute and I'll be fine."

"The hell ye will, sar," Angus growled and moved in to lend a hand. Adrian's cursed insistence that he could walk on his own caused the Scot to glare a muttered apology at the lieutenant before hauling back and punching him solidly on the jaw. Adrian fell sideways over MacDonald's arm, and with a deft maneuver Angus had him up and slung over his shoulder without a hint of further protest.

"I ken he'll travel easier this way," Angus snorted and started walking up the slope, leaving the doctor and the sergeant staring after him in stunned silence. After a moment, Matt and Rowntree exchanged a glance, then a shrug, and the sergeant headed up the slope behind Mac-Donald.

"Come along then," Matt said to Dickie and Courtney. "We have a way to go before sunrise."

Courtney looked past him to the cove, to the dark, concealment available on the far shore.

"You can go if you want," Matt sighed. "I won't try to stop you. I assume Shaw is heading east?"

Courtney's deep green eyes were turned to his, her face blank and unreadable in the moving shadows.

Matt put an arm around Dickie's shoulders. "I can understand your reluctance to come with us, Court. And your reluctance to trust us, or to believe in Adrian. But he's a good man. A good friend. If he lives through the next few days, it's my guess he'd put himself and his reputation on the line for you. And since he and I are the only ones who know who you really are —"

"What do you mean, if he lives?"

Matt exhaled slowly. "I don't have to tell you his wounds are pretty bad. He's lost a lot of blood. If the shock doesn't kill him, the heat and flies and God knows what else just might. You obviously know a little doctoring. I was hoping you'd know of some plants or herbs that grow in this area . . . anything that might help. . . ."

She looked up the darkened slope.

"I'll come with you," she murmured. "I'll even help you if I can. But the first reasonable chance I get, I'll go my own way."

"If that's what you want."

"It's what I want," she said firmly.

"Then when the time comes, I'll do everything I can to help you. You have my word on it."

Courtney uncurled her fingers, releasing the pressure of her nails from her palms. Cool, slender fingers slipped tentatively into her hand, and she felt a reassuring squeeze from Dickie Little. She looked down and responded faintly to his smile, then allowed herself to be led up the slope after Matthew Rutger.

# Chapter Twenty-One

By noon of the following day, the air was sweltering. The sun had climbed steadily in a cloudless blue sky and offered no relief from the flies and sweat and the dry breezes that carried sand and dust into mouths and eyes. The coast was alternately rugged — with jagged rocks and short, stubby scrub trees — and barren — with stretches of hot white sand that burned underfoot and attracted the scorching rays of the sun. Often the straggling party of a hundred-odd men were forced to slow to a snail's pace, and rest stops were called when they could seek relief in the shallow surf. Two ships had been sighted, both bearing the square-rigged sails of the Moroccan Xebecs. Rowntree had commanded the men to remain low and out of sight until they passed, since the crews would be less sympathetic than the pirates they had just escaped from.

When Rowntree estimated they were ten miles west of the cove, he ordered the men to scout ahead for a place to set up a temporary camp. The wounded men, carried laboriously on makeshift litters, could travel no farther without rest, food, and fresh water. A location was found at the base of a steep wall of rocks. Lookouts situated on top could see a mile of beach in either direction and detect any approaching threat from land or sea. Armed parties were dispatched to forage for food. Others were sent to scout the shore for driftwood and brush. Fires for warmth would be essential for the cold night ahead, and to signal if an American patrol ship was spotted.

While the watches and the foraging parties went about their duties, the remaining third of the men, on Rowntree's orders, curled up beneath the shade of the rocks and tried to steal a few hours of badly needed sleep.

"Ye should take ye're aen advice, laddie," MacDonald growled. "Ye're about tae drop in ye're shadow."

"Look who's telling who to rest," Andrew rejoined wryly. "You've carried the lieutenant nearly every step of the way down this miserable beach."

"Aye, an' I'd dae it again, if need be. He's nay lookin' good. I could feel the fever risin' in him e'en afore we stopped."

The two marines looked silently to where the doctor was kneeling over Adrian Ballantine. Courtney was beside him, her hands outstretched to accept the bloodied, sodden bandages as they were carefully peeled away.

"You'll have to wash them, I'm afraid," Matt said, his voice raspy from exhaustion. "We've none to spare. Damn . . . if I only had a few of my instruments. A needle and thread. Anything to close these wounds."

"Can't you seal them any other way?"

"You mean cauterize them? Yes, I could. But if this fever is from shock, I don't want to risk the strain on his heart."

"And if it's from infection?" she asked softly.

"If it's from infection, I'd need a saw, not a hot iron." Matt leaned back and dragged a hand wearily across his brow. He saw Courtney's shocked expression and attempted a reassuring smile. "He had a good dunking in the water, and the wounds bled freely enough. The chance of infection is slim. As for the others —"

Matt's smile faded as his eyes scanned the other litters. There were a score of minor wounds, a score of men as badly off as Ballantine, and some whose best hope was a quick and merciful death. He had thought the conditions on the deck of the *Falconer* were hell on earth; he was at a loss for words to describe what he thought of this environment.

Courtney had no idea how to respond to the anguish she saw on Matt's face. She could not hate him or treat him with cold disdain as she had resolved to do, nor did she trust herself to keep her emotions under guard with Adrian so helpless, so obviously in pain. His complexion had taken on a yellowish hue; his face and torso were bathed in sweat. He was failing so rapidly it frightened her, and she knew she could not bear to watch and do nothing.

"I'll wash these bandages," she whispered and took the soiled cotton strips to the knee-deep surf to scour them in the fine sand. Some of the men had waded into the shallows and were scrubbing the sweat and grime of the battle from their skin, bathing their injuries. As she knelt on the beach, they stopped what they were doing to stare at her.

The water was cold and refreshing. There was still mud caked in her hair and in her clothes, chafing against her skin. She was sorely tempted to wash but she was still wary of these Yankees.

They knew she was a woman; there was no hiding the truth since she'd had to tie her shirt in front to compensate for the lost buttons. Her slender waist drew speculative gazes, as did the creamy vee of flesh that showed at her plunging neckline. So far no one had ventured to speak to her, much less touch her, and she could only assume it was because of Ballantine's protection. How long that immunity would last she dared not even guess.

After spreading the torn strips of shirting on a rock to dry, she walked back to where Matthew was fussing over another wounded marine.

"I saw some plants back along the shore," she said without emotion. "I think they were the kind the Arabs use in poultices."

"Fine. Fine. I'll use them if you think they might help."

"I'll go along with you," Rowntree said, rising from his seat by the base of the rocks, and Courtney's eyes flashed her contempt.

"Are you afraid I might run away?"

Rowntree flushed. "No, miss. You could've done it ten times over if you'd wanted to. I just thought you might want help."

"Well, I don't. I'm quite capable of carrying a few leaves and berries."

Rowntree's flush deepened — more so when he heard the Scot's full-bellied chuckle. "There's tellin' ye where ye can poot it, laddie."

Andrew stared after the retreating figure and, with a grim frown, followed her. Courtney detected the shuffle of footsteps in the sand behind her and whirled around, her fist raised defensively, the dirk she clutched winking ominously in the sunlight.

Rowntree halted at once, his gaze meeting the challenge in her eyes. "I was only wanting to make up for last night," he said tautly. "I had no idea you were a . . . a woman. I wouldn't have fought so rough if I'd known."

"Well, I would have killed you, Yankee," she replied calmly, "had it been the other way around."

Rowntree's eyes flicked to the knife, then back to her face. "Yes, miss. I believe you would've. But the way I see it now, we're both sort of after the same thing. On the same side, so to speak. I mean, after what you did for the boy, and what you're doing for the lieutenant. . . ."

"I'm not doing anything I wouldn't do for a wounded dog," she grated.

The crimson stain rose in the young sergeant's face again, and he spoke through clenched teeth. "Yes, miss. But if it's all the same to you, I'd like to help anyway."

Some of the tension went out of Courtney's stance and with a disgusted curse, she tucked the dirk back into the wrist strap. "Suit yourself, Yankee. I don't care."

Rowntree was glaring at the leather sheath. "I see what the doc meant about the knives. I could've sworn that was the one I knocked off you last night when you were about to stab the lieutenant."

"I was not going to stab him," she countered evenly. "I was going to cut away the end of my shirt where he was holding it."

With that she turned and strode down the beach. Rowntree stubbornly followed, his eyes burning into the back of the narrow shoulders. During one of the few lucid moments the lieutenant had had during the arduous walk, he had ordered Rowntree to guard her with his life, and by God she was going to be guarded whether she liked it or not.

Courtney veered off the coarse sand and wandered along the bordering brush, bending now and then as a plant caught her attention. She found a patch of coriander and another of marigolds, the seeds and flowers of which could be brewed into tea to reduce fevers. She found the thick, rubbery leaves she had seen the women on Snake Island use to tie on wounds to draw out the poisons and parsley and fig leaves to crush and apply to burns. When the pouch formed by her shirt ends was filled, she turned and found Rowntree standing wordlessly behind her, stripped to the waist, his shirt held out to take the overflow.

"Where are you from, Yankee?" she asked with narrowed eyes.

"Virginia, miss."

She grimaced and continued walking. "I should have known."

They stuffed his shirt with edibles — dates, figs, wild onions, and carrots, then started back toward the cliff. They passed a small stream on the way, and Courtney knelt beside it, luxuriating in the taste of the cool, clean water, and the feel of it splashed on her steamy skin. She could not resist pouring handfuls of it over her head to rinse out the mud and sweat, nor could she pass the opportunity to let it trickle down her neck in shivery rivulets.

"Miss?" Rowntree was positively glowing red. "If you'd like, I could go over yonder behind those rocks and you could . . . well, you could bathe proper. I'll see no one disturbs you."

Courtney's first impulse was to refuse, but before she could speak Rowntree threw her a quick smile and trotted off behind the barrier of rocks.

The bath was indeed refreshing. Courtney washed out the shirt and breeches as well, knowing they would dry rapidly in the hot sunlight. What she had not considered until it was too late was that the damp black silk would cling to her every curve. The look on Rowntree's face when she emerged from around the rocks, set her temper on edge all over again, and she did not speak another word to him on the trek back.

Rutger hurried over to meet her and rummaged feverishly through the herbs she had gathered. Some were met by a quick grunt, others a smile, still others a frown of curiosity. But for the most part he was pleased and said so.

"It isn't a herbalist's dream, but it will help. Perhaps if we could risk a small fire and brew up a broth of sorts. . . ."

Courtney was staring past the doctor's shoulder to where Ballantine was stretched out on the sand. "How is he?"

"The same," Matt sighed. "Worse, maybe. I don't know."

Courtney looked closely at Matthew. His exhaustion was growing more pronounced by the minute. The lines around his mouth seemed to be carved deeper; his eyes were puffed and underscored with heavy dark smudges. He couldn't have had more than a handful of hours of sleep since the *Eagle* was first attacked, and he was obviously in danger of collapsing.

"Why don't you rest?" she suggested quietly. "I'll look after things here."

"I don't need —"

"Your hands are shaking; you can hardly see straight. You need to rest or you'll be no good to anyone."

Matt opened his mouth to deny it, but he closed it again, knowing she spoke the truth. He licked his dry lips; the words had difficulty forming. "Maybe . . . for an hour or so. No more. Yes, I'll rest for an hour and then I'll be fine. I'll find a bit of shade —"

Adrian groaned in his fitful sleep, and Matt's hazel eyes went immediately to him, as they did to every other man who flinched at the flies or turned or took a sudden deep breath.

"Not here, you won't sleep," Courtney said firmly and glanced at Rowntree. "Sergeant, will you escort the doctor back to the stream. Make him bathe and sleep, even if you have to knock him flat to do it."

"See here," Matt protested. "There's no need to go to such lengths. I'll sleep perfectly well right . . . there." He pointed to a small square of shade in the lee of the rocks.

"If you don't do as I say," Courtney said to Rowntree with a shrug, "you'll be burying the doctor alongside the other men he kills."

"Doc?"

Matt backed up a step. "But who will look after these men? What if I am needed? What if —"

"I'll look after them," said Courtney patiently. "And if I need you, for any reason, I'll send someone to fetch you. I swear I will. Now please —" She bit her lip, conscious of the concern creeping into her voice.

"She's right, doc," Rowntree agreed. "You don't look so good. I'd hate to see you make a mistake you wouldn't normally make."

Matthew stumbled back, his face showing his anger and confusion. He heard a drawn-out sigh behind him and half-turned, just as Angus MacDonald's fist dealt out a stiff right uppercut to his jaw.

"This is beginnin' tae wear on ma nairves," the Scot grumbled. "Two officers in two days: it's nay a healthy skill tae be honin'."

Courtney touched her own tender jaw. "It seems to be the only thing you Yankees are good at."

The Scot grinned sheepishly and took up the limp burden on his shoulder. "I ken where the stream is, lassie. I'll take him. An' if ye need me afore the watch tonight, Andrew, ye'll find me layin' doon aside the doc, takin' a wee snork masel'."

Rowntree shook his head as he watched MacDonald trudge off along the beach. "I don't know how he does it."

"He reminds me a great deal of —" Courtney stopped herself just as Seagram's name came to her lips. The sergeant was watching her, surprised at the tenderness in her tone. She stiffened and hardened her gaze. "If you could find some coconuts and split them, it would be a useful task for you to be about, Yankee."

Rowntree's smile faded. "Yes, miss. Anything else?"

"Some palm branches for shade and for fans to keep these blasted flies away. And you could start someone digging a firepit so that these men can have some hot food in their bellies."

"Yes, miss. I'll get right on it."

Courtney detected a new gleam of admiration in his eyes and she resented it for the way it softened her to his youth and earnestness. He should hate her for what her father's men had done to the *Eagle*, to her crew; just as she should hate the Yankees — every last one of them — for their interference in her life.

She left Rowntree standing by himself and beckoned to Dickie Little, who had been watching her with eyes as big as saucers. She gave him brief instructions and set him to work crushing the coriander seeds and the marigolds. A huge iron pot, salvaged by an enterprising sailor and carried the long miles from the cove, was filled with water and propped over a fire of smokeless pine knots. In a short time a strong broth was prepared for the wounded men, scooped into empty coconut shells, and encouraged down their feverish throats. The pot was immediately refilled, and this time the onions and carrots, parsley, roots, and berries went into it, along with three unlucky quails that had wandered into a sailor's path. More men returned to the campsite with figs and dates; two carried a spitted sheep between them. At least there would be no shortage of food or water, and the men's spirits were kept high.

Courtney remained vigilant by Adrian's side, grudgingly allowing the sergeant to help her with the other men. She wondered at the source of his energy and persistence; surely he'd had no more sleep than many of the others. Even she found herself succumbing to heavy eyelids and sagging shoulders as she sat in the heat of the sun. She might even have dozed in the early hours of twilight, when the heat left the sand and the first of the cooling breezes brought relief. But the coolness quickly increased to a chill, and Rowntree ordered the fires stoked, the sound of his voice jarring Courtney alert.

Adrian was moving restlessly. His face was drenched with sweat; the droplets slid along his jaw and glued his hair back in greasy strands. His complexion had gone grayish-white; his lips were caked with salt. His eyelids trembled convulsively; his head thrashed; and his hands spasmodically shuddered into fists. He was shivering, though the sweat poured off him, but there were no blankets, no sources of heat other than the fire. Rowntree, with the help of two other men, had carefully moved him, and the other wounded men, closer to the blaze but it seemed to have little effect. Courtney kept wiping his brow with a cool, damp cloth, and frequently his eyes would open, grateful for the comfort, but she knew he didn't see her, did not see anything through the pain and fever. She checked his wounds often, fearful that his erratic thrashings would keep the wounds open, but although they stayed raw and red, the bleeding seemed to be under control. She replaced the cotton strips with those she had washed earlier in the afternoon and was relieved to see only minimal staining.

She propped up his head and forced him to swallow the strong herbal tea. When he coughed and would have choked it aside, she only held his head more firmly and tilted the filled shell between his lips until she was satisfied he had swallowed a fair quantity.

The hours dragged by, marked by the pounding of the surf. When she was not staring at Adrian, or the fire, she watched the action of the sea, the curling waves that sparkled and foamed within the faint reflections of light. The moon, she knew, would not make an appearance until shortly before dawn, and the wait seemed interminable in the darkness. She dozed again, her chin cradled in her hands, and when she woke she was pleasantly surprised to find the sky distinctly brighter.

"Good morning."

She glanced toward the sound of the whisper, startled to see the gray eyes open and fastened on her face. His voice sounded clear enough but she could see by the way his mouth was pressed taut, it was taking a great deal of effort to grasp and hold onto a rational thought. And yet his eyes were clear. Too clear, for they seemed to pierce cleanly through the armor of indifference she sought to hide behind.

"I was always told women looked their worst in the mornings," he murmured. "I can see I was lied to."

Courtney frowned and laid the scrap of cotton across his brow to soak up the moisture. His eyes closed briefly, but there could not have been much relief from the dry, warm cloth.

"I'll get some fresh water," she said and started to pull away, but his right hand lifted and reached for her wrist with fingers that were as hot and dry as the kindling by the fire.

"Don't go. Stay and talk to me."

"You mustn't talk at all, Yankee. You need your strength to fight the fever."

"The rest of the men . . . ."

"They're fine," she assured him. "We've made camp and posted plenty of guards. There's food and fresh water in plentiful supply, but your sergeant seems to think it won't be necessary. He thinks we'll be picked up some time today."

"Matt?"

"He's still resting, I imagine. He was nearly falling over from exhaustion."

Her voice faltered and she found she was holding her breath. His gaze was so intent on her, she felt seared by it. She tried to cover her discomfort by sponging back the damp locks of his hair, but somehow the gesture was transformed into a caress.

"Courtney . . ." His fingers tightened around her wrist, forcing her to lean closer. "You won't leave me, will you?"

"Leave you?" Her heart began to throb against her rib-cage — a trapped bird fighting to escape.

"I'd like a chance to prove I'm not as much of a bastard as I've let you believe."

Courtney caught her lower lip between her teeth to keep it from trembling. She knew it was just the fever speaking. She knew a person's thoughts and actions were distorted by delirium; what a person said or did often had no foundation in reality. Yet she could not still the rapid beating of her heart, nor could she prevent a soft pink flush from flooding her cheeks with a blatant message for his hungry eyes.

For a brief moment she was transported back to the greatcabin of the *Falconer*. She was lying on a mattress of scattered clothing; her body was betraying her, denying her the control she had fought so hard to maintain over the years. He had demanded an admission then, words he did not need to hear, words already spoken eloquently by her body. The bright shine in her eyes joined the blush in her cheeks to tell him the truth now.

"Sleep," she murmured. "Sleep and we'll talk later, when you have your strength back."

"But you won't leave me. Promise you won't leave me."

"Sleep," she whispered, her vision drowning in a pool of tears. "I won't leave you. Not like this."

"Sleep," he muttered, and his eyes closed. The terrible intensity relented and although he did not relinquish his hold on her wrist, his chest heaved with a contented murmur and his head rolled gently to one side. The sweat continued to run off his face in rivers, but he was quieter. The shivering stopped. The anguished thrashing stopped. Only his thumb continued to move for some time, over and over, gently, tenderly stroking the back of her hand.

Matthew Rutger rejoined the main body of the camp just as the sun burst into the cloudless sky like a great golden eye. The doctor looked rumpled and grumpy. There were still shadows under his eyes but the puffiness and the redness had gone, leaving only a faint bruising on his stubbled jaw.

"I suppose you were going to wake me eventually," he grumbled when Courtney looked up at his approach.

"Eventually," she agreed smoothly. "When I thought your disposition had improved."

He smirked and knelt beside Adrian, his hand pressing immediately against the flushed throat. "Hmm. Fever seems to have broken somewhat."

"He's resting quietly, if that's what you want to know."

"He wake up at all?"

"For a few minutes. He wasn't really making any sense though."

"Hmm. What about the others?" he asked, swiveling on his heels in the fine sand.

"See for yourself. I haven't poisoned any of them, or strangled them."

He glowered at her a moment then moved quickly, efficiently along the rows of wounded men, stopping beside each one to peer under bandages, check dressings, touch a forehead, or lift a man's eyelid. Courtney followed close behind, wondering how many faults he would point out in the way she had handled the job. While she waited, she glanced at the company of men and tried not to look too disturbed that they were watching her, probably ready to tear her to pieces if Rutger gave them a sign.

High overhead, the lookouts paced across the top of the cliff, their arms folded across their chests, muskets cradled in the crook. Back and forth they patroled, their eyes alert to any movement on land or at sea. Several men were gathered around the huge iron cauldron chopping vegetables, roots, herbs, and the left-over mutton into a bubbling bath of water. Seagulls circled in broad sweeps, alerted to the smell of fresh food. The air was fragrant with the morning dew as it rose off the border of vegetation. Tiny spirals of sand and ash spun like dervishes in the hustling breezes that brought ashore the salty, clean smell of the golden-gray Mediterranean.

"Much as I hate to admit it," Matthew said and straightened, "it appears that you've managed quite well without me. The only complaint I have is that you didn't find time to sleep yourself."

Courtney flushed under the unexpected praise. "I slept a few hours."

"Too few," Matt said and raised a hand to gently brush a coarse sprinkle of sand off her cheek. The early sunlight was flirting with her skin and hair, bathing one in a warm glow, causing the other to gleam with streaks of fiery gold. "He probably won't even know enough to thank you."

The emerald eyes flicked away. "I don't want his thanks."

Matt's searching gaze came away with enough of the truth to bring a faint smile to his lips. "He does tend to have that effect on people."

"He has absolutely no effect on me," Courtney retorted angrily — although she could not have said at whom she was angry.

"You don't care what happens to Adrian?"

"No," she said stubbornly. "I don't. And I certainly don't want him to care what happens to me."

"Is that why you stayed with us? And is that why he took you off the *Falconer* at the risk of his own life and the lives of his men?" He smiled again at the startled look on Courtney's face and tilted his head slightly. "Come on. Walk with me. Talk, if you like. I'm a good listener."

"There's nothing to talk about," she insisted.

"All right. Then I'll talk; you listen." He started walking toward the glittering water's edge, and after a moment's hesitation, Courtney followed.

"You are undoubtedly worried about what will happen to you when we reach Gibraltar. Well, don't be. As I've said before, Adrian and I are the only ones who know who you are and neither of us is going to volunteer the information. Do you honestly think we've gone through all of this just to see you thrown behind bars?"

Courtney's eyes burned as hotly as her cheeks. "I don't know what to think anymore. Everything has changed so quickly. I don't know if I even want to go free." She saw the frown on his face, and her voice took on a bitter harshness. "You've taken away everything I value in this life, everything I could call my own. You've destroyed my home, my family, my friends. You've forced me to look back and admit —" She stopped and chewed viciously on her lip.

"Forced you to admit what?"

"To admit I don't belong in my father's world. But I don't belong in your world either. I can't go back. I can't go forward."

"Good heavens, you talk as if you're an old woman of ninety, set in her ways, unable to adapt to something new. You're how old — sixteen? Seventeen?"

"Nineteen," she said through her teeth.

"Well, whatever — young enough to change."

"I've changed once already. I don't think I could do it again. Besides, dresses and jewels and fancy manners wouldn't change the way I feel inside. They wouldn't change the way I feel about sipping tea and eating magnolia blossoms on some plantation veranda."

Matt's mouth trembled at the corners. "I'm sure they wouldn't. But by the same token, I don't think these hands" — he lifted her slender, chafed ones in his — "were meant to be as familiar as they are with muskets and knives."

"I made my choice years ago," she said quietly. "I can't go back."

"The choice was made *for* you," he corrected her gently. "And you don't have to go back. Just move forward."

Courtney pulled her hands from his and turned to face the sea, her bare toes stubbing into the wet sand and kicking it into a small hillock. Matt studied her profile in silence, noting the fine lines of her cheek and nose and throat, and remembering what Adrian had mentioned once, briefly: that she had claimed to have blood of the French aristocracy flowing through her veins.

"Have you any family left alive in France?" he asked casually. The emerald eyes leveled on his, and he flushed. "Adrian said something about your mother, about her being guillotined. I don't mean to pry, but —"

"They're all dead," she said bluntly. "My grandfather's château was on the outskirts of Paris and was one of the first to be overrun by the righteous citizens of the revolution."

"And yet you escaped?"

Courtney bristled at his tone, and her explanation came with more vehemence than was warranted. "Grandpère was an ugly, brusque man, and his servants loathed him. They even opened the gates of the château when the mobs came out from the city. But my mother . . . she was sweet and gentle and she'd been so dreadfully mistreated by her father that the servants hid us — Mother and me — and lied to the citizens' committee by convincing them we were north, in Gascony. When the danger passed, they smuggled us out and away from the château, but grandpère and grandmère, the great Count and Countess de Villiers, in all their finery, were dragged to Paris behind an oxcart and were offered to Madame Gillotine. Any other questions, doctor?"

He felt the bite of sarcasm in her voice, but ventured another inquiry regardless. "Did you say de Villiers? The name sounds familiar. . . ."

Courtney looked back down at the sand. "Mother rarely talked about him. Duncan never did. I gather he was quite important — an advisor or confidant to the king. I know he had something to do with the French merchant fleet; that was how he and Duncan Farrow met, and how Duncan and my mother met."

"There were no aunts, no uncles?"

"No one left alive," she said bitterly. "So you see? Two lifetimes, two families wiped off the face of the earth. Perhaps someone" — she angled her eyes upward sardonically — "is trying to tell me something."

"Perhaps He's telling you not to give up."

"He has a hell of a way of giving encouragement. But don't worry about me, doctor, I'll survive. The wicked always manage to survive, didn't you know?"

"I would hardly call you wicked."

"Oh? You'd call me chaste and innocent? These hands, remember. They're not only familiar with muskets and knives, they've *used* them. How many of your socially upright, irreproachable countrymen would care to keep company with a woman who knew more about killing than giving birth? Would you, Doctor Rutger? Would he?"

Matt followed her glance to where Adrian lay on the sand. "I can't answer for him. . . ."

"Then answer for yourself. What kind of woman are you going home to? You *are* going home to someone, aren't you? Someone soft and sweet and lily-white? Never mind, you don't have to answer me: it's written all over your face. I only hope she knows how lucky she is."

Matt was startled by the compliment and flushed again under the intensity of her gaze. "How will you live? How will you get by? Gibraltar's a British port. I don't imagine they'll be too receptive to the Farrow name."

"But French names and titles hold a lingering fascination for them. And I have this —" She dug into the pocket of her breeches and produced the emerald ring. Matt's brow's lifted appreciatively, and his lips puckered around a low whistle.

"Nice trinket. I thought I'd only dreamed seeing it on your finger last night."

"Garrett stuck it on me. I was only just able to oil it free this morning." She met the surprised hazel eyes and grinned wryly. "Is it so hard to believe I could attract a man like Garrett Shaw?"

"Why no. No, not at all. I just —"

She sighed. "Then again, maybe he's no better than I deserve."

"You deserve a damn-sight better," Matt argued. "And I wish you would stop insisting otherwise."

Courtney only smiled and turned the emerald and diamond ring over in her palm, watching the sun's rays refract into hundreds of colored sparks. "At any rate, it will come in handy, if only to save me from begging in the streets. It might even pay my passage to America."

"America?" Matt's train of thought was shunted off balance again. "You plan to go to America?"

Courtney was not listening; she was gazing out over the bright slash of sea and sky. "Well, well. Your sergeant should be pleased with himself."

"What?" Matt was about to turn himself when he heard other shouts from the cliff top and the sound of running feet coming toward them.

"A ship!" Rowntree gasped eagerly, and slid to a halt beside them. He held a hand, like a visor, over his eyes and squinted in the direction of the blot of white on the horizon. "She's one of ours. I'll wager my stripes, she's one of ours!"

Hoots and cheers went up along the beach as the word spread. The sergeant dashed off again and ordered wood to be set near the fire in readiness. He sent men to call in the scouts and foraging parties. Extra lookouts were posted, and the men with the keenest eyesight were challenged to give the earliest identification. Within ten minutes of the sighting, three pairs of hands cupped around three mouths and shouted a simultaneous recognition of an American gunboat — one man even going so far as to name her.

"She's the *Argus*, sir! Eighteen guns! Lieutenant Allen commanding!"

Rowntree waited an additional ten minutes to satisfy his own sense of caution, then ordered the signal fire stoked with every scrap of wood they could lay a hand to. Dozens of somber, sweating faces looked seaward, marking the swift progress of the gunboat that seemed bent on sailing obliviously past. But, with a puff of smoke from her bows and the rolling echo of a cannon shot, she took a sharp tack toward shore, toward the eruption of laughing, leaping, wildly cheering men.

Courtney followed Matthew back to where the wounded were being readied for the rescue. She could not help but share some of the exhilaration and relief of the men around her, yet at the same time, as she sank to her knees beside Adrian Ballantine and let her hand slip into his, she was overwhelmed by a sense of sadness and impending loss.

# Chapter Twenty-Two

The world was buzzing. Bright colored lights, a dusting of shadows, and an infernal hum closed in oppressively, adding to the heat and the flies and the sticky stench of the sweat pouring between his shoulder blades. Adrian tried to moisten his lips but the effort was too much and the spittle too valuable to waste. He had been in the fields all day. The sun was boiling down mercilessly, frying the top of his head, turning the leather of his saddle mushy and acrid. The air was steamy with summer humidity; the sweet aroma of tobacco mixed with the pungent leather, horse lather and his own grime to cloy at the back of his throat like a layer of tar. There was no breeze to wash the heat away. No salt air to cool his skin. No snap and crack of canvas overhead to break the monotony of the azure blue sky.

The slaves worked lethargically. They examined each green leaf of tobacco for dirt and worm, then carried them one by one to the paltry stack at the end of the mile-long row. Adrian wiped a hand across his brow, and it came alway slick with sweat and blood. He must have forgotten his hat — either that or it had melted in the heat. The collar of his shirt was choking him. The heavy broadcloth frockcoat was pricking his skin; the satin waistcoat was glued to him like weighted armor. Black Amos, the overseer, was standing in front of Adrian's horse, grinning. He was pointing at the swollen sun and shouting something about it being a nice cool day for working. Over and over: cool day for working, Massa Ballantine. Cool day . . . Black bastards, didn't they ever sweat? Adrian could feel it running in rivers down his neck, down his back, pouring into the hole in his thigh where someone had thoughtlessly cut his breeches so the sun could blister his flesh raw. He reached down to cover it and was horrified to realize he was groping air. Groping air with a stump where his left hand and forearm should have been.

Someone was screaming. Adrian let go of the cantle of the saddle to cover his mouth. Everyone was staring! To his shame, he felt himself beginning to fall off the horse. For some reason, the crash to the ground didn't hurt — not right away — because he had fallen on something soft. He opened his mouth to scream again, seeing Falworth's face, but in the next instant the brown eyes became a clear, vivid green, and she was smiling up at him. Courtney was smiling. She was wrapping her arms around him and holding him close. And he felt so safe. So cool. So *healed*.

"Adrian?"

"You didn't leave me. You didn't."

"Adrian?" A pause. "I think he's coming around, thank God. Will someone fetch the doctor?"

"Courtney?"

A cool hand was laid briefly against his brow. "The fever has broken; he'll be all right now. You should try to get some sleep, Miss."

Voices. Adrian could hear voices but he could not convince his eyes to open. Courtney was there. He could *feel* her, by God. But he did not recognize the other cool, crisp voice. Another woman? Who was she?

"Courtney?" Good God, was that his voice? It sounded like a child's whine.

"Yes, Adrian, I'm here. You're going to be all right. The doctor will be here soon and he'll tell you himself. I . . . I only wanted to hear your voice again, to know you were going to make it."

"Courtney . . ." Why couldn't he say anything else? His mouth felt like it was stuffed with cotton wool and . . .

Something cool was pressed to his brow. Not a hand. It touched his brow and his cheek and then his lips, and he could taste a salty sweet wetness left behind.

"Courtney?"

There was no answer this time. The warmth that had seemed to surround him left suddenly, and there was only a hollow chill in its place.

"Courtney? Please . . . Courtney?"

Adrian lifted his hand and circled it feebly in the air, hoping to come into contact with something solid. There was nothing. Nothing. And the effort brought on a darkness, a deep, descending darkness and he had no choice but to fall into it. . . .

"Adrian?"

The lieutenant frowned and tried to open his eyes.

"Adrian . . . It's Matt. Are you in there?"

"Matt?"

"In the flesh. It's about high time you came out of it, old friend. We've had a hell of a time keeping the weeds from growing between your toes."

Adrian groaned and opened one eye a slit. Matt was standing by the side of the bed. He looked disgustingly clean and cheerful, his shirt and breeches a dazzling white.

"We were beginning to think you would sleep forever, you lazy bastard."

"Sleep?" Adrian queried. "How long?"

"Five days now."

Adrian frowned and tried to raise a hand to knuckle himself fully awake — but his arms wouldn't move.

"We had to strap you down, old buddy," Matt explained as he moved quickly to unfasten the cotton strips. "From the sounds of it you relived and refought every battle you'd ever been in. You grew up all over again, had fights with your brother, your father, your commanding officers. . . . Thank you, Sister Agatha, I'll manage the rest."

Adrian turned his head and caught a glimpse of a white wimple surrounding a red, cherubic face.

"Where am I?" he asked, craning his neck to see the rows of beds on either side of him.

"The military hospital in Gibraltar."

Adrian moistened his lips with difficulty. "How. . . ."

"We were picked up by the *Argus* and brought here. Mind you, when her captain heard about the *Falconer* he was set to run after her, overcrowded decks or no, but Rowntree managed to talk him out of it, at least long enough to transport the wounded back here. We made record time getting into the base, I can tell you, and Lieutenant Allen was turned about with all sails set within a couple of hours. Rowntree went out with him, and MacDonald — bandages and all."

"They went after Shaw?"

"With blood in their eyes."

Adrian laid back and cursed his incapacitation. A memory returned, and he lifted both his head and his left arm, and was relieved to see a hand at the end of the thick padding of bandages. His thigh was heavily wrapped as well, but it was there, with movement and feeling.

"You were damned lucky on both counts," Matt said quietly as he read the relief on Adrian's face. "But don't thank me until you see the scars."

Adrian tested his arm and flexed his hand carefully. There was a great deal of pain and stiffness, but it would come back in time. "I don't have to wait to thank you for my life," he murmured and clasped his hand over Matt's.

"Hell, I owed you ten times over. Besides, I had help.

Now — can I get you some hot soup? Are you hungry?''

"Starving," Adrian admitted. "But I'd trade a bucket of soup for a single glass of cold water."

"Done." Matt grinned and poured some out of a nearby pitcher. He noted that Adrian forced his damaged arm to reach out to accept the cup and he frowned. "Because I know you so well, I'll only warn you on principle: don't push it with the arm or the leg. Too much too soon will undo all the good work I've done. Oh and, as soon as you're up to it — I'll decide when that is — Commodore Preble is anxious to see you. He's even been to the hospital twice to look in on you."

"He has?"

"With a small regiment of brass in tow." Matt's grin broadened and he tilted his head in amusement. "They've made you out to be quite the hero, you know. The escape is the talk of the town as well as a triumphant coup for the navy. Even the Brits are impressed."

"Why? Because I lost the *Eagle* to the corsairs?"

"Jennings' incompetence lost the *Eagle*," Matt reminded him. "And had you done nothing about it, the *Eagle* would be sitting in an Arab port at the moment, and we would be clinking around in iron bracelets. Before Rowntree and MacDonald left, they gave a full report to the Admiralty about how you planned and organized the escape; how you insisted on destroying the *Eagle* even if it cost every last life (although I do believe they exaggerated shamelessly there — or at least, I hope they did). They even told the commodore how you hung in the shrouds for twenty-four hours through a thunderstorm and still came away spitting vinegar. I must confess, it all sounded heroic."

Adrian scowled and raked a hand through his dark blond hair. "The last thing I wanted was any special recognition. Every last man on board deserves equal commendation for what they did and what they went through."

"Agreed. And they'll get it, don't worry. Preble's already sent a courier home with the news. But unfortunately they feel they have to single out a particular head to wear the laurel wreath and, my cocky friend, that head happens to be on your shoulders. Good Lord, how could they pass you up? Look at your record: from court-martialed renegade to national hero in under six months. The folks at home will eat you up. Hell, your father might even admit to a passing acquaintance with you. Don't fight it. Think of it as leverage, both at home and in the navy. Now, relax. Doctor's orders. I'll see about getting you that soup."

"And something stronger than water?"

"I might be able to scrape up a jug or two of ale. Don't go away, I'll be right back."

"Matt?"

The doctor stopped.

"Where is she?"

"Who?" Matt asked blithely, stalling for time. He had been expecting the question, yet had almost escaped before having to face it. He made a pretense of straightening the blankets at the foot of the bed, but it was no good. His smile faded and he was forced to meet the iron gray eyes.

"She's gone, Adrian. She left last night."

"Gone? Gone where?" He struggled to prop himself up, and Matt hurried over to his side. "What do you mean she left? Where the hell did she go?"

"She left the hospital late last night. She stayed as long as the fever was in you, but as soon as it broke and she knew you would be all right —"

"And you let her go!"

"I couldn't stop her. You couldn't have stopped her either, even if you'd tried."

"Tried? Goddammit, I was unconscious! It was up to you to make sure she stayed here — at least until I had a chance to speak to her."

"And what would you have said? Stay with me and be my love?"

"That's not fair and you know it." Adrian snarled.

"A lot of things in her life haven't been fair lately. Adrian, you're my friend and I know you mean well, and no doubt you care for her more than she thinks you do — but what good would it have done either of you?"

"What good? Why you self-righteous —" Adrian pushed Matt's hands away from his shoulders. "Let me up, you bastard. I'll go after her myself."

"Go ahead and try, if you want to kill yourself." Matt stood back, his hands clenched by his sides as he watched Adrian strain ineffectually to push himself upright. He was still weak; his intentions were a good deal stronger than his abilities, and the combined agony of his arm and thigh sent him collapsing back against the pillows with a gasp. The doctor bent over him, his hands and eyes probing the bandages on the lieutenant's forehead, his arm, his leg. When he straightened, Adrian's gaze was locked to his with a painful urgency.

"Do you know where she went? Have you any idea? She didn't . . . she didn't go back to him, did she? To Shaw?"

"No. No, that much I'm certain of. She didn't go back. I gather she was going to try to pick up the pieces of her life. Pieces which you and I were jointly responsible for breaking, although I suspect you played a bigger part than I."

Ballantine searched Matt's face, surprised and taken aback by the anger he saw there. "I didn't set out to deliberately hurt her. God knows I didn't set out to do anything at all."

Matt backed away from the bed, and the harsh gleam faded from his eyes. "I know you didn't. You never do. And I'm sure she wasn't too happy about falling in love with you either. Maybe she thought it was for the best to just cut away quickly before anyone was hurt any more deeply."

Adrian's shock deepened. "In love with me?" he whispered. "She told you she was in love with me?"

"She didn't have to. And since she could hardly hope to overcome your pride as well as hers, I can't say I wouldn't have done exactly the same thing."

"My pride? What has *my* pride got to do with her running away?"

"Think about it my friend. The answers might surprise you."

From a sitting position in his bed, Adrian was able to stare out the window of his room. He had spent a goodly number of hours staring out the window, watching the activity in the busy harbor below. British ships, American ships, Spanish ships came and went in flotillas with the tides. Gibraltar was a port of call for most trading vessels en route to or from the Atlantic, as well as home for hundreds of fishing boats of all sizes and shapes. Towering over the lot was the United States frigate *Constitution*, forty-four guns, her regal masts strung with miles of rigging, her decks gleaming beneath the hot sun, her gracefully curved hull barely hinting at the power behind the closed gunports. She was one of only six massive warships the fledgling American navy boasted. She was Commodore Preble's flagship and mother hen to the dozen smaller schooners, sloops, and gunboats that formed the fighting force in the Mediterranean.

Adrian shifted uncomfortably against the pile of soft pillows and grimaced at the stab of pain in his thigh. Matt had not exaggerated about the time it would take to heal his wounds, nor had he underplayed the ugliness of the scars. The wounds in his leg and arm had been cauterized on board the *Argus*, and it was doubtful if either would regain their former appearance. Thankfully, he was right-handed, so he would not lose his skill with sword or musket. It would take weeks, however, if not months to mend properly — a fact which the commodore had pointed out as delicately as his dour, irascible temperament would permit.

A gaunt, sharp-featured New Englander, Commodore Edward Preble had strutted into the hospital ward in the midst of an argument Ballantine was having with Sister Agatha about the need to have her assistance in using the chamberpot. He had been on the verge of banishing her in most unholy terms when the commodore arrived, and he was greatly relieved to hear his senior officer order the nurse to remove her person so that he might have a few private moments with the lieutenant.

"Thank you, sir. They treat me like a prize goose around here, or a child who hasn't the strength to see to his own business."

The commodore's mouth twitched in a brief smile and he signaled an adjutant to bring a chair to the side of the bed. His pale brown eyes moved with concern over the bandages on Adrian's temple and arm, and to the thick padding beneath the blanket.

"You do indeed look as if you've been through rough weather, Captain Ballantine. My compliments and my gratitude seem paltry at best."

"Sir, I'd rather the men have your compliments. They are far more deserving than I."

"False modesty, Captain? It hardly becomes you. Of course the men are deserving of my praise and their country's praise and indeed they shall have it. But it is you who spurred them on. You who led them. You who accepted a dangerous and thankless mission and succeeded far beyond what could humanly be expected of you. I have read the formal statements submitted by your Sergeant-at-arms, Mister Rowntree, and by Marine Corporal Mac-Donald — but I have also listened closely to the scuttlebutt which, even as we sit, is spreading from tavern to tavern like wildfire. This war needs heroes badly, Mister Ballantine, and you happen to fit the mold perfectly."

"And if I'd prefer not to?"

"Then you should have failed. You should have allowed the *Eagle* to fall into Pasha Karamanli's hands. You should have allowed your men to suffer a life of slavery and degradation. You should have allowed the traitor to go free and unpunished so I could have chosen another young pup, eager to prove his mettle. That sir, would surely have demonstrated a preference for anonymity."

Ballantine returned the commodore's steady gaze. Hero or failure: there never had been any middle ground.

"I see what you mean, sir," he murmured.

"Do you? Perhaps it will ease your distress for me to tell

you I share your repugnance for fame and notoriety, but alas, it is a burden we must learn to bear with some amount of grace."

"Yes, sir. But how can you be so certain I've succeeded one hundred percent in my mission?"

"Because if you hadn't, I dare say you wouldn't be here now. Well, Captain? Am I permitted to hear the details, or are you too tired to satisfy my curiosity? If so, I can return at a later time."

"No, sir! All I've done for the past five days is sleep."

"Indeed, and you should sleep five more. The doctor has recommended a recuperation period of several months, which I whole-heartedly agree with."

"Several months?" Ballantine shifted uneasily. "I'm sure it won't take that long —"

"Nonsense. You need the time to heal in spirit as well as in body. The navy can stumble along without you for a while — or do you consider yourself indispensable as well as humble?"

Parry and thrust. A conversation with Commodore Preble was like a duel of wits. Perhaps it was why Ballantine admired and liked the old soldier. He had a sharp, no-nonsense attitude; he respected the intelligence of his men and did everything in his power to see that even the lowest ranked cabin boy won recognition if it was deserved. Loyalty down begets loyalty up: it was his staunch belief.

"Not indispensable, sir. Merely unwilling to sit out the war in relative ease."

"While my other captains are making names for themselves? Decatur, Lawrence, Stewart . . . they are indeed earning the right to wear their sabers proudly, as I knew they would. As I knew *you* would. As for sitting out the war in relative ease — the Secretary of the Navy has plans for you, m'boy. He knows how you gambled with your life and your reputation for the sake of keeping all of our sabers shining, and you'll not be overlooked when the next postings for promotions come due. You have my word on that. And if you decide to return to active duty, I dare say you'll have your choice of navy branches to serve: intelligence, or a command at the helm of your own ship.''

"*If* I decide?"

Preble chuckled and there was a glint of conspiracy in his eyes. "I understand you have a fiancée eagerly awaiting your return to Norfolk. Edgecombe, isn't it? I know her father well — and I've heard a great deal about Samuel Ballantine. I warrant the two families will have their own ideas on how you'll spend your future days."

"Their ideas are not necessarily mine," Adrian said quietly.

Preble studied the stern, confident features a moment, then smiled again. "Good. I was hoping to hear you say that. Now then, from the beginning, if you don't mind."

Adrian accepted one of the commodore's cigars and after a quiet moment of savoring the first taste of the harsh tobacco, he took the commodore back, step by step, through the attack on Snake Island and the events of the subsequent two weeks. The commodore's face remained impassive throughout; only the pale eyes betrayed any sign of anger or disgust or sympathy. He interrupted infrequently, and Ballantine sensed he was only filling in gaps left by Rowntree and MacDonald for the actual sea battle, capture, imprisonment, and escape. Only when he began to speak of Otis Falworth's involvement did the questions become more pointed. The confrontation in the sail locker was met with a grunt and a nod; the name of Falworth's informant on the commodore's staff caused the officer to stand and pace to the window, his hands clasped angrily behind his back.

"And did you believe Falworth about Mister Winthrop's naïveté?"

"I believe the boy could be a braggart and easily swayed by Falworth's guile."

"He had you fooled, didn't he?" Preble said, not unkindly. "A lesser man would have been putty in his hands. Still, when a man comes to a position of trust and responsibility, he must be trustworthy and responsible. I can tolerate no disloyalty, regardless of the fellow's culpability or lack of it. He'll be dismissed and brought before the naval court on charges. As for Captain Jennings'' — Preble turned from the window, his thin face tense with displeasure — "the man should have been drummed out of the service years ago. Incompetence has no place at the helm of a ship, not when hundreds of lives and the pride of one's country is at stake. Damn, but I'd truly hoped he was our man; it would have left a better taste in my mouth. Publicly, you realize he'll be regarded as a martyr — death by torture tends to paint people that way. And I suppose it would serve morale no good measure to brand the man a coward and tyrant — men seem to shy away from enlisting if they hear too many tales of despots at sea." He grimaced and added, "At least, that is the basis of the argument my superiors will give me."

Ballantine leaned back on the pillows, his throat dry from talking, his energy deserting him suddenly — a condition which Preble noted instantly. He glanced at a gold pocketwatch.

"Good heavens. It's past four o'clock. I've kept you talking well over two hours."

"Time well spent, sir," Ballantine said. "I hope I haven't left anything out."

Preble pursed his lips thoughtfully and snapped the lid of the watch shut. "There is this matter of the young woman both you and the doctor say gave you invaluable assistance . . . Courtney Brown?"

Ballantine's gaze slid away from Preble's. "I don't know if it was her real name, sir. She seemed reluctant to trust us fully in the beginning."

"Understandable. And yet from all accounts she trusted you with her life, and you trusted her with yours."

"She'd only been with the corsairs a few years, sir, and I don't think their ways were too deeply ingrained. She helped defuse the situation on the *Eagle* when the prisoners broke out of the hold. She won decent treatment for our men on the *Falconer*; helped in the actual escape; then helped later with our wounded until the *Argus* came. I'd like to petition for a full pardon for her, sir.''

"Mmmm. Only the fourth such request.''

"Four?''

"Messers Rowntree, MacDonald, and the good doctor. I hardly see how I could refuse. Very well then, Captain, I'll leave you now. I'm afraid you'll be here a fortnight longer until the *Carolina* sails for home. She's a good swift ship; she'll get you back in time for the parties and celebrations.''

"Thank you, sir,'' Adrian said dryly.

The commodore retrieved his bicorne from the small wooden table where he had left it, and tucked it up under his arm. "Get yourself well, Captain Ballantine. I need good men like you. With a little help and the grace of God, we'll win this blasted war in no time. We'll have these corsairs on the run and drive every last one of them, down to their sons and daughters, into the sea!''

# Chapter Twenty-Three

Courtney Farrow adjusted the hood of her cloak to keep her face in shadow as she stepped from the coach to the boardwalk. She thanked the driver and settled a coin in his hand, then hurried the few steps into the cosy warmth of the waterfront teashop. A tiny bell on the door announced her arrival to the homely man behind the counter, and he hastened over, wiping his hands on a snow-white apron as he ushered her to a small table near the window. From there, she had an excellent view of the waterfront, the docks, the frenzied activity on the wharfs as one ship docked and another was being loaded with last-minute provisions.

"Aye, Miss? How can I serve ye?"

"Just tea, please," she answered, looking up at the proprietor.

"Aye, a luv'ly cupp'a should warm the cockles of yer 'art. Mayn't I ask if ye're just comin' or just goin'?"

"Going."

"Ahh. On the *Sirius*, then?" He glanced out the window and nodded toward the activity on the wharf. "Bound for America?"

"Yes."

"Luv'ly place, that. Luv'ly place. The wife and I visited near ten year back when our son wed himsel' to a planter's daughter and brought a luv'ly pair of twins into the family. Boys, they was; real charmers. But we've t'ree daughters here who've wed themselves to Spaniards and my Bess is dead against leavin' them alone too long with the Papists. So we runs the teashop, and we hears the gossip comin' and goin'. Travelin' all alone, are ye?"

"Yes, my . . . husband went on ahead."

"Ahh. Well, ye've picked the proper ship to book on. Captain Pettigrew's a foin gentleman, a foin sailor. Runs a clean, fair ship, he does. Here now, an' I'd best be after ye're tea or the flag's'll be up before ye're half done. Won't be but a minute."

He beamed and hurried away, his portly body constructed in such a way that most of the movement was done from the knees down. Courtney sighed and pushed the hood back, using the opportunity to glance surreptitiously at the other patrons. The teashop was small, crammed between two towering warehouses, but it smelled deliciously of fresh scones and aromatic teas. There were three other couples sharing the English atmosphere and talking among themselves in low, relaxed tones. None of them looked her way but briefly; no one stared or raised a brow in curiosity.

She felt as though they should. She felt stiff and unnatural in the prim, high-collared traveling suit she had purchased for the occasion. Her feet were sweating and itching inside tight leather shoes, and the cloak, though lightweight, felt like a wooden yoke on her shoulders. She had sold the emerald ring for enough to buy the suit, the cloak, and several frocks, as well as to book passage on the merchantman *Sirius*, bound for Boston and Norfolk. She had money left over to find a comfortable hotel once she was in Norfolk, and to spend on maintaining her disguise as a refugee from France. To that end she had assumed the name de Villiers and practised long and hard in front of a mirror until she felt reasonably sure she could walk in shoes and skirts and foolish underthings without tripping and splatting inelegantly at every turn.

Out of the corner of her eye, she noticed a man smiling at her from across the teashop. She raised a hand nervously and patted the bottom row of auburn curls that lay softly against the nape of her neck. The salon she had visited earlier in the day had trimmed and styled her ragged coiffure into something she was assured was most fashionable. Since then she had noticed several passersby on the streets turning to cast an approving eye along her newly garbed figure — a consequence she had been forewarned about by the enthusiastic dressmaker who had labored over her transformation.

"Here ye be, m'dear." The proprietor returned to the table, his wide, flat hands balancing a tray laden with a cup and saucer, a teapot and cozy, condiments, and a plate of dainty cakes and scones. "Eat hearty whilst ye have the chance, 'at's what I always tell me guests. First day out the ship's likely not to follow any regular schedules and goodness only knows when ye'll be served a proper meal — although Captain Pettigrew is a bit of a toff when it comes to his food. He likes to dine with his passengers whenever he can, and he likes to put out a real fancy spread. Ever sailed before, Miss?"

"Some," she admitted with a wry smile.

"Best thing for ye's a dry biscuit with a spot o' jam if ye start feeling queasy. Not too heavy in the belly, if ye knows what I mean."

"Thank you. I'll try to remember."

His brow folded like an accordian as he fussed with the

plates and cutlery. "Odd, an' I can't seem to place yer accent. It's a luv'ly lilt ye have — mayn't I ask?"

Courtney glanced hastily around. There were now two men and a woman showing some passing interest in their conversation.

"I'm from Paris originally, but I've spent time in Italy and Spain recently."

"Ahh," he smiled knowingly. "Turrible troubles yer country's had, Miss. Turrible. And this here Bonypart's a mite cocky for his own good 'ealth. He's due for a comeuppance, ye ask me. Our Admiral Nelson tromped him a good one in Egypt already; ye'd think the pompous sod'd take a lesson, but no. Seems we'll have to do it all over again. Ahh me, well . . . Whup! There she is! Flags goin' up on the *Sirius*. Ye've an hour before she sails, Miss, an' if I don't have a chance to speak at ye again, luck on yer voyage. And don't you take no never mind about portents and old wives' tales about storms bodin' ill luck for a sea voyage — ye're very own face has enough sunshine in it to light up the whole Mediterranean."

"Thank you," she smiled again and tried not to shiver visibly. The sky was indeed growing darker by the minute, a thick gray ceiling of cotton wool descending over the harbor. Courtney's attention was drawn to the *Sirius*, a three-masted barkentine, smaller than either the *Falconer* or the *Eagle*, with most of her space occupied by cargo. Courtney had been lucky to be able to book passage on her; the next available berth was not for three weeks.

The flags were up, yet the wharf was still crowded with cartloads of provisions, wicker cages filled with chickens, barrels of salted beef and fish. Men were already up in the rigging, swinging from yard to yard to ready the sails and do a final check on the tackles and lines. Men were streaming up and down her gangway plank to herd the supplies on board. A tall, dark-haired man in a navy peacoat stood on the foredeck, overseeing the operations and shouting orders through a hailing trumpet. Farther out in the bay, the tugs were making ready to attach their tow lines to guide the heavily laden bark out to the open sea lane.

Courtney's dark green eyes wandered over the forest of masts and rigging, reluctantly finding and settling on the one ship she had avoided thinking about since hearing of its return to Gibraltar two days earlier.

The *Argus* showed no signs of a skirmish on her clean, polished decks. Courtney had even dared to slip into her breeches and shirt and mingle with the raucous tavern crowds to see if she could hear any news of the *Argus*'s venture. But either the gunboat had failed to take up the *Falconer*'s scent, or she had been limited to a two-week patrol, for she had come back with no news of Garrett Shaw. It was as if the Farrow ship had fallen off the edge of the earth.

Courtney had, however, heard a great deal about the Yankees' newest war hero — Captain Adrian Ballantine. Stories made him out to be godlike and indestructible; some even made it sound as if he had met the entire crew of blood-thirsty, fire-breathing corsairs single-handedly. He had been released several days ago from the hospital and was due to ship out of Gibraltar on the naval cutter *Carolina*. A royal send-off had been planned for the morrow, and Courtney was thankful she would miss it. She refused to let her thoughts linger on the painfully clear image of the boldly handsome officer. She knew she was taking the only wise and prudent measure available by slipping quietly and quickly out of sight. It would not have taken long for him to resent her presence, to see her faults, to laugh, even, at her shortcomings. She had been almost his equal at sea. On land, in the foolish role she had assumed for herself, she would have been a glaring embarrassment.

Stirring herself, Courtney drained the last of her cooling tea from the cup and left the appropriate number of coins on the table. The proprietor, busy with another customer, looked over and waved.

"Luck again, Miss. 'Ope ye find 'appiness and good fortune in America."

She nodded and smiled, and promptly erased his chubby face from her thoughts as she stepped out into the busy mainstream of traffic. The smell of fish and floating garbage instantly replaced the comforting teashop aromas, and she pulled her cloak tighter against the chilly breeze. She was pushed and jostled the hundred yards or so to the end of the wharf and needed a few moments of respite beside some tall, stacked crates before she could bolster the nerve to walk down the pier and climb the gangway to the *Sirius*. Gulls screamed in endless flapping circles overhead. Hawkers pitched their wares to the departing crewmen and passengers. Merchants and bankers conducted business meetings in hurried, arm-waving sessions the full length of the dock. ·

Courtney took firm hold of her courage and walked toward the gangway. She breathed deeply of the familiar scents of wet canvas and pitch, and took some small comfort in the crack of sails as the topmost royals were let loose and drawn taut into their braces. She had deliberately timed her boarding, hoping to blend in in the last-minute confusion. She had her papers out and clutched in her gloveless hand. Her eyes locked on the dark-haired man she had seen earlier, who now stood at the head of the gangway.

She had one foot on the wide plank and was well into her second step when she noticed a man partially hidden from view by a stack of wooden crates. He had his broad back to the gangway and was conversing with the dark-haired man. Courtney's breath caught in her throat as she forced another step. His hair was sun-bleached gold, impatiently wisping free of the neat clubbed tail at the back of his neck. Another hesitant step earned her the attention of the first man who had a plain, square face which verged on being handsome when he smiled. He did so now, and extended a hand to Courtney to assist her the final few steps.

The blond head turned, and Courtney gasped. At the same time the hem of her cloak was whipped by a sharp gust of wind and tangled around her ankles, causing her to stumble forward into the quickly outstretched hands of both men.

"Hup! Watch your step, ma'am," the darker of the two said after he had steadied her. "The roll takes a bit of getting used to after you've been on land. First Mate Lansing, ma'am, at your service . . . and Captain Jeffrey Pettigrew."

The captain smiled and seemed reluctant to release her arm as he steered her into a cleared square on the deck. On a closer inspection his hair was not exactly the same gleaming gold of Ballantine's, nor were his features as sharply defined or his eyes as probingly direct. But the similarities in their height and build had sent a flush into Courtney's cheeks, a flush that was openly admired by both officers.

"Y'all will have to excuse the confusion, ma'am, but we're about to set sail. Might Ah be so bold as to inquire the nature of yoah business on board mah ship?"

"Wh-why yes, I. . . ."

"Miss de Villiers is traveling with us to Norfolk," the first mate said, handing Courtney back her papers with a courteous nod. "She's the last one to check off against the passenger manifest, sir."

"In that case, ma'am, yoah arrival is most timely," Captain Pettigrew drawled. "Ah trust yoah belongings are aboard? Good. Mistah Lansing, perhaps you could spare a moment and show Miz de Villiers to a prime spot by the rail — that is if y'all wish to see the casting-off?"

"Why yes, thank you, but there's no need to trouble yourself. I can find my own way."

"Why it's no trouble a'tall, ma'am. Ah only apologise for not being able to do it mahself. But Ah trust y'all will be able to join mah officers and yoah fellow passengers tonight for suppah? We can have a chance then to get all acquainted. Eight bells?"

"I . . . Thank you, yes."

"Ma'am." The captain inclined his head and discharged her into the care of First Mate Lansing. He, in turn, guided her around a stack of crated, cackling chickens and found a place for her to stand by the forward shrouds before excusing himself to rejoin the captain.

The *Sirius* carried no armaments aside from two small swivel guns in the bow and a second pair in the stern. Her decks, therefore, were wide and would be refreshingly clear once the last of the provisions were stored below.

Courtney rested her hands on the rail, her emotions mixed as she let her gaze sweep over the bustling waterfront, along the crowded shore, then higher to the dominating bulk of the gigantic rock that had guarded the exit to the Atlantic since the beginning of time. The town, the ships, the people were dwarfed in its mighty shadow, and Courtney found herself wondering if she would ever seen the likes of its majesty again. She was setting sail for the unknown. She was leaving her two lifetimes behind her and embarking on a third. Would it be her last? Would her father be waiting somewhere at the other end — waiting just as eagerly, just as hopefully, to see a familiar face in the crowd? Would she ever see a familiar face again?

"Courtney?"

It was just a gasp. A breath snatched by the wind.

"Courtney, is that you?"

She whirled about, her eyes searching frantically for the source of the shocked whisper. He was there. Less than two feet away, very real, very alive.

"Davey!" she cried softly, the disbelief welling along her lashes, burning at the back of her throat until she thought it would choke her. "Davey . . . what are you doing here?"

She took a step toward the short, gruff figure but his hand shot up in an abrupt warning. "Nay lass, nay! Ye mustn't let on ye know me — for your sake as well as mine!"

Courtney swallowed hard and blinked the unshed tears out of her eyes, her mind racing through the thousands of questions she was burning to ask. The best she could manage and the most inadequate, was a breathed, "You got away?"

"Aye, but only by the skin o' my arse." He grunted and his eyes darted along the deck. "I were luckier 'n the *Falconer*."

"She's gone?"

"Burned the bloody night and day through, she did How the piss we made it as far as we did, I'll never know but make it we did, with Shaw throwin' everything over board that weren't tied ner bolted down. Damn near threw me off fer dead too, along with the others, but for a little un-corpse-like ass wind. I thought ye were gone, lass. I thought whatever bleedin' thunderclap caught me on the brain-box caught you too!"

"Oh, Davey, I. . . ." How could she tell him? How could she begin to explain?

"No mind, lass. Ye're alive and that's all what matters. And ye're usin' ye're noggin too. Good. Good! We'll catch the bastards sure!"

"Catch them? Catch who?"

"Shaw and his tart, o' course. Who else would I be willin' to follow halfway to hell just for the pleasure of slittin' his eyelids an' stakin' him to an anthill? They were the first ashore when the *Falconer* grounded, and the first to offer gold to the local thieves to carry them to Gibraltar."

"They're here? *Garrett and Miranda are here*?"

"Whsht! Damn and blast, girl, ye'll have the clappers on us yet! Aye, here. And here's where I follered 'em and lost 'em, God rot their souls." The red beard — sadly reduced to a quarter-inch of stubble — shifted and a stream of tobacco juice spurted out over the rail. "But I know where they be bound. Where *I* be bound, and now you."

"Norfolk?" she whispered, her thoughts reeling. It hadn't even occured to her that one or both of them could have disguised themselves as she had done and fled the Mediterranean. "But . . . why Norfolk?"

" 'Cause Norfolk is where yer father's gold is," Dunn said, as if explaining something to a very thick-headed child. "I *tole* ye he was sniffin' after it, and if he thinks ye're dead — which he does — then there ain't nothin' to stop him from takin' that whore-bitch to Norfolk — which he's doin' — and usin' her to claim Duncan's fortune."

Courtney's face paled as she stared at Davey Dunn. Conversely, his darkened as his keen blue eyes darted past her shoulder. A curse took him to the rat lines, and he pretended to fuss at a length of cable.

"That first mate has eyes in the back o' his head," he

scowled. "We can't talk no more, lass. I'll have to think on a signal or the like, what we can use to arrange a meetin'. I've signed on this bucket o' bilge for the crossin'. Used the name 'McCutcheon' after the nose-picking sod what fathered me. Fer now ye look all right — all prim and proper." He straightened suddenly and grinned. "Jest don't slip up and tell these lubbers how to set the riggin' — Jaysus! It's a wonder this bucket even floats!"

With that and a hasty scowl at the first mate, Davey swung himself nimbly up into the shrouds and climbed hand over hand to the mizzen topgallant, where he was lost to Courtney's view behind a billowing sheet of canvas. She lowered the hand that had been holding her hood in place and pressed her cold, trembling fingers to her lips.

She was somewhat relieved that she was not totally alone. Yet the mere thought of having to face Garrett Shaw and Miranda again in Norfolk raised a tiny spray of fine hairs at the nape of her neck. Since morning she had not been able to shake the feeling of dread she had wakened with, and now she knew why.

A pipe shrilled and her composure was further fragmented as the gangway was taken aboard and the rail dropped and bolted into place. Men on shore let loose the mooring cables, and tugs took up slack on the tow lines. The dock began to slide past, and the activity on the wharf ground to a standstill as the workers stopped and planted their hands on their hips, or dragged cloths across their sweating brows while they watched the *Sirius* glide out of her docket. The wind gusted gently, snapping the canvas, and within minutes the sails were carved into hard white curls against the gray sky.

Courtney's gaze went to the *Argus* as they passed, then to the cutter *Carolina*. She was bedecked and beribboned for the festivities that were slated to begin at noon the next day and end when her lines were cast off and she left the harbor to take Adrian Ballantine home.

She turned away from the rail, away from the salty

breeze that brought a veil of tears glimmering into her eyes.

Courtney's cabin was sparsely furnished, but comfortable. The trimmings consisted of a bed, a nightstand with commode and washbasin, a shelf against one panelled wall, and a three-foot-square rag rug to add a touch of hominess. Hers was one of five cabins on the lower deck set aside for passengers willing to pay extra for the luxury of privacy. A larger storeroom below was lined with bunks and transported those who could only afford to share accommodations with goats, sheep, and chickens. First Mate Lansing had escorted Courtney personally to her cabin, and had filled in details of the six other guests she could expect to meet at dinner: two American businessmen returning home, a middle-aged couple who he thought had made a pilgrimage to Rome, and a young Spanish woman journeying in the care of her duenna.

Courtney's first test of patience had come at the same time. Tongue in cheek, she had asked the first mate if the sea lanes were safe, what with the absence of any cannon with which to defend themselves against attack. The only maurauders, she had been assured, were the French, and they were too busy these days worrying the British convoys. Corsairs? No, ma'am. They never strayed too far from their home bases along the Barbary Coast, and anyway, hadn't she heard — the Farrow brothers had been caught weeks ago and there wasn't another band of chicken thieves foolish enough or powerful enough to attack Atlantic shipping.

Chicken thieves!

Courtney had clutched her locket in a savage grip. A ship such as the *Sirius* would have been frightened into chicken *fodder* on a single bow shot from the *Wild Goose*. Taking of her cargo and crew would have been hardly more than a boring exercise.

Several hours had passed since then and she was still

seething inwardly. While she dressed for dinner, her emerald eyes kept straying to the small oval mirror over the nightstand. The stranger who looked back at her was not even faintly reminiscent of the Court Farrow she had felt so confident, so secure with a month ago. Seeing herself now, in a pale amber frock and short green bolero jacket, she could hardly believe she had run barefoot and bedraggled along the sands of Snake Island, had laughed and worked alongside burly men in the rigging of the *Wild Goose*, had fought with sword and musket and had been as familiar with the intricacies of breaking down and cleaning a flintlock pistol as she had been with washing her hands. What would First Mate Lansing's reaction be to those revelations, she wondered?

Court Farrow. Courtney de Villiers. Were they two people or were they one? Could she don a mask and take it off again at will? Could she see this masquerade through to its conclusion regardless of what she might find at the end? *Was* Duncan alive? Was Garrett Shaw really the traitor?

Courtney pressed her fingertips to her temples and massaged the throbbing veins. In the distance she heard the hollow tolling of the ship's bell advising the crew of the hour: eight bells. Courtney was expected to dine in the captain's wardroom even though she had no appetite for food.

She straightened with a sigh and brushed an errant curl off her cheek. Her hand was trembling, and her stomach fluttered unsteadily, reminding her she'd only eaten a single scone all day.

"Right, Courtney my girl," she muttered and tugged the velvet bolero jacket into order. "You've chosen to travel like a lady; I guess you'll have to act like one."

A last quick clasp at her locket for luck, and she stepped out into the corridor. All five passenger compartments were located in the stern, all five doors faced a sturdy flight of steps leading to the maindeck. Courtney heard a second door opening just as she finished setting her own latch. When she turned, it was to meet the startled gaze of Adrian Ballantine.

# Chapter Twenty-Four

It seemed as though an eternity passed as they stood in the dimly lit corridor and stared at one another in stunned disbelief. Events of their turbulent two weeks together flashed like a kaleidoscope in front of Courtney's eyes — seeing him tall and arrogant on the beach of Snake Island; seeing him in the surgery when he had condemned her to those long, dreadful days in the cage. She remembered the look on his face when he first discovered her to be a woman, and then the subsequent hard, blazing desire that had raged in his eyes when he had carried her to the bed on board the *Eagle*. And she remembered the soft plea in his voice when he lay wounded and hurting. . . .

"Courtney?"

The sound of his voice triggered a thousand more memories, but she pushed them ruthlessly aside and kept her manner deliberately cool.

"Yankee. What on earth are you doing on the *Sirius*? I thought I'd heard you were supposed to leave Gibraltar on the *Carolina*."

His eyes gleamed like molten silver as they washed over her face, her dress, her lustrous crown of auburn curls. "I'm not much of a party man," he murmured. "I thought I'd avoid the crush and leave quietly. And you? If I had to guess the last place I would ever find you, it would be on a merchantman bound for America."

"I have . . . business there."

"Business?" he said, and there was a faintly amused curve to his mouth. "Not in the same profession, I trust."

Courtney's cheeks blushed a soft pink. Her eyes were wide and dark, like receding mirrors as they sized him up warily. He could see himself the way she viewed him. He was dressed to fit the part of a businessman, in a dark blue frock coat and black breeches. His waistcoat was pale gray brocade threaded with blue pinstripes; his shirt was starched white, the neckcloth and collar rising high beneath his chin to boldly define the mahogany of his skin and the golden sheen of his hair. A deep, savage scar ran from the tip of his eyebrow into his hairline. There were still vague signs of strain underscoring his eyes, but the irises were sharp and clear and as willfully disturbing as she had ever seen them.

"I see you have recovered fully from your wounds."

"The arm is still a bit stiff," he murmured, "but it's improving."

"The doctor — he isn't with you?"

"It would have been difficult for the two of us to sneak away. I volunteered him to stay behind to accept the wreaths and speeches on my behalf. He'll sail on the *Carolina* tomorrow as planned."

"I see. And the others?"

"The boy will be going home with Matt tomorrow; Rowntree and MacDonald both elected to stay in the Mediterranean and accept postings on the *Constitution* . . ." He paused and looked at her in a way that made her knees quiver. "If you care so much, you could have stayed instead of running away by yourself — although" — his appraising gaze moved slowly over her — "you don't appear to have suffered for the absence. I must confess, I've never encountered such an inventive chameleon. From pirate to cabin boy; from nurse to seductress. . . ."

Courtney stiffened slightly. "Indeed. And I can see your own charm has not been affected in the least either."

His startling white teeth flashed in a cat's grin, and he bowed in a mocking acknowledgement of the compliment.

"Much as I long to continue this conversation, Yankee, I'm afraid we'll have to postpone it to some other time. I'm already late for a previous engagement."

"Previous engagement?" he mused softly, his brow remaining arched. "We have adapted quickly to our new role, haven't we?"

Courtney's cheeks flushed darkly, and her hands clenched into fists. "Listen, Yankee —"

"Lieutenant Yankee," he reminded her wryly. "Rather, I should say, it's Captain Yankee now, but no matter. I trust you will allow me to escort you to dinner, Miss Farrow? You're absolutely correct; we mustn't keep Captain Pettigrew waiting."

Adrian stretched out his hand to her, but she knew there was no possibility of her surviving a direct contact, not with her heart hammering so and her emotions vascillating between fury and temptation. Instead, she imperiously gathered the folds of her skirt together and swept past him, her cheeks burning and her eyes staring adamantly ahead. She could feel his laughter warming the back of her neck as he fell into step behind her. She stopped so abruptly, his lean thighs were treated to a swirl of muslin before she could recover.

"The name is de Villiers," she told him archly. "I would appreciate it if you could try to remember it?"

"I will concentrate on nothing else for the next six weeks," he promised, his eyes probing hers. She was saved by a rumble of friendly laughter from behind them, and she turned quickly and hurried toward the well-lit wardroom.

First Mate Lansing shot to his feet instantly upon seeing

Courtney at the entryway. The captain rose as well, his homely face broadening in a smile as he greeted Courtney with a relaxed bow. Introductions were made around the table: Mr. and Mrs. Santini returning to Boston from a visit to Italy; Mr. Franklin Cordel, a banker; Senorita Maria del Fuega and her duenna, Doña Dolores. . . .

"And this heah gentleman," the captain said, turning to Adrian, "is our very own genuine hero of the Barbary wars, Captain Adrian Raefer Ballantine."

The captive audience was suitably impressed, and Courtney was relieved to have the bulk of the attention shift to Ballantine. She hastened to the vacant seat beside First Mate Lansing and studiously avoided Adrian's eyes throughout the pre-dinner amenities. She also avoided the lure of the deliciously sweet, strong red wine which accompanied the meal of succulent roast chicken. Her appetite had deserted her completely, and her dinner, for the most part, went untouched.

Six weeks! Six weeks of shared meals, shared lodgings, and unavoidable encounters on a ship half the size of the *Falconer*! Perhaps if she pleaded illness — the plague or the pox — Captain Pettigrew would set her ashore before they reached open water. Perhaps if she begged, pleaded, or bribed the captain he would maroon her on the Canary Islands when they came within range. Six weeks! She knew Ballantine would not be content to leave her be. She knew that gleam in his eye well enough to fear it and having just fought and won an inner battle to free herself from his influence, she knew she was not strong enough to survive another.

When the meal ended, Courtney was the first to jump to her feet and ask to be excused. Doña Delores nodded solemnly in agreement and ushered her shy charge away from the heady attractions offered by the tableful of attentive gentlemen. Adrian stood along with the other men to bid a casually polite "good evening" to each of the ladies in turn, but only Courtney earned an extra, faintly portentous glint from the smoky gray eyes.

Never, she thought wildly. Never. She would never let him touch her again; never even let him close enough to threaten the fragile hold she had on her emotions. When she was safely inside her cabin, she locked and barred the door. For added measure, she tipped the rail-backed chair against the oak panel and wedged it firmly beneath the brass latch. She undressed swiftly and extinguished her lantern, then crawled beneath the single layer of blanket and huddled under it. Her eyes remained glued to the narrow slit of light that fanned across the floor from the bottom of the door, and she lay wide awake, listening.

She was startled tensely alert sometime later by the sound of boots and quiet laughter out in the corridor as the Santinis bid goodnight to Franklin Cardel, and separated at their respective doors. Courtney held her breath, waiting, but there were no further sounds of movement beyond her door.

Her eyelids grew heavy and the pillow grew softer. The anxieties of the day pulled and tugged her thoughts into a kind of sluggish resignation, and she let herself drift into a troubled sleep; one dominated by a sternly handsome face and a white, wolfish smile.

When Courtney awoke again the cabin was bathed in a misty sunlight that crept in through the shuttered porthole. The chair was still in place, undisturbed, beneath the door latch. Her clothes still lay in an untidy heap on the floor, and for a moment, the disappointment was as acute as the relief. He hadn't come to her door during the night. He hadn't attempted to wake her or win an entry. For all she knew, he hadn't even returned to his cabin.

She dressed and left her cabin to take a brief stroll on deck before breakfast. Adrian had apparently decided on the same means of clearing the residue of sleep from his system, as had the Spaniard and her duenna. He saw Courtney and paused in the middle of a smiling exchange with the dark-eyed beauty to bid her a pleasantly bland good morning. Senorita del Fuega did not trouble herself to tear her eyes away from the tall American of-ficer — with good reason. He wore a loose-fitting, open-throated linen shirt and dark breeches, drawing attention to the muscles across his chest, the leanness of his waist, the hard sculpting of his thighs. He must have been elab-orating on the extent of the injuries he had sustained in battle, for the senorita rested a hand on his forearm as she stared up at him, wrapt with concern.

Courtney muttered a suitably dry greeting and walked in the opposite direction. Without a moment's contempla-tion, she smiled charmingly and returned the tentative salutation offered by First Mate Lansing and accepted the offer of his company for the duration of her stroll. She even went so far as to fake a small stumble when they rounded the forecastle, prompting the mate to supply his arm for balance. Courtney was aware of Adrian's frown-ing glance and deliberately pressed closer to Lansing, as if his description of currents and underwater rifts was the most intriguing thing she'd ever heard.

Adrian's interest waned after the first two circuits of the *Sirius*'s upper deck. Instead, he directed his attentions elsewhere: to the demurely responsive Senorita del Fuega.

Courtney elected to remain in her cabin most of the day, and took all of her meals with the exception of dinner, alone. She appeared in the wardroom wearing a white batiste gown patterned with tiny sprigs of mauve flowers. She had added a short cashmere shawl as protection against the dampness of the passageways and exchanged the awkward leather shoes for a pair of delicate satin slip-pers. She had no idea if her selections were appropriate, and she was somewhat disconcerted to find the other women wrapped to the throats and sporting thick, protec-tive wool overdresses. Doña Dolores was as scandalized by Courtney's apparent lack of concern for lung rot and other dampness-related diseases as she was by Courtney's ob-vious disregard for propriety.

First Mate Edward Lansing assumed the brazenness was

for his benefit and relished it accordingly. Even the staid and mustachioed Mr. Santini relaxed from under the glare of his stout wife long enough to wink admiringly. Courtney would almost have enjoyed herself if not for the quiet amusement in Adrian Ballantine's eyes as he, in turn, catered to the refined sensuality of the senorita.

To the surprise and chagrin of her dinner companions, Courtney again excused herself early and retired to her cabin. She went alone this time, the senorita adamantly refusing to obey the whispered commands of her duenna. Courtney's thoughts were in such a turmoil that she had the latch of the cabin door turned and the door half opened before she realized that someone had followed her along the corridor.

Her gasp was stifled in her throat as she recognized the short, burly outline of Davey Dunn.

"Davey! You frightened me half to death! Come inside quickly before anyone sees you."

"I've nay but a minute to spare, lass," he grunted as he ducked inside the cabin. "I only come to warn ye."

"About the Yankee lieutenant being on board? Yes, I know. I've already supped in his company twice."

"Eh? An' he said nothin' to ye?"

"Nothing yet. Has he seen you?"

"Dunno. But I seen him on deck today and near lost my water. He's a wily bastard, that'un, and I ain't about to wager the family name he ain't seen me, beard or no."

Davey did look drastically different without the halo of red fuzz surrounding his face, but Courtney knew there was not much that escaped Ballantine's notice.

"Like a regular masquerade ball, this 'ere ship is," Dunn muttered. "You and me; the Yankee — all goin' in circles after our own tails. Never mind, lass, I'll think on some way to get rid o' him what won't cause too many questions."

"Davey" — she reached out a tentative hand to his arm — "I don't think he'll cause any trouble. He more or less told me he was willing to let bygones be gone and done with. He . . . he just wants to go home and recuperate from his wounds.''

"He blew up yer 'ome, girl.''

"I know. And we blew up his ship.''

The pale blue eyes screwed down into slits. "It were him what thumped me on the head, weren't it? And it were him what took ye off the *Falconer* before hell busted loose, weren't it?''

Courtney did not need to offer an answer to either question; he knew them already.

"Damnation,'' he exploded. "And I suppose this were no accident either, you an' him on the same ship?''

"No! You're wrong there, Davey. Dead wrong. I took the first passage that was available. *He* was supposed to leave Gibraltar on the *Carolina* with the rest of the Yankee war heroes. His being here was as much of a surprise to me as it was to you.''

Dunn did not look convinced. The surly disbelief was etched on his face.

"Davey . . . you have to believe me. I don't like trusting him any more than you do, but what other choice do we have? You can't just kill him, for heaven's sake; I doubt if anyone would believe it was accidental. We'll just have to wait and see what happens. Six weeks is a long time.''

"Aye, an' we're bound to hit a storm or two. I'll watch him, all right. I'll watch him real close and if I think he's up to nay good, he'll be in the drink before a blink warns him. As fer yersel', girl'' — he lifted a stubby finger and wagged it ominously — "remember, ye're a Farrow. Think on what Duncan'd say if he know'd ye were warmin' it with a Yankee.''

Courtney's mouth dropped open, but he was already turning back to the door. He flung it wide, his anger slamming back at Courtney. He was gone before she could take any measure to stop him. She went to the door, but after a moment's indecision, her hand fell away from the latch without opening it. She leaned her brow on the wooden panel and did not try to staunch the flow of hot tears over her lashes.

Tears! What on earth was she crying for now? When was it going to end?

A brisk tap on the door jolted her head upright.

"Davey?" she whispered and yanked the door open . . . but where she expected to see the short, gnarly-faced corsair, she found Adrian.

"What are you doing here?" she gasped. "What on earth do you want?"

She backed away from the door, her hands flying to her cheeks to dash away the shiny film of tears.

"Why can't you leave me alone? Why can't you just go away and leave me alone! What more do you want from me?"

After the slightest hesitation, he held up the cashmere shawl she had worn earlier in the wardroom. "You forgot this. I thought you might need it for the morning."

Courtney blinked furiously at a fresh flood of tears and snatched the delicate garment out of his hand. "Thank you. Now will you please go away and . . . and see if the senorita wouldn't appreciate your concerns more."

She spun away from him and bunched the shawl into a tight ball. She heard the door close, and she released her breath on a sob — one that was stifled midway as she heard his quiet baritone behind her.

"Courtney? What's wrong? What has upset you?"

"Upset me?" She whirled again, her eyes alight. "Upset me? Since when have you started to care if something upsets me?"

"It *was* your idea," he said, unscathed. "You started it, remember."

"What idea?" she demanded angrily. "What did I start? He's going to kill you! He knows about us; he knows what happened on the *Falconer*!"

Ballantine's frown deepened as he watched her tears course down her cheeks. "Lansing knows who you are?"

"Lansing?" Courtney cursed under her breath and raised a trembling hand to soothe the sudden ache at her temple. "Not Lansing . . . *Dunn*! Davey Dunn! He's on board the *Sirius*. He saw you on deck today, and he was just here . . . to warn me. And when I told him we'd already spoken . . . he guessed what had happened on the *Falconer* . . . and I just *know* he knows the rest."

"The rest?" Adrian inquired politely, and took a step closer.

"The rest. The *rest*! You know damn well what the rest is." She dropped her hand, and her eyes met his, the tears brimming with damnable persistence. "The rest is . . . that I'll be lucky if he doesn't kill me along with you when the first storm hits."

Adrian pursed his lips to contain his smile. "Is that what he's planning to do — toss me over on the first wave?"

Her breath left her on a tiny sob. "Davey is no joke. He can be mean and dangerous, and —"

"And so can I. I'm listening to you, Irish. I'm taking your warning to heart, believe me." Somehow his hands found their way onto her shoulders, his long fingers resting lightly on the curve of her throat. "But the fact is, I simply have more important things on my mind at the moment, such as: Why is it you still don't think you can trust me, even after all that's happened between us?"

"Nothing has happened!" she insisted. "And as for trusting you, every time I thought it was safe to trust you, you used me. On the *Eagle*, on the *Falconer*. . . ."

"I also recall saving your life a couple of times," he murmured.

"I didn't ask you to. And how do you know what would have happened to me if I'd stayed on the *Falconer*? Davey escaped, Garrett escaped, Miranda escaped —"

"Shaw escaped? The *Falconer* didn't burn?"

"She burned, no thanks to you, but close enough to shore for the crew to abandon her."

Adrian exhaled thoughtfully, and after a moment, his fingertips resumed their gentle, caressing strokes along her neck. "So you're telling me you wish I'd left you to live happily ever after with Garrett Shaw? Should I have believed Miranda when she told me you and he had set up house together in the aftercabin?"

"No! She was lying!" Courtney gasped. "Garrett Shaw never touched me. Oh he wanted to, all right, and he tried to but —" She caught her breath; his hands had tightened on her shoulders to draw her forward. His head was lowering toward hers. His mouth was brushing her temple and trailing a tender path of kisses across her cheek.

*"No!"* she cried and pushed out of his arms. "No, I won't let you do this to me again!"

"Do what, Miss de Villiers? *Rape* you, as I did on the *Eagle*? Or ravish you until you cry out for more, as you did on the *Falconer*?"

Courtney's cheeks flushed a deep crimson, and she stumbled back but there was nowhere to take refuge from the intensity of his eyes. She turned away to break their hold, but she could still feel their heat searing through the sheer fabric of her gown.

"Please . . . please go away. . . ."

Adrian came up behind her and placed his hands on the narrow indent of her waist. She gasped softly at the touch of his lips on her shoulder, at the back of her neck.

"Please," she whispered. "You mustn't —"

"I asked about you everywhere," he said, his voice muffled against her skin. "I haunted every tavern in Gibraltar, every rooming house, every hotel. I tore strips off a dozen innkeepers I suspected of lying to me."

Courtney's eyes widened. "Wh-why?"

He laughed quietly, and his breath tickled the fine hairs at her nape. "Well, for one thing, my perceptive young beauty, I did give my word to Seagram, if you'll recall, to see that no harm came to you. And as you've accused me so often in the past, I am an honorable bastard. Too damned honorable, I've also been told."

"But . . . I released you from your bond. Several times."

"Maybe I didn't want to be released," he said pointedly and pressed a kiss on the warmest nook of her neck. His lips traveled to the tip of her ear. "And maybe there was a second reason. Maybe it occurred to me, lying there in that godforsaken hospital bed, that seeing you again, touching you again, holding you was all I could think about. It was all that kept me going."

His hands slid upward until he had the thinly clad firmness of her breasts cradled in his palms. She felt her flesh tighten under the gentle insistence of his thumbs; she felt her nipples constrict and send shivers down her spine at each demonstrative stroke.

"When I saw you yesterday," he breathed, "do you know how close you came to being picked up, carried into my cabin, and ravished then and there? I spent a long cold night walking the decks because I knew if I came below, you wouldn't have stood a chance."

His hand lifted to her chin and cupped it, turned it, angled it so he had access to her mouth. A flush of heated blood set the length of her body on fire.

"Please," she tried one last time. "don't. . . ."

Lips that had only been grazing hers closed over the plea and silenced it beneath a demanding kiss. Hands that had been content to merely taunt her, descended boldly to her waist again and turned her around, forcing her fully into his embrace. Tears poured hot and fast over her lashes, and his mouth broke away from hers to try vainly to capture the shiny rivulets and dry them.

"Do you know how much I want you? How much I need you?"

Courtney's heart soared at the ragged honesty in his voice. "But . . . it isn't right. It can't happen. . . ."

"It's as right as we want it to be. And I'm afraid, Irish" — his mouth was warm and so very convincing — "I'm afraid it *is* happening."

For a full minute Courtney could do little more than savor the taste and feel of his lips as they moved possessively over hers. She dared not think — she could hardly breathe through the heady rush of sensations that welcomed each slow, probing thrust of his tongue. Her hands crept up the broad plain of his chest and curled around his neck. Her body pressed closer to his. She felt his hands slide down from her shoulders and begin a slow assault on the row of buttons at the back of her dress. She felt the material part and the warmth of his flesh smooth against hers. He slipped the gown off her shoulders and released the delicate ribboned belt beneath her breasts. The dress fell in a pool of batiste around her ankles, followed by the sheer silk shimmy.

She cried out weakly as he abandoned her lips to travel to the curve of her shoulder. Her knees shivered and threatened to fold, but he moved on. He moved down. His hands molded to the roundness of her breasts, and his mouth captured the aroused and straining peaks. Over and over, his tongue flicked and circled the aching flesh. His lips pulled and suckled and tormented her until her hands were balled into fists and her cheeks were wet with new tears. She curled her lower lip between her teeth to stop the choked gasps of pleasure, but it was futile. A sigh bent her head forward, and she laid her cheek on the thick golden waves of his hair; her trembling fingers moved to release the velvet bow that confined his shiny mane.

It was wrong, but she didn't care. It seemed wicked and wanton to stand naked in his arms — and him still fully clothed — but he seemed to be in no hurry. Courtney took the initiative, sliding her hands beneath his broadcloth coat and pushing it off his shoulders; she fumbled with the buttons of his waistcoat, the starched white neckcloth, the pearlized studs of his shirt.

Adrian's eyes were smoky-dark with passion. He kept his gaze locked to hers as she unfastened the last of the buttons and spread her hands over the steely hard surface of his chest. She ran her fingers through the wiry mat of hair, and she leaned forward so her brow touched the stern line of his jaw. The scent of his skin was intoxicating. The feel of his flesh sent such raw need coursing through her body that her mouth became the aggressor — tasting, sampling, exploring the hard-surfaced contours until she felt tremors in his arms. Her hands were greedy now to know and feel what her stubbornness had almost denied her. The strong column of his neck, the muscled rack of ribs, the tapering funnel of curling hairs that led to the waist of his breeches — she explored it all. Slowly. Deliberately. And when she pucked at the waist of his snowy white nankeen breeches, she heard his sharp intake of air, but it was she who chose to ignore reason now, to ignore everything but the surging flesh that pushed boldly, vigorously into her hands.

His hands twined into her hair and tilted her mouth roughly up to his; his arms scooped her off her feet and carried her to the narrow berth, where she was left untended for the few brief seconds it took for him to remove what remained of his clothes and join her on the bed. Courtney's thighs parted to welcome him, her hands caressing the tautly muscled flanks as they bore down on her. Hot and pulsing, iron hard and sleekly determined to find the deepest, most forbidden reserves of ecstasy, the vaunted flesh shuddered within her. It stroked and probed and thrusted to the core of her passion. When Courtney could no longer control her own arching hunger, Adrian willingly assumed the rapturous duty. He held her and moved for her, with her, within her, until they were both lost to the sweet, blinding madness.

Courtney purred and stretched with contentment. There was not much room to maneuver in; the berth was built to accommodate one person in any degree of comfort. Two were a test of the thin wooden supports and the equally thin ticking. Still, with arms and legs entwined, with her head cradled in the hollow of his shoulder and her breasts pressed against his chest, the arrangement passed muster.

Her attempt to stretch out a cramped muscle triggered an instant response from Adrian's sleeping form. His hand shifted to shape to the roundness of her breast. A smile tugged at his lips as he felt more sensitive areas of his body stir. He turned his head slightly, and his eyes opened a slit to study the lithe young body that had intruded on his dreams.

"It's probably well past breakfast," she murmured.

"Probably."

"Don't you think the captain might wonder what has become of us?"

"Undoubtedly." His lips moved into the crown of auburn curls, and he drank in the sensuous fragrance of her hair. "And if he did come looking for us, and if he stood outside the door for any length of time" — his hand skimmed down to her waist — "then he knows exactly what has become of us. Poor Mister Lansing; he'll be crushed."

"Poor Senorita del Fuega," she countered evenly. "Although her duenna should say her beads a thousand times in gratitude that her innocent charge has been saved from such a lustful beast."

"Lustful?" he mused, and warm hands were suddenly turning her, guiding her beneath him on the narrow cot. "*Me*?"

"Aren't you even hungry?" she asked, blushing furiously.

"Ravenous," he admitted, and his lips moved into the curve of her throat. Courtney was well beyond feigning any resistance. She simply closed her eyes and savored the sensations tingling through her body.

"I suppose it would be foolish to suggest to you that we should try to avoid one another for the rest of the voyage," she said in a whisper.

"You wouldn't have much success," he agreed. "Why? Have I run out of ways to please you already?"

"No," she gasped and curled her body against his. "No, I just . . . I mean, you *are* a returning hero. You *do* have a fiancée waiting for you. The last thing you need are rumors and gossip following you off the ship."

His eyes were unscrutable as they sought hers. "Do you think it matters to me what a few gossips say?"

"It did at one time," she answered quietly. "You were quite explicit when you pointed out my shortcomings . . . ill-bred, smelling of a slops jar —"

"The circumstances were a little different," he reminded her.

"Perhaps the circumstances, yes, but I still fall well short of your fine Virginia ladies. I can't dance. I can't sing or play the pianoforte. I stab my fingers when I try to sew. I barely know which is the front of a dress and which is the back. I'd rather go barefoot then squeeze my feet into shoes, and I have almost as many scars on my body as you do."

Adrian considered the imploring emerald gaze for a long moment then smoothed back the fine spray of disheveled curls from her neck. Her argument was quelled by the gently exploring lips.

"I was never fond of dancing myself," he murmured. "And you shouldn't belittle your voice until you've heard mine. As for your loathing for dresses, madam, or shoes, or clothing or any kind . . . at this precise moment, I applaud it."

"I'm still Duncan Farrow's daughter, and you're still Adrian Ballantine, Yankee officer, member of a rich, upper-class family. You know full well, regardless of how we feel, we'll have to go our own separate ways when we arrive in Norfolk."

The nuzzling stopped, and the shaggy blond head lifted again.

"I know no such thing."

"Adrian . . . I still have to find my father. Nothing has changed. My reasons for going to Virginia are the same."

"Your father? Courtney —" His frown deepened and she pressed her cool fingertips against his lips to forestall the next obvious statement.

"*You* think he's dead. *I* don't. I never have."

"The *Wild Goose* was captured and destroyed . . . even Shaw told you —"

"He told me he saw the *Goose* burn and he told me he

found no trace of Duncan. He assumed my father died. No doubt he'll assume I died in the fire on the *Falconer* since he's found no trace of my body either."

"Courtney —"

She wriggled out of his embrace and stood. She plucked from the floor the first garment she saw — his linen shirt — and pushed her arms into the sleeves.

"You thought the *Falconer* was destroyed," she reminded him. "And yet she magically appeared on the horizon to fight the *Eagle*."

"Yes, but —"

"No buts, Yankee. I know Duncan Farrow is alive. I can feel it . . . in here." She pressed her fist to her chest. "And I'm not going to stop looking for him, or for the man who betrayed him."

"The man who — !" Adrian sat up and swung his legs over the side of the cot. "And just how the hell do you propose to go about all of this by yourself?"

"I won't be doing it by myself. Davey Dunn will help me. He's convinced that Duncan is still alive, and so was Seagram. You asked me once what Seagram said to me on the deck of the *Eagle* just before he died. Well, he told me to find Duncan, to keep believing my father was alive, because no one could have killed the Seawolf that easily."

Adrian's attention was jolted away from the arguments forming in his mind. "What did you just say?"

"It wasn't what I said, it was what Seagram said." Courtney walked back to the side of the bed and dropped to her knees in front of Adrian, her hands reaching out to his while she angled the full power of her eyes up to his. "Seagram told me to find Duncan. To find Seawolf. It was the last thing he said before he died."

"Seawolf?"

Courtney smiled at what she thought was Adrian's confusion. "Years ago, when we were in France and he needed a way of sending messages to my mother, he sent them encoded and signed 'Seawolf.' He kept up the practice later in order to confuse anyone who might intercept communiqués between himself and Garrett or Verart. They all had code names: Verart was 'the Eel,' Garrett, 'the Cobra' " — she stole a sidelong glance, but the name raised no flicker in the gray eyes —"and Duncan was 'the Serpent.' "

"I thought you just said Duncan used the name 'Seawolf.' "

"Ten years ago, yes. But he never used the name once he moved to Snake Island. He couldn't . . . not without thinking of Mother." Adrian cradled her head between his hands. The gray eyes were intent upon hers; the strong, finely formed mouth was pressed into a grim line. "What is it? What's wrong?" she asked.

"Nothing," he said. "Nothing is wrong. I just . . . I don't want to see you put your heart and soul into something that could cost you your life."

"It has to be done. You of all people should be able to understand why. You went back for Falworth, didn't you?"

"Yes."

"And you found him?"

Harshly: "Yes. I found him."

"But you didn't stop to worry that your ship was burning or that the *Falconer* was burning, or that your chances of getting off either ship alive were minimal at best." Her hands tightened on his. "If you *had* been forced to worry about all those things and if you *had* been forced to leave the ship without settling with Falworth and if, later you discovered he *was* still alive — would you have shut your eyes and walked away? Would you have been content to put an ocean between the two of you and simply forget what he did to you, to your men, to your ship? Can you ask me to forget what was done to my father and my friends?"

The impassioned plea sent the blood pounding into Adrian's temples. Dear God, her eyes. Eyes he had been wary of from the very beginning. He had thought them dangerous then; he considered them deadly now. How long could he hope to hide the truth from her? Duncan Farrow was Seawolf, the man who had been selling information to the American navy.

It didn't make sense, and yet the more he played it through his mind, the more logical it became. Farrow wanted out of the game — Courtney had admitted as much. He had not taken her or his brother on the final doomed run through the blockade and again, by a later admission, Courtney had said both she and Verart were supposed to have sailed to Algiers for supplies. If they had not delayed, they would have been away from Snake Island when the *Eagle* had attacked. And since Duncan Farrow had no way of knowing they hadn't gone for supplies, he would have had no reason to show himself to the *Falconer* when Shaw had returned to search for survivors at Moknine.

Oh yes, he thought savagely as he looked down at Courtney, I believe you now. I believe the bastard is still alive. He never would have been stupid enough to have been caught by his own scheming hand. No, he stayed alive so that his daughter could join him in America and he could continue to bask in her blind devotion. But what were the contingency plans if she were to discover the truth? Would he kill her as cold-bloodedly, as ruthlessly as he had planned the deaths of all other witnesses?

"Adrian?"

"What?" He blinked the rage out of his eyes with an effort. "I'm sorry, I was . . . I was thinking about the ironies: two sides, two traitors. And you're right. I wouldn't have been able to turn my back. I won't now. The man you're after played as big a part in destroying the *Eagle* as Otis Falworth did, and I want to find him just as badly as you do."

Courtney's eyes widened. "You mean you'll help me? You'll help me find the man who betrayed us?"

"I'll help you," he grated harshly. "Providing you trust me. Trust me and believe me when I say I will never deliberately do anything to hurt you again."

"I believe you," she said with a frown, bewildered by his sudden vehemence.

"And you'll trust me?"

She hesitated a moment, then nodded.

"How are you supposed to contact your father if he's alive and if he's in Norfolk?"

"Through a lawyer. Prendergast."

"A friend?"

"I've never seen him before. It was just a name Verart whispered in my ear before he died, although it wasn't hard to remember. Prendergast was Duncan's mother's maiden name."

"A relative then?"

"No. At least, I don't think so. It was just a habit of my father's, to associate names with things out of the past."

"I see. What were you supposed to do — just walk in to the lawyer's office and introduce yourself as Courtney Farrow?"

Again she hesitated. "No. I'm to give him the name 'Longford.' "

"Longford?"

"It's the name of the county in Ireland where Father was born."

"Does anyone else know about this?"

"Practically everyone but me, it seems," she said dryly. "Verart and Seagram knew, Davey Dunn . . . Garrett knew there was something going on but I don't think he had all the pieces of the puzzle until Miranda threw in with him."

"Why Miranda?"

"Because he tried to get me to cooperate, but I wouldn't do it. Miranda used to interpret captured documents and manifests from prize ships. She speaks, or understands, four languages besides English and was often left alone for hours at Duncan's desk to sort through papers. I remember a violent argument they had once when Duncan found her going through his personal papers. If he had any correspondence with Prendergast —'' She shrugged and left the sentence unfinished.

"They could both be going to Norfolk to look for your father," Adrian suggested. Courtney shook her head.

"Garrett is firmly convinced Duncan is dead. He's going to America to claim whatever profits my father managed to set aside."

"Surely he made a fortune along with Duncan all these years."

"Money falls right out of Garrett's pockets. And now that the *Falconer* is gone, he can't even do what he does best, not until he finds a way to buy another ship."

Adrian was quietly thoughtful for a few moments, his fingers content to stroke absently through the shiny auburn curls.

"Twice you've mentioned this inheritance — it must be sizable for so many people to be chasing after it."

"I don't know," she said honestly. "Both Verart and Davey implied that Duncan had been trying to establish himself as a respectable businessman in America — to buy land, build a home, settle down. I know he was getting tired of the killing and the bloodshed, and of Garrett's insistence that they attack more and more ships. I've never really thought about it, but looking back over the years, Duncan never spent much money. He bought things we needed, for the Island and for the ships, but he was never a showman like Garrett. He used to try to buy things for me, but even that stopped when he realized I wasn't really interested in fancy clothes and jewels. Maybe that's why he kept his plans for retiring a secret. Maybe he thought I would've argued and refused to go."

"Would you have refused?"

"I don't know," she whispered softly. "I think the idea would have terrified me. It does now if I think about it too much — which is why I have to concentrate instead, on finding the traitor before he finds Duncan."

"You have someone in mind?"

The large green eyes faltered and looked away. "Davey has an idea. It didn't seem possible at first, but with everything that's happened . . ." She looked up again. "He believes it was Garrett who sold us out."

"Shaw? What makes Dunn suspect Shaw?"

"He would have known all of Duncan's plans in advance: his raids, his schedules for running the blockades, his meetings with Karamanli."

"A dozen people could have known."

"A dozen people couldn't come and go as they pleased. A dozen people didn't have contacts in Gibraltar and Tangiers and Tripoli, and a dozen people didn't claim to have sources high in the American Admiralty office."

"He was Falworth's conduit?"

"He took gold with him to Gibraltar and he came back with valuable information."

"Damn," Adrian muttered softly. "Then Shaw was the Englishman Falworth spoke about."

"The Englishman?" Courtney frowned. "No, it wasn't Garrett. He said *his* contact used the name 'Englishman' — whom I assumed was your Lieutenant Falworth. Especially since Garrett seemed to know him well enough on the *Falconer*."

"Well, if Shaw isn't the Englishman and Falworth claimed not to be — who the devil is?"

"Adrian . . . you said the man your navy dealt with in Father's camp used a code name . . . ?"

It was Adrian's turn to stare. He couldn't tell her their contact had been Seawolf, not yet anyway. He blurted the first foolish name that came into his head; a nickname he dredged out of his memory from childhood days.

"Swordfish. We knew him only as Swordfish."

"Swordfish?" A shadow flickered behind her eyes, and the disappointment sagged heavily on her shoulders. "No. No, I don't remember ever hearing it."

Courtney rested her cheek on Adrian's knee and he leaned forward to bury his lips in her hair. Her answers had pointed out some nagging inconsistencies — things which had troubled him during his period of recuperation in the hospital when he'd not had much to do but think. Everything had pointed to the fact that the naval leak came from a high position, but a sub-lieutenant, even one with access to the commodore's order memos, was hardly likely to have information to sell as sensitive as that which had been finding its way into Duncan Farrow's hands. Shaw had been in possession of the most recent code book — he had given the correct responses to the raised signal flags on the *Eagle*. But while Falworth's cousin might have had access to blockade orders, he would not have been able to get his hands on sealed code books. And there was still Alan. Always Alan. Always the picture of the neat bluish puncture wound beneath his breastbone, something which only Adrian and Matthew Rutger had seen. It had been Matthew's idea to let it stand on the log as an accident; to sit back and wait and watch for someone to make a mistake. But no one had. Not Falworth, not Jennings, not a single member of the *Eagle*'s crew. Matthew hadn't known Adrian's real mission on the *Eagle*. He hadn't even known he'd numbered among the prime suspects in the beginning. For that bit of deception, Adrian had felt like a traitor himself for weeks. It made him feel all the more guilty as he sat holding and loving Courtney Farrow.

"Promise me something," he whispered.

"More promises, Yankee?" she murmured, tilting her head up off his knee. "You demand a great deal from your captives, don't you?"

He did not return her smile. "Promise me you won't go after Shaw — or whoever it is — on your own."

The emerald eyes searched his warily, and her voice mocked his concern. "Why the sudden confidence in my ability?"

"It's because I know too well what you're capable of, that I'm worried."

"Should I be flattered?"

"You should be careful. And you shouldn't be too

damned stubborn about using my help when it's offered. I have *some* abilities, you know."

"Now who's asking for flattery? Very well, Yankee, I'll say it: your abilities are awesome."

His gaze moved down to the moist, supple lips and remained there while his hands slipped to her shoulders and gently eased aside the folds of the linen shirt.

"Are we referring to the same abilities, madam?" he murmured.

She leaned into his kiss, her tongue darting between his lips, luring his into a game of thrust and parry.

"Swordfighting, is it?" His arms tightened to lift her onto the bed. His hand smoothed its way down to her belly, down to the fine thatch of red-gold curls. She gasped as she accused him of foul play, but his fingers were already engaged too deeply in the counterattack to pay any notice . . . and in the next breath, she did not want him to.

# Chapter Twenty-Five

The *Sirius* took seven weeks to reach Boston harbor. Spates of poor weather extended the journey into the first week of October, and Courtney's first glimpse of America was of a land painted in the bright crimsons, ambers, and golds of autumn. Captain Pettigrew, aware that most of his passengers had spent their time on board the *Sirius* in various stages of illness, elected to remain in the sheltered harbor for a week, three days over the four he had originally scheduled, in order to repair the storm damage his ship had suffered and to allow the weary passengers to recoup their color.

For Courtney, who had suffered nothing more than a minor queasiness in the last few mornings aboard the *Sirius*, the delay meant a full week of exploring the shops and taverns, of eavesdropping on the broad nasal twang of the Bostonians, of sampling the elegance of fine restaurants, and of spending long, langorous hours snuggled with Adrian in front of the blazing warmth of a fire. It was a welcome change from their enforced restraint on board the *Sirius*. Aside from the occasional stroll on deck and the polite ritual of sharing the mealtimes, they had maintained a discreet civility in front of their fellow passengers. Only when the ship's company was asleep did an equally discreet tap on Courtney's door signal an end to the formalities. Even then, the nights seemed disproportionately shorter than the days, and since most of their conversations were undertaken in whispers, their time together seemed furtive as well as brief.

Once ashore, all pretense was suspended. Adrian took a suite in a large, expensive hotel and spent the first full day ensconced in an enormous feather bed with an uncommonly receptive pirate wench. The days were spent exploring in the city; he bought her so many clothes and accessories she grew reluctant to show an interest in the window displays they passed. He introduced to her new food, new customs; he took her to an opera one night and spent the entire evening watching the bewildered expression on her face. He marveled at her curiosity over things he had taken for granted: the proper fork and spoon to use, the correct way to sit, to stand, to walk. She even demanded a demonstration of waltz steps — an exercise that ended in a tumble of arms and legs on the thick carpet. And gradually she learned how to laugh. Or at least, she learned not to keep it hidden from him, or to regard it as a sign of weakness or betrayal. As he had suspected, it was a husky, deep-throated sound that turned heads, and would have warmed the coldest of hearts. It won his completely.

As slowly as the laughter had come, the distrust and wariness began to fade from the emerald eyes. It had been there almost constantly the first few weeks of their turbulent relationship, surging and receding like the tides of the sea. On board the *Sirius*, she'd had nowhere to run from him, nowhere to hide. She could not retreat behind her anger for very long — it waned by day, by night it perked only until she heard the sound of gentle tapping at her door. She still argued with him, still found ways to test him, but he was as determined to tear through the last of her defenses as she was to hold some back. He still feared what lay ahead for her in Norfolk, but otherwise he was as honest with her as he could be; as honest as he was with himself. The lie about the codename was his one small concession to winning her trust and confidence, and perhaps it was a mistake to keep it from her; but he knew he would lose her before he had a chance to win her if she knew the truth about Seawolf. Her intense loyalty truly frightened him; if it was bruised or damaged too badly, she might not ever come out of her shell again.

By a mutual understanding they never talked about Norfolk, or about Garrett Shaw, or Duncan Farrow . . . or Deborah Longworth Edgecombe. They knew the *Carolina* would have passed them somewhere in the Atlantic and that, without the need to stop over in Boston, she would be in Norfolk a full two weeks ahead of the *Sirius*. Adrian's family — and Deborah — would be alerted to his arrival, as would a public clamoring for a hero.

"Maybe I'll just send a courier on ahead and tell them I've decided to go north, to Canada," he suggested wryly on their last night in Boston.

"Coward," she declared. She was seated cross-legged on the floor and was wearing a loose-fitting cambric night-gown. She had a box of bonbons on her lap. Her fingers were sticky with chocolate; her eyes were as sparkling and mischievous as a child's. She had only recently emerged from a hot bath, the firelight was behind her and made her damp hair glitter in a coppery-red nimbus around her cheeks and throat.

Adrian was also seated on the floor, his long legs stretched toward the warmth of the fire, his upper torso gleaming nakedly in the russet light. He watched her select a bonbon and scrape the sweet coating away with her teeth to uncover the treat in the center.

Courtney glanced over and scowled. "Something wrong with the way I eat, Yankee?"

He smiled and sipped at his brandy. "Not if you're four years old and have never seen a chocolate before."

She stuck out her tongue and proceeded to lick each

sticky finger. The smile in his eyes lingered as they dropped to the balloon glass he held cradled in his palm. The firelight flickered blood-red in the brandy; the heat of his hand warmed it so that when it touched his lips it glided, like honey, down his throat.

He sensed Courtney's eyes upon him and he lowered his left arm, still self-conscious about the ugliness of the scars.

"I wasn't staring at that, you vain rogue," Courtney chided softly. "And even if I was, those are your medals; you should wear them proudly."

She leaned forward and brushed her lips lightly against his, escaping before his hand could capture the nape of her neck. Instead, she caught his hand and held it while, first her fingertips then her lips traced a tender path of caresses along the pink, shiny welts that distorted his forearm.

Adrian felt an immediate and powerful response in his body. In eight weeks his hunger for her had not diminished in the slightest. If anything it had grown the nearer they came to Virginia. Fear of losing her? He did not know. It was as if she had seeped into his blood and altered its chemistry so that he would never feel whole without her. What indeed would the Ballantine family think of her? He was under no illusions as to the kind of woman Samuel Ballantine considered acceptable to welcome into the family. And yet Adrian would no more think of trying to mold Courtney into a demure, vapid southern belle as he would . . . well, trying to fit himself into his brother's shoes. Rory loved the land and the security he found there. The last thing Adrian wanted out of life was a sprawling, sleeping plantation house with nothing more stormy in his existence than the weather.

A life with Courtney Farrow would be nothing but storms. In the way she loved and the way she hated, there was only instinct and passion to guide her. Deborah was gentle, obliging, calming almost to the degree that she melded with the background. He had known Deborah all of his life, had known his father's plans for their marriage from the day she was born. He had offered the proposal and she had accepted, but they had been strangers going through the motions. There was no fire, no test of will, no challenge to keep him hungry. Not like Courtney: There was passion in Courtney's body, even in repose. She could seduce a man with a single glance if she chose to, and promise more with one of her petulant, defiant pouts than she ever dreamed.

As if to confirm his observation, he brushed his fingers against the fire-gilded silhouette and waited for the emerald eyes to rise to his. He set the brandy glass aside, his gaze locked to hers while he unfastened the delicate row of satin ribbons that descended from her neck down the front of the gown. The cambric trembled away from the soft round flesh and he twined his hands around hers to pull her closer. She came willingly, her mouth tasting sweet and chocolatey as he possessed it.

"You must be the Devil, Irish," he muttered against her fragrant flesh. "You must be, for you're in my blood and I'm damned if I know how to get you out."

"Do you want to get me out, Yankee?" she asked, her hands at his shoulders tracing the bronzed, rippling muscles. The cambric was open almost to her waist; with a casual flick of cloth, he had both breasts bared to his searching fingertips.

"I fear it's too late, madam. Far too late." He pulled her down onto the thick carpet and fused his mouth to hers. If she needed a further answer, it was in the heat of his flesh as it filled her. With soft cries she welcomed him and moved with him, loving him as she always did: as if each time was their first and their last.

They left the bitter chill of Boston behind and sailed south to Virginia where the wind still carried an autumn bite but the sun seemed determined to keep the trees and grass green. The harbor was crowded with vessels of all shapes and sizes: from single-masted sloops to three-masted frigates. Adrian's sharp eyes singled out the *Carolina*, and his expression turned grim. Fishing boats had already scurried on ahead to announce their arrival; the docks were teeming with people and the waterfront stores flew colorful, patriotic displays of flags.

Adrian had donned his uniform for the first time since leaving Gibraltar. The stiff navy blue tunic with its gold braid and high standing collar made him look exactly the part of a returning hero, and Courtney's heart pounded with a combination of pride and nervousness.

"I think I'll wait below until you've left the ship," she said quietly, eyeing the mass of humanity waiting on the dock.

"You'll do no such thing. If I'm forced to endure this, I'll damn well endure it with you by my side."

"But all those people —"

"By my side," he insisted. "And no more arguments or I'll ask Captain Pettigrew for a pair of manacles to keep you bound to me by force."

"It would be a fitting way for me to enter Norfolk," she mused, her gaze darting here and there as the distance steadily narrowed and more and more of the uniforms waiting on the dock became distinguishable from the plain cloaks and greatcoats of the civilians.

Adrian sensed her distress and tucked a comforting arm around her shoulders. "You have nothing to worry about. We Yankees are most hospitable to pretty young exiles from foreign lands."

Courtney smiled half-heartedly at his attempt at humor, but her thoughts were rife with doubts for the first time since leaving Gibraltar. Why had she thought she could get away with this masquerade? Why had she come to America, of all places? Why hadn't she simply sent someone else in her place to find her father and tell him she was alive and waiting?

She glanced surreptitiously into the *Sirius*'s rigging and saw the familiar froth of red beard and hair. She had only spoken to Davey Dunn twice in the eight weeks they had been on board the ship, both times on her initiative since he had apparently decided to shun her. She knew Adrian had talked to him — she had seen bruises on both men as proof — but whatever agreement they had reached, she was not privy to, having only received a grunted assurance from Adrian that there would be no more trouble. Knowing Davey, he would vanish within seconds of stepping ashore and not rest until he had located Duncan Farrow.

If he was here. More doubts! Doubts about her father, doubts about the wisdom of crossing the Atlantic to search for him and, worst of all, doubts about her dependency on Adrian Ballantine. He had promised to help her find Duncan, but what then? As an officer of the American navy he was honor-bound to take Duncan to the authorities. Would he? Despite everything that had happened, the promises exchanged . . . would he believe in her enough to at least give Duncan a chance to get away?

He had said that she was in his blood, but a man could be cut and the blood would drain away . . . He had changed her life: there was no question about that. He had shown her gentleness and tenderness and he had encouraged a return of all the emotions and feelings she had fought so hard over the years to forget.

He had loved her through battles and captivity; when he was hurt and in pain; on the sea. But there had been only the two of them — and no one to compare her to. He had rarely mentioned Deborah in all the time they had been together on board the *Sirius*, but Courtney found herself thinking more and more about the specter she had never met, but whom she had come to dread. Especially now.

Matthew Rutger had said Deborah was beautiful and elegant, refined and gracious — by implication everything Courtney was not. Would she be waiting on the dock to greet Adrian? Of course she would, unless she was a complete fool. How would Courtney handle the meeting? Why was she more afraid of meeting this woman than she ever had been of meeting the meanest, ugliest pirate along the Barbary Coast?

The ship sidled toward the main wharf, and the activity in the rigging took on a frenzied note. The steering sails were hauled in; the mooring cables were snaked from their capstans; and First Mate Lansing shouted a steady stream of orders into his hailing trumpet. The captain, standing on the forecastle bridge, waved to someone ashore, and his homely face split into a wide grin. He removed his cap and held it aloft, as did several of the laughing crewmen. They were home. Their wives and sweethearts were on shore waiting, smiling, eager to hear the news from abroad and to convey the gossip from home.

The cables were released, and a dozen helping hands on shore grabbed for them and slung them around the thick wooden pilons. The *Sirius* came to a sliding halt, jerking slightly as she nudged up against the dock. First Mate Lansing's trumpet relayed the order to clear the gangway hatch and lower away. The captain descended from the bridge and collected his log and manifests from a cabin boy, then walked across the deck toward Adrian and Courtney.

"Captain Ballantine, Miz Courtney: a pleasuh to have y'all aboard. Ah hope yoah journey was a pleasant one?"

"Thank you, Captain Pettigrew," Adrian said, returning the friendly salute before he extended his hand for a warm shake. "A pleasure indeed."

"The vultures appeah to have sniffed y'all out." The Captain grinned and indicated the milling confusion on shore. "Best not keep them waitin' too long or y'all are apt to start a riot. Again, ma'am, mah absolute pleasuh."

Courtney smiled, the best she could manage with her tongue fastened to the roof of her mouth. Her thoughts were all for the crowd, for the harsh sounds, for the smell of oil and tar and smoking fish that pervaded the air.

"Come along, my brave Irish hellion," Adrian murmured in her ear. "Fate awaits you."

Courtney looked up, startled, but there was no mockery in his eyes, only gentle understanding. She let him steer her toward the gangway where the other passengers had gathered to bid one another farewell. Each vied for a last word with Adrian, or lingered in the hope of disembarking from the *Sirius* at his side. But he held fast to Courtney,

and she wondered briefly if it was not as much for his protection as for hers.

Immediately, when he set foot on the gangway the air
clanged and crashed with the sounds of a military band
welcoming them ashore. A cheer went up in the crowd and
hats were torn from heads and waved gleefully. Courtney
felt very small, very insignificant in the wave of admiration
for the tall, smiling officer by her side. He assisted her
from the gangway ramp onto the dock then turned to acknowledge the salute of a young naval lieutenant who murmured a greeting and pointed to the reception committee
waiting a dozen paces away. Two commodores and a rear-
admiral stood before a starched and stiff-necked row of
captains and junior officers, but Adrian's eyes flicked past
them to the small group of civilians by their side. Courtney
followed his gaze and found it returned by a man who
could only have been the patriarch of the Ballantine family.

Samuel Ballantine was as tall as Adrian and would have
been as broadly built in his prime, although there was
nothing gaunt or sagging about him now to suggest any
loss of power or esteem. He wore a towering black beaver
hat over a shock of wavy gray air. His face was broad and
as cragged as a lion's; every line and crease seemed to
represent years of command and every line led to the
domineering presence of his eyes. A darker blue-gray than
Adrian's, they were flat and cold. They radiated power,
but no compassion.

Beside him stood a younger, thinner version of the
weathered body and harsh, uncompromising face.
Adrian's brother, Rory Ballantine, could have been just as
cold, just as formidable a barrier to cross, but for the
smile — no, the grin — that softened the composition of
his face.

"Adrian! Dammit" — he came running across the
separating gap and clapped his arms around Adrian's
shoulders — "it's good to have you back! Let me have a
look at you! We should have known you'd come back with
bells ringing and flags flying. I won't believe half the

stories they're telling us about you until I hear it from your lips — even then, I'm not sure I'll swallow them all."

Adrian laughed and turned to Courtney. "I did warn you about my family, didn't I? Rory will take some getting used to, but once you come to know him, he's really quite harmless. Courtney de Villiers: Emory Ballantine."

Rory swept his hat off his head and bowed to Courtney, but the shock showed in his soft blue eyes. When he straightened, they were on Adrian. Adrian's face remained challengingly blank and his brother's gaze flicked back to Courtney.

"Welcome to Norfolk, Miss de Villiers." His smile had turned polite and forced. "I hope you'll find your stay here a pleasant one."

"For heaven's sakes, Rory Ballantine, don't keep him all to yourself!"

Adrian glanced toward the source of the impatient shout, and a smile creased his handsome face. A petite, red-faced, very obviously pregnant woman detached herself from Samuel Ballantine's arm and held out both hands to welcome Adrian.

"Helen! Good to see you! What the Devil has my little brother been up to, or need I ask?"

The woman blushed prettily and raised a gloved hand to contain her giggles. "It's good to have you back, Adrian. We're all so proud of you! The boys talk of nothing else all day long but their famous uncle."

Adrian leaned to one side as he caught a glimpse of two peeping heads huddled in the shadow of his sister-in-law's skirts. The twins, Neil and David: they'd been babes in arms the last time Adrian had seen them.

"Has it only been a year?" he murmured, after coaxing a handshake out of the shy pair before they scurried behind their mother's skirt again. "It seems more like ten."

He straightened and turned to Samuel Ballantine. For a long, hard moment the two men stared at one another, each acknowledging the other's stubborn pride. The elder man relented first, and he lifted his hand to his son.

"Adrian. You were determined to prove your way was the right way, weren't you."

"An inherited trait, I suppose. It's good to see you, Father."

"Good to see you," Samuel conceded quietly. "I hope this last episode puts an end to your wanderlust, boy. It's high time you settled down and made a proper home. Deborah! Don't be so blasted shy, girl. Step up here and say hello to your husband."

Past the shield of Adrian's broad shoulders, Courtney saw a slim, elegantly dressed woman step away from Samuel Ballantine's shadow and offer a shy smile of welcome. Courtney felt her heart slide into the pit of her belly, and from there turn to liquid terror. She needed no one to tell her that this stunningly beautiful creature was Deborah Longworth Edgecombe. Her face was as finely molded as a porcelain figurine's; her hair was silvery blonde and piled in an abundance of glossy curls.

"Adrian." Deborah's voice was a hushed whisper. "Welcome home."

"Deborah." He took both of her gloved hands in his and pressed them to his lips. One of them escaped his grip and, like an elusive butterfly, caressed his bronzed cheek.

"We were so worried. We heard you were wounded. We heard you'd been in a hospital for weeks and weeks."

"Ten days," Adrian corrected her with a smile. "And Matt was with me all the time. Where is he, by the way? I saw the *Carolina* out in the harbor. . . ."

Adrian's eyes swept the front line of the crowds, then glanced toward the patiently waiting naval committee. Matt's wry countenance was nowhere to be seen — odd, since it would have suited his sense of humor to watch Adrian squirm with all the attention.

"Adrian —" Samuel's voice tugged him back. "There is one other person most anxious to meet you."

Deborah's gaze faltered, and she lowered her lashes before Adrian could question what he saw there. She half-turned and murmured something to the young woman standing by her side, and when she faced Adrian again, she was holding a bundle wrapped in a long white wool shawl. Adrian's frown was answered by a quiet gurgle and coo from the squirming bundle. Deborah looked up at him, her eyes wide and pleading. Her lips were white and bloodless, her pale skin almost ashen with apprehension.

"Well, sir?" Samuel demanded in a voice loud enough to be overheard by the crowds. "Have you nothing to say to your wife for presenting you with a fine baby daughter in your absence?"

Adrian could only stare at his father, at the deep blue eyes that seemed to be saying, 'We'll do it my way now, boy.'

"My . . . daughter?"

"Naturally we were all surprised to hear the two of you had eloped before you left Norfolk — another little display of independence? Never mind, m'boy, we'll forgive you. I can forgive anyone who presents me with a beautiful daughter-in-law and an equally beautiful grandchild. My dear" — he smiled at Deborah — "give the child back to her nurse and take your place by your husband's side. I believe Rear Admiral Morris is waiting to begin the formal ceremonies."

"Yes, Papa," Deborah whispered and covered the child's face with the shawl before handing her to the nurse.

Adrian felt the anger build inside him, but this was no time to vent it. He could not deny the elopement in public, not while he could still see the haunting plea in Deborah's eyes. He felt trapped and cornered, and he could only pray that Courtney. . . .

Courtney!

Adrian whirled around, but she was nowhere in sight. He vaguely recalled feeling her hand slip out of the crook of his arm when he had greeted Helen, but he had assumed she was still behind him.

Damn . . . damn!

He searched the laughing, waving throngs, but she was not among them. There was not even a glimpse of her cloak to indicate which way she had gone; no disturbance in the crowds to tell him which way to shout, to run.

No, dammit! He was not going to lose her again!

He took a step in the direction of the crowd, but a strong hand grasped his elbow and stopped him.

"Adrian, don't be a fool," came the hissed warning. It was Rory, and there was genuine panic in his eyes. "Don't make a scene now. It isn't worth it. Wait! Good God, if Father sees you like this . . . if he thinks that girl means anything to you —"

"That girl is my wife," Adrian snarled. "My *only* wife. We were married on the *Sirius*."

# Chapter Twenty-Six

Courtney ran until her legs threatened to tumble her into the dusty streetside ditch. Her lungs burned; her eyes were stinging although there were no tears to show for her foolishness. There was no reason to cry, nothing to be gained by admitting how deeply this new betrayal had stunned her.

Several passersby on the street cursed as she pushed around and through them, but she barely noticed. She was angry, hurt, humiliated. She had allowed her heart to rule her head and now she was paying the price. She had loved him, truly and honestly loved him, and she had thought he loved her. She had believed it, had even let him convince her there were selfish reasons for admitting it.

"Marry me," Adrian had said. "We belong together, you and I. Marry me and I can keep you safe . . . loved . . . happy."

*Safe*? He must have seen how the word had lodged in her

mind like an iron spike even though her first instinct had been to refuse.

"I can't marry you. I can't marry anyone."

"Why?"

"Why? Do you have to hear me say it?" Her temper had come to her defense, but he had been expecting it. "Because I don't belong. You know what my life has been like these past ten years. You know what I've done."

"You have the scars to prove it," he murmured. "And you wear them proudly, like medals. Believe it or not, I'm proud of them too. I wouldn't have you any other way."

"But I've been a thief! A pirate!"

"Aye, and you've stolen my heart and plundered my soul, madam," he chided softly.

"These hands —" She thrust them out. "Do you know what they've done?"

Adrian caught them and held them to his lips. "They've wielded cutlasses and guns and knives like no other hands I've seen. The mere thought of what they're capable of will keep me honest and faithful to my dying day, of that you can be sure."

Tears flooded her eyes. "But my father —"

"We'll find him together." A shadow had flickered across his eyes, but the smile had remained. "And if he helps me, I'll help him."

"Help you, how?"

"I want the Englishman just as much as you do, remember?"

There it was, and she had missed it. Either missed it or deliberately misread the promise that had been in his eyes — the hesitation, the lie! It had been there all along, and she hadn't seen it. Hadn't wanted to see it because she thought, she *believed* she loved him and he loved her despite their differences. Her heart as well as her body had betrayed her, and both would carry the scars forever. One moment of blind foolishness had cost her everything — her pride, her self-respect. She had stood on the sun-drenched deck of the *Sirius* and exchanged vows with a man who had played on her emotions as coldly, as expertly as if she'd been putty to fit to a mold.

Well, he had not gotten away completely unscathed. Courtney had seen the look of horror on his face when his sweet Deborah had proudly presented his child for inspection. He hadn't known about her little surprise, had not anticipated his own well-laid plans going awry so early in the game. What would he do now? Even if he hadn't actually exchanged vows with his Deborah, he was more married to her than if he wore a brand and an iron yoke. Honorable, upright, socially conscious officers and gentlemen simply did not turn their backs on their own kind, not even if they had wed another. Of course she, Courtney Farrow, a mere pirate wench, would be expected to understand and adjust — to what: to become his mistress? Had that been the other emotion she had seen in the cold gray eyes — relief? Naturally he would still offer his protection . . . as long as she still gave him the information he wanted.

Clever, she thought, her brow streaming, her legs weakening, her lungs heaving for air. Clever, cunning bastard. Had that been the ploy from the beginning: to win her trust and her love in the hopes of her leading him to Duncan Farrow? Was Captain Ballantine vying for another quick promotion — to commodore, perhaps?

She had to get off the streets! She had to work quickly to find her father and leave Virginia as soon as possible. She would have to locate the lawyer — Horace J. Prendergast — and she would have to use him to alert her father to the dangers closing in around him. Together they would hunt down Garrett Shaw and confront him with what they knew. Davey Dunn was in Norfolk as well. He had witnessed her marriage to Adrian Ballantine, and there had been nothing but cold contempt in his eyes. If he found Duncan first. . . .

Courtney reeled dizzily around a corner and knew she could not run much longer. There were cramps in her legs, in her chest, and a steady throbbing pain in her abdomen. Invisible hands were tightening around her belly and squeezing, each steely finger digging for buried nerves. Her clothing stuck to her in soaked patches; her hair clung wetly to her neck. She saw a hotel halfway along the grimy side-street: not too big, not too small; not expensive, not cheap. The Seafarers Inn looked as though it catered to the nondescript clientele of Norfolk, the ones who were neither rich nor poor. It would do.

Courtney stumbled across the narrow street and paused by the double oak doors while she tried to regain her breath. She could not use the name "Farrow" or "de Villiers." Ballantine's influence in Norfolk would be considerable and for whatever motives, he would send out inquiries for a lone French emigrée using either name.

McCutcheon! It was the name Davey had used, and if he had seen her run from the dock, he might look for her. . . .

Courtney closed her eyes and stifled the sob of despair before it could choke past her sealed lips. Davey wouldn't look for her — he would avoid her like the pox. Ballantine wouldn't look for her — he knew enough already to sniff out Duncan Farrow on his own if he was determined to do so. Garrett Shaw might look for her, especially if he had followed the commotion on the docks, and if he'd heard of Ballantine's arrival with a woman — a small, dark-haired woman with an odd French name. . . .

Courtney pushed away from the cool stone façade and entered the dark, cheerless foyer of the Seafarers Inn. It smelled of musty wood and sickeningly cloying whale oil, and Courtney's stomach took a worse turn. Her mouth went suddenly dry, and her vision blurred. It stayed blurred through a haze of dancing, cartwheeling lights, and a hum rose in her ears — a hum that all but drowned out the sound of her own name being called from the foot of the wide winding staircase.

The spate of dizziness passed as quickly as it had gripped her, but the shock of seeing the familiar oval face staring at her immobilized her as effectively as if she had fallen in a dead faint. She tried to warn him away with her eyes, but it was too late. With a second, head-turning cry of recognition, Dickie Little flung himself across the distance of the foyer and ran straight into her arms.

Adrian Ballantine tolerated the pomp and ceremony for two long hours. By the time he was able to finally close the door to his suite in the very expensive, very fashionable Carelton Hotel, he was barely able to see through the build-up of pressure behind his eyes.

"I don't suppose there is anything to drink around here?"

"There's whisky," Deborah said haltingly. "Or bourbon. I'll fix it for you if you like."

"Bourbon. No water. And make it a strong one. It's been a hell of an afternoon. Rory?"

"Nothing, thanks. Look, you two probably want to be alone —"

"On the contrary," Adrian insisted silkily. "The last thing I want at the moment is to be alone, especially since I appear to be the only one ignorant of whatever grand conspiracy is going on here."

"There's no conspiracy," said Rory as he reached for his hat.

"No? Let me make myself clearer then: Take one more step toward that door and I'll break both your legs."

Rory glanced up, startled. Adrian's eyes were as cold as his voice, and both nailed the younger Ballantine to the spot as if his feet had been skewered by arrows.

Deborah's long slender hands shook visibly as she poured out the strong spirits, but to her credit, she did not avoid the dangerously calm gray eyes as they flicked from Rory to her. Adrian took the drink in silence, finished it in silence, then shattered the tension with a harsh inquiry.

"I want somebody in this room to tell me what the hell is going on — and I want the truth, dammit, starting with that child in the next room. Whose is it?"

Rory's mouth dropped open, and despite the warning, he started to sidle for the door. "Adrian, for God's sake, you don't want me to hear this."

"I told you to stay put! As for someone hearing this . . . I could have denounced the child back on the dock during that touching welcome-home scene, but I didn't. I chose to wait — at what cost I don't quite know yet — and for that bit of decency, by God, I want the truth."

Deborah lifted a trembling hand and smoothed a wisp of hair off her cheek. "It's all right, Rory. It's only as much as he deserves. I'm grateful for what Adrian did, and he's perfectly justified in being angry. The child isn't his. She couldn't be. We never . . . I mean . . ." Her voice failed and she lowered her eyes.

"We never eloped," Adrian provided, "And we never shared a bed."

"No," she whispered. "Never."

Some of the coldness melted from Adrian's eyes. Rory let out a long sigh and muttered, "I think I'll have that drink after all."

"Do I get an explanation?" Adrian asked, moving closer to Deborah.

"There isn't much to explain. After you left Norfolk, I discovered I was with child. I had to tell someone, so I . . . I told Mother. The next thing I knew it was after midnight and there was a carriage pulling up to the house and . . ." — she looked up, her eyes swimming in tears — "and it was your father. He demanded to know who the father of my child was and I . . . I lied and . . . and said it was you. I know it was wrong of me and cowardly of me, but I needed time to think and . . . and we *were* engaged. I knew they expected me to name you as the father, and I was so frightened. They were all so angry. I didn't know what else to do."

Adrian watched the flow of tears and tried to keep Courtney's face from intruding on his thoughts. He couldn't blame Deborah for taking what she thought was the only safe way out of a disastrous predicament. She would have been ostracized by family and friends if she had borne a child out of wedlock.

"What about the real father? Where was he during this?"

"He . . . was away also. He'd left Norfolk and I . . . I had no way of letting him know what was happening until he wrote me with an address. But that took almost four months and by then. . . ."

"By then you were 'married'?"

Deborah nodded. "It was your father's idea. He said it was best for everyone concerned. The only way. He said he could arrange it; he could buy the legal documents to support my claim of an elopement. The child would be born a Ballantine, with your name and wealth to protect her. And . . . and he said chances were good you'd be killed in the Mediterranean anyway. You were such a hothead."

Adrian could only stare.

"I couldn't go through with it," she whispered fiercely. "I told them I wouldn't do it — couldn't do it. I told them I lied, that you weren't the father, that you'd only proposed to me because you were under the same kind of pressure I was. I told them you didn't love me and I didn't love you . . . not in the way that counts. I mean . . . I do love you" — she twisted her hands together, desperate to find the words to ease the bleakness in the gray eyes — "I've loved you ever since I was a little girl, but with a little girl's kind of love, not a woman's love. You were my handsome prince. You were going to rescue me from the dreaded castle . . . Can you understand what I'm trying to say?"

Adrian's anger waned, then dissolved completely as he raised both of her ice-cold hands to his lips. "I think so. If it helps any, I've loved you the same way: enough to have gone through with the marriage, but not in a way that would have been fair to either one of us. But it still doesn't explain how we came to *be* married."

Deborah's chin quivered, and her eyes filled again.

"They forced me to do it. Both of them: your father and mine. They told me if I refused, they would have the baby taken away from me. They told me I would never see her, never know what happened to her — if she was healthy or sick, well cared for or left to starve."

"The bastards!" Rory exclaimed.

Adrian's eyes never left Deborah's face. "So you agreed, of course. What choice did you have?"

"None," she wept softly. "I had some money, but not enough. I didn't know what to do. Oh Adrian, I'm so sorry. I've ruined everybody's life: mine, yours, Lori's."

"Lori?"

"Yes, I . . . I named her Lori. Florence, really." The brief wistfulness in her voice turned bitter at another recollection. "Your father wanted me to name her Jessica, after your mother, but I wouldn't do it. I had to give her something of her father's."

"Did you ever write to him? Does he know?"

Deborah shook her head and whispered, "I couldn't. I don't know what it would have done to him. He was counting on the time too, to think, to find a way around the obstacles . . . obstacles that were in *his* mind only! I told him it didn't matter that he had no money, no position, no listing in the social register. I told him I was willing to go anywhere with him, in any capacity — wife, mistress, servant — as long as he loved me as much as I loved him. And he did. I know he did. He was just so damned honorable. Why do men have to be so blind? So pig-headed?" Her lips continued to tremble, but there were no more words.

Adrian's hand tightened on her shoulders, and he drew her into his arms, his fingers stroking down the finespun gold of her hair. His eyes met Rory's.

"I knew he wanted to tie you down, but I didn't realize to what lengths he was prepared to go," Rory said of their father. "God knows what he'll do when he finds out you're already married."

Deborah stiffened slightly and raised a tear-stained face.

"Married? Oh Adrian . . . no! Oh no, what have I done?"

Her complexion turned ashen, and the strength in her knees gave out. Adrian swept her up in his arms and carried her to the settee.

"The girl," she gasped. "The one on the ship . . . she was your wife?"

Adrian could see no way to blunt the edge of the truth. "Her name is Courtney. We were married two days ago, on the *Sirius*, just after we left Boston."

"But . . . where is she? Where did she go? Oh, Adrian! How you must hate me!"

"Why would I hate you? None of this was your doing. You had no choice."

"I did. I did!" she cried hysterically and began to twist out of his grip. "I could have said no and run away."

"Run where?" he asked gently, holding her hands very tightly. "You don't think they would have let you go, do you? If I know nothing else about Sam Ballantine, I know he's a bastard who keeps his promises — and his threats. He'd have taken his anger on you out on Lori, make no mistake of it."

"Lori," Deborah sighed miserably. "My Lori! What will happen to her now?"

"Absolutely nothing will happen to Lori. You have *my* word on it," Adrian said firmly. "Will you believe me? And trust me to find a way out of this for all of us?"

"I . . . I do trust you, Adrian, but —"

"Then go and wash those tears away. If I'm not mistaken, if these ears of mine haven't been at sea too long, that sounds like a baby crying."

"Lori," she gasped and glanced at the door to the adjoining room. "Oh dear, I've forgotten all about her. I was so worried about everything else. She's probably starving."

"Then you'd better go to her," Adrian said and kissed her tenderly on the cheek. "And stop worrying. That's why I had Rory stay behind; he may be a bit of a mule, but he's got a good brain on his shoulders. We'll think of something."

She gave each of them a tremulous smile before wiping her cheeks and walking to the door at the far side of the room. The sound of wailing came briefly louder, then faded again as the door closed. Adrian continued to stare at the closed door, his eyes no longer forced to guard against revealing the anger or apprehension he felt.

"Who the hell does he think he is playing god with people's lives?"

Rory came up quietly behind Adrian to hand him his refilled glass and offer a derisive toast. "To Father. To wishing I had the backbone to tell him precisely what I think of him at this minute. To knowing that look in your eye even after a year's absence. I'm sorry to see it. It would have been good to have you around for a while."

"Good for who? And for God's sake, stay sober. I wasn't joking when I said I needed your brains."

Rory looked down into his glass and after a moment, nodded and set it aside. "Deborah had a good question. Where would Courtney have gone? Does she know anyone in Norfolk?"

"No one it wouldn't curl your hair to know. To answer your question — no, dammit, I don't know where she'd go. She'd run. She'd try to lose herself, probably along the waterfront where she'd feel safe in the crowds. She hasn't much money — if any — so she'd be limited to the smaller taverns or rooming houses. And the first thing she'll do is look up a lawyer."

"So quickly?"

Adrian shook his head. "For a different reason entirely. But she has to find him before she does anything else — what the Devil was his name? If she does find him, he'll lead her to her father, or worse, he'll lead her to Garrett Shaw. In which case, she's as good as dead."

Adrian paced as he thought aloud and missed the increasingly astounded look on his brother's face. "Dead! Adrian, you're not making any sense."

"It's a long story, little brother. And there are just too many pieces missing for my liking. If only she'd just stayed . . . waited until I could explain! God knows which direction her mind has taken her in. She'll be hurt, angry — no, not angry . . . furious! She'll think back on all the questions I asked and she'll put all the wrong reasons to them. She'll think I was using her. Using her to get to Farrow . . ." He stopped pacing and his jaw turned to a stone ridge. "And if she finds Farrow before I do . . . without knowing who he is, what he is . . . ." The tic shivered alive in his cheek, and he met Rory's stare.

"You're talking as if you're after a dangerous criminal, not your own wife. How far could she get in a strange city, all alone? How long could she hide?"

"You'd be surprised to know what she could manage on her own. And if Courtney Farrow was alone in a roomful of the worst criminals Norfolk could offer — I'd feel sorry for the criminals."

Rory's eyes narrowed. "I think you'd best start at the beginning and tell me the whole story — missing pieces or no."

"There's no time —" Adrian began, but Rory cut him off before he was midway to the door.

"You can't go running off half-cocked without even any idea of where to begin looking!"

"The lawyer —"

"Whose name you don't remember?"

"I'll find him if I have to tear apart every barrister's office in the city."

"On Sunday? The shops and offices are all closed, remember. No matter how urgent your business is, you have no choice. You have to wait until tomorrow . . . and *so will she*. Look — it's already dark outside. No one is going hunting for anyone tonight. Not you, not her."

"Well, I'm not going to bloody well sit here and do nothing," Adrian snarled.

"No, you're not. You're going to bloody well sit here and tell me everything. Then we'll decide what has to be done. By the sounds of it, you're going to need more than just my brains. You're going to need my help."

"Courtney is the one who needs help, the little fool, though she'll never admit it."

"In that case, you sound like the perfect couple," Rory said dryly and added, "Now sit yourself down, brother mine. You're about to tell me more about yourself than you ever have before. And possibly get drunker than you've ever been before, if I have anything to say about it."

Adrian still hesitated, and Rory took the initiative by sitting himself on the settee and placing the full bourbon bottle beside him.

"You can start with that absurd court-martial no one seems to know anything about, and no one — including S.B. himself — could get anyone to talk about."

Adrian walked to the window and stared out over the growing dusk. Courtney, dammit, where are you?

He turned and started talking.

Courtney stood in the gloomy doorway of the hotel room and waited for her eyes to adjust to the shadows. Dickie surged past her, and when she saw where he was headed, she gasped and closed the door quickly behind her. Matthew Rutger lay sprawled on the bed, his arms askew, his head lolled to one side, his mouth gaping and dribbling spittle into a darkly wet spot on the bed linens. At first she thought he was horribly ill, but as she moved closer, she caught the odor of sweat and cheap whisky.

"Dear God, what happened?" she asked, gagging on the smells as she crossed to the window to throw the shutters wide.

"Doctor's been like this three days, Miss. Won't stop. Won't talk. Won't get out of the bed."

"I can see that, but why? What brought it on?"

"Dunno, Miss. He won't talk to me, just to send me for more whisky."

"Yes, well, that stops here and now," Courtney said firmly and unfastened her cloak. Her nose wrinkled as she approached the bed and saw the chamber pot full almost to overflowing. "Dickie —"

"Yes, Miss. I'll do it," he said quickly and scampered to pick up the disgusting container. He carried it gingerly to the door and glanced back at the sound of his name.

"Coffee," she managed to gasp over the sudden wave of nausea churning in her stomach. "Strong and hot. And order a bath, if they have such a thing here."

"Yes, Miss." He looked at the doctor. "Will he be all right?"

"If we can survive this, he damned well can," she declared, kicking at the pile of soiled laundry at her feet. She stood over Matthew for a long moment and ascertained he was indeed still breathing, then she set about removing his stained shirt, breeches, and stockings. By the time Dickie had returned she had stripped Matt naked and was rolling his clothes and linens into a huge bundle.

"See if the hotel has a laundry. If not, throw these things away, and we'll buy him new ones. Is the bath coming?"

"Yes, Miss. Clerk said ten minutes or so."

"Good. Help me sit him up, and we'll try to get some coffee into him. Did you ask for it strong?"

"Smells strong," he said, grimacing as he poured a cup of black liquid sediment into a cup.

"Doctor Rutger? Doctor Rutger . . . Matthew, can you hear me?"

"Eh?" Matt's head rolled, his neck seeming to lack all strength. "Doan blame you. Never blamed you."

Courtney bit her lip and frowned as Matt's head swung in a drunken semicircle across his chest. He kept babbling under his breath, his stupor disturbed by the rough handling.

"Matthew? It's me — Courtney. Will you drink this for me? It's coffee. It will make you feel better."

"Doan wanna feel bedder. Doan wanna feel anything."

He started to roll backward, to slide out of Dickie's grasp, and Courtney leaned across to catch him. His head was brought sharply up against her bosom, jarring the bleary hazel eyes open.

"Nice," he muttered into her left breast.

"Doctor Rutger!" she cried impatiently. "It's me, Courtney. *Court*! Can you hear me?"

"Doan need to shout," he grumbled, and the red-veined eyeballs rolled upward. "Court? Court is that you?"

"Yes. Yes, Matthew, it's me. What on earth have you done to yourself?"

"Been drinkin'," he confessed thickly.

"Why? Why have you been drinking? Has something happened?"

"Courtney?" His hand swam up and groped around her arm. "Why did she do it? Why did she marry him? She didn't love him. She loved me. I know she loved me."

Courtney shook her head helplessly. She vaguely recalled his mentioning a woman when they were waiting to be rescued by the *Argus* but that seemed like lifetimes ago.

"I'm sorry, Matthew. I'm sorry she didn't wait for you."

"I doan blame him. She's beautiful . . . beautiful . . . like my sister, Lori. She was beautiful too. She died when she was jus' a li'l girl. Li'l Lori . . ." His head sagged to a more comfortable resting place on her breast. "I jus wanna drink, tha's all. Jus tonight."

"It's the middle of the afternoon," Courtney announced, "and you'll be having no more to drink."

"Just wanna sleep. Jus want my Deborah back. . . ."

"Deborah?" Courtney felt a cold shiver run down her spine.

"Beautiful," he sighed. "Beautiful. Should've known she didn't mean it. Shoulda known she only used me to make him jealous."

"Make *who* jealous, Matthew?" she asked carefully.

"Who?" He looked up and there were tears in his eyes. "The only man I could never say anything to. Can't blame im neither, 'cause I know he doesn't love her . . . he loves ou. But what can he do? What can any of us do now?"

"Adrian," Courtney whispered. "You're in love with Adrian's Deborah?"

"She was *my* Deborah first," he said angrily. "*Mine*. And we were gonna tell him . . . we were gonna tell them all . . . but. . . ."

Courtney saw his mouth move soundlessly, anguish filled his eyes, and his body trembled with the same sense of hopelessness she had felt while running away from the dock. What a dreadful, cruel thing love was. How it twisted people's lives and destroyed them!

"Stay with me," he pleaded and his arms went around her waist. "Doan leave me . . . doan . . . ."

"I won't leave you," she whispered and stroked her fingers through the curly mop of brown hair as he pressed his face into her bosom. Her thoughts were abruptly diverted by a faint knock on the door, and she met Dickie's eyes with a nod. "It's probably the bath. Have them set it near the fire. We don't want him catching pneumonia now on top of his other troubles."

Dickie went to the door and opened it a cautious crack. The impact of a fist slamming the door back sent the small boy spinning across the floor. Courtney's arms were hindered by Mathew's deadweight, and she could not move fast enough to free the dirk strapped to her wrist. By the time the shock had registered and cleared, and her hands were in motion, the intruder was already looming over her, his gun cocked and leveled at Matthew's head.

# Chapter Twenty-Seven

Adrian lit a cigar and stood at the open french window. He had an overview of the tantalizing shimmer of the harbor with none of the filth and confusion of a waterfront hotel. The squalor was concealed by the row of buildings directly across from the Carleton Hotel, but he still had a full view of the tall ships riding easily at anchor. Adrian needed the reassurance somehow, that life existed beyond the luxurious extravagance of the high vaulted ceilings and crystal fixtures. He needed to know the wind and the sea were out there waiting for him. For him and Courtney.

Where was she? What was she doing? Had she found a decent place to spend the night? Was she alone? Frightened? As brave and spirited as she was, he knew she had her limits. To be thrust out on her own, in a strange city, with strange people, customs, styles, and little or no money . . . believing the man she had finally grown to trust with her heart and her soul had betrayed her. . . .

He had sent a messenger to the docks late the previous

night to inquire if anyone had claimed her luggage. If no one had, the orders were to remain until someone did, to follow that someone and learn the final destination of the cases. He was not underestimating Courtney's intelligence. She would no doubt anticipate just such a move on his part and would arrange for the bags to take a twisted, complicated route to wherever she was staying. A thousand-dollar bonus would ensure Adrian's man kept a sharp eye. If someone claimed those cases, he wanted to know who.

*If* someone claimed the cases. She could always choose to ignore them; abandon the contents and revert to breeches and a shirt — cheap and easy to purchase anywhere. She was wearing her locket, the only possession she seemed to treasure.

Adrian cursed and exhaled a cloud of smoke. He rubbed the scar on his forearm absently, kneading the muscles and flexing his hand into a fist over and over again. He had regained almost full use of the hand and arm, thanks to Matt's expertise and Courtney's insistence that he exercise it to the point of agony. The same was true of the wound on his thigh. She had kept him to a strict regimen of exercise to rebuild the damaged muscles, without which it might have taken months for the recovery. She knew a great deal about fighting, about survival. He shuddered to think where her instincts might lead her.

Adrian's eyes were on the sunrise, his thoughts on Courtney, and he did not hear the faint rustle of silk behind him until he caught the flash of a pale yellow gown out of the corner of his eye. Deborah had spent as restless a night as he and Rory; they'd heard sounds of her pacing until the small hours of the morning. She looked no worse for wear in the strengthening sunlight — her eyes were like two clear chips of the sky, her skin was pale, but not from weariness or strain. Her hair, brushed free from its comb and pins, cascaded down her back in a silvery-soft water fall.

Adrian could see why he had not resisted the family pressures overmuch. She was beautiful. She would hav made a beautiful wife and mother, and hadn't those been his only prerequisites a year ago? A home, a family, a wife . . . anything to keep the peace, or to placate the family. But that was before Courtney had swept into his life. He hadn't meant to fall in love with her — good God, who would have expected it of the stolid, arrogant Adrian Raefer Ballantine? In love he was, however, and he would go to any lengths to win her back. Any lengths.

"Did you get any sleep at all?" Deborah asked quietly.

"Some," he lied. "You?"

"Not much."

"If you're worried about Matt, don't be. He'll understand what you did and why you did it."

Deborah's startled blue eyes looked away from the window. "You knew?"

"I've had a little time to think things through. I didn't remember until a while ago that he had a sister named Lori. A twin. She died when they were eleven or twelve."

"Eleven. He said he always felt as if a part of himself was missing afterwards."

"Maybe you can give it back to him."

Deborah bowed her lovely head. "He hasn't even tried to see me. The *Carolina*'s been in port almost ten days and . . . and he hasn't even called to pay his respects. Or to question the marriage. Or to demand an explanation. I expected — prayed for at least that much. Oh good Lord, look at me: I'm crying again. I didn't think I had any tears left."

Adrian smiled gently and slipped an arm around her shoulders. She went willingly into the comfort of his embrace and laid her wet cheek against his shirt. "What will we do, Adrian?"

He stared at the smoking ash at the tip of his cigar and took a deep breath. "First, I'm going to find my wife. Then I'm going to find Matt and drag them both here by the scruff of the neck if I have to. After we straighten them out on exactly who loves whom, we'll take them — or drag them again, if need be — to a church to tell the whole blasted world who belongs to whom. Does that sound reasonable to you?''

Deborah swallowed hard and looked up at him, suddenly breathless with newfound hope. "What about your father? And mine?''

"We'll invite them, naturally. I'll be interested to see how they worm their way out of the scandal. There will be quite a scandal, you know.''

"I don't care," she vowed. "Matt's home is in Pennsylvania. I can make new friends there.''

"And your family?''

The blue eyes chilled. "They deserve whatever they get. I owe them no loyalty. They gave me none when I needed them the most.''

"Then all we have to do is find this lawyer who provided the documents supporting our 'elopement.' I don't suppose you remember the name of the man they used? Harris was the family lawyer.''

"No." She frowned and sniffled delicately. "It definitely wasn't a family lawyer, and I only overheard the name once. Polder? Pruder?''

"*Prendergast*?''

"No. No, nothing quite so — why are you looking at me like that? Have I said something funny?''

Adrian was grinning. "Not funny, just damned timely. Here I've been wracking my memory all night trying to think of Prendergast's name —''

"The lawyer Courtney will go to see to find her father?" Deborah blushed and raised a hand to her lips. "I'm sorry. I didn't eavesdrop on purpose. I was wide awake and I could hear you plainly through the door.''

Adrian brushed aside the apology. "It doesn't matter. The important thing is, you made me think of the name.''

"Penderton.''

"What?''

"Penderton. The name of the lawyer your father used.''

Adrian's grin broadened. "I shall be only too happy to pay both illustrious gentlemen a visit today."

"No," came a yawned rejoiner from the settee. "You take Prendergast, I'll cope with Penderton. If we separate we can get twice as much ground covered, and I do believe haste is of the utmost importance in both cases."

Adrian turned to watch the disheveled form of his brother prop itself on the edge of the couch. His dark hair stood on end; his eyes were puffy and showed their lack of sleep. The frown was permanently grooved on his brow as he glared belligerently at the sunlight.

"What time is it?"

"Six o'clock. Thereabouts."

"Good God. Helen will be bristling like a porcupine. Six o'clock? Did you get any sleep at all?"

Adrian glanced at Deborah. "Some."

"Well —" Rory scratched both hands through his hair, ruffling it even more. "A pot of coffee would go down good about now. A side of bacon, half-dozen eggs, ham and cheese . . . maybe some hotcakes."

"The life of a country squire," Adrian mused. "Are you planning to eat the morning away?"

"Just the first hour of it. And you should too. All of us should. We'll need the fuel. Are you planning to speak to Father today?"

"If he crosses my path, no doubt I'll think of a word or two to spare on the bastard. Other than that, no. I don't plan to go out of my way to tell him what I think of him. He'll find out soon enough."

"Will you tell him about Alan?"

"There's nothing to tell. Not yet anyway."

"You've no idea who murdered him?"

"Theories, yes. None that I can prove. And even if I could — it's difficult to kill a dead man."

Rory pursed his lips and nodded. "More's the pity, you can't even kill a ghost."

Adrian stared at his brother and tried not to acknowledge the cold shiver his words sent along his spine. Luckily, he was distracted further by the sound of a knock on the door.

The three exchanged a glance in silence.

"Who do you suppose it could be this early in the morning?" Deborah whispered.

"One way to find out," Rory said and pushed to his feet. "Perhaps it's a kitchen maid who's read my mind."

He had a hand on the brass latch before the alarm bells jangled a raw alert inside Adrian's brain. Rory's name was forming on his lips, his body was lunging forward even as his arms were outstretched and shooting for the chair where his tunic jacket and saber had been discarded the previous night. He saw the startled look on Rory's face a split second before he heard Deborah scream. The door was open. Something heavy crashed against it and fell inward. The bloody hand that had been grasped to the jamb for support left a crimson smear all the way down the wall from eye level to floor.

Courtney opened her eyes slowly. At first she thought it was the middle of the night, it was so dark around her, but then, as her senses began to prick awake, she realized the blackness was caused by a thick blindfold. Her ankles were bound. Her hands were lashed together at the wrists and tied to the cane slats on the back of the chair she was sitting in. From somewhere she heard the sound of dripping water. The air was chilly and damp — a cellar? — and smelled of mildew and rot. There was another odor, a strong odor she could not identify other than to determine it was extremely harsh and unpleasant. Her mouth, surprisingly, was not gagged. She noted it with a cool detachment — no gag meant whoever had brought her here had no fears of noise bringing discovery.

There were no distinguishable sounds other than the steady, hollow drip, drip, drip, of water. It was a cavern sound. An ancient, primitive sound, that spoke of a crypt.

Courtney forced such thoughts out of her mind and *concentrated*. She did not remember being brought here or tied into the chair, or . . . or stripped! That explained the cold. She was no longer wearing the layers of muslin and linen. She wore something loose — a shirt or a smock perhaps. They had obviously searched her thoroughly and now wanted to keep her feeling completely defenseless.

She did not want to make any overt moves. Because she could not hear anyone else in the vicinity it did not mean she was alone. In fact, she sensed she was *not* alone. Someone else was nearby — watching her? Waiting for her to show signs of wakening?

Slowly, with as little motion as she could manage, she began an assessment of her body's condition. No horrendous pains meant nothing broken. There were bruises, to be sure, and scratches on her flesh from the struggle she had put up before the explosion in her skull had darkened her world. She had been sitting on the bed with Matthew — *Matthew! Dickie! No. No! You can't think of them just yet.* Clear everything out of your mind! Think! *Remember!* You were sitting on the bed! . . . Sitting on the bed. A knock on the door. Dickie had gone to answer it. No! Wait! Too late — he was on the floor. Someone was bursting through the doorway, a gun out. Pointed. At Matthew.

"Move and he's dead," the voice had hissed. "Anybody moves and he's dead."

Dear God, it was Garrett, and he had looked like a wild man! He hadn't shaved for weeks, and his eyes had seemed strangely sunken, with dark bluish semicircles beneath them, carved deeply into his skin. *One of his hands was missing!* She had seen the grossly misshapen stump reaching out to knock the dirk out of her grasp before she could swing it up to use. The sight had startled her as much as the touch of the steel barrel against Matthew's temple. And behind him, she had heard a laugh, had seen two more guns aimed through the doorway, had lifted her eyes to meet a pair of blazingly hate-filled amber ones.

"Well, well," Miranda had spat. "If it isn't the little princess. All dressed up in her finery. All sweet and cozy with another one of her Yankee lovers. Straight out of the arms of one into the bed of another . . . tsk tsk tsk. No wonder she didn't have time or bedspace for you, Garrett."

"She'll have it now," he growled and hooked his stump under her arm to drag her to her feet. "I made her a promise back on the *Falconer*, and by God, I intend to see it through."

Dickie had moved then. He had picked himself up off the floor and hurled himself at Garrett Shaw like a slender, frail fury. Shaw felt the sting of teeth and nails and roared out a curse as he turned to fling the boy aside. He had looked away from Courtney for a split second, and moved the gun away from Matthew's temple long enough for her to lunge at it. She grasped the cold steel barrel in her hands and wrenched it around. She thrust a finger behind the trigger to lock it as Duncan had shown her, and she clawed out for Garrett's eyes with her free hand. A second roar brought the horrible, grotesque stump up to strike her fully on the side of the neck. The world had spun and darkened dizzily for a moment but she had not released her grip on the gun. She held it and fought for control . . . and Garrett had struck her again and again, and his knee had come up and slammed into her belly. Miranda had been laughing, goading him on. Matthew had been struggling to his hands and knees on the floor, swaying, crawling drunkenly toward Dickie's unmoving body. Garrett had struck again, and Courtney's fingers had opened finally releasing the gun. She had doubled over in agony, waves of agony that had robbed her of any ability to move, or to scream. . . .

Courtney swallowed past the rage and pain, but it remained like a lump of fire at the back of her throat. She forgot her resolve not to move, and her hands jerked at the ropes that bound her wrists to the chair. She stiffened as she heard a satisfied chuckle several feet away.

"So, you are awake. I thought as much." She heard a

faint scraping of a chair leg and then footsteps on the stone. Her mind was still in a whirl of confusion. Pain and anger, hatred, resentment, fear for Matthew and Dickie all crowded in on her ability to think and remain calm. The voice . . . it was vaguely familiar. It was not Garrett's, but it was a man's voice and it rang with arrogance and authority.

"I've been watching you for some time, Miss Farrow, waiting for you to waken — indeed, wondering if you would. The captain was unnecessarily brutal, I must say. Such lovely skin, to be so bruised."

Courtney flinched back as a hand brushed against her cheek. There was a moment of hesitation, and the hand stroked her throat, then roughly cupped her chin and held it.

"You are hardly in any position to resist me, my dear."

"Get your filthy, sodding hands off me," she hissed.

"Why? Are you afraid I might touch something that belongs to your valiant Captain Ballantine?" The mention of Adrian's name lodged a greater horror in Courtney's mind, and she felt the hot, rasping breath of her tormentor on her cheek as he leaned his face closer to hers. "I plan to do more than simply touch you, my dear. Much more. How could I pass up such an opportunity?"

Courtney ground her teeth together to keep from hurling a stream of oaths at the disembodied voice. The voice. The voice! Concentrate on the voice! She knew she had heard it before, but where? Don't think of what he's saying! He wants you frightened. He wants you terrified. He wants you making mistakes. *Show your fear and you're lost:* Duncan's words. Duncan's warning. And she was Duncan Farrow's daughter, by God. She was Servanne de Villiers' daughter. She was Adrian Ballantine's wife!

"Who are you?" she asked coldly. "Why have you brought me here?"

She could sense the amusement. She could almost see the ace!

"Who I am is of little consequence, but I'm sure you'll

find out in due time. As to the whys and wherefores, it is a simple matter of compensation — or at least it was; now it has become much more. But originally we came all this way in expectation of reaping a veritable fortune for our troubles.''

"Davey was right. Garrett only wanted Duncan's money.''

"Fortune, my dear, fortune. Are you truly so naïve as to doubt that there are millions involved here? And can you really blame us for being slightly distressed to get all this way only to find out Duncan Farrow is alive and well and waiting for his daughter to turn up?''

"Duncan?'' she gasped. "He's alive?''

"Ingratiatingly so. And unfortunately he is not the most generous of men. He wouldn't think to offer us a few hundred thousand for our trouble, not without some gentle . . . persuasion.''

"Me?'' she said scornfully.

"Among other things, you. I had quite a time convincing Miranda of your usefulness. She was all for removing you permanently. I gather she is tired of seeing you resurrected from the dead. But the *ways* she suggested of removing you . . . tsk tsk. Such disturbing appetites in a woman of such amazing charm. Although, in all honesty, I cannot find fault with her basic reasoning — pain tends to loosen the tongue as readily as money.''

He released her chin abruptly, and she heard his footsteps pace slowly around the back of the chair.

"Of course it would simplify matters if we knew where Duncan's lair was. He seems to have gone to ground, as they say, and taken that wretch Prendergast with him. You wouldn't by any chance happen to know where they might have gone?''

"Go to hell,'' she spat.

"Mmm. Stubborn. Garrett warned me you might be difficult. But don't misread me, my dear. I'd as soon watch you writhe in agony as see you writhe in ecstacy. It's completely up to you if you choose to live or die, and in what condition. Frankly, if your stubbornness stems from loyalty, I'm afraid the gesture is a wasted one. Your search for Seawolf should be proof of that.''

Courtney stiffened. Seawolf? How did he know about Seawolf?

''I see you are familiar with the name? I don't wonder. Garrett tells me your search for the man who betrayed you is almost an obsession.''

''Betrayed —?'' The whisper escaped before she could catch it.

''Seawolf has become a popular name in the Admiralty offices. You can imagine, he has saved our illustrious Commodore Preble thousands of dollars in equipment and lives — not to mention time. The information he has sold has led to the removal of half a dozen pirate dens along the Barbary Coast — or did you think it was just your father's band he betrayed?''

Courtney's mind was reeling. What was he saying? What was he talking about! Seawolf was the traitor? No. No! Impossible! Adrian had told her the code name — Swordfish. Not Seawolf! Not Duncan! Duncan Farrow would never sell out his own men. It was a lie! A ploy to throw her off guard.

''What? Did you say something, my dear?''

''You're the one Garrett calls 'the Englishman,' aren't you?''

''Astute as well as lovely.''

''Then you should know all about betrayal,'' she ground out through her teeth.

The voice chuckled again. ''Indeed I do. I know about deception and guile. I know about greed. I know about vengeance.''

''Then you know Adrian will kill you when he finds you.''

The voice moved lower so that it hissed in her ear again. ''If the valiant Lieutenant Ballantine had to choose between killing me and saving you, which would he do? And your father — do you think he'll pay more to arrange your freedom or to have a chance to settle accounts with Garrett Shaw? So many choices, so many intriguing combinations. I haven't even mentioned Garrett! Your lover cost him his ship, his hand, his dreams of collecting a fortune. He's eagerly looking forward to killing Ballantine. And you, my dear. Who would you save if you could barter for the freedom of one life: Your father's? Your lover's? They've both played games with your life; they've both used you. My *God*!'' — the voice was strained with excitement — ''I couldn't have planned a better denouement myself . . . regardless of who lives and who dies!''

Adrian knelt beside the bleeding body and grabbed it by the shoulders and chest to turn it on its back. Davey Dunn cursed his pointed lack of gentleness with as strong an oath as Adrian emitted on recognition.

''Don't you Yankees ever piss?'' Dunn gasped. ''I been waitin' two hour in the closet down the hall. Scair't the wind out o' two nigra maids an' a bootboy fer me troubles.''

''Where the hell have you come from? What happened to your shoulder? Rory, for Christ's sake, help me drag him inside before we have half the hotel up in arms.''

With Rory's assistance, Adrian lifted the stubby corsair to his feet and steered him into a nearby chair. Deborah, her hands still clapped over her mouth and her eyes still wide and rounded with disbelief, skirted well clear of the three men as she ran to the door to close it.

''Oh dear, dear, dear,'' Davey droned as his gaze settled on the empty whisky bottle on the table beside him. ''Have ye nay more where that come from?''

Adrian glared at him. ''After you answer a few questions.''

''On a dry throat? Ye're a rare cruel man. No' the kind o' man Duncan'd expect his daughter to marry.''

Adrian clenched his jaw and nodded to Rory to fetch another full bottle from the sideboard. The younger Ballantine, clearly astonished by the corsair's audacity, brought the bottle and three glasses, filling them all to the brim.

"Well?" Adrian demanded when the first glassful had been drained to the vapors.

"Well, I got news fer ye, Yankee. None good."

"I'm listening."

"So's half the bloody town," Dunn spat, drilling his gaze first into Rory, then Deborah.

"They both know everything that's happened over the past few months. I'd prefer they hear what you have to say. Unless —" He glanced at Deborah but she shook her head and remained standing by the door.

The small, squinty eyes peered up at Adrian through the fuzz of red lashes and brows. "Ain't healthy, Yankee, but it's yer choice. They got her. Her an' the doc an' the kid."

Adrian's face froze. "Courtney?"

"Aye, Court. I seen them on the dock yesterday when the *Sirius* dropped anchor. Waited to see who it were they was interest'd in afore I showed meself. Figured it was you, since ye burned his ship."

"Garrett Shaw?"

Dunn nodded. "An' his whore. Bold as brass, they was, jest standin' there, but then I don't suppose no one'd know who they was. 'Peered like they'd jest come fer a look-see and instead they seen a ghost. Cain't say as how I blame 'em. I thought sure Court were dead too till I seen her on the ship. Anyhows, they seen her hie on out o' there and damme if they didn't near trip on their chins follerin' her. Natur'ly, I follered them. Went up and down and along a few twisty bits till I reckon Court run out o' wind, cuz I seen her walk kind o' tottery-like into a hotel."

Adrian said nothing. Not a muscle quivered or an eyelash blinked, not even when Deborah moved slowly away from the door and slipped her arm through his.

"Shaw 'n his whore stood ten minutes on the street debatin' what to do and finally he leaves and she stays to watch the front o' the hotel. 'Nother twenty minutes or so an' he's back with a wagon. It didn't look too good, so I give 'em five minutes, then I went in after them. That's when I got me this here pinprick.'' He pointed disgustedly to his shoulder. It sloped at an odd angle from the thick stump of his neck; the bullet had obviously smashed through bone. The sleeve of his shirt and the front of his leather vest were soaked with blood, most of it dried and caked brown.

"I come flyin' through the door and the first thing I seen was Court an' Shaw grapplin' over a gun. The other two — the doc an' the boy — were on the floor. I didn't know if they was dead or alive. I couldn't see Miranda a-tall.'' He stopped and shook his head. "Stupid. Stupid. I weren't thinkin'. I were in too much o' a hurry. She steps out from behind the door, an' . . . *blam!* Down I goes.''

Adrian's features were becoming tauter, whiter, colder as Dunn's story progressed, but he did not interrupt.

"She were all fer killin' me then and there — guess she figured she'd seen enough ghosts fer one day — but Shaw stopped her. Said as how I'd come in useful fer deliverin' messages an such.''

"Messages?''

"Aye. Two o' them. One fer Duncan, invitin' him to a party tonight. Midnight. A warehouse near the edge o' town. He's to bring money. Lots o' it.''

"Farrow's alive? He's in Norfolk?''

"Hell o' a place for ghosts, ain't it, Yankee?'' There was a strange flicker behind the pale blue eyes as he studied Adrian closely. "Must o' shook up their plans some, hearin' about Duncan.''

"Plans?''

Dunn grimaced. "You an' Court must've done *some* talkin' in that cabin o' hers every night. Plans! Duncan's money! The whore fancied herself up an' hoofed into the lawyer's office tryin' to tell him she were Court. Spoke the right words, give the right names, but when she didn't have the *locket* to show him, he tol' her the act weren't worth a goose fart an' if'n she knew what were good for her, she'd skunk-tail on out o' there. A week ago that were, so the pair o' thieves must've been broodin' on it since. Now they got Court and they must figure she'll do better than any locket. Damn, but I ain't jawed so much in ten year. Throat's about burned dry.''

"How do you know all of this?"

"Seen Duncan," he grunted and held out his empty glass to Rory, who filled it without a second thought.

"You've *seen* him?"

Dunn screwed up his face. "Ye deef? Or maybe ye think I'd come to you first without seein' the captain?"

Deborah had kept her silence long enough. She dropped Adrian's arm and stepped forward. "Matthew . . . is he all right?"

"Eh?" Dunn squinted up at her. "Aye, far as I could see. Leastwise, he were movin'. Boy had a busted leg though, and Court were unconscious when Shaw carried her out."

A nerve shivered in Adrian's cheek. "You said you had two messages."

"Aye. One fer Duncan, one fer you. Seems there's someone wants you invited ter the party too. Calls his'self 'the Englishman.' ''

Adrian's hands tightened into fists. "The Englishman. He's here?"

"Regular masquerade ball, ain't it?" He raised the glass of whisky to his lips with a sly grin, and Adrian turned away. He paced to the window and stared into the bright glitter of the water in the bay.

"How much do they want from Farrow? Does he have enough to cover their demands?"

"Considerin' they asked fer 'everythin' . . . I dunno. Ye offerin' to throw in yer fancy saber an' gold braid?"

Adrian looked around slowly, his eyes cold and deadly, but Dunn continued.

"I'm thinkin' it ain't the money they're after. And if'n it is, they don't know 'zactly how much 'everythin' is, so Duncan reckons he might have an edge. Sum'mit ter bargain with."

"What kind of an edge?"

"Ign'runce, boy," Dunn clucked derisively. "Pure ign'runce to wed a girl without knowin' nothin' 'bout her, nothin' 'bout her grandpappy."

"De Villiers? What does he have to do with any of this?"

"Plenty, considerin' who he was."

"Who was he, other than a French nobleman?"

"He were Louis' personal banker. King Louis, that be, and by personal, I mean *real* personal."

"Go on," Adrian insisted.

Again Dunn hesitated and eyed Deborah and Rory.

"I'm not a man who likes to repeat himself too often," Adrian grated harshly. "And I'm rapidly running out of patience."

Dunn stared at him a moment then shrugged. "What the hell, we'll all probl'y be dead by mornin' anyway. It started with the troubles back in Paris in '89. Louis panicked when the Bastille was overrun, and he gave the royal treasury to de Villiers for safekeepin'. Bloody September come around, and the king were locked up, mobs were bangin' on everyone's doors wavin' torches and honin' the guillotines. Ol' Gaston, he know'd his daughter were the only one of 'em had any chance o' sneakin' away, so he give her the two biggest chests and ordered her to hide them real good, fer the sake o' king'n country. She carried them damn things with her four years, near as we can figure. When Duncan got 'round to openin' them — expectin' they was full o' clothes and such fer young Court — he seen diamonds the size o' yer thumb, rubies like fists, gold chains and crowns and rings enough ter string 'round yer waist like a belt! I can tell ye, he pert 'near choked on his own bile."

Adrian was stunned. "I'd heard stories of a vast treasure that went missing during the early days of the Reign of Terror, but I assumed it was just that: stories."

"So did the committee what took over the government

Robespierre weren't about to admit his citizens stole the treasury, and since the records were all burned, nobody knew 'zactly how much there'd been in the first place. And Duncan weren't about ter come for'ard, not after what them bastards did ter his wife. But he know'd he couldn't keep the chests on the *Goose*, ner on the Island neither, so he brung 'em here. Since then he jest been addin' ter the 'estate', hopin' one day ter give it all to Court to make up fer the bad years.''

"And you say Shaw knows nothing about it? How can you be so certain?"

"Ain't but four people ever seen what was in them chests, aside from Duncan's wife. Me 'n Duncan 'r the only two left alive what knows about them, an' even I don't know where he's hid them. Never wanted to know. Never asked."

Adrian patted his pocket absently in search of a cigar. It didn't make sense. Why would Duncan Farrow be sitting on a fortune in unclaimed gems; a second fortune in gold from his raiding ventures over the years — yet sell out his ship and mates for a few measly thousands of dollars and incredible risks? And there was Courtney. She was just too damned canny to be completely blinded by affection. Their own relationship was proof of that.

"How many people knew about Seawolf?" he asked gruffly.

"Eh? Seawolf? How in blazes —"

"That was the name Farrow used to send messages to his wife, wasn't it?"

"Aye, but —

"It's also the name someone has been using to sell Farrow out to the Americans. If it's Shaw, which you and Courtney seemed convinced of, and which I am only now coming to believe, then she's dead regardless of what Duncan tries to buy her freedom with. So are Matt and the boy, and anyone else who gets in his way."

"Ye're a cheery bastard, ain't ye?"

Adrian ignored the sarcasm. "Farrow and I have to have a long talk before this goes any farther. How do I get in touch with him?"

"Ye walk to the door, Yankee. He's out in the hallway waitin' on my decision to either trust ye or kill ye."

The dripping was constant, incessant. Courtney had even begun to imagine what it looked like. A crack in the ceiling. A slow, swollen bubble of water stretching, stretching, then breaking free like a weighted sphere to cause a small explosion on the surface of the tiny pool formed beneath it. Pools. Drops. Water. She was thirsty and cold. She didn't know how many hours she had been sitting alone, whether it was day or night. The chill had gone clean through her flesh to her bones, and she shivered almost constantly. There was absolute silence beyond the drips. There was only the rush of her own breath and the steady throb of her heartbeat to disturb the monotony of the *drips*.

The Voice had gone away and not returned. He had said his piece and planted both the doubts and fears firmly in her mind, then left her to brood upon them. Left them to fester and eat away at her self-control. Of course she didn't believe a word of his lies; not about Seawolf. Someone was obviously using the name, hoping to cleverly throw suspicion on Duncan.

But who? No one *knew* the name. No one knew the intimate details of her flight from France. Only Verart Farrow, Seagram, Davey Dunn, and Duncan. And only they would have known about Seawolf. Verart and Seagram were dead. . . .

*Seagram*! He had told her to find Seawolf. He had commanded her to find Seawolf with his last gasp of breath.

*Find Seawolf*! Had it been a command . . . or a warning? No, not a warning! He had said Duncan had *been* betrayed, not Duncan *had* betrayed. What else had he said? What *exactly* had he said? Think think think.

*Drip . . . drip . . . drip. . . .*

Find him. Warn him. Verart knew. Only a matter of time to put a face to the name . . . calls himself . . . *drip* . . . *drip* . . . *drip*. . . .

*Calls himself*! *Calls* himself Seawolf! *Find the man who calls himself Seawolf*!

Courtney gasped aloud, and her entire body clenched through a wave of pain. Her wrists . . . she had been working her hands and wrists to try to loosen the knots in the ropes and the dreadful concentration had sent the twine burning into her flesh. She didn't care. She didn't care! Duncan was Seawolf, and Seawolf was brave and strong and cunning. He would know about Garrett's treachery. He would know about The Voice. He was probably looking for her now, tearing the city apart to find her. Seawolf and Adrian. . . .

Adrian! Adrian had lied about the code name — but had he lied to protect her? Was that the cause of the shadow she had seen in his eyes. The lie, the hesitation . . . was it because he had known about Seawolf — about the *name* Seawolf! Oh God, she wished she could see him, talk to him! If Adrian thought Duncan was the traitor, then The Voice would have won. And if Adrian found Duncan before either of them *knew*, there could well be a fight to the death.

How long had she been locked in this blasted room? Hours? Days? She was so thirsty it might well have been weeks! Was it morning or night? She hadn't been able to distinguish between the two in the cage either, but at least she'd heard the voices of the other prisoners to hold her sanity together. Seagram had been within a shout's distance. Could anybody hear her now if she *screamed*!

"Calm down," she ordered herself. She ignored the agony in her wrists and resumed the steady, twisting, sawing motion against the ropes. The pain sharpened her senses. It kept her from succumbing to the tension of the *drip* . . . *drip* . . . *dripping*. Tense people made mistakes. Frightened people made mistakes.

Adrian . . . Duncan . . . please hurry. . . .

# Chapter Twenty-Eight

Duncan Farrow did not possess Adrian's height or Garrett Shaw's breadth of chest, but he was none the less a formidable man. Each of his moves was calculated and wary. His walk was fluid, like a panther's — soundless, controlled, the energy conserved for the kill. His eyes were bottomless and emerald green; his hair was a dark shade of auburn, shot through at the temples with silver. The clothes he wore could not disguise the air of restrained deadliness. The high white collar did not conceal the scar that sliced down his neck from his hairline. The conservative gray broadcloth coat was immaculately tailored but did not soften the impact of the weathered mahogany complexion. His hands, although held easily by his sides, were large boned and powerful enough to evoke thoughts of swords and cutlasses and smoking cannon. The face was the face of a handsome man who had lived forty-three years with the bitterness of painful memories.

He stood in the rain-slicked shadows, his frame just ou

of range of the yellowish halo of light from the solitary street lantern. His eyes were the only thing that moved. They searched the recesses and darkened windows for any signs of an unwanted presence. There would be watchers in the darkness, he knew. The invitation had been for midnight, and it was five minutes before. He had been standing in the shadows for more than two hours.

Garrett had chosen the district well. The warehouse was the last one before the hard-packed road turned abruptly to rutted earth. Docks were behind the building; two rickety sheds and an abandoned mill were the only other structures on the lonely stretch of road. There were no taverns, no rooming houses, no reason for curious pedestrians to be in the area this hour of the night. Duncan had to smile at Garrett's audacity. The sign over the door read 'Wm. Longford, Import Export.' It was Duncan's own warehouse.

The sky had clouded over in the late afternoon and it had rained lightly since then. Everything was damp. The air smelled of wet wood, the scum that formed on the shore, and the forest that lurked just beyond the verge of civilization. It was deadly quiet, however. Only the gentle lap of trapped waves against the jetty disturbed the silence.

Duncan moved away from the wall he had been leaning on and, by habit, flexed the muscles in his arms — his knife sheaths were secure. He could feel the solid presence of the pistol strapped at the small of his back; he knew the first search would locate the weapons but if he came wearing none at all, Garrett would be doubly suspicious.

His eyes went a last time to the copse of trees on his left, and he nodded even though he knew he could not be seen. Dunn was in place, his broken shoulder doubtlessly causing more agony than he should have been able to bear, but nothing about Davey surprised Duncan. He was thankful for the stolid support. Grateful that if he were to die tonight, it would not be alone.

Duncan walked slowly across the rain-swept road and paused before the wooden door of the warehouse. There were no lights visible. He had expected none. He pushed the door wide and stepped inside, his senses adapting to the surroundings.

Nothing. Not the slightest movement. Not a single wary breath.

Garrett was confident Duncan would come alone, as he had been instructed. They had worked too many years together to require the services of outsiders. They respected each other's skill and courage; there would be no hired gunmen ready to shoot him in the back, no burly guards for insurance. Life or death would be decided between the two of them. It was the law of the sea. The law of a corsair. The one uncertainty was the Englishman. He was a coward and a sneak, driven by greed and treachery. But Duncan was not worried about the Englishman — he was Ballantine's concern.

He smiled again as he thought of his new son-in-law. He could see why the golden-haired Yankee had won Courtney's heart. He was arrogant and ruthless, not afraid to demand explanations and challenge them on receipt. The Yankee reminded him so much of himself he was sure they would come to like each other immensely — if they both survived.

The warehouse was three storeys high. The main floor was large and cavernous, stocked top to bottom, row upon row, with bales of fresh-picked cotton. The smell was oppressive. The top floor went only half the length of the building and housed the offices. The bottom floor was stone and had large swinging bays that opened out onto the dock. A huge hole in the main floor supported winches and cables; directly underneath were the weight scales.

Downstairs, Duncan decided. Access to the outside, an easy escape. There was probably a boat tied to the jetty.

The stairwell was on the far side of the room, and he was well aware of the noise his footsteps made on the creaking boards. The descent was a steep one, the steps changing from wood to stone halfway down. As he neared the bottom he could see a halo of pale light, and he slowed his pace, not wanting to lose his night sight too quickly, not wanting to be hampered however temporarily by the change to lamplight.

He finished the slow count to fifty that he had begun at the street door and continued down to the lower landing. There were more bales of cotton stacked on either side of the exit, as well as barrels of tar, oil, and pitch.

A foot scraped, and Duncan's eyes moved slowly to the ring of light. A lantern was on a rickety table in the center of a small clearing formed by the walls of cotton; candles were placed at either end. The table had three chairs, one of which was occupied by Garrett Shaw. Their eyes met and held a long moment, each acknowledging the other's resourcefulness in having come this far by such different means.

Duncan's eyes broke away first to continue his inspection. A man and a boy were tied back to back in a corner. Their mouths were tightly gagged; their immobility was assured by the lengths of rope that circled their chests. The boy's head lolled forward; he was in a state of semi-consciousness and held a roughly splintered leg straight out in front of him. The man's worried hazel eyes were red-rimmed from fatigue, yet still they were bright and intense as they tried in vain to convey a message to Duncan Farrow . . . or was it a warning?

Duncan's gaze followed Matt's to where a fourth chair stood half hidden by a bale of cotton. Courtney was seated on it, her arms bound behind her. She was dressed in a loose-fitting smock and must have been freezing in the damp chill of the air. She looked pale and vulnerable, but otherwise unhurt. Her eyes were covered by a blindfold but Duncan knew she had sensed his arrival.

"Court?"

"Father? Oh Father, is it really you?" She bit back the rest of what she wanted to say, to cry, to scream, and instead concentrated on pinpointing his voice.

"It's me," Duncan said and glared at Garrett. "Take the blindfold off her. It serves no purpose."

Garrett's eyes flicked briefly to the shadowy figure who stood behind a stack of baled cotton, out of Duncan's line of vision. He caught the shrugged nod and crooked a finger in Miranda's direction to have her remove the black silk scarf. The dark-haired beauty looked less than pleased by the request, knowing that in order to do so she must move out of the dim light and thus earn Duncan's full attention.

Courtney's whole body tensed as she felt the short, jerky tugs that freed the scarf from around her eyes. Her pulse was racing, her heart sending up a clamor in her chest and ears. She had been kept in total darkness since the kidnapping. She had been moved from the cold storage cellar only an hour before and had not been told what to expect, or whom. Not until she'd overheard Garrett and Miranda bickering did she realize Duncan would be coming. Not until she actually heard his voice did she believe they had a chance of succeeding with their treachery — the three of them: Garrett, Miranda, and the Englishman.

She felt the scarf loosen and fall away from her eyes, and she fought back the instant rush of tears as the sudden brightness exploded on her senses. She sought out Duncan immediately, and the relief in her eyes clouded over with a thousand questions.

"Are you all right, Court?"

"Yes. Yes, I'm fine."

"Did they hurt you in any way?"

"Hurt me?" Could she count the hunger and the thirst, the cold and the isolation? "No, they haven't hurt me."

"And we won't, as long as you both behave," Garrett said. He crooked his finger at Miranda again. "Search him. I want no surprises."

Miranda walked around the table, her breasts undulating within the thin white blouse, her hips swaying provocatively beneath bright blue taffeta. Her amber eyes were locked unwaveringly to Duncan's as she approached, and there was undisguised sensuality in the motion of her hands as she ran them down his ribs, around to his back, down the inside and outside of his lean thighs. By the time she finished the search, the knives were on the table, the gun was tucked into the waist of her skirt, and there was a half-smile pulling at the corners of her mouth.

"You came alone?" Garrett asked impatiently. "I specifically sent the invitation for two."

"Two?" Duncan feigned ignorance. "You expected Davey to return in the condition he was in?"

"Don't play games with me, Duncan," Garrett snarled. "Where is he? Where is the Yankee bastard who did this to me?" He raised the pink and shiny gnarl of flesh that should have been his right hand, and added quietly, "I owe him."

"I presume you mean this Ballantine I've heard so much about? Why should I know or even care where he is? I fully expected him to be here already — if he intended to come at all, that is. I confess I'm not surprised he's failed to show — what does he care if we kill one another?"

"Dunn gave him the message? The full message? The time and the place . . . and the sender?"

"Ahh yes, the Englishman. Does this mean I finally get to meet your private source?"

"He was more interested in seeing Ballantine."

"Then he'll have to make other arrangements, won't he?" Duncan said, letting a trace of irritation scrape into his voice. "Frankly I'm more interested in what the hell you're trying to prove here tonight by kidnapping my daughter and holding her to ransom."

"I'm not trying to prove anything," Garrett grinned, "Except perhaps that crime doesn't pay — for you. It's a perfectly honorable part of our profession, isn't it? Kidnapping? Isn't that why you kept all this" — he waved the stump airily to indicate the warehouse — "so secret? She'd've been kidnapped every other day if word of this was common knowledge."

"I suppose I could ask here, how you came to find out?"

"You could. And I'd give you a simple enough

answer — I followed Verart into Algiers one day. He met with the captain of a merchantman, and the next thing I knew, there were packets changing hands and crates, and barrels . . . Did you bring money with you tonight?''

Duncan smirked. ''What, no inquiries after my health? No curiosity as to how I made it away from Moknine alive?''

''How did you get away?'' Miranda drawled. ''Garrett said you were trapped. He said the *Goose* was in flames, escape impossible.''

''Her magazine took a direct hit,'' Duncan nodded, his eyes not leaving Garrett's face. ''I remember being blown overboard when she went up, but not much after that. When I woke up — I must have floated ashore on some timber — quite a few hours had passed and I couldn't find another soul alive anywhere around me, or a ship in sight, friendly or otherwise. I knew enough to get away from there before the scavengers moved in, and I started walking eastward, hoping to run into a friendly village or encampment. I walked a day, two days, I don't know. I remember cursing the flies and cursing the sun, and falling down so many times my knees were raw to the bone. The next solid memory I have is of waking up in a sheepskin tent with half a hundred Bedouins outside it debating my fate.''

''You obviously got away,'' Miranda said dryly.

''I helped the debate along by offering them enough gold to pay for their winterings for the next ten years or so. All they had to do was take me to Algiers.''

''So you could get on a ship and sail cleanly away, while we were taken captive on board a Yankee warship bound for Gibraltar and the hangman's gibbet.''

Duncan nodded again, slowly this time. ''Aye, the news of Snake Island falling to the Yankees spread along the coast like a wave of the pox, but I didn't think they'd be about hanging you in Gibraltar. They would more likely have wanted to create a sensation with public trials and long prison sentences — or terms of indentureship.

thought if I arrived here ahead of the prison ships, it would have been a simple enough matter to put in the bids for your labor contracts. But of course, none of that was necessary, thanks to the *Falconer*'s intervention.''

"Intervention that cost me my ship and my crew," Garrett growled.

"*Your* ship?"

"Law of the sea, Duncan. You abandoned her."

"And you lost her within a week to a handful of half-starved, unarmed Americans." Duncan pursed his lips. "Something tells me you didn't deserve her."

"They had weapons," Garrett declared, surging to his feet.

"One in particular — named Ballantine?" Duncan's gaze reverted to Courtney. "As I understand it, he stole several things from you, and not all of them through violence. But I'm a forgiving man. Release Courtney, and I'll buy you a fleet of ships to replace the *Falconer*."

"A fleet, is it now?" Garrett scoffed. "As I recall, you were none too willing to deed me ownership of the two you had and were tired of."

"I offered them to you at a fair price."

"A price you knew full well I couldn't meet."

"Is that why you decided to steal them from me?"

"The law of the sea, Duncan! I stole nothing! You were gone; vanished without a trace. I had no choice but to assume you were dead."

"You've a choice now," Duncan said evenly. "Let Courtney go and let us walk out of here and I'll not look over my shoulder to see which way you've run."

Garrett hesitated, his fist still raised, his eyes glittering.

"You don't believe him, do you?" Miranda cried scornfully. "He wouldn't let you walk away from this. Not after you've touched his precious daughter. We started something, damn you, now we've got to see it through. Tell him. *Tell him*!"

Duncan looked at her with mild amusement. "Your loyalty is touching, my dear. As touching as Garrett's."

"Loyalty?" she spat. "I gave you four good years of my life and what did I get in return? Did you ever treat me with respect? Did you ever treat me like anything other than your whore? Did you ever once touch me with gentleness or kindness? Did you ever once consider me part of your life?"

Duncan stared at her a long moment, at the tears of indignation that were gathering along the fringe of her lashes. He raised his hands and clapped slowly and deliberately, the sound echoing like a thunderclap in the room. "Bravo. A fine performance. And one that might have worked had I not known that you'd sleep with any man who waved a trinket before you. You brought them into my house, into my bed. You took the greatest pains to ensure you never conceived my child, although for that I find myself exceedingly grateful. Yes, I used you, Miranda. But it was a fair exchange. I don't recall you ever acting like anything other than a whore."

Miranda bared her claws and started to push past Garrett, but the corsair's hand shot out and held her back.

"We've no time for this," he said angrily. "Did you bring the money? Yes or no?"

The dark green eyes moved lazily to his. "No. But I brought something just as good."

Duncan's hand moved toward a breast pocket, and a gun appeared instantly in Garrett Shaw's fist. It was fully cocked, the muzzle aimed between Duncan's eyes.

"Documents," Farrow explained easily. "In my pocket. No tricks."

Garrett's eyes narrowed, and he followed the progress of Duncan's thumb and forefinger as they reached beneath the coat.

"There's a letter of attorney here, giving you access to all of my assets and bank funds. There is a deed to my property, bills of sale for my home, my businesses. They're all quite legal and irrevocable. They only require our two signatures."

Garrett was instantly suspicious. "I know nothing o

legal papers. Nor do I trust them. Fancy words and fancy seals . . . how do I know it isn't a trap or a lie? How do I know you own everything you lay claim to. That it isn't just words?''

"You gave me less than twenty-four hours to make arrangements, and twelve of those were on a Sunday — a day of rest in the civilized world. The documents are real. You have my word on it. But they aren't valid or legal without my signature, and that you won't have until my daughter is cut free.''

Garrett dragged the stump of his hand across his upper lip to cover a second of hesitation and hissed to Miranda, "Do it. Cut her free."

"*What*?''

"You heard me. I said cut her free!''

Miranda planted her hands on her hips and glared at Garrett, her eyes blazing furiously, but in the end she crossed to the chair where Courtney sat and began to pick at the bloodied knots of twine that bound her wrists. Duncan watched her for a moment, then glanced cynically at Garrett.

"Odd you should use the word 'trap' so freely. I should think you'd be able to smell one out after all this time. Out of curiosity — how much did the Americans pay you to set up the rendezvous at Moknine?''

Garrett's head whipped around. "What? *Me*? Pay *me*? Are you mad?''

"No madness. I've had a great deal of time to think through the coincidences that have been plaguing us over the past eighteen months: the Americans knowing where to intercept the grainboats we were smuggling through the blockade at Tripoli; the Americans sending a warship instead of a sloop to patrol a harbor where we make regular supply purchases; the Americans knowing where and how we were to meet with Karamanli's envoy — knowing the sequence of the signal lamps, knowing enough to have three gunboats waiting to block the mouth of the bay.''

"Damn your eyes, Duncan Farrow! Are you accusing

me of *knowing* those damned Yankees would be on shore waiting for us?''

"You made the initial arrangements."

"I was as surprised to see those gunboats as you were!"

"Were you? Is that why, when we did manage to break out — thanks to Davey Dunn *who now carries your bullet in his shoulder* — is that why you let the *Goose* go out alone to meet them?''

The shock of the accusation drained the color from Garrett's cheeks. "A boom," he whispered hoarsely. "I lost a boom. My topsails were down. I had no steerage. By the time we were clear, the *Goose* was aflame. The three gunboats were around her like maggots, pouring shot into her . . . I saw the magazine blow —''

"Aye, and I saw the wind blowing at your back, Garrett."

The stump slammed down on the table. "I've never run from a fight in my life, Duncan Farrow! We went back! We ran one of the bloody sows to ground and we blasted her into splinters. We chased after the other two, but they were too fast; they had the wind in their teeth and they were running. We scoured that bloody harbor for hours, searching for survivors. We searched the shore; we search-ed the hills; we even leveled a Berber village because they'd taken three of our dead boys for sport. I didn't want to believe you were dead. I didn't want to leave until we'd found some sign of what'd happened, but the lads were starting to look over their shoulders more'n they looked ahead. They feared the Yankees would double back with reinforcements. We *had* to leave! We didn't *want* to, but we *had* to! Ask Dunn. Ask him if I didn't say straight out that something smelled foul in that bay. Ask him if I didn't put on all sail and head for Snake Island, suspecting some taint of treachery touched there too.''

"Or maybe you already knew it had touched and you went back to scavenge through the pieces.''

Garrett's jaw dropped. "Duncan . . . for God's sake I'm a thief, aye. A whoremonger and a cheat . . . *but I'n no Judas*! Good Christ, you can't be thinking *I'm* the one who betrayed us?''

Miranda abandoned her half-hearted efforts with Courtney's bindings and straightened slowly, her amber eyes going from one hard, strained face to the other.

Courtney took advantage of Miranda's inattention to pull and twist the twine further. She could feel the ropes cutting deeply into her flesh, but she didn't care. They were so loose, it would only take the right combination of twists and turns to break them apart. She had to be careful. She was aware of the watcher in the shadows. She had seen the glint of a musket barrel, and although she had tried to catch her father's eye to warn him of the unseen threat, Duncan was too engrossed in exposing Garrett's lies.

''Verart told me he was close to finding out who it was selling us out time and time again . . . to the Yankees, to Karamanli, there didn't seem to be a preference. Only a pattern. And it had to be someone who knew our plans, our schedules, our business arrangements. Someone who knew the one name to use whose association with betrayal would cause more pain than any of the treacherous acts combined. A name out of the past that would guarantee the cooperation of the French and British, and now the Americans. You, Garrett. You had the means and the opportunity. You had the greed and the ambition for power.''

''No!''

''You knew about France. About my working for the British to run guns in and aristocrats out.''

''*No*!''

''You knew the code name that would trigger memories of the past, open doors, loosen purse strings. . . .''

''No, damn you, listen to me —''

''You knew I was getting out. You knew the party was going to be over soon. No more raids, no more prize ships, no more profits in the slave markets. You knew about what I had here . . . and you wanted it all.''

"No! I knew about this" — he gestured wildly with the stump to indicate the warehouse — "and yes, I'll even admit to some envy —"

"You wanted my ships; you wanted my daughter, my mistress. I just never dreamed you would go to such lengths to get them. I didn't think you would betray your own kind. *The law of the sea*, Garrett," he hissed, "remember it? Our law? Absolute loyalty to your own kind."

"It wasn't me, you bastard! It wasn't me." Garrett's chest was heaving, his brow streaming sweat.

"And this was none of your doing either?" Duncan raged. "The kidnapping. The ransom demand. Whose idea was it if it wasn't yours?"

Garrett's eyes went to Miranda. "You said it would be easy. You said we could do it without anyone getting hurt."

"Shut up, you fool," Miranda cried. "Can't you see what he's doing? He's accusing you on purpose. He wants you blind and stupid so he can prove he's smarter than you. Don't listen to him, for God's sake. We're so close . . . so close to having it all!"

"I don't want it all. Not this way! Not if it brands me a Judas!"

"You're not a Judas," she said harshly. "Didn't you hear what he said? Weren't you listening? The French and the British know him as Seawolf. *He's* the one who's afraid of being blamed for selling us all out, and for all we know he's guilty. How else did he get all of this? Look at him, Garrett, then look at yourself. Tell me who has been paid to sell out whom!"

Garrett looked haltingly at Duncan, but Duncan, suddenly, had eyes only for Miranda. His face had become like a terrible stone mask.

"How did you know?" he asked quietly. "How did you know about Seawolf?"

Miranda stared at him, the amber cat's eyes showing a trace of fear for the first time. "Wh-what? You told me

You bragged about it, about your exploits in France, about working with the British —"

"No." Duncan shook his head slowly and advanced a step. "I never told you about France. I never told anyone about France."

Miranda's tongue darted across her lips to moisten them. Her gaze was locked to Duncan's. Her breath was backed up somewhere in her throat. "You're just saying that to frighten me, Duncan. Of course you told me. How else would I know about it?"

Duncan took a deep breath and cursed it free. "The *ledgers*. The old logbooks. You were reading them when I found you at my desk one day. Verart had made some entries —"

"Then that must be it," she said with annoyance. "So what of it? If I saw the name in some old ledgers, what does it prove?"

"It proves you had access to charts and maps as well. It proves you knew our plans, knew our ways and means of communicating with Tripoli. You knew our signals, our contacts along the Barbary Coast . . . goddamn you knew the location of most of the camps. They've been picked off and cleaned out one by one over the past few months. Snake Island was the last stronghold. And it would have been impregnable with a full force of men, with our two ships for support —"

"What is he saying?" Garrett demanded. "What have you done?"

"He's saying nothing! I've done nothing! Garrett, don't listen to him. Would I betray you? Would I betray the only people who ever gave me a home and welcomed me into their midst?"

"Aye," Garrett said harshly. "If the price was right, you'd betray your own mother. Now give us the truth, girl. The truth, and it may not go as hard on you."

Miranda looked from one cold face to the other and then to the watcher in the shadows. He was smiling. He was enjoying the show immensely. She could hope for no support from that quarter, despite all that she'd done for the bastard, all that she'd endured.

Miranda reached into the waistband of her skirt and withdrew the pistol. With her free hand, she grabbed a fistful of Courtney's hair and jerked back on it so the gun had a cozy resting place on the curve of her throat. "*Get back*! Both of you get back or I'll kill her."

Duncan had taken an instinctive step forward when he saw the pistol, but halted at the sight of it digging into Courtney's flesh.

"Miranda, let her go!"

"Let her go? When I've come so far, gone to such lengths for the sheer pleasure of seeing the pair of you squirm the way you're squirming now? What's the matter, Duncan? Does she remind you so much of your brave and valiant Servanne?"

Duncan's lips started to curl back over his teeth in a snarl, but the curse was forestalled by a bitter laugh from Miranda.

"I wasn't as clean, or as pure as your martyred French wife, but I made you cry out her name time and time again — did you know that? Did you know her name drove me to read your ledgers? I wanted to know who this goddess of virtue was you worshipped with your heart and soul and left nothing for me but contempt. And you" — the amber eyes flashed to Garrett — "you, with your bragging and your boasting, your lofty plans of gaining a fortune and sharing it with me . . . you had no intention of sharing anything with me. You only wanted what you couldn't have, and you couldn't have *her*."

She drove the barrel of the gun deeper into Courtney's neck for emphasis, and the involuntary gasp of pain spurred movement from both Duncan and Garrett.

"*I said get back*!" Miranda screamed. "Get back or I'll pull this trigger and you can both watch her die in front of your eyes! Peacocks! Preening, self-righteous peacocks! Well, I proved I was every bit as clever as either one of you. You think *she's* so brave and cunning because sh dresses like a man and fights like a boar? You didn't notice how brave and cunning I was to slowly clean out every rival band of thieves along the Coast. A word in the right ear, a cryptic message in the right hands, and the Yankees did the rest. I gave you *power*! I gave you *control* of the seas! But did you treat me any differently? No! You gave more of everything to your precious Courtney — more love, more attention, more respect. Well, now *I* want more. I want it *all*. I want those papers signed — *to me*! And I want them *now*, or you'll see blood!''

Duncan tore the packet open and laid the papers flat on the table. He took a small vial of ink and a sharpened stub of a quill from his pocket and hastily scratched his signature on the five documents. He straightened and caught his breath as he saw the gun gouged even deeper into Courtney's throat.

''I'm not stupid, Duncan,'' Miranda hissed. ''Use your seal. The wax from the candle will do.''

His jaw clenched, Duncan leaned over the documents again, touching each with the melted end of the candle and imprinting the wax with the head of his ring. When he straightened this time, it was not to stare at the smile of triumph on Miranda's face, rather it was to see the shadowy figure of a man step out from behind the bales of cotton. The newcomer carried a smooth-bore, double-barreled musket and held it level with Miranda's.

''Well done. Collect your papers, my dear. I'll watch the girl.''

Courtney could not hold back a second gasp as she recognized the corpulent figure. Matthew Rutger, bound and tightly gagged in the corner, jerked so hard against his bindings, young Dickie's body went rigid with the pain. It was The Voice. It was the man Garrett called ''the Englishman,'' and although his uniform had been replaced by poorly fitting civilian clothes, there was no mistaking the pompous, porcine features of William Leach Jennings.

''Right, Yank. Duncan said give 'im fifty, we give 'im fifty.

Ye want the back way, ye'd best get movin'." Dunn adjusted the crude sling his arm was cradled in and rearranged the two guns it gave comfort to as well.

"Stay by the front door," Adrian commanded. "Don't let anyone in or out."

"I know'd my job, Fancy Britches," the corsair growled. "Ye just make damn sure ye know yer own or I'll be down yer throat like a bad case o' rot."

Adrian grinned and slapped the corsair on his good shoulder for luck before he crouched and ran along the side of the warehouse to the rear jetty. The building was wide and deep and was built into the slope of the hill so that half of the lower floor was carved out of the land, like a cave. The grade to the dock was steep, and Adrian had to use brush and weeds and jagged rocks for handholds. When he slithered out onto the flat rock at the bottom, his breeches and shirt were smeared with mud.

The huge loading doors at the rear of the building were closed but not latched. A small ketch was moored to the pilons, and Adrian ducked quickly back around the corner of the building when he saw the dark shape huddled in the bow. Shaw had placed a guard on the dock in case of a hurried departure. Probably armed. Probably ready to give off a signal at the first sign of trouble. It also indicated the meeting was being held on the lower floor, near a ready exit to the open water.

He finished his own silent count to twenty and knew Dunn would be in position at the front door. He took a deep breath and crouched again, falling soundlessly forward so that his body hugged the cold stone. He drew his knife out of the sheath at his waist and clamped it between his teeth, then began inching forward. According to Duncan Farrow, the water was deep in the inlet. The jetty was built on a lip of stone, and from there the bottom dropped away. Adrian slid along the rock until he reached the edge of the water, then silently rolled himself into the inky depths.

Moving hand over hand, keeping just his head above the

water, he followed the dock around to where the boat was moored. He paused several yards away to steady his breathing, then took a deep lungful of air and sank beneath the surface.

The guard heard and saw nothing until it was too late. A single splash of water, a flick of wetness on his sleeve, and there was an iron band around his throat. There was a cold hand gripping his chin and mouth, twisting his body up and over the bulwark as a knife sliced in a clean arc across his throat.

Adrian held the body under long enough for the last of the bubbles to pop to the surface. He let the corpse drift free and hauled himself dripping onto the dock, his knife once again clamped between his teeth. He darted to the bay doors and carefully eased one open a crack. It was well oiled, and there were no creaks; he slipped inside and pulled the door shut behind him. He was closed in on all sides by walls of baled cotton and tobacco. A rectangular patch of blackness directly overhead was the opening in the main floor, and he could make out the outline of ropes, cables, and hooks suspended there.

A light was glowing to the extreme right side of the building, and it was from there Adrian could hear faint snatches of voices. He started working his way around the columns of cotton bales, and the closer he came to the light, the less the conversation was muffled. He was in position beside the last row in time to hear the final shouted accusations, but he was as taken aback as Duncan and Garrett to hear Miranda threaten Courtney. He dared not move in case he startled a shot from the pistol. He was starting to maneuver around them when he was stopped dead in his tracks by the sound of an unmistakably familiar cackle of laughter.

"You look surprised, my dear," Jennings said to Courtney. "Were you expecting someone else?"

"I was told you died on the *Falconer*," she said tautly.

"I was told by both of my avaricious companions that

*you* had died on the *Falconer*." Jennings looked up and frowned. "Miranda? The papers — you were so desperate for them a moment ago, by all means collect them."

Miranda had eased the pressure from Courtney's neck, but she had not moved or removed the gun. "I'm not taking orders from you."

"No? Well let me rephrase it to a request then. Please get the documents, and please deposit them in my hand."

"Why should I?"

"Because" — Jennings fingered the trigger of the musket — "I could care less if this young lady dies by your hand or mine. You, however, should care, because if she dies you lose your leverage and these gentlemen will tear you apart limb from limb. And besides, the party is about to become infinitely more exciting, and I know how excitement affects you. *Mister Ballantine? Do come out from wherever you are and join us.*"

After a moment's silence, Jennings laughed again. "Don't make me do anything so mundane as to count to three and blow your lover's ear off; it hardly becomes any of us to indulge in such childish antics."

Courtney's eyes darted to the far end of the clearing, to the figure who moved out from the bales into the open. Adrian. *Adrian!*

"Good heavens, you do look a sight, Lieutenant. Shall we assume by your appearance that the man we left on guard is no longer with us?"

The cold gray eyes moved up from Courtney's face and locked wordlessly onto Jennings.

"And I thought never to live long enough to see you speechless," Jennings mused dryly. "Come, come. Close to the light. Join us, by all means. I believe you know everyone here. In that respect I appear to be the only surprise guest. Good heavens, Lieutenant, I can see the questions fairly bursting to come out of you —"

"You knew it was the *Falconer*," Adrian said quietly. "That was why you insisted on a surrender. You knew you could talk your way to freedom."

"I *guessed* it was the *Falconer*. Hoped it was, actually, since Captain Farrow and I had never been formally introduced."

"Falworth. Where did he fit in?"

"A pawn, nothing more. A bit player in a drama that was far too complex for his greedy mind to grasp. He came rather cheaply, I'm disappointed to say, but he was convenient in the end."

"Alan?"

The single, softly spoken name sent such a surge of hatred through Courtney that she closed her eyes briefly. She saw Seagram, broken and bleeding, Nilsson . . . even Matthew, his back torn and raw. She had seen enough bodies to envision a ten-year-old, his skull crushed by Jennings' hand . . . a face much like Adrian's . . . .

"He saw something he shouldn't have," Jennings shrugged. "It was unfortunate, but necessary. As was this unholy alliance —" he gestured with his free hand to Miranda and Garrett — "but I had no idea I was bedding the notorious Seawolf." The beady eyes gleamed in Miranda's direction. "That was as much a shock to me now as my appearance must have been to her on the *Falconer*."

"I was enjoying the idea that you had died in unbearable agony," she said through her teeth. "I was wishing Garrett had given me first cut with the hot knife."

"Charming," Jennings frowned. "And not at all the attitude I'd expect from a partner."

"Partner?" she spat. "If you think I'm going to help you now —"

"I *know* you're going to help me. We're going to help each other — unless, of course, you'd prefer me to just walk out now and leave you here alone with your friends?"

Miranda glanced at Duncan, then Garrett. There was no chance she would survive five minutes alone with either one of them, regardless of what she promised.

She lowered the gun and squared her shoulders.

"Much better," Jennings said. "And now, if you please, the papers?"

Miranda started to move toward the table just as Courtney's hands sprang free of the twine. The jolt was so sudden and so unexpected, she had no time to think the action through as she brought her arms up to grab at the musket. She had hold of the barrel, had it pushed away from her neck and aimed harmlessly into vacant air when she saw Duncan lunge forward into its path on the one side, and Garrett leap toward Miranda on the other.

Courtney screamed a warning just as the musket exploded in her hands. Miranda, in turn, reacted to the sudden shout and fired her pistol point blank into Garrett Shaw's belly. Adrian, in motion before the echo from the first blast had settled, dove across the width of the room, his hands outstretched and clawing for Jennings' throat even as the captain was fumbling to cock the second hammer of the musket.

Courtney ran foward to catch her father as he staggered under the impact of the shot. Miranda, as shocked by the force of the recoil as she was by the sight of the bloody cavity in Garrett's belly, stumbled back against the bales of cotton and watched in horror as he kept walking toward her, his eyes burning into hers, the stump raised and prepared to strike. He roared and staggered to his knees, his weight behind his shoulder as it smashed into the bale of cotton where Miranda stood. The whole column toppled with the impact, and the candle that had been balanced on the top jumped from its dish, splashing wax over the dry white bales. The flames leapfrogged from one spash to the next and finally dribbled eagerly into a half-filled drum of oil. The surface caught, and the flames shot up against a second column of bales, and in moments the smoke was spreading thick tentacles into the air.

Courtney glanced up from her father long enough to see a flash of blue taffeta disappearing into the blackness of the stairwell. When she looked back, Duncan's face was ashen, his hands groping for the source of blood on his rib and arm.

"I'm all right," he gasped. "I'm all right."

The emerald eyes went to the darkened stairwell again, then to the pair of knives Miranda had removed from Duncan in the search. She sprang to her feet and delayed only long enough to slice through the rope and gag that kept Matthew Rutger immobile against the wall of cotton.

"Fire!" he croaked the instant his mouth was freed. "The cotton's on fire. We've got to get out of here. It'll go up like tinder."

"Get my father out of here!" Courtney shouted and raced for the stairwell.

"*Courtney!*"

She ignored Duncan's shout and plunged into the darkness, stumbling awkwardly up the steep flight of stairs until she reached the top. She stood there a long moment, her mouth open to swallow air into her pumping lungs. She could hear a noise ahead somewhere. Running footsteps . . . the sound of a curse as a knee or shoulder found a harsh edge of a crate. Behind her, Courtney could hear the fight between Adrian and Jennings — the crash of wood as the table legs collapsed under their combined weight. She forced herself to concentrate on the darkness ahead, on locating Miranda before the woman had a chance to find the door.

Adrian was surprised by the determination in Jennings arms. Not devastated, merely surprised. The strength in his own arms gave him more cause for concern. Jennings had swung the musket and caught Adrian's forearm in the same place as the recent injury caused by Miranda's knives. The agony had blinded Adrian for a costly few seconds, and by the time he had shaken his vision clear of the pinwheeling lights, Jennings had run between the columns of cotton and was making a dash for the bay doors. Adrian sprinted after him, his powerful legs enabling him to catch the bulbous figure before Jennings had gone three rows. A tackle had them both on the cold stone floor. A pair of well-aimed, well-delivered punches across the multi-chinned jaw had the fleshy lips opened and squealing for mercy.

"Mercy?" Adrian spat. "I'll show you as much mercy as you showed the men who were flogged to death on your ships; as much as you showed the men who died on the *Eagle* because of your treachery!"

Adrian grabbed two fistfuls of shirt and flesh and dragged Jennings to his feet. Rage and fury gave his arms the strength needed to haul the protesting body along the floor to where he had seen the weigh scales, the cables and hooks.

"Wh-what are you going to do?" Jennings screamed. "You can't take the law into your own hands! This is murder!"

Adrian pulled on a length of cable until he had a loop freed. He placed the loop around Jennings' neck and yanked it to tighten the slack.

"It's murder! *It's murder! Aughhhhh!*"

Adrian put his weight on the cables and Jennings danced on tiptoes, his arms flailing the air, his eyes bulging in fear, his mouth gaping and foamed with blood and spittle.

"You're forgetting," Adrian said calmly. "You're already dead. You died a hero's death on the *Falconer*."

Adrian leaned more of his weight into the ropes and felt the rachet wheel click into place high above. His face poured sweat, but he pulled and pulled, and when he could pull no more, he tied the ends of the cable around the bar protruding from the wall. Jennings was twitching. His arms, his legs, his jiggling belly . . . they twitched and flopped with the last gasps of life.

"For you, Alan," Adrian said and stared at the grossly distorted, discolored features. The flickering light tore his attention away from the swinging body. The fire was spreading quickly. The air was choked with fumes and smoke; the roaring was so loud Adrian could not hear his own voice shouting into the inferno.

Miranda stopped halfway across the cavernous room and

whirled lightly on the balls of her feet. Someone was behind her. Someone had followed her up the stairs to the main floor of the warehouse. Courtney! It had to be! No one else was capable of moving so quickly, so stealthily.

Miranda pressed herself against a wall of bales and kicked her skirt high enough to reach beneath it for the knife strapped to her thigh. The papers she had grabbed from the table in her dash past, she stuffed into the bodice of her blouse. She melted back along the bales, moving soundlessly now, alert to the slightest creak of wood.

Courtney stopped and held her breath. She could taste the sting of the smoke at the back of her throat. It had grown stronger in the last few seconds. There was a dull red glow mushrooming up from the rectangular hole over the loading bay, and she knew the fire was not far behind her. The boards under her feet were warm already, and it felt as if the air she was exhaling was being sucked below for fuel.

Courtney crouched to stay beneath the creeping streamers of smoke. If she could see in the growing brightness, she could be seen, and she was not about to underestimate Miranda again. Seawolf! Miranda had sold them all out — for what? A few pieces of silver? A fit of jealous rage?

Miranda cursed softly as she scuffed her shin for the twentieth time in as many seconds. She waved a hand to disperse the smoke, but there was too much of it. Her pulse was racing with the knowledge that the fire was already bursting out in the bales closest to the loading bay; if she could reach the street door in time to block it somehow, the green-eyed bitch would be trapped. Garrett was dead. Duncan was dead or dying. Courtney was the last obstacle between the past and a rich, brilliant future.

Damnation, where was the door? The heat and smoke were confusing her, the rows of cotton seemed to never end.

There! A swirl of clean air, and. . . .

Davey Dunn was blocking the door, the only exit from the warehouse. Miranda saw him and hesitated long enough to conceal her knife in the folds of blue taffeta before she ran toward him, her eyes wide and filled with terror.

"Davey! Davey! You have to help — quickly! It's Garrett! He's gone mad! He's shot Duncan and he's shot Courtney and he's chasing after me!"

"After . . . what? Eh?" Dunn shoved her out of the way and raised his pistol toward the sound of the approaching footsteps. The pain in his shattered arm and the confusion of the smoke distracted him, and he remembered too late that it was Miranda who had shot him. He did not need to hear Courtney's voice shouting a warning to him to realize he had made a fatal mistake.

Miranda held the knife in both hands and brought it plunging down between the muscular shoulders, sinking the blade deep enough to kill him before his body had struck the floor. She dove for the latch of the door and pulled for all she was worth, but the door was wedged fast by Dunn's feet. She started to kick them aside, but the sound of a choked gasp of disbelief made her spin around and press her back against the door.

Courtney was standing there in a mist of smoke, the glowing, throbbing light of the fire behind her. She was staring down at the body at her feet. In her right hand she held a knife but the blade pointed straight down to the floor, as if she hadn't the strength to lift it.

Miranda's eyes were drawn to the darker gap in the wall beside Courtney. It was a second staircase, leading to the upper-floor offices and loft. Miranda glanced back at Courtney but the girl still hadn't moved, hadn't twitched a muscle.

Miranda slid a foot sideways a few inches . . . still no notice . . . a few more . . . then she bolted for the landing. She heard the whisper of steel, and it seemed to take an eternity before she felt its bite at the base of her neck. The single bite flared into a million pinpoints of pain that washed through her body, draining her of strength. S staggered against the wall and gasped out a name. Her jaw sagged and her eyes stared up into the cool clean air beckoning from the top of the stairs. Her hands clawed the walls as she pulled herself forward, but her legs refused to follow. Her head fell forward, dragged by the weight of her hair, a weight that was suddenly so great that, exhausted, she let herself slump down on the stairs. Something white fell on the stair in front of her. Papers. They were spattered crimson, then streaked by the dragging cascade of her hair. She was tired. So tired. She heard voices. Shouts. A rush of cool sweet air . . . then nothing.

Adrian fought his way up the smoke-filled staircase to the main floor and weaved his way blindly through the maze of burning bales. He heard shouting up ahead and recognized Rory's voice, but he couldn't see through the hot, stinging clouds of smoke. The air was so dry it scorched his lungs. He could feel the flames licking at his arms, his legs, his hair, and he remembered a vivid scene from a nightmare — of flesh melting off bones and dripping in pools of fiery gore.

"Courtney!" It was nothing more than a gasp torn from his throat.

"Adrian? Adrian!" It was Rory. "Good God, man, hurry! The ceiling is about to go!"

"*Noooo*! *Courtney*!"

"She's outside! *Adrian*!" He had spun around to go back into the furnace, but Rory grabbed him and shouted in his face again. "Courtney's all right! She's outside! Now move! *Move*!"

Strong arms pulled him, pushed him, propelled him out the door seconds before the upper story of the warehouse collapsed into the burning core. The force of hot, crushing air hurled Adrian and Rory to the ground, and in the next instant there were hands tearing at him again, at both of them, peeling the burning scraps of clothing from their bodies.

"Was there anyone else inside?" Rory asked, his hands cupped around his mouth to direct the shout in Adrian's ear.

"Around back. We got them into a boat. Matt and the boy . . . Duncan . . ." The gray eyes halted their frantic search at the edge of the road. A small, pale shape was huddled in the mud beside Davey Dunn.

Adrian climbed shakily to his feet, shrugging off the helpful hands as he walked toward Courtney. As he came closer, he realized Dunn was dead. His blood was smeared on the shapeless white smock she wore — at least, he prayed unashamedly that it was Davey Dunn's blood. He noticed her hands: the wrists were raw from rope burns, and he could not help but recall the same marks on her when he'd first seen her in his cabin on the *Falconer*. Since then he had promised to protect her. To love, honor, and protect her. To keep her safe.

"Courtney?"

The green eyes were swimming with tears. Tears streaked her cheeks, dampened the front of her smock. She was staring at the spectacular horror of the fire, and he had to repeat her name three times before she sought his face.

"She killed them all you know," Courtney droned tonelessly. "Verart, Seagram, Davey, Garrett, Duncan" — Adrian dropped to his knees beside her — "Matthew, Dickie —"

"No. *No*, Courtney!" His hands went to either side of her face, cradling it gently, tilting it to his, turning her so she couldn't see the fire. "Your father's alive. Matt's alive. The boy's alive."

"They're . . . alive?"

"Yes!" He kissed her tenderly, fleetingly. "Yes. They're alive. Oh, my darling, yes. And you're alive. . . ." He kissed her eyes, her cheeks, her temples.

"Matthew?"

"Yes. Yes, he's alive."

The emerald eyes looked up into his solemnly. "Sh

doesn't love you, you know. She loves him. She loves Matthew.''

Adrian stared at her a moment, then slowly grinned with comprehension. "I know she does. And I know Matt loves Deborah, too, so . . . where does that leave us?"

"Together?" she dared to whisper.

His hands tightened; his fingers ran into the auburn curls and he brought her mouth to within a breath of touching his. "Does this mean you've finally stopped running away from me?"

Courtney leaned forward in silence to answer him.

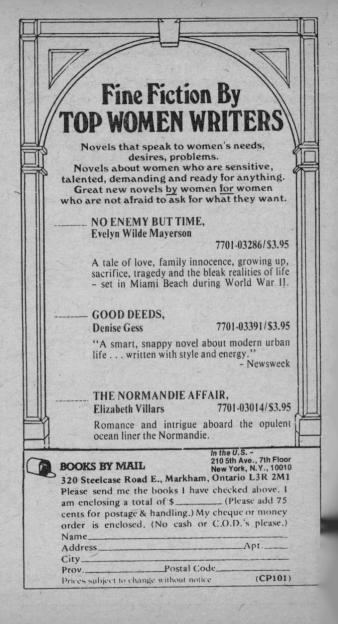

# Innocent People Caught In The Grip Of TERROR!

**JOHN BALL**
AUTHOR OF **IN THE HEAT OF THE NIGHT** INTRODUCING, **POLICE CHIEF JACK TALLON** IN THESE EXCITING, FAST-PACED MYSTERIES.

# FREE!!
# BOOKS BY MAIL
# CATALOGUE

BOOKS BY MAIL will share with you our current bestselling books as well as hard to find specialty titles in areas that will match your interests. You will be updated on what's new in books at no cost to you. Just fill in the coupon below and discover the convenience of having books delivered to your home.
*PLEASE ADD $1.00 TO COVER THE COST OF POSTAGE & HANDLING.*

**BOOKS BY MAIL**

320 Steelcase Road E.,
Markham, Ontario L3R 2M1

*In the U.S. –*
*210 5th Ave., 7th Floor*
*New York, N.Y., 10010*

Please send Books By Mail catalogue to:

Name_____
_____(please print)_____

Address_____

City_____

Prov._____ Postal Code _____

(BBM1)